Defenders at the Gate

Book One of the Defenders Series

J. E. MAXWELL

Edited by
C. M. Reeves
https://www.linkedin.com/in/maxwellreeves

Table of Contents

PROLOGUE

The three in the huge Fortress orbiting the swelling red giant star were silent. It was finally time to go. They were there at the beginning ... well, not the Creation *beginning, but they were there eons ago when events on the third planet from the star changed everything. Their memory spanned all that had happened since then. Now all of the planets and moons – even the asteroids and comets - were gone, and it was time for them to follow. But first, they remembered ...* **The Defenders at the Gate.**

"Each man must for himself alone decide what is right and what is wrong, which course is patriotic and which isn't. You cannot shirk this and be a man."

— Mark Twain

PART 1 – THE CHASE

Chapter 1

A full moon augmented the glow from widely spaced floodlights shining on the unpainted concrete building. A combination of shadows cast by boxwood hedges and irregularly spaced recessed windows created angular bands of light and dark on the walls. Several failed lights, the result of long neglected maintenance, added randomness to the patterns. The sight reminded him of a camouflaged warship, hull painted in shades of gray and black to disguise its silhouette.

Nicholas MacEwen stood in the dark, staring at the building in the distance. This was his first attempt at sabotage. Actually, it was far worse than sabotage. There were overtones of infanticide since he was bent on ruining his own project, the project which he had fought for years to inaugurate; the prototype which he perpetually felt was on the verge of working. If Defender was not literally the fruit of his loins, it was at least the sweat of his brow and the love of his life. Tonight he would thrust it as far back from the brink of success as he could.

The building squatted on an isolated lot at the back of an industrial development which had begun on the edge of a large metropolis in the latter stages of a business boom - a boom that had since gone bust. The nearest activity was an occasional car passing by on a tree lined, two-lane road on the far side of a large plowed field behind the structure. The only sounds he heard from his observation point on a dark side street came from an occasional piece of windblown litter skittering past him and the quiet whooshing sound made by the passage of those distant cars. Heat still radiated from the pavement beneath his feet even though it was several hours past sunset. The air was warm and moist, and the sporadic breeze carried the combined scents of many blooming plants as well as the rotting vegetation smell common to newly turned earth in this part of the country.

Nick was a large man, almost 6 foot 4 inches weighing about 240 pounds. His broad face was highlighted by bright blue eyes, capped with prematurely graying hair and underlined with a full beard and mustache. His physique was in keeping with his heritage - were he a little younger, Nick would look right at home as a Highland Games contestant.

He stood staring at the peaceful scene before him, feeling slightly nauseated. Finally, Nick returned to his white crew cab pickup truck and drove the remaining distance, long since convinced no one was working late on a Monday night and angered by his own procrastination. Circling to the rear of the plant, he left his vehicle in a corner of the dimly lit parking lot.

There was a white trailer parked next to the rear door of the building. It was the type of trailer commonly used as a temporary office at construction sites. This one contained his prototype. But he walked past the trailer towards the door at the back of the building. He wanted the damage to be thorough but undetectable, and that would require some preparation.

He entered a security code on a keypad at the employee entrance, disarming the alarm and briefly unlocking the door. Not for the first time he thought, *we really should have a biometric scanner instead of a keypad ... and we should have facility wide video surveillance as well.* He proceeded down the hall through widely spaced pools of light from the few overhead fixtures left on at night. *But that would cost money, and money has been tight for a long time. In any case, I'm glad we don't have that kind of security tonight!*

His sneakers squeaked on the freshly waxed tile floors of the empty, dimly lit corridors, and the high-pitched echoes of his passage returned from the unoccupied spaces. *At least the cleaning crew did a good job earlier this evening. About the only thing the country has plenty of now are people willing to work hard for low wages. Any job is better than no job.*

Nick entered the windowless engineering lab, turned on the main overhead lights and closed the door behind him. Scanning the room, he selected a computer workstation at random. Nick could have used his Personal Integrated Digital Device (PIDD – commonly pronounced "pid") to log on to the network, but he was old school and didn't like the feel - or rather the lack thereof - of a virtual keyboard as well as he liked the old style mechanical keyboards in the lab. In fact, the computer equipment and the software were years out of date, as were most of the equipment and furnishings in the plant.

At the workstation, he logged on to the network with a user identification and password combination which gave him full system administrator access rights for the entire network domain, including the server. *Computer access should be biometric also.* His first action was to delete the entries in the system logs of both the server and the workstation pertaining to the beginning of his computer session.

Less than an hour's work yielded a copy of the original software for the field generator control, and a copy of a new altered version. In keeping with habits developed over many years, he immediately backed up both versions by encrypting and copying them to his PIDD which was still paired to the network. The modifications were subtle, consisting of random changes in constants and the arrangement of variables in the computation subroutines. All of the basic control routines were untouched, so the field generator operation would appear to be unchanged. *In other words*, he ruefully admitted, *it would still fail to function properly*. However, the altered code should thoroughly frustrate any attempts to pick up the project where he left off.

After deleting the original software from the server, Nick entered the file management program and changed the dates on the altered files to match the original versions. This subterfuge would never survive close examination by a data retrieval expert, but there would be no reason for anyone to suspect that the files had been revised. Then he copied the revised code into a tiny flash memory integrated circuit using the programmer in the lab. This newly programmed integrated circuit would replace the one currently serving as program memory for the microprocessor installed in the field generator control unit. Finally, he cycled the workstation's power without logging off. The system log would show the brief power outage, but such occurrences were not terribly uncommon in this part of Houston these days. More importantly, the log would not show his session ending.

Sliding his PIDD into the PIDD-pocket in his pants – much larger than its distant ancestor, the watch pocket - and carrying the flash memory, Nick turned off the engineering lab lights and retraced his steps down the hall. He walked slowly from one widely spaced pool of light to the next, pausing at each to look around at the sights he knew so well. As he arrived at the last pool of light just inside the employee entrance, Nick turned around and stood still, taking one last look at the place where he had worked for seven years. He felt like an actor in a long running play, basking in the final spotlight before leaving the stage for the last time. *But there will be no applause for me.* He then turned and entered the security code on the inside keypad to unlock the door and exit the building.

Nick walked over to the trailer, smiling at the triangular orange and black radiation warning symbol on its door. There really wasn't a significant radiation hazard, but the implication of one discouraged unwanted visitors.

Nick climbed the two wooden steps positioned at the entrance. The old trailer had a door lock requiring an actual physical key, which Nick pulled from his pocket. Nick unlocked and opened the trailer door, leaving it open so he could see well enough to close the blinds on the trailer's single small window before turning on the lights. But the door swung closed behind him when the trailer rocked on its ancient springs as he walked to the window. He hurriedly completed the task from a combination of memory and feel, propelled by a sudden surge of irrational fear. His pulse and irritation both subsided as soon as he was able to examine the interior of the trailer in the glow of its ceiling lights.

The Defender prototype looked a little like an old style dentist's x-ray machine. A cream colored equipment cabinet with a two-section movable arm on the top right side of the unit stood against one wall of the trailer. A cube with one concave parabolic face was mounted on a ball joint at the end of the arm. Conductive metallic strips arranged in spiral strip line antennas of various sizes covered the concave surface. At the moment, the arm was oriented so the concave surface faced straight down.

The equipment would look vandalized to an outsider. Equipment panels were off, wires hung out of openings, and electronic components covered every horizontal surface in the trailer. Nick surveyed the familiar work-in-process surroundings with a sense of warm nostalgia, abruptly replaced with anger as he remembered that he was in these comfortable surroundings for the last time.

Replacing the flash memory only took a moment, since it was mounted in a socket to ease programming changes during the prototype phase, and the field generator control unit was among those currently missing its cover.

His mission accomplished, Nick started to leave, but had second thoughts. He didn't want anyone hurt as a result of his sabotage. The modifications shouldn't cause the equipment or its surroundings any damage, but he wanted to be sure. Nick peeked out through a couple of slats in the blinds to verify the parking lot was still deserted. He could see his pickup truck, and beyond that the field leading to the trees and road. The only motion he noticed was June bugs mindlessly assaulting the building's remaining floodlight beams.

Returning to the equipment, he reached out to the main power switch. Turning it on produced no adverse reaction, but he really didn't expect one. Still, he noticed he was standing as far away from the equipment as possible and holding his breath. After relaxing a little, and self-consciously checking for the smell of smoke, he sat down in a chair in front of a small shelf mounted on the front of the equipment rack. The touch screen display for the computer which ran the Defender supervisory program was mounted at eye level in the rack before him and a virtual keyboard glowed softly on the surface of the shelf. He touched the icon on the screen for the self-test routine. The results of the self-test, arrayed on the display a few seconds later, showed all parameters were within tolerance, and the equipment was ready to operate. This confirmed that his alterations to the control unit microprocessor programming would be very difficult, if not impossible, to detect. Thus encouraged, he touched the icon to energize the field. Touching this icon should cause no useful reaction; the energy radiated by the antennas mounted on the end of the arm should fail to form the Defender field, as always.

Suddenly, the trailer lights dimmed and he heard a hum and a soft rustling noise, followed shortly by a loud beeping alarm. Instinctively, he slapped a large, red, palm-sized emergency switch mounted on a panel to his left, interrupting the power to the field generator. Only then did he allow the flashing message on the computer display to register. It was a substantial overcurrent condition on input power — unprecedented, but within the operating limits of the equipment. Curious, he changed the power alarm settings in the supervisory program before resetting the emergency disconnect and retouching the energize icon. Again the lights dimmed and he heard the hum — which he now realized was from the equipment's power supply, only louder than normal — and the soft rustling noise, which he still did not understand. It occurred to him that there was an odd odor as well.

Glancing at the area a few feet below the generator's movable arm, he was startled to see what appeared to be a horizontal black circle suspended in the air. Nick slowly rose from his chair and cautiously approached the dark circle. It was about a double hand's width in diameter and was hovering about waist high. As he watched, a pair of small white lights moved across its surface from right to left accompanied by a combination whooshing/sighing sound. He froze. He couldn't decide whether to turn back and hit the emergency disconnect switch again or to investigate the apparition. The internal debate raged until his fear ebbed and his curiosity won out.

He thought it didn't look right, and then was amused at the notion that he should know how it was supposed to look. As he edged closer, he decided it looked wrong because it did not seem to have any thickness. He crouched down so the edge of the circle was right at eye level and it seemed to completely disappear. When he squatted even lower, he found himself looking up at a perfectly circular mirror reflecting a view of the trailer floor. The circle appeared to exist in only two dimensions.

Standing up again, he noticed the circle was only dark in comparison to its surroundings, not totally black. As he tried to make out the faint patterns he could see in its surface, another pair of lights began to progress across the circle. He suddenly realized with considerable amazement that he was looking at the road behind the plant! The lights were car headlights, the sounds were from the passage of those cars and the wind in the trees, and the odor was from the freshly turned earth in the field.

At that very moment, a June bug buzzed straight up out of the circle toward the trailer's ceiling lights and nearly scared him to death.

Chapter 2

Earlier that same Monday, Jimmy Barton was in his newly redecorated office at Instrument Technologies Corporation standing behind his U-shaped, burled walnut desk. The office was more than large enough for the oversized desk, a couch, a love seat, and half a dozen chairs all done in dark brown leather. The couch was accompanied by matching walnut end tables and a coffee table, all resting on a thick sand-colored carpet. The walls were covered in tan suede accented with a number of original paintings all done by a popular southwestern artist. Golf trophies, a few of which he had actually won, decorated the shelves of a large walnut hutch positioned against the wall opposite his desk.

He leaned forward, reviewing the overhead projector transparencies for the board of directors meeting, ready to pounce on Sheila if there were any mistakes. Transparencies were getting more and more difficult to find and he was furious when they were wasted. People thought he was crazy to use an antiquated overhead projector, but all of the newfangled computerized projection equipment was ridiculously expensive and he could never get them to work right anyway.

Jimmy could feel drops of perspiration trickling across the large bald spot in his unruly light blond hair. It was a hot, humid day, and the temperature was nearly 80 degrees Fahrenheit in his office. Every thermostat in the plant had a locked cover to which he possessed the only key. Ignoring the irony represented by his office décor, Jimmy knew the value of a dollar, and he also knew the high cost of air conditioning.

At ITC, Jimmy was the energy management system. There was no need for expensive and unreliable computers and software just to fiddle with thermostats when he already knew exactly where they should be set. He considered turning his office thermostat down a little, but rationalized that the heat was more noticeable at the moment because he was in a hurry and angry. Everything was a last minute panic, as usual.

It wouldn't be so bad if I didn't have to do everything myself, he silently grumbled. He looked up from the stack of overhead projector transparencies and shouted toward the open door of his office, "Where's the new income statement?" *I've carried this company on my back ever since my father died.*

His father, James Buchanan Barton – "Buck" when in the presence of family and close friends - had been the president and the chairman of the board of ITC until his death six years ago. Jimmy's first name was also James, but his middle name was Marvin - his maternal grandfather's name. "Jimmy" was his boyhood nickname, and although he wasn't terribly enamored with it, he was happy that his middle name kept him from being called "Junior" or something like Jim Bob or Jimmy John. He made sure that his employees knew that he was "Mister Barton" to them.

"Here it is," Sheila Thompson said as she walked into Jimmy's office carrying the missing transparency. "Frank made the changes you wanted."

Sheila, a petite, grey-haired lady in her late-sixties, was Jimmy's executive assistant. Her title derived mostly from her knowledge of where a lot of bodies were buried, dating back from when she was his father's secretary. Secretaries - a.k.a. administrative support a.k.a. executive assistants - had become a bit of an anachronism. Many of their functions had been taken over by electronics in the computer age. Nevertheless, some remained employed as status symbols, or by technophobes that would have otherwise been helpless. In this case, it was by a status-seeking technophobe.

"Took him long enough," Jimmy grumped. He wondered how his father would deal with the company's current problems if he were still alive. *When I was just an infant, he found a way to turn a desperate business situation into a huge success. However, unlike me, he wasn't trying to do it in the middle of a depression.*

* * * * *

Buck Barton got his start as a physicist in the early days of the atomic age, when any company with the word "nuclear" in its name was considered a gold mine. Stock options and predictions of personal wealth lured him to ElectroNuclear Inc., a startup company which designed electronic instruments for the nuclear industry. Years later, the environmental and health hazards of working with radioactive materials became more evident and nuclear became a dirty word almost overnight. ElectroNuclear's sales plummeted and the company hit the skids. At Buck's suggestion, his partners gratefully signed over their stock to him and sought their fortunes elsewhere.

He had a plan. An industry originally driven by wild optimism and speculative growth was now driven by the fear of liability. He needed a different strategy targeted to the new market realities. That strategy was corporate acquisition.

He began to call the owners of small nuclear industry companies to explain his proposition: ElectroNuclear would buy them out for less than the liquidation value of their assets. The mounting legal liabilities related to dealing with radioactive materials over the years would transfer to ElectroNuclear with the purchase, so the previous owners would be in the clear. He would then immediately close the purchased company and sell off the assets for a quick profit.

He was selling financial absolution to the fiscally desperate. How hard a sale could that be?

His plan was a great success. He became highly skilled at lining up acquisitions and liquidating assets quickly. As this technique generated more and more money, he was able to offer the deal to larger companies. ElectroNuclear eventually purchased and liquidated twenty-seven firms representing hundreds of millions of dollars in potential liabilities while earning tens of millions in liquidation profits.

Finally, he purchased one more company. At the time, Instrument Technologies Corporation was a medium-sized manufacturer of electronic instruments used for oil and gas exploration. Many of their products were in the form of sophisticated down-hole tools. These were cylindrically packaged sensors designed to be lowered into oil wells in order to test the physical properties of the surrounding ground formations. Since it was a combination of electronics, physics, and geology, the company was a good fit for Buck's background, and running it would prevent him from being counted among the idle rich. It would also provide a good disguise for ElectroNuclear and its single remaining asset — cash. Since he was the sole stockholder, it was easy to pass a motion to merge ElectroNuclear into Instrument Technologies Corporation. Shortly after that, all of the corporate records of ElectroNuclear and its subsidiaries were conveniently misplaced during the process of moving to the ITC plant. For all practical purposes, ElectroNuclear, and all of the nuclear industry companies it had purchased, disappeared.

Of course, all of this left thousands of workers from those twenty-seven companies without jobs and without recourse in case of long term health problems. It also left other companies holding the bag when the government started handing out bills for the cost of cleaning up nuclear waste dumps.

Buck's personal destiny was significantly better than those abandoned workers. An Arab oil embargo caused a tremendous increase in the cost of oil soon after Buck purchased ITC. There was a resulting boom in exploration and ITC's sales increased tenfold in just a few years. Buck added many millions to his already considerable wealth.

There is an old German saying that "der Apfel fellt nicht gerne weit vom Baume" – the apple does not usually fall far from the tree.

* * * * *

"Thanks, Sheila," Jimmy said as she handed him the new transparency. "You know, if brains were dynamite, Frank wouldn't have enough to blow his nose. He knows better than to show a loss on Winter Path." Jimmy shook his head angrily. "We'll just have to move more expenses over to cost-reimbursable contracts. He knows how we handle these things, but as usual, I have to do his job for him." Jimmy fumed, *I'd love to fire both Frank and Sheila, but they know too much.*

* * * * *

Jimmy went to work for his father at ITC right out of college as a salesman. Many of ITC's customers were owned by families whose sons grew up with him in the River Oaks section of Houston. A typical sales call consisted of a round of golf or game of tennis with a former high school or college classmate. Eventually, he became director of Marketing and limited

12

himself to handling only the big accounts, which typically meant taking customers deep sea fishing or gambling in Las Vegas.

But nothing lasts forever. Ten years after Jimmy started at ITC, a candidate ran for the office of president of the United States on a progressive, environmentalist, feel good, form-over-substance campaign. He was a perfect fit for postmodern voters and won the election. Within two years, new oil leases dropped to its lowest level in history and the number of working rigs decreased drastically. ITC was suddenly struggling. Jimmy urged his father to take their turn at the public trough and diversify into defense contracting.

Government stimulus spending was on the upswing under the current administration as a response to the recession caused by the Housing Bubble burst that occurred while the economy was still shaky after the Dot Com Bubble burst. Trading on his father's background in physics, ITC's experience with electronics, and, admittedly, a gross under-bid due to inexperience, Jimmy got ITC its first government contract in the field of directed-energy weapons. It quickly became apparent that the company was in over its head. Falling back on old habits, Jimmy's father arranged a merger with a small cash-starved company known for its technical prowess in the field, and the newly reinforced ITC did well enough to become a mid-sized player in the industry. Other contracts, classified and usually assigned names consisting of two randomly chosen words to mask their purpose, followed. Government contracting served the company well, greatly cushioning the effects of the collapse of the energy exploration market and the generally poor economy.

Shortly thereafter, Buck Barton died and Jimmy became the president and chief executive officer of ITC. Unfortunately, he was not the chairman of the board - his mother, Martha, controlled everything by way of the Barton Family Trust, set up by his father during ITC's rapid growth years. ITC was now a closely held corporation with the Barton Family Trust holding the majority of the stock. Martha Barton did not want to engage in business matters directly, but was talked out of giving Jimmy a free hand in ITC's operation by his two siblings. So she signed over a token amount of stock to her younger brother, Ken Wilson, a bank president, and elected him chairman of the board of ITC as a check and balance over Jimmy.

Ken advised his sister to resist Jimmy's entreaties for additional capital infusions from the Barton Family Trust when defense spending began to decline. So, with Ken's blessing, Jimmy convinced two of his lifelong acquaintances to invest in ITC and become members of the board of directors. Dave Litchfield and Rick Kramer attended the same prep school and university as Jimmy. They had all joined the same fraternity. Rick - with a particularly poor sense of priorities in Jimmy's opinion - actually took enough time out from partying to graduate.

Jimmy dreamed of eventually gaining majority control and throwing Ken out on his ear, but solving a more immediate problem took priority. The company was strapped for cash in a seriously down economy and its contractual backlog was declining rapidly.

Chapter 3

"Board members are starting to arrive," Sheila said as she departed Jimmy's office.

If it wasn't for Ken, thought Jimmy, *we wouldn't have to waste time with board meetings.*

Jimmy finished gathering up the overheads and left his office by way of a side door into a short hallway. Passing his private bathroom on one side, and his private building entrance on the other, he walked through the door to his private conference room.

The conference room was paneled in dark grained tiger stripe mahogany and had a matching conference table. High backed burgundy leather chairs trimmed with large brass brads surrounded the table. One side of the room was entirely glass. The uninspiring view was of the large empty lot across the street in front of ITC's building. Past and to each side of the empty lot were the other industrial park buildings, over half of them unoccupied. In the middle distance, a highway shimmered in the heat.

Two directors were already in place. Dave Litchfield was seated at the side of the table facing the window. Trim, about average height, wavy light brown hair with just a few gray hairs beginning to appear near the temples, he sat tipped back in his chair, almost reclining. He had a twinkle in his pale blue eyes and a slight upward curl at the corners of his mouth. Dave always looked like he had just heard a good joke and was looking for an opportunity to pass it on. In this case, the joke was an old one - the overhead projector sitting in the middle of the conference room table. Jimmy insisted on using the projector because it was cheap and reliable, but Dave knew it was really because Jimmy was a computer phobic. *Where the heck does he get the transparencies,* Dave wondered once again, *and does the Smithsonian know that a projector is missing from their antiquities display?* Belying the impression of continual mirth, Dave was a serious businessman who was doing well as the president of his family's business - or at least as well as the present economy allowed.

Ken Wilson was seated at the head of the table nearest Jimmy's connecting hallway door. Jimmy could only see the crown of Ken's head protruding above the back of the chair until swerving to take a side chair.

Sitting down, Jimmy saw that Ken was immaculately attired and groomed, as always. Seemingly mindless of the heat, Ken continued to wear his suit jacket even though Jimmy and Dave were in shirtsleeves. Ken's expensive clothing, carefully coiffured full mane of white hair, diamond pinkie ring, and gold encrusted Rolex watch all attested to his standing as a distinguished member of Houston's business elite. His face was slightly thin and long, enhancing his aristocratic appearance. Ken retained the soft southeast Texas accent, with its hint of Cajun influence which marked him as the descendant of generations of Houstonians. It was subtle, and didn't come to the fore except with the use of certain words - such as "special" which came out sounding like "spatial."

Jimmy felt the same surge of irritation he always felt when he saw Uncle Ken at the head of the table. *He's sitting in* my *place!*

* * * * *

As he watched Jimmy enter the conference room, Ken noted his nephew's appearance. Jimmy's collar was unbuttoned, his tie was loosened, and his shirttail was one inch away from complete freedom in the back. There was also a loose shirt button at the apex of Jimmy's pot belly. *That boy always looks like he slept in his clothes and didn't so much as comb his hair when he woke up.* Ken thought of Jimmy as a boy even though there was not really that much difference in their ages. Jimmy's round, pudgy face had always made him look younger, but to Ken, it was a matter of deportment, not appearance. Jimmy would always be a boy compared to Buck.

Ken knew that some people might question his late brother-in-law's business techniques, but Buck had been a winner. In business, as in war, the victors get to write the histories. He scanned the variety of plaques representing business awards that covered the conference room walls - all of them predated Jimmy's presidency. Ken believed Jimmy was trying to compete with his father's accomplishments and was always looking for some gimmick which would lead to instant success. Whatever the cause, ITC fared poorly under Jimmy, steadily shrinking to a shadow of its former self.

I wonder what Jimmy would say if he knew what the employees call the company behind his back. They took the initials, ITC, pronouncing the first two as the word "it," and adding the last letter, came up with "itsy" which was naturally followed by "bitsy." Some of the cruder employees hinted that the term also applied to a certain part of Jimmy's anatomy. It was a shame Martha's ITC stock probably wouldn't be worth much before long. Fortunately, there were many other investments made by the family trust that would see her through.

Jimmy said, "Rick won't be here. He's tied up with some out of town customers."

"He's only been to one board meeting this year. Maybe we should look to replace him," said Ken.

"We have a quorum with the three of us," said Jimmy, ignoring Ken's comment about a replacement. After all, Rick was Jimmy's friend while Ken certainly wasn't.

Frank Palmer, ITC's vice president for finance and administration, entered through the conference room's main door. Frank was not a member of the board; he only attended to present the financial reports. He wore a wrinkled seersucker suit in a compromise between decorum and temperature. It was of

16

noticeably poor quality and looked at least one size too small. He appeared rushed and nervous, with a frown and knitted eyebrows riding under somewhat rumpled reddish-brown hair. Ken wondered, not for the first time, whether anyone at ITC knew how to groom properly.

Sheila followed a moment later and closed the door behind her.

Well, Ken thought, *I stand corrected. I forgot about Sheila. She is always dressed very tastefully.*

Sheila was there to take the minutes. Dave Litchfield was officially listed as the secretary of the corporation, but he simply signed the minutes prepared by Sheila. She circled the table handing out copies of the minutes from the previous board meeting, and then sat in a chair in the corner of the room looking disinterested.

As usual, Jimmy folded his hands, bowed his head and said a prayer at the beginning of the meeting.

As usual, Ken was sickened by Jimmy's hypocritical piety. According to Martha, Jimmy hadn't seen the inside of a church since he left for college.

After a slight pause, Ken called the board meeting to order and asked, "Are there any corrections to the minutes from the previous meeting?" Jimmy and Dave glanced down at the copies they so recently received and had not read, but no one spoke.

"Very well," said Ken. "We'll proceed to the presentation of the financial data."

Ken leaned forward, placed his elbows on the conference table and interlaced his fingers just below his chin. The little finger on his right hand began to twist the pinkie ring on his left hand around and around. When the large central diamond reached the proper angle, it reflected light from the ceiling fixtures - it was like having a miniature lighthouse at the head of the table. Although Ken remained expressionless, he was highly amused by the obvious aggravation this caused Jimmy.

The reference to financial data was Frank's cue. He rose and went to the front of the conference room. As Frank passed the wall-mounted control panel, he dimmed the lights — which unfortunately dimmed Ken's lighthouse also — and activated the motors which lowered the projector screen and closed the drapes.

Jimmy flipped the first transparency on top of the overhead projector sitting on the table. When he turned the projector on, the profit and loss statement appeared on the screen next to Frank. The statement showed the revenue resulting from, and the costs associated with, each of ITC's contracts. There were columns for the present and previous quarter for comparison. The statement continued through other income and expense entries resulting finally in a figure for earnings per share of stock.

Frank tugged at the end of each coat sleeve in turn and began, "As you can see, we showed a profit for the quarter just ended even though sales continued a downward trend."

He looked like a man who didn't believe a word he was saying. Ken mentally translated: *As you can see, we fiddled the figures again.*

"This was accomplished by aggressive cost control measures aimed at achieving maximum efficiencies in a revenue-poor environment."

This was accomplished by cooking the books.

"For example, at Mister Barton's suggestion, we canceled our guard service. During normal working hours, we've moved an accounting clerk to the lobby so she can double as a receptionist, and at night we'll rely on our alarm system."

Well, Ken thought, *we do need to cut expenses, but we'll probably get ripped off some night, lose our facility security clearance, and be out of business.*

"Are there any questions?" Frank paused.

Without waiting for a response, Jimmy removed the income statement and replaced it with the balance sheet transparency. The balance sheet listed all of the assets and liabilities of the company in various categories. It portrayed the overall financial condition of ITC with an accounting of net worth.

Frank continued, "The primary item of interest on the balance sheet is the value of the short term debt, which shows that we have continued to use our line of credit with the bank to cover current operating expenses. As a result, we had to negotiate a higher ceiling amount for our loan last month. During those negotiations, the bank insisted on adding guarantors to the note."

Ken was silently thankful that the bank auditors had insisted that it would be a conflict of interest for his bank to maintain the ITC operating account when Ken became the company's chairman. Fortunately, they had not seen any problem with maintaining the Barton Family Trust funds.

Frank nervously glanced around the room before continuing. "Ken's employment contract with the bank prohibits him from guaranteeing loans. Dave and Rick are already signatories on notes for their family businesses and can't sign any additional loans. So, Mr. Barton offered stock and long term employment contracts to our vice presidents in exchange for their signatures on the note. There is an action item for the Board of Directors to issue the promised stock and produce the required employment contracts."

Ken arched one eyebrow. *Frank obviously wants someone to make a motion to that effect, and based on Jimmy's frown he is against it. I'm not going to get in the middle of this one. Convincing the vice presidents to sign was Jimmy's idea. I'll bet dollars to donuts that Jimmy has no intention of honoring his promises. Oh well,* thought Ken, *the VP's probably were all aware that the real offer was to sign or lose their jobs.*

When the silent interlude reached an uncomfortable length, Frank reluctantly proceeded. "Our financial ratios are still within the requirements of the loan limitation formulas, but we don't have a lot of room left to maneuver. If we win the Pavilion Mast contract, we may have trouble passing the government's pre-award financial responsibility test without more contributed capital."

Jimmy quickly interjected, "The Pavilion Mast proposal probably won't finish audit and evaluation by the government for at least two more months, then the procuring agency will request a minimum of one Best and Final Offer from the bidders. The government will review the BAFO's before they call for any financial responsibility audits and I'm sure we can tidy up our financial position by then ... and I have a good feeling about our chances for winning the contract." Jimmy gave Frank a cold stare.

Ken's eyes narrowed and he momentarily stopped rotating his pinkie ring as he took advantage of Jimmy's interruption. "Cutting right to the bottom line, Frank, why are net assets down so much? I understand that the operating loan liability increased, but you actually show enough profit on the income statement to offset a fair amount of that."

Jimmy looked startled, and then angry as he said, "That's a good question. What's the problem, Frank?"

After glancing up at the ceiling briefly, Frank returned his gaze to the group around the conference table. Appearing to choose his words carefully, he said, "I made a last minute correction to the income statement and didn't get a chance to correct the balance sheet."

"Well I'm tired of these kinds of mistakes," Jimmy snapped, "and if you don't get your act together we'll be looking for a new financial officer. Do you understand?" When Frank did not respond immediately, Jimmy loudly repeated, "*Do you understand*?"

His face turning red, Frank looked at Jimmy and answered, "Yes sir." Then Frank focused on Ken and asked, "Are there any other questions?"

"I've got a question for Jimmy," said Ken. He had a pretty good idea who was actually to blame for the discrepancy — and which of the conflicting numbers was really right — and he was trying to remove the focus from Frank. "Where are the costs for MacEwen's research project? I was under the impression that we've had a number of people finishing the prototype assembly and that the testing phase has begun, yet the total expense for research and development shown is small and unchanged from last quarter."

"Well," Jimmy responded, "as you can see, the company can't really afford an investment in this project right now. On the other hand, we don't want to approach the government for money either. Research conducted using funds reimbursable on defense contracts becomes the property of the government. We feel Nick's project, if successful, would be a valuable asset for ITC. If the government owns the design, they'll put the production contract up for competition. We don't want that. We want to be sole source and charge an amount in keeping with what the market will bear."

Ken appeared confused and asked, "But didn't you tell me once that government sole source contracts are negotiated on the basis of estimated costs plus a relatively small profit? How is that 'in keeping with what the market will bear'?" *What's going on here?*

Jimmy, frowning, shifted in his chair and answered, "Yes, but as long as we are sole source, we can be very flexible with our cost estimates."

Ken tried again, "But you still didn't answer my question about the cost of the research work. There's nothing shown under non-reimbursable expenses and I don't see a deduction from pretax profit for it either." *Is there some legality here that could threaten Martha?*

Jimmy gave Ken a belligerent look. "We have been very creative in our cost accounting for this effort."

Worried now, Ken asked. "How is that possible? MacEwen strikes me as a straight shooter and he has to approve expenses on his own project, doesn't he?" *Is there some legality here that could threaten* me*?*

Frank suddenly blurted, "We alter the cost account numbers on the time sheets and purchase orders after he signs them."

Jimmy jerked his head around to give Frank a furious glare, and then quickly looked at Sheila to see if she was writing any of this down - Jimmy didn't allow her to use any electronic devices during the meetings. She sat unmoving with her pencil and pad sandwiched between her lap and folded hands. Jimmy's relief prevented him from noticing that Sheila's bored expression now included a veneer of disgust.

Jimmy turned back to face Ken and looked like he was going to say something. Visibly changing his mind, he remained silent.

After a considerable pause, Ken said, "I'm really concerned about the corporate culture you're developing here at ITC, Jimmy."

"Oh come on, Uncle Ken," a form of address Ken despised, "a culture is something biologists grow in petri dishes. We're talking business here."

Flushed with anger, Ken loudly added, "And I don't want to hear about any trumped up cost estimates, creative accounting, or altered records." *What am I going to tell Martha?*

Jimmy hotly replied, "It doesn't matter anymore, I've decided to suspend the project until we can afford to continue. You should see the electric bill we get every month because that thing spikes our peak demand every time it's turned on! And it doesn't work anyway!"

Ken, coldly furious now, asked, "*You've* decided? Don't you think the decision to abandon a major research project that has continued for many years should be made by the Board of Directors? Besides, my understanding is that Buck promised Nick that he would be allowed to finish his prototype once his company was merged with ITC." *Jimmy's got his father's drive, but lacks his father's sense of direction.*

The fire intensified in Jimmy's eyes as he answered, "We aren't abandoning the project, just putting it on hold. I'll worry about Nick. We don't have a choice anyway – we don't have the money!"

Dave, very careful to stay out of the fray thus far, broke the ensuing silence by asking, "Hey isn't it about time for lunch?"

Seizing the proffered lifesaver, Jimmy quickly answered, "It sure is! Where do you want to go, Ken?"

After a few more moments of silence, Ken relented. *Oh well, this company is probably going to be in the dumper pretty soon anyway, and going to lunch after a board meeting is traditional. Besides, it's the only pay I get for being chairman of the board!* Giving Jimmy an angry glance letting him know that the discussion wasn't over, he leaned back in his chair and answered, "How about Chinese?" He knew that Jimmy hated Chinese.

After Dave and a reluctant Jimmy both nodded their agreement, Jimmy said, "Let's close with a prayer."

Chapter 4

"... tink ... tink ... tink ..." The June bug kept bouncing off the ceiling light in the trailer as Nick stared at the circular vision fixed in midair. The sound mocked his own silent exhortations to ... *think ... think ... think.*

What have I done? What am I going to do now? He glanced over at the computer display again to verify there was no flashing message or any other indication of impending equipment malfunctions. He saw a simple declarative message never displayed before: FIELD ESTABLISHED. Everything else was normal except he noticed a slight uptick in power consumption whenever a new June bug flew in. *But this isn't the field! The field is supposed to be a defense against energy weapons and should be spherical in shape.*

* * * * *

Nick had always been interested in military history. As a youth, he read about the ways weapons technology had changed the balance between offense and defense over the years and how the course of history had changed as a result. The American Civil War was a clear example. In the early part of the war, aggressive attackers were often at an advantage. Due to the limited range, poor accuracy and time-consuming loading procedures of smooth bore muskets, defenders often fired no more than a single effective volley at attackers before hand-to-hand combat was joined. At that point, the physical and psychological momentum generated by the charging attackers was often enough to tip the balance in their favor. Later in the war, when firearms with rifled barrels and breech loading cartridges were available, defenders could fire multiple effective volleys at attackers before they could attain close quarters. Generals who continued to believe in the superiority of the attack throughout the war contributed greatly to the massive casualties suffered. The abilities of the North to manufacture the improved weapons in quantity, and also replace casualties from a larger population pool, were the decisive factors in the outcome of the war.

Nick's studies convinced him that defense remained superior throughout World War I due to massed, accurate artillery fire and inventions such as the machine gun and barbed wire. As World War II started, offense and defense were somewhat more balanced due to the introduction of large armored formations and the effective use of air power. But offensive weapons regained clear superiority by the end of the war with the detonation of the atomic bomb. The subsequent development of hydrogen bombs and intercontinental ballistic missiles reinforced the superiority of the offense. In fact, the superiority of the offense had grown so great as to force the world's super powers to adopt the strategy of Mutually Assured Destruction. Nick felt that the world would be a much safer place without fingers hovering over "Armageddon" buttons, but that would require a reliable counter to nuclear weapons.

Still fascinated with military technology, he graduated from college with Bachelor and Master of Science degrees in electrical engineering and joined General Armaments, the country's largest weapons company.

At GenArm, Nick advanced rapidly and became involved with directed-energy weapons development. True to his calling, he started thinking about developing an effective defense against such weapons. He wanted to investigate high energy electromagnetic fields in an attempt to form some sort of a barrier to radiated energy. A number of his peers ridiculed Nick for trying to invent a force field, declaring it an artifice relegated to science fiction novels. But Nick reminded them that many energy weapons already produced by GenArm were considered fictional devices only a few short years before.

In any case, he wasn't having much luck generating support for the necessary research and development funds among senior management. Some of those managers were old enough to have witnessed the political and public relations fallout of the Strategic Defense Initiative - nicknamed "Star Wars" by the press in the 1980's - but more importantly they saw the level of government spending on SDI remain insufficient to the task over the intervening years. Some systems got as far as pre-deployment testing but no further. Most of these systems were based on destroying a ballistic missile in flight, either in its boost stage with an interceptor missile or in its terminal stage with directed-energy weapons.

Ultimately, the Executive Committee became convinced that anything threatening the Mutually Assured Destruction balance of offensive weapons between the super powers would not be deployed for international political reasons and therefore not worthy of scarce research and development funds. Although Nick pointed out that nuclear weapons had spread well beyond superpower control - thus creating a threat that transcended the ghoulish logic of MAD - the committee would not relent.

Nick was aware of the dearth of R&D funds caused by the early stages of what eventually developed into the Second Great Depression. Given the prevailing economic conditions, Nick became convinced that the primary reason for senior management's reluctance to fund his research was because they couldn't afford to have two horses in the race and were placing all of their bets on their airborne laser system candidate. Even so, Nick was dismayed that a potentially important contribution to the defense of the country was being ignored, so he brought the subject up at every opportunity. Once it was obvious that he had worn out his welcome, he left GenArm and started his own company, MacEwen Systems Inc., and the Defender project was begun in his garage. Nick was thrilled to finally begin work on his dream, but he couldn't have predicted how bad an already weak economy would become.

His company grew slowly by taking on small directed-energy weapons study contracts but his financial limitations, aggravated by the recession cum depression, eventually outweighed his ambitions. It also didn't help that the majority of his time and all of his profits were going into the Defender project.

He eventually had to allow the absorption of his company by ITC in a quasi-merger on the condition that he was allowed to continue his attempts to create a defensive field. In return, he accepted the position of vice president of engineering for the combined company and quickly resolved significant technical issues ITC was experiencing on a pivotal government contract. He frequently regretted his decision to give up on building his own company, but never so much as he regretted it now.

* * * * *

The dark circle levitating in the trailer tonight was not what he expected. *I don't know what this is! I'm going to have to go back to the lab and modify the software again.* Nick started to return to the console to turn the generator off, and hesitated. *I can't just ignore this ...* he looked again at the phenomenon as his subconscious gave it a tentative name ... *this "hole."* Cars could be heard through it. The bug flew through it. He could even smell the turned earth of the field through it. It was not an image, it was a hole! From the looks of it, the other side of the hole was somewhere in the field behind the plant. *What am I going to do? I can't stay here all night fooling with this thing. Everyone will be coming in to work in the morning.*

First, he just had to know if it was really a hole. Picking up a pencil from one of the work tables, Nick slowly lowered the sharpened end down into the opening. There was no resistance to the motion, but the display showed a slight uptick in power. He stopped with the pencil only halfway through - he didn't feel comfortable with the idea of sticking his fingers in the hole. After hesitating briefly, he released the pencil. It fell the rest of the way through and disappeared along a curved trajectory. *What the ...?! It didn't fall straight down! What's going on? Wait a minute.* He thought furiously. *When I saw the car headlights pass, it looked like I was seeing them from the side instead of from above. But I'm looking down on the hole! ... Shouldn't I be looking at the ground?*

Momentarily abandoning his earlier caution, Nick rushed out of the trailer without turning off the lights. He jogged out into the plowed field, and then slowed as he realized he didn't want to blunder into physical contact with the other end of the hole. He stopped and tried to figure out about where it should be, based on the view of the road he remembered. Figuring it would have to be somewhere almost directly ahead of him, but at least halfway across the field, he proceeded in that direction very carefully as his eyes adjusted to the dark. Stumbling across the furrows slowed him even further.

As Nick approached the middle of the field, he advanced one step at a time, carefully looking all around for anything out of the ordinary.

There's something over there! A little constellation of lights hung in midair ten or twelve yards to his front left. As he came closer, Nick could make out a small mirror image of the floodlit plant behind him. *So this must be the back of the hole out here.* As Nick edged around to the other side, he was almost blinded by the light radiating from the front. It was just the interior of the trailer, made to seem much brighter since it was surrounded by the dark in the field. *This is what attracted the June bugs. If I don't turn it off soon, the whole trailer will be full of them!* Nick shook his head in disbelief. *That's a funny thing to be worrying about in light of all this ... in* light *of all this! Ha! I'm a regular comedian!* Nick suddenly realized he was bordering on hysterics.

He looked away from the hole in order to regain some semblance of sanity as well as his night vision. After a few moments, the moonlight was enough for him to find the pencil lying on the ground directly below the hole. *So the hole out here is vertical. That's why I was looking at the road from the side and the pencil curved after it dropped through the hole.*

Then Nick took the pencil and tried to toss it back through the hole into the trailer. It came straight back out and fell on the ground at his feet again. *And the side of the hole in the trailer is horizontal, so the direction of gravity on that side is toward me. I'm looking at the field projector boom and the ceiling of the trailer - it seems like I could reach through and touch the boom, but the hole isn't big enough. None of this is making any sense!*

He had to do one more quick experiment. Picking up the pencil again, Nick held the eraser end between his thumb and forefinger. Facing the hole, he inserted the pencil halfway through, and then moved it straight down. *At least this direction is down on this side of the hole. In the trailer, it's either right or left; I'm not sure which.* He felt no resistance to the motion as his hand continued smoothly down past the edge of the hole. Holding the pencil up to the light coming from the hole, he saw that the pencil was apparently unharmed.

Next, he held the pencil below the hole and moved the pencil up very slowly. As soon as the pencil moved inside the hole, he carefully looked around to the back of the hole and saw only the mirror-like surface – no protruding pencil. Looking at the front side, he could see the pencil extending into the trailer. As he continued to move the pencil higher, it disappeared from the trailer, and he could see the entire pencil above the hole here in the middle of the field. *It's like this thing is only two-dimensional. There's absolutely no thickness to it. Or it's so thin that it moves between the molecules of the pencil without disturbing them noticeably.* Nick moved the pencil up and down through and beyond the circumference of the hole without noticing any obstruction to the movement.

Now, he moved to the side of the hole and reoriented the pencil, which was a little longer than the diameter of the hole, so it was parallel to the plane of the hole. Nick then tried moving the pencil back and forth. The pencil moved freely when traveling from front to back, but not in the other direction. *There are some weird boundary effects going on around the circumference. The front side will accept objects that are smaller than its diameter but simply ignores larger objects, the back side rejects everything, and edgewise it's like the hole wasn't there at all.*

What have I done? Nick stared at the pencil for a moment as an ancient quote from the <u>Rubaiyat</u> came to mind unbidden: "The Moving Finger Writes; and, having writ, Moves on: nor all your Piety nor Wit Shall lure it back to cancel half a Line, Nor all thy tears wash out a Word of it."

Chapter 5

Frank left the conference room and headed for his office as soon as Jimmy, Ken, and Dave went for Chinese. Grabbing a paper bag from his briefcase, he bucked the flow of people swirling down the hallway to the lunch room as he proceeded toward the engineering area and Nick MacEwen's office.

When Frank joined ITC, he sought Nick out from a combination of courtesy and curiosity. He frankly wondered how ITC had been able to recruit someone of Nick's caliber. The relationship grew from acquaintance to mutual professional respect and on into a friendship. Now the brown bag luncheons in Nick's office were habitual, and evening or weekend social encounters including Frank's wife, Susan, were not uncommon. Frank discovered Nick had few real friends and seemed to be disinclined to develop relationships – certainly all of Sue's attempts at matchmaking had failed miserably. Frank initiated every new aspect of their association: the initial ice breaking, eating lunch together, and the first activity outside of the workplace. Frank concluded that his bachelor friend's only true love was named Defender.

Nick looked up from his computer and smiled as Frank entered the office. "Hi, Frank. Grab me a Dr. Pepper while you're in there." Nick was wearing a white dress shirt with the sleeves rolled up just below his elbows, a red and blue striped tie, and khaki pants. A blue blazer hung on a hanger on the back of his office door. The combination was practically a uniform for GenArm professional personnel - old habits die hard.

Frank went over to a small, waist high refrigerator in the corner of the office. The soft drink machine in the cafeteria did not include Dr. Pepper, so Nick bought the refrigerator and kept it stocked rather than forego his favorite refreshment. *He must go through a couple of six packs a day,* Frank thought as he pushed a chair aside so he could open the refrigerator door. Once their lunch routine set in, Frank kept some fruit juices in the refrigerator as well. After a momentary search for a clear spot on Nick's desk, he set down the requested Dr. Pepper and picked out a can of grapefruit juice for himself.

Nick's and Frank's offices were the same size — small. There was barely enough room to squeeze in a normal sized desk, two visitors' chairs, a filing cabinet, and the miniature refrigerator. Nick's office looked even smaller because of the clutter of books and papers covering every flat surface. In fact, Frank had to move several books off of a chair before he could sit. There was no window, and the walls were bare, but as small and plain as the offices were, Frank and Nick were privileged compared to the open bays or occasional partitioned cubicles endured by most of the staff. Years ago, as ITC shrank, the large plant in northwest Houston was sold to generate cash and the company moved into a much smaller, leased facility on the southwest side. At the moment, it made for pretty cramped quarters. Frank often wondered how much larger and more luxurious Nick's office had been at General Armaments. As much time as he spent with Nick, certain aspects of his friend were still a mystery.

"So how did the board meeting go?" Nick asked with a look of mild amusement. A loud protesting screech punctuated his question as he swiveled his chair and extracted a lunch bag from a desk drawer.

"Terrible," Frank replied. "Jimmy changed the numbers again at the last minute and Ken caught him. Then Jimmy blamed it on me and threatened to fire me. Of course, that's nothing new."

Nick's brow furrowed and he nodded sympathetically as he emptied the contents of his lunch bag on a stack of papers and asked, "So, what did you bring for lunch, Frank? Anything you want to trade?"

Nick's eating preferences formed the basis of a running joke between the two and elicited an immediate response from Frank. He smiled and said, "No way, Nick! You've probably got something obnoxious like peanut butter and bologna sandwiches again! How can you stand that stuff?"

"Well, nobody ever accused me of being a slave to convention," Nick replied while peeling back a corner of his sandwich to reveal the accuracy of Frank's prediction.

Frank said, "I've got ham and Swiss cheese, with lettuce, tomato, and mayo - a respectable sandwich which your barbaric tastes couldn't possibly appreciate."

Both men smiled, obviously comfortable with the familiar banter between them. But as they began to eat, Nick's mood slowly darkened. Several minutes passed in silence except for the occasional rustling of a potato chip bag.

Finally, Nick cleared his throat and said, "Speaking of changing numbers, I've got a problem. I needed to return some defective parts that were delivered for the Defender prototype. I went to the Purchasing department and pulled the paperwork to make sure who the vendor was and whether or not I needed return authorization numbers before we shipped them back."

Nick selected several papers from the top of one of the piles on his desk and handed them to Frank. There was no smile in evidence when Nick said, "The charge numbers on the purchase orders aren't right."

A few seconds passed while Frank considered his response. Making up his mind, he continued, "We're altering the charge numbers on time sheets and purchase orders after you sign them. Your research work is not being charged to R&D."

Frank was surprised when Nick's expression changed from concern to sadness, instead of the anticipated anger. Nick finally asked, "What is it being charged to then?"

"Well," Frank explained, "Jimmy thinks I am spreading the expenses around on our cost-plus contracts so the government is paying for the research without knowing about it or being able to claim title to it later. In reality, I'm altering the account numbers so the work is charged to our fixed price contracts. That's one of the reasons Winter Path was going to show a loss this month until Jimmy changed it."

"Why are you doing that?"

Frank answered with a shrug, "This way the R&D cost is coming out of profit as it should. I'm trying to do what I can to make the ultimate results turn out right ... assuming two wrongs can make a right. Of course at this point no one can tell what either your research or the fixed price contracts really cost."

Nick just shook his head and mumbled, "We are never more foolish than when we attempt to fool ourselves."

He leaned forward in his chair and looked across the desk at Frank. "You're taking a pretty big risk doing this behind Jimmy's back, aren't you?"

Frank replied, "Yes and no. If he finds out, he'll fire me on the spot and try to blacklist me to boot. But Jimmy is not nearly the financial expert that he fancies himself to be. I occasionally screw up some obvious but fairly meaningless number to distract him. You know, kind of like magicians do - make the audience look anyplace except where the actual sleight of hand is occurring. If he catches on to what I'm doing, I'm toast. But keeping a job is not worth committing fraud. Anyway, it's pretty unlikely that he will catch on to what I'm really doing."

"Yeah, I've noticed that about Jimmy," Nick said, "There's very little he doesn't miss."

Nick put down his sandwich. "But how does Jimmy expect to explain the existence of a prototype if there are no visible costs associated with its design and construction?"

"If it comes to a showdown, he intends to insist the work was done by employees after hours, on their own time, using scrapped or rejected material having no residual value," Frank answered in a mechanical way. It sounded like he was reciting a memorized statement. Nick wondered if Jimmy made Frank rehearse the response.

"Surely he doesn't think anyone will believe that."

Frank merely shrugged.

"Does he really expect the employees to back him up on such an outrageous story?"

Frank replied, "Sure. In his view, he can trust all of his managers because he has bought them with exorbitantly high salaries." Nick and Frank both laughed at that. "He expects the rest of the workers will do anything in consideration for the great honor and privilege of being employed by him."

"Well, now you're just being sarcastic." Nick said with a smile.

"Not really," Frank said. "Jimmy frequently comments on the universal love and admiration of his employees."

Nick leaned back in his chair and frowned. "Jimmy might be right about the employees backing him up. Unemployment rates in the high thirty percent range makes for some pretty loyal employees."

"It turns out that his 'on their own time' explanation would blow up in his face anyway," Frank added. "The Fair Labor Standards Act prohibits non-exempt employees from volunteering time performing the same or similar functions for which they are normally paid. Jimmy would be required to pay back wages plus a stiff fine.

"What sweet justice that would be," Frank continued with a faraway look. "Jimmy paying employees for work they had already been paid to do, only because he said that he hadn't paid them!"

Nick laughed, picked up his unfinished sandwich and began eating again, although the frown eventually returned. After Nick finished his lunch in silence, he said, "Look, don't misunderstand me. I'm not complaining about economic realities. We are living in very difficult times. I'm just saying I think the best way to improve your lot is to perform better, not cheat more.

"Anyway, I understand what you're telling me about the Defender project cost accounts and I appreciate your honesty," Nick continued. "In return, I have to be honest with you. If it weren't for you telling me how you are correcting the miss-charges as you go, I would be compelled to blow the whistle."

Frank somberly replied, "Thank you for giving me a chance to explain the situation first."

Nick threw his lunch refuse in the trash can and asked, "What does Ken think of all this?"

"Well," Frank smiled as he replied, "in the meeting today Ken said 'I don't want to hear about any trumped up cost estimates, creative accounting, or altered records!' So I'm sure Jimmy will happily make sure that Ken doesn't hear about them."

Nick laughed, but Frank's smile faded away as he remembered how the morning's board meeting had ended. Unable to look at his friend directly, he hung his head and said, "Nick, there's something else I need to tell you."

Chapter 6

Well, I guess that proved an object can *be in two places at the same time,* Nick thought. He looked up at the nearly cloudless night sky as if suddenly aware he was outside. A gust of wind seemed to chill him - which was ridiculous considering the temperature - and he shivered. *Speaking of being in places, I'm standing in the middle of a field at night, illuminated by a circle of light floating in midair, and another car could come down the road at any minute!*

Lost in thought, he tossed the pencil aside as he quickly retraced his steps across the plowed field and the parking lot to the trailer. Once inside, he paused, wanting to investigate further. But remembering the telltale light in the field, he turned off the Defender field. The hole, and by inference the light floating in the field, disappeared. Everything was back the way it was except the number of June bugs attacking the ceiling lights had increased.

His deep breathing, caused by exertion and anxiety, was the only sound in the trailer other than the June bugs. He stared at the bugs without really seeing them as he tried to organize his thoughts. *Why do things like this happen to me? I can't even trash a bunch of software properly. I changed several dozen equations in ways that should have prevented the equipment from ever functioning, and instead, it shows real signs of life for the first time.*

The heat and humidity were very uncomfortable in the closed trailer. Wiping beads of sweat off of his forehead with a handkerchief, he thought about turning on the trailer's roof mounted air conditioner, but didn't want to make any more noise than was absolutely necessary. As his breathing slowed, he mentally reviewed the progress of the Defender project to date as he searched for explanations.

The Defender was based on creating interference patterns among a controlled set of circularly polarized electromagnetic fields of different frequencies and phases. The idea was to cause standing waves where the signals would reinforce each other in densely packed layers of opposite polarities. Varying the frequency and phase relationships between the signals should control the size of the field and its distance from the projector - the antenna array - on the generator. Laboratory experiments with breadboard circuits and cobbled together test equipment proved the desired patterns could be achieved at low signal strengths. The prototype was built to generate the field intensities necessary to determine if a field could be formed which would deflect significant amounts of energy. The real trick was to deflect more energy than was required to maintain the generated field.

The prototype was constructed in a trailer for three reasons. First, there was little room for it anywhere else due to Jimmy's husbandry of the facilities. Second, some of the employees who knew about the laboratory experiments were worried about possible side effects when the field energy levels were increased. *Those people may have been prophetic!* And finally, Jimmy wanted as few people as feasible aware of the prototype's progress.

Nick continued to reexamine the evening's events in his mind, then thought of another quick test he wanted to try. It required turning on the hole again, but he didn't want a light shining out in the field behind the plant, and that meant turning off the lights inside the trailer. *It's stupid to be uncomfortable in the dark.* But he couldn't help it. *It won't really be so dark in here with the equipment on. The computer display puts out a fair amount of light. It will be like watching late night TV with the lights off.* Ashamed at his hesitancy, he rose, stepped to the switch next to the trailer door, and extinguished the lights. Once his eyes adjusted, the glow from the computer monitor and status lights on the equipment panels were sufficient to see quite well.

Returning to his seat, it only took a second to click on the icon to energize the field again. He picked up a small screwdriver and walked over to the hole floating beneath the projector. This time, he leaned over and tried to push the screwdriver up through the mirrored bottom side of the hole. It did not yield. He tapped the screwdriver against the surface. It sounded like he was striking metal or glass. *It's obviously a hard surface on this side. It reflects light, so maybe it's reflecting other radiated energies as well. This could be a closer relative to the Defender field than I thought. I wish I had more time to figure it out!* He returned to the equipment rack and turned off the field generator again, then turned the lights back on.

I don't know what it's doing, but I know it's not generating the Defender field as it was originally envisioned. It will take a lot of time and testing to determine what's really happening, how to control the process, and what the usefulness of this mode of operation might be, and I don't have any time left! I've got to get out of here! He took a deep breath and tried to relax.

Some of the possibilities were fairly obvious to him. It appeared to somehow connect two points in space together, reducing the distance between them to zero. Matter, even living organisms, could pass through apparently unharmed. He looked up at the June bugs still bouncing off the lights. *It's a complete failure as a bug zapper, that's for sure!* The process required a fair amount of power which might limit the range. Even so, there could be beneficial applications in communications and transportation as long as there was a way to control where the other end of the hole opened. *Assume for a moment the range is not limited. Maybe we could put a man on the moon again ... wait a minute! The other side of the hole would be in a vacuum. That could be a real problem!*

He got up and began to pace up and down in front of the equipment racks while his mind raced. *I guess there could be a number of other illegal uses, too. It looks like a great burglary tool. The walls of the trailer certainly didn't interfere with it. I wonder if it can penetrate thicker walls, like bank vaults! It could be used to commit the perfect crime. The old windowless room, door bolted on the inside, murder conundrum. Just open up a hole and fire a bullet through it. No sign of entry, no murder weapon found. Political assassinations would be a snap!*

There are also possible military applications. You might be able to move troops through a hole if it could be made big enough. Or open a hole inside an enemy's headquarters and shove a bomb through. Maybe shove a nuclear bomb through! That sure would thwart any strategic defense programs I know about. They're all targeted at the delivery systems! There wouldn't be any defense against a bomb delivered with no warning through a hole. That's just great. The Defender *field generator may turn out to be the perfect* Offensive *weapon!*

Chapter 7

When the Board of Directors returned from lunch, Ken departed for his bank in downtown Houston, but Jimmy asked Dave to stay a while longer.

Once they were seated in Jimmy's office, he started the conversation. "Guess who I ran into at the last American Defense Industry Association conference." Dave did not respond as Jimmy swiveled in his chair, leaned back, and put his feet up on his desk.

Dave sprawled in one of the visitor's chairs just in front of the desk. Jimmy's desk and chair rested on a well camouflaged three-inch high platform. Dave knew that Jimmy felt he gained a psychological advantage over visitors by literally holding the higher ground. At least it was one way to make people look up to him. Dave's posture accentuated the difference in elevation, but he couldn't care less.

"It was none other than Vance Billingsly." Jimmy wore a smug expression as he raised his arms and clasped his hands behind his head.

Dave thought for a minute, and then asked, "You mean the president of General Armaments?"

"The same," Jimmy confirmed. "After introducing himself and engaging me in a little small talk about the conference, he said he wanted to warn me about Nick."

Dave felt some trepidation over what would come next. He was instrumental in recruiting Nick to ITC. He'd seen a news vid about Nick's struggling young company on a business blog site streamed to his PIDD. He knew the challenges ITC was facing back then, and saw the potential for a serendipitous arrangement between the two companies. The initial contact and first few meetings with Nick were handled by Dave. Dave also acted as a go-between when Jimmy, acting on his ailing father's behalf, was negotiating the offer with Nick. Nick wanted an employment contract — not at all unusual under the circumstances - but Jimmy threw a fit. He insisted his word was his bond and his family had conducted business for years based on nothing more than a handshake and he wasn't about to change that now. Buck had intervened at Dave's bequest and proposed a compromise merger agreement describing how the companies would be combined and what Nick's role would be in the organization. Dave worked hard to convince Nick to trust the Bartons and sign the merger agreement. Dave shifted in his chair and sat a little straighter.

Jimmy continued, "He told me Nick was a trouble maker with a holier than thou attitude and an unrealistically inflexible approach to doing business." Jimmy smiled. "I think he was just trying to feel me out. When I agreed with him about Nick, he asked me if I was free for dinner."

Jimmy removed his feet from the desk, turned his chair to face Dave squarely, and leaned forward as if he was about to share a great secret.

"The dinner conversation was fascinating. Vance knows everybody in the energy weapons industry — at government agencies and at contractors alike. To make a long story short, he described an unofficial relationship between the heads of most of the companies in the business. They cooperate to practically guarantee sufficient profitable contracts for all. He said he could arrange it so we would win the Pavilion Mast contract even if we increased our bid at BAFO."

"You're talking about price fixing," Dave said. "That could be very risky. Why would Billingsly offer to do such a thing for us?"

Jimmy answered, "Because he wants to team with us on the Defender research."

"What? How did he even know about that?"

"He seems to know a lot about us," Jimmy replied with a slight smile. "He's good. He knows we're in the prototype stage and things look promising. I suspect he knows one or more of our employees a little too well. That's something we need to track down and fix later. I'll tell you one thing, though. It isn't Nick."

"Why do you say that?"

"Because Vance said Nick has to go."

"Go? You mean we're supposed to fire him?"

"That's right," said Jimmy. "Vance feels there's no way we'll be able to keep the government from claiming rights to the results of the research efforts if Nick is involved. We could even end up with a big investigative audit of all our contracts. He says, one way or another, Nick will eventually find out we're charging the work to cost-plus government contracts and blow the whistle."

The surprises were coming too fast and furious for Dave's liking. "He knew about altering the cost account numbers? How could he know about that? I didn't even know until this morning!"

"I told you he knows a lot about us, but I think he was guessing about the accounting. Frank wouldn't risk losing his cushy high-paying job by telling anyone. Anyway, I confirmed Vance's suspicions," answered Jimmy.

Dave raised his eyebrows and shifted uncomfortably in his chair. The normal twinkle in his eyes was long gone and now he was frowning. "Why did you admit it? How do you know you can trust him?"

Jimmy smiled broadly at Dave's discomfort and said, "I told you I was making a long story short. We had quite a discussion. He's one of us. He believes in the Jimmy Barton Rules of Business."

Oh yes, thought Dave, *The Jimmy Barton Rules of Business.* He'd heard them often enough. *Rule Number One: 'You have to cheat in order to succeed.' Rule Number Two: 'All people are fundamentally lazy, incompetent, and dishonest in varying proportions.' Rule Number Three: 'Employees who are mostly lazy or incompetent are a waste of money, so try to hire people who are mostly dishonest and they will help you cheat.' Jimmy probably felt hiring Nick violated Rule Number Three.*

Dave knew that the only quality Jimmy valued in an employee was loyalty. Jimmy would periodically post blind ads on employment sites with job descriptions matching those of ITC's key positions. Then he would fire any ITC employee who responded to the ad for disloyalty.

"So," said Dave, "how will we complete the project without Nick? He's the one who knows the most about it and has done the majority of the work."

"Vance says he has a guy who can finish the work," Jimmy answered, "one who doesn't concern himself with where the money comes from as long as he's well paid."

"Wait a minute," said Dave. "Nick told me he couldn't sell the Defender concept at GenArm when he was there years ago. Why is Billingsly so interested now?"

"I asked Vance the very same question," replied Jimmy. "He said things have changed since the breakup of the U.S.S.R. and the widely proclaimed end of the Cold War. Before that, GenArm didn't think defensive weapon systems would sell. SDI ran into trouble because it would threaten the MAD balance and might even precipitate a preemptive strike by the Soviets. There was also criticism based on the expectation SDI would not be perfect - some of the payloads launched would still get through.

"After that," Jimmy continued, "the concern became focused on a small number of weapons in the hands of a third world country or some group of terrorists who are not deterred by MAD, but that threat didn't really promote SDI funding since the terrorists didn't have access to the delivery systems that SDI proposed to intercept.

"Vance told me that the game changer is the Depression combined with the ongoing religious wars. The standard of living in third world countries was already low, and the Depression has further reduced supplies and increased prices of essential goods worldwide. This fosters greater unrest among the populace that fans the flames of current conflicts while making revolutions or new hostilities between neighboring countries more likely. Many of those poorer countries are aligned with one or more major countries that might intervene, causing the conflict to spread.

"In the meantime, national security analysts are pointing out a dangerous side effect of the large reductions in armed forces and conventional weapons stores among the world's major nations during the Depression - if a war breaks out, the antagonists could be forced to employ unconventional weapons very quickly, at least on a tactical level, and things could escalate from there. Vance told me the government's interest in defensive measures of

36

all kinds is now high and rising."

Jimmy smiled and added, "When you think about it, World War II ended the First Great Depression. Maybe World War III will end the Second Great Depression."

Jimmy almost seems happy discussing the possibility of war. I guess he's already starting to count the money he'd make on Defender if he can get it to work. After reflecting for a moment, Dave said, "Okay, so he's changed his mind about the market. But we've carried Defender to the prototype stage without him. Why does he think we should cut him in now?"

"Well, his real message was kind of a carrot-and-stick approach. If we scratch his back, he'll scratch ours. On the other hand, he implied we would fare poorly against the coordinated strength of the rest of the industry if we didn't cooperate. But his official position was to claim partial rights to the development - he maintains Nick actually did a lot of the conceptual work while he was still an employee of GenArm. Vance insists they have an ethical, if not a legal, right to participate in the continued project."

Dave sat bolt upright and exploded, "Ethical right? He talks about price fixing and threatens us with restraint of trade by way of an illegal industry cabal, and then talks about *ethics*?"

Jimmy laughed. "Well, Dave, you've heard of situational ethics haven't you? Basically, Vance is just saying we're either with him or against him. If we're with him, we have a responsibility to support him, and the favor will be returned."

Dave was not happy with the situation and mentally searched for pitfalls. "What will Ken say about this? He's already asking very pointed questions about Defender."

"Actually, I couldn't care less what Ken says," answered Jimmy. "But appeasing Ken happens to be a side effect of Vance's proposal. Ken is concerned about abandoning the Defender project and the arrangement with GenArm will provide ample funding for Defender research. In fact, I bet I can figure out a way to classify the whole project as an asset and declare the amount supplied by GenArm as revenue for ITC while spreading the costs over the years as depreciation. That will allow us to show a tidy profit this year." Jimmy smiled broadly, obviously pleased with himself for thinking of another game to play with the books.

Dave tried again. "We can't discharge Nick for cause - his performance has been excellent. What if he sues us for wrongful termination?"

Jimmy smiled and said, "He's smart enough to know that suing us would cost a lot of money since we could tie him up with legal maneuvers for years. He won't have that kind of money because I'm not going to give him enough severance pay for him to do anything more than worry about how he's going to make his next rent payment."

Dave winced and took another tack, "What are you going to do for an Engineering Manager? Are you going to promote Jack Davis?"

Jimmy snorted, "No. I don't want any European-educated engineer as my Engineering Manager."

Dave was confused. "What do you mean by 'European-educated'?"

"Well, he's from Australia isn't he?"

Now Dave's mind reeled. "Australia isn't a European country; it's a continent in itself! You must be thinking of Austria." *I know that Jimmy partied his way through school and never got a degree, but this is ridiculous!* "Besides, Jack immigrated with his family as a teenager and his engineering degree is from Rice University right here in Houston."

"Wherever he's from and wherever he went to school, he came to ITC with Nick during the merger. I don't want a Nick Loyalist as my Engineering Manager."

Dave was becoming more and more uncomfortable. He tried one more ploy. "What if Nick goes out and competes against us?"

That elicited a big laugh from Jimmy. "Nick? Compete with us? You've got to be kidding! He doesn't have it in him. He's a sheep, not a wolf ... and a deluded sheep at that. He's his own worst enemy! Did I ever tell you about his hubcaps?"

"Hubcaps," Dave responded, "what do hubcaps have to do with this?"

Jimmy answered, "Somebody stole the hubcaps off his truck. He complained that replacements cost several hundred dollars at the dealer. I told him to stop at one of those hubcap-covered shacks on the side of the highway and he could probably buy back his own set for less than half the dealer's price. Do you know what he said?"

Jimmy didn't wait for an answer before continuing. "He said buying from road side shacks supports the market in stolen hubcaps. If everyone bought factory replacements from legitimate outlets instead, the thefts would stop. I told him there was no way everyone was going to stop buying stolen hubcaps and he was just throwing his money away. He said my argument could be used to rationalize anything - responsible behavior had to start somewhere, and it might as well be with him. Can you imagine?

"Besides, he'd be afraid to start another company," Jimmy chuckled. "His first one failed didn't it? He's not a risk taker. Shortly after he came to ITC he drove us to lunch. He wouldn't park in the No Parking zone right in front of the restaurant like I always do. He said he'd enjoy his lunch more if he wasn't worrying about his truck getting towed! He's totally gutless! And you're concerned about competition from a guy like that?" Jimmy laughed. "He'll never be a victor; he's a born victim! Don't make me laugh any more - my sides hurt!"

Turning serious again, Jimmy said, "Listen, Dave, I want you to come with me in a minute to give Nick his notice."

Dave slumped back in his chair, defeated. He didn't like any of this, but close relations between his family and Jimmy's family went back many years. The bond that existed between the two groups of fellow upper-economic strata travelers is the only reason he agreed to purchase stock and sit on ITC's board. The Bartons would have done the same for him or any other Litchfield if asked. Dave certainly did not consider ITC a good investment. He fully expected to lose every dime of his money. But he would have to go along - to Nick's office and beyond. "So you've already made up your mind to cooperate with GenArm and let them in on Defender."

"Yes, the help Vance is offering us is going to be extremely valuable," Jimmy answered. "We're certain to get the Pavilion Mast contract this way. In contrast, we don't even know if the Defender will ever work. So we're trading a share in an uncertain thing in return for all of a sure thing. What could be better? GenArm is a lot bigger than us, but I think we'll make a good Mutt-and-Jeff team." Jimmy chuckled at his analogy.

David and Goliath is more like it, thought Dave. *And Goliath is trying to talk us out of our slingshot.*

Chapter 8

Nick stopped pacing and faced the equipment again. *If the phenomenon can be controlled, if the range can be extended, this thing could have enormous potential for mayhem. Actually, there is a respectable potential for mayhem already. In the wrong hands it could be a devastating weapon. But what am I going to do? I don't want to destroy it. In the* right *hands it could be enormously beneficial. But who are the right hands? Me? ... First things first - if I'm not going to destroy it, I need to protect it, and how am I going to do that?*

Pacing back and forth again, he considered his options. *To begin with, I have to do something about the software on the computer system inside the plant. Who would have guessed that my attempt at making sure that the Defender would never do anything would actually cause it to do something! Whether I decide to destroy or protect the equipment, I have to eliminate any information that could allow anyone else to make another operable prototype.* He was glad that years of conditioning had compelled him to make the backup copies of the original software as well as the altered version. Patting his PIDD-pocket reassured him that his PIDD was still there. That reminded him to check the time.

"What time is it, Agnes?"

"Ten minutes and twenty-three seconds after eleven P.M., Nick," Agnes' voice came from his PIDD-pocket.

Nick sighed, and headed for the door.

Twenty minutes later, he was back in the trailer after replacing the original software files and once again eliminating any record of his work session on the computer system. He returned to stare at the equipment. *So now I'm back where I started. Well, sort of ... with the minor addition of a likely world shattering technological breakthrough. Now, do I try and tear this thing apart? I sure don't want to. I've spent a good chunk of my adult life trying to make this thing work! I want to see what it can do. But I can't do that here, and it's too big to steal.*

He felt a tingling sensation down his spine as he had an outrageous thought. *Or is it? It's in a trailer, after all, and I've got a trailer hitch on my truck! ... Where would I take it? ... Is the trailer really road worthy?*

He decided to inspect the outside of the trailer before worrying about destinations. Between the moon and the building floodlights he could see well enough. The hitch looked like it was the right size. The safety chains were there. The tires looked good. *Where does the power come in? ... There it is.* The power cable entered on the lower back corner of the trailer next to the rear wall of the plant. His eyes followed the cable to an electrical box mounted on the plant wall. The electrical box had a hasp on its hinged lid that fortunately was devoid of any lock. Nick sighed, *probably another one of Jimmy's cost saving measures. Padlocks cost money.* He raised the lid of the box and verified that the power cable from the trailer was attached to a large circuit breaker with spade lugs. He could interrupt the power by throwing the circuit breaker open and simply unscrewing the connections with a screwdriver - there were plenty of tools in the trailer.

So I can drive off with this puppy anytime I want. He shook his head as he finished his circumnavigation. The irony of the situation was obvious. Here was a project deserving of extreme security measures from the outset - and was even more deserving now - yet the prototype was totally unprotected, a plum ripe for picking.

They might build another one, he thought, reentering the trailer, *and then they might stumble across the same software changes I did ... extremely unlikely, but not impossible.* Then he remembered the design drawings. *But I have the only accurate drawings.* He had annotated the drawings stored in his PIDD whenever a change was made to the prototype hardware. The changes had not yet been incorporated on the master drawing files in the CAD system thanks to another of Jimmy's cost saving measures - he discharged several of the CAD operators in a lay off several months ago, and prioritized contract work over R&D. *So if I take the trailer, they'll be left with seriously out of date drawings and dysfunctional software. That sounds fair to me!*

But where will I go? A possible destination came to mind, but it would take many hours of driving. The magnitude of what he was considering suddenly hit him. *What am I doing? I can't steal this thing! But I can't leave it here either!*

His internal conflict was resolved when he remembered the importance of the discovery and his overwhelming desire to keep it away from the wrong people. *I don't want to believe that good guys always finish last, even though there's a lot of supporting evidence for it, but in any event I'll try to make sure the bad guys don't finish first this time.*

With adrenaline-aided quickness, he combed the inside of the trailer, securing loose objects and turning off equipment. Then he turned off the lights. He decided to leave the door open while he hitched the trailer to his truck - maybe the floodlights outside would entice the June bugs to leave the darkened interior. *All ashore that's going ashore!* He wondered at feeling so chipper while his attempted sabotage transformed itself into grand theft. He picked up the wooden stairs, turned them sideways, and shoved them into the trailer. As he walked to his truck, he looked around the parking lot to verify he was still alone. Satisfied, he entered and started his truck, then pulled in front of the trailer.

The trailer's tongue was resting on cinder blocks, but was equipped with an integral jack. Once he jacked the trailer up slightly and moved the cinder blocks to one side, he was able to back his truck up using the rear view camera to position the ball hitch underneath the mating socket on the trailer.

He was relieved the ball fit perfectly when he lowered the front of the trailer. Scooting under the truck on his back, he hooked the trailer's safety chains on frame members. Then he rose and stepped back to inspect his work.

Looks like I'm ready to go.

He got in his truck and glanced in the rear view mirrors before putting the truck in gear. He could see the trailer door gently swaying back and forth in the breeze. *I left the door open!* He got out of his truck, walked to the side of the trailer, reached up, locked and slammed the door. *If there are any June bugs left in there, they are about to go on an unexpected journey.* Returning to the driver's seat, he put the truck in gear and pulled slowly away from the building.

A second later he heard a loud bang and felt a sharp jolt. Near panic, he mashed the brake pedal and looked in his rear view mirrors. He couldn't see anything. Getting out of his truck yet again, he walked back to the trailer. There, on the rear corner, he saw the electric power cable dragging on the ground. On the plant wall a few feet behind the rear of the trailer was a recently mangled electrical box. *I'm really off to a good start!*

Chapter 9

Nick looked up from his computer as Jimmy and Dave walked into his office. "Well, to what do I owe the honor of a visit by this august group?" he asked. Neither of them offered a rejoinder as Jimmy settled himself in the one empty visitor's chair and Dave moved books off of the other chair in front of Nick's desk and sat down. *I guess this is when they tell me that it has been decided to put Defender on hold. I hope they're in the mood for an argument. Thanks to Frank, I've had a little time to prepare.*

Nick glanced at Dave who was trying very hard to remain expressionless. It made him appear quite distressed in contrast to his normal amused countenance. This visit obviously was not an occasion for joking or light banter.

Also unsmiling, Jimmy started by saying, "Nick, the Board of Directors has decided it's time to make a change. The Defender project has cost us a lot of money and we still don't have anything to show for it."

Nick momentarily considered calling Jimmy's bluff. According to Frank, Jimmy thought the Defender costs were being charged to cost-plus contracts and reimbursed by the government, thereby costing ITC nothing. But Nick couldn't think of a way to point that out without getting Frank in trouble, so he remained silent.

Jimmy continued, "So we've decided we must drastically cut costs. I'm sorry to say we can't afford to keep you on the team. But don't worry; we can carry you until the end of the month."

Nick blinked and stared at Jimmy in disbelief. *What's going on here? Can't keep me on the team? He's firing me? That's not what Frank said. Of course they wouldn't talk about something like this in front of Frank. I can't believe this is happening! Why? And what's this about the end of the month? That's only a couple of weeks away! He can't be serious about any of this!*

Nick looked over at Dave again to see if he could detect any indication this was some sort of practical joke. Jimmy had a reputation for them. Nick hated practical jokes and was ready to blast Jimmy if this was one of them. If anything, Dave looked more miserable than before. *Jimmy is serious!* Nick felt a knot in his stomach as his muscles tensed. He didn't know what to do or say. He'd never been fired before. In fact, just the opposite - he was always praised and promoted. Even at GenArm, where some very powerful people were unhappy with his resistance to unethical business practices, he'd survived numerous layoffs during the recession and been a rising star until he decided to leave.

Time seemed to stand still. The room felt uncomfortably hot. There was a rushing sound in his ears. Nick realized he probably appeared flushed. He lowered his eyes in embarrassment and discovered he wasn't breathing. Now he was angry over being embarrassed. *I should be mad at Jimmy, not myself! I haven't done anything wrong! I've done a lot for this company! I've put them on the weapons systems map!* But he couldn't shake the feeling of shame - the shame of being fired. He tried to take a deep breath silently even though his body was willing him to gasp for air. *There's got to be a way to change his mind. Surely he wouldn't abandon Defender now.* "Why would you want to give up on Defender when we're this close to making it work?"

Dave shifted — squirmed was a better description — in his chair. Jimmy hesitated before responding. "I didn't say we were giving up on Defender. We just have to cut costs."

"But how can you continue the project without me?" Nick exclaimed. *Ouch! That sure sounded like a self-important whine. Nobody but Jimmy is indispensable in Jimmy's world! Although, getting anyone else up to speed in this case would certainly require a lot of time and a bundle of money. But I already know money is not the real issue here. I wonder ... what is the real issue?*

"Based on an agreement reached in discussions between Vance Billingsly of GenArm and myself, our two companies are going to team up to finish Defender," Jimmy answered. "ITC has carried the ball this far and GenArm will finish up. That will cut our remaining costs to almost nothing, which is about all we can afford."

For a moment, Nick's jaw went slack and his mouth gaped open. *Bingo! That's the real issue. Vance Billingsly has figured out a way to reach out and touch somebody. He's getting back at me for not cooperating with his schemes at GenArm.* Nick took a deep breath ... *No; Vance would not actually spend money just for revenge. He'd already blacklisted me at all the major weapons system contractors. Vance must really want to get his hands on Defender. How did Jimmy and Vance get hooked up? I wonder if Jimmy knows he's swimming with sharks.* "Jimmy, you'd better be real careful dealing with Vance Billingsly. He can't be trusted."

Jimmy was obviously angered by Nick's warning. *Uh oh,* thought Nick. *Too late! He's already trusted Vance and now he's mad at me for suggesting he was gullible. Of course, what do I care if he's mad at me? He's firing me! And, based on what Frank told me at lunch, plus this GenArm connection, I should be glad to get out of here.* Instead, Nick's feelings of anger and humiliation grew as he silently scolded himself for being so fearful for his personal future. *What am I going to do? I don't have much in the way of savings – I don't know anybody who does have any significant savings these days ... Well, maybe Jimmy does.*

"My relationship with Vance is not your concern, Nick. I just want you to help bring GenArm's engineer up to speed on the project before you go. If you don't think you can do that, then maybe you should leave now instead of at the end of the month."

Nick's complexion flushed anew. *There's that end of the month thing again!* Nick felt like punching Jimmy in the mouth - or at least physically throwing him out of his office - but he knew it wouldn't do any good. *I've got to remain calm. If I antagonize him, it'll just get worse.* "The end of the month is coming up pretty fast, Jimmy." He was ashamed of the quaver in his voice. "That's not much notice." *Particularly when I probably can't get a job anywhere else in the industry and I'm not prepared to retire, either emotionally or financially. I've got too many obligations. I'm even signed on the company's debt! ... Wait a minute, he must be forgetting about the employment contract.* "What about the long term employment contract you promised me for co-signing the company's note last month?"

Jimmy grinned at Nick as he rose from his chair and Dave slowly followed suit. Then he asked a question Nick would never forget before turning and leading Dave out of the office without waiting for an answer:

"Do you have that in writing?"

Chapter 10

Nick MacEwen shook his head in disgust as he returned to his truck. *I'd better put my brain in gear and stop making stupid mistakes or I'm going to get caught before I get started. I can't believe I forgot to disconnect the power.* Now the loose power cable was wrapped around the rear bumper of the trailer and secured in place with some electrical tape. He looked back over his shoulder at the scene of the crime as he tried to think of any other potential problems.

He had restored the original software on the computer and the log was clear. He had the program files on his PIDD and the only accurate drawings were also stored in the PIDD. *I'm glad Jimmy didn't arrange for extra security or ask me to turn in my trailer key. He probably didn't think I'd have the nerve to do something like this. Or maybe he thought I'd enjoy being fired after I was promised an employment contract ... all while remaining jointly and severally responsible for the company's bank loan.* He felt that he had done everything he could to do at this point to prevent Jimmy and Vance from benefitting from their actions. Nick climbed behind the wheel and slowly pulled out of the parking lot. He was not used to towing and frequently checked his rear view mirrors to make sure the trailer looked all right.

Unnoticed by Nick while he concentrated on his driving, the pale light from a PIDD display appeared in the window of a dark room in one of the empty buildings across the street from ITC as the truck and trailer passed by. At about the same time, a dark silhouette separated itself from the shadow of an industrial trash bin near the back of ITC's parking lot and watched the truck and trailer recede towards the front of the industrial park. The intruder then proceeded into the field and started a flashlight lit search.

At the front of the industrial park, Nick turned south on the access road and took the entrance ramp for U.S. Highway 59. If anyone saw the trailer leave the area, he wanted them to remember it was heading out of the city toward Mexico. Once he was far enough away, he would turn north, circle back past his apartment in northwest Houston and grab some essentials.

The circuitous route would take time that he could ill afford, but it was better than towing a stolen trailer south to north the length of the city. He needed to both limit exposure and avoid certain notorious areas of the city where the residents' speculations regarding the marketability of any items being transported in the trailer might induce an attempt at a hijacking. He was not that well equipped to resist the attempt and would be unwilling to report it even if he survived the encounter.

The moon was high in the nearly cloudless sky, but he was still too close to the city lights to see many stars. The traffic on the fringes of Houston at this time of night was fairly light excepting the interstates. *Maybe I'll take Texas Highway 6 northwest to Waco instead of Interstate 45 north towards Dallas after I go by the apartment. That will keep me off of the freeway and less in the public eye.*

Nick thought about the long trip ahead. He intended to drive straight through, stopping only for food and gas. *I don't want to use my PIDD to pay - the charge records could reveal my route.* Banks had stopped processing checks years ago, so he needed cash. Although Congress had debated closing down the mints and requiring that all financial transactions occur electronically, a number of contributors gave key Congressmen practical demonstrations of the importance of cash to the underground economy and the proposal died in committee.

Now cash was king in the depression. *I'll stop at an ATM and get some money.* However, automatic teller machines also produced a record which included the location of the transaction. *The information age must create a lot of problems for criminals ... like me.* Actually, he knew the information age also created a lot of opportunities for criminals as well.

Criminal activity in general had increased greatly in direct proportion to the depth of the depression. Technical crimes such as embezzlement, identity theft and fraud were growing, but nowhere near as fast as less sophisticated crimes like armed robbery and burglary. There had been riots and looting in some cities, including Houston, as inner city mobs ranged out into the suburbs in an ultimately futile attempt to steal the good life. The mobs discovered that the good life was in very short supply these days.

Houston is the largest city in the country that does not have zoning laws, resulting in a patchwork quilt of industrial, retail, and residential developments of varying size and quality. Thankfully, Nick's apartment was in a middle-class neighborhood that was out of the price range of the financially desperate while simultaneously not appearing to be worth the effort for looting mobs. The owners of the homes and apartment complexes in the area were more than willing to perpetuate that appearance by avoiding most exterior maintenance, so Nick considered the neighborhood relatively safe.

Nick decided to use an ATM located in the same sector of the city, the northwest, as his apartment. He was about to command Agnes to plan his route when he thought better of it. He remembered that Global Positioning Satellite data from PIDDs was now used by the government to automatically collect speeding fines and tolls, so he couldn't risk using his PIDD to direct his travel.

To be safe, I should just turn it off. The Administration had recently proposed a law against driving a vehicle without a functioning PIDD - presumably to make sure that speeders and toll deadbeats were caught - but the only reason they had not implemented it already was that more and more people were unable to afford a PIDD given the economic conditions. New legislation was in the works to distribute government-provided PIDDs to those who couldn't otherwise afford them.

With his newfound perspective of a fugitive, Nick wondered if fine and toll revenue was all that the government wanted out of GPS-based surveillance. *Maybe that's why PIDDs don't have an on/off switch.*

Nick pulled off at a tree-lined roadside rest stop and parked behind a short line of darkened semi-trucks. Somewhat fearfully, he opened up his PIDD's battery compartment, removed the battery, and put both the PIDD and battery in his truck's glove compartment. *Can they tell that I have dropped off the grid? Are alarms sounding somewhere? ...* Well, there was nothing he could do about it even if there were. *Get a grip, Nick! Get moving!* He was back on the road a few minutes later feeling very vulnerable with a quiescent PIDD. *I'll just have to navigate by memory.*

So Nick continued around the western fringe of the city. This was mostly ranch country, with the horizon interrupted only occasionally by a patch of woods, a church spire, or the boxy silhouette of a rural manufacturing plant showing in the pale moonlight. Most of the factories were abandoned, victims of the depression. The only lights were in widely spaced farm yards or clustered around the odd open gas station in the small towns he passed. Nick could see plenty of stars now. Occasionally his headlights would briefly illuminate the dark hulk of a deserted house near the road as he passed. It saddened him to realize that each of them represented a displaced family - probably due to foreclosure.

He noticed a brief streak of faint light in the night sky. He saw a few more over the space of several minutes while he divided his attention between the road ahead and the relevant patch of sky. *Meteor shower*, he realized. Nick thought about what would happen if those streaks in the sky were missiles instead of meteoroids. Without the multilayered space and ground-based defenses proposed as part of the SDI program, the country could only respond in kind, dispensing wholesale death and destruction, tit for tat ... *Revenge, not victory.* The air in the truck suddenly felt chilly. He increased the temperature setting a couple of degrees on the climate control.

As the miles went by, Nick peered ahead in the dark watching for road signs to gauge his progress, but the very few he saw were unlit and worn too badly to make out. Apparently, the priority on providing highway signage had diminished over the years due to a combination of the depression and the use of PIDDs for travel directions. Finally, he passed a sign that was legible – "DO NOT PASS." Nick chuckled. *Are you breaking the law if you pass a 'Do Not Pass' sign? Is this another crime I have committed this night?*

He encountered very little traffic except when he crossed over or under major highways. Nick was grateful for the nearly empty roads as he was running below the speed limit, partially because he was still trying to get used to towing the trailer and partially because the condition of the road surface seemed to deteriorate the further he traveled from the city proper. Finally, he was just a little northwest of Houston. Now he was ready to make his money run.

Chapter 11

Shi Rui Xian awoke to the music his PIDD was playing to announce an incoming call. Shi Rui Xian was listed as the Agricultural Attaché at the Chinese Consulate in Houston. In reality, he was the station chief for the Ministry of State Security (MSS) responsible for intelligence operations in Alabama, Arkansas, Florida, Georgia, Louisiana, Mississippi, Oklahoma, Texas and Puerto Rico, with a rank equivalence of Colonel. The particular musical piece that was playing was from the modern Peking opera *Da Tang Guifei* which meant that the call was from one of his agents.

Colonel Shi rolled over and snatched his PIDD from the induction pad on his night stand. Glancing at the screen, he saw that the call came from Xue Jian Heng, one of his agents assigned to Defender surveillance. The call was audio only in accordance with his instructions, but the time was 11:48PM. *This is not a scheduled call, so something important has happened.* Colonel Shi tapped the icon for a secure connection and waited while both PIDDs contacted the secure server in Beijing via satellite to obtain a one-time encryption key. Once the Ānquán - the Chinese character for safety - appeared indicating that the PIDDs were secure and synchronized, he said in perfect English, "Good morning, to whom am I speaking?" to which Agent Xue replied, "Chu Long," which was the correct pass phrase as well as a humorous reference to a Houston butcher shop named Chu Long Meats. Of course, it was only funny in English. The whole conversation would be in English because his agents were instructed to never use Chinese since they might be overheard. Their speech, dress and mannerisms were all designed to make them look like second- or third-generation native born Asian Americans, as some of them actually were.

Face-to-face meetings were the preferred method of communication between Colonel Shi and his agents, but encrypted calls from agents in the field were allowed for scheduled reports using innocuous phrases to indicate status. The phrases were agreed to in advance during the face-to-face meetings and changed on a regular basis. But preplanned phrases might be inadequate to convey the necessary information in an emergency situation. In that event, the agents were instructed to use ordinary sounding phrases to get their message across even though they were using a secure connection. This was so the conversation would not reveal any important information even if one of the participants was the focus of remote listening surveillance or if the communication was intercepted and the encryption eventually broken. Colonel Shi was cautious and took what westerners would call a belt-and-suspenders approach to his duties.

He said, "What can I do for you this morning Long?" *Maybe if I keep saying 'morning' he'll get the message that I am not too happy about being awakened at this time of night.*

Agent Xue replied, "The bird has flown with the coop."

The bird has flown with *the coop? That's not one of the pre-arranged phrases and could only mean one thing - so much for Chinese inscrutability.* Forgetting his annoyance over the early hour, Colonel Shi considered that for a moment and asked, "Are you able to follow the bird?"

Agent Xue answered, "Not with current resources."

Of course! Xue is alone on the night shift. He probably couldn't get to his car fast enough to follow, and even if he did it would be too easy for the bird to spot the hawk on his tail.

Even having one agent watching ITC during the night when the plant was closed had been considered overkill by his superiors, but he had insisted that Defender's potential for upsetting strategic balances justified extraordinary measures. He argued for at least two agents at night, but was allowed only one. This event would prove the value of his caution, but that might be a hollow victory if the bird got away.

"Were you able to observe the direction of flight?"

"Southwest," Xue answered.

That would be toward the gulf, or maybe Mexico, thought Colonel Shi, *which makes no sense. Why would they move the Defender prototype at all, let alone in the middle of the night? Maybe they are going to a remote location for some sort of secret field tests - possibly the Chihuahuan Desert in the Big Bend area of Texas.* "Were there multiple birds or coops in the flight?"

"One of each, and it was *the* bird with *the* coop."

This is very strange – and very troublesome. We don't have enough agents in place to follow MacEwen and the prototype, and not enough information to guess where he and it are going. "Please continue to observe the perch in case the bird returns. I will call you back if I can determine the bird's path of flight by other means."

Colonel Shi broke the connection and then tapped in an unlisted number belonging to the Chinese Embassy in Washington, D.C. from memory. He had memorized all of his contacts' information. He could have stored them in his PIDD where they would be available with a voice command or a few finger taps, but Shi was risk averse; he even deleted the PIDD's history files after every call. American counter-espionage agents wouldn't get any useful leads should his PIDD ever fall into their hands.

Shi verified that the video mode was still turned off, and then tapped the Send icon. The call connected immediately, but was answered with silence. He then tapped the icon for a secure call and after seeing that key synchronization and encryption had been established said, "This is Colonel Shi Rui Xian in the Houston Consulate. I need to speak with the duty officer."

"This is Ni Bin, Colonel Shi, I have the duty. How may I help you?"

"Ah, good morning Major Ni, you may not be pleased, but I am glad you have the late shift. I need a PIDD's current location right away – one that you have been monitoring for some time. I expect it will be in motion. If so, please determine the direction of travel."

"I will check with the communications center on it right away. What is the number?" Major Ni wrote down MacEwen's PIDD number and promised to call back as soon as possible with the requested information.

Colonel Shi broke the connection. *The Americans can be unbelievably naïve sometimes. They want their privacy, so they design PIDDs with encrypted connections and biometric security. Then they have all of the PIDDs built in China! No PIDDs ever leave China without a back door electronic protocol that allows remote access to all stored data, including the GPS readings.*

It will take the embassy personnel a little time to sort through the data and report back, and I'm thoroughly awake now, so I might as well get up and drive over to MacEwen's apartment just to make sure he didn't go there. Colonel Shi reached up and turned on the nightstand lamp. He could have used a voice command to turn on the light, but he had turned off the built-in apartment management computer as soon as he moved in. Colonel Shi was a belt-and-suspenders risk-averse paranoid.

Chapter 12

Turning southeast, Nick returned to the Houston suburbs and stopped at an open convenience store near his apartment. The store, sitting in a pool of light from its street sign and gas pump island portico, stood out from the surrounding, mostly dark buildings. There was only one car parked in front of the store. He pulled in on the edge of the lot where the trailer wouldn't block access to the pumps or store parking spaces and took his PIDD out of the glove compartment to replace the battery before entering the store.

Once inside and standing in front of the ATM, he glanced over at the clerk and the store's only other customer for signs of undue interest in his activities before placing his PIDD on the ATM's induction pad to communicate his banking information. Shielding the ATM display from view with his body, he touched the icon to withdraw the maximum amount allowed for a single transaction — eight hundred dollars in twenties — from his bank account. *There's a piece of good luck. What are the odds of an ATM machine in a convenience store having eight hundred bucks this late at night in Houston?* Of course, he was not anywhere near the nightlife hot spots, nor was the nightlife as lively as it used to be. Without turning around, he quickly jammed the bills into his pocket without counting them, more willing to trust the machine than the people in the store if they glimpsed the size of his withdrawal.

Nick headed for the cold drink coolers next. He grabbed two six-packs of Dr. Pepper while the other customer concluded his business and left. As Nick approached the checkout counter, he noticed a display of pre-paid PIDDs and had a sudden thought.

"Excuse me," he said to the clerk. Pointing at the display he asked, "How much are the PIDDs?"

Pre-paid PIDDs were temporarily activated and could be reactivated for an additional fee, or thrown away. Most mass market electronic hardware was inexpensively manufactured robotically in Pacific Rim countries and considered disposable. The fee was primarily for the use of the data infrastructure, and usually billed based on data packet usage, although some plans were available based on unlimited data packages over a specified period of time. The distinctions between types of communications - audio, video, text - had essentially disappeared over the years as they all eventually boiled down to moving digital data from one place to another, hence data packets became the coin of the industry.

Besides communicating, the PIDDs could run many different kinds of applications, most of which were preloaded, and the remainder could be downloaded without additional charge. New applications were funded by the data service providers since they encouraged the use of additional data packets. The so-called PP-PIDDs were primarily used by individuals who had poor credit ratings and could not qualify for a monthly-billed account - an increasingly large percentage of the population. Young children, of course, always giggled at the many jokes revolving around PP and PIDD-ling.

The clerk simply pointed to a sign that listed the plans and prices. Nick looked them over and said, "I'll take the unlimited plan for one month," as he placed the rest of his purchases on the counter. The clerk took one of the PIDDs from the display and set it on the CIDD's (Commercial Integrated Digital Device, pronounced "sid") induction pad embedded in the counter. He touched an icon on the CIDD's screen. A form came up on the display and a virtual keyboard appeared on the counter in front of Nick. The clerk pointed at the form and the keyboard in turn as he looked up expectantly at Nick. It was an activation form for the data service provider. *It's time to take a gamble.* Nick filled out the form with a fictitious name and address. *And in this economy I think I will win the bet.*

"ID," said the taciturn clerk as he held out his hand. Nick was expecting this, because he knew that every PIDD was required by law to be registered to a specific individual. Nick reached into his pocket, pulled out a twenty dollar bill and handed it to the clerk. The clerk raised one eyebrow, glanced at the form on the CIDD screen, and smiled slightly as he slid the twenty into his shirt pocket.

"Thank you, Mister Jackson," responded the clerk as he touched the icon to activate the PIDD and then turned to ring up and bag Nick's Dr. Peppers. Nick took out his regular PIDD, placed it on the CIDD's pad and transferred the requisite amount from his bank account. He didn't care if anyone knew where he was at the moment since he was near his apartment.

Returning to his truck, Nick threw the Dr. Peppers in the truck's console refrigerator and then pulled up to the gas pumps in front of the store.

While he was waiting for the truck's dual tanks to fill, he noticed an old electrical charging pole at the end of the pump island. He smiled slightly as he remembered the short-lived electric car fad.

Electric cars were supposed to reduce the emissions caused by burning fossil fuels, and therefore ease global warming. But about eighty percent of the electricity generated in America came from burning fossil fuels, and the inefficiencies of generating, transmitting and distributing the electricity required to charge the batteries in an electric car meant that only about one-third of the energy produced by burning the fossil fuels at the generating plant actually reached the consumer. So roughly three times as much fossil fuel would be required to provide the same amount of energy to an electric car as an internal combustion car that burned the fossil fuel in situ. Once the facts were widely understood, the electric cars quickly disappeared from the roadways.

Nick started to think of ways that Defender's unexpected behavior might untie the Gordian Knot of clean energy production and distribution, but he was awakened from his reverie when the pump dinged to signal full tanks.

He looked at the total on the pump's display with dismay. On an intellectual level, Nick knew that the price of gasoline had been rising meteorically, but being suddenly unemployed put a whole new personal emphasis on that information. Even though his income had been much higher than average, he had barely been getting by – and he was a confirmed bachelor! He couldn't imagine how people with an average or lower income could support a family. Prices had been rising faster than wages for many years.

Nick paid using the pump's induction pad with his regular PIDD. Even starting with a full tank, he knew that eight hundred dollars would not be enough to cover gas for the trip he was facing. *I'll have to figure out how to get more cash as I go. Right now I just need to get going*, Nick thought as he drove to his apartment.

At his apartment, Nick looked around at the furniture and saw nothing that he really cared about. That was a good thing, since he didn't have the time or the space to load any of it. He grabbed what few clothes he had out of his closet and dresser drawers, threw them on the bed, pulled the bedspread up over the pile and tied it off. Looking a bit like Santa Claus with a big bag of toys over his shoulder, he went out to the parking lot and threw them in the trailer. He similarly swept all of his toiletries out of the bathroom cabinet into the empty grocery bag from the convenience store. *Ah, the life of a bachelor. Not very fancy, but very efficient!* Finally, he rounded up the important things, those items that he really cared about. Taking the boxes down off the shelf in his closet, he carefully carried them out to the trailer.

Back in the apartment, Nick placed both his regular PIDD and the PP-PIDD on the kitchen table. Sitting down, he pressed the workstation icon on his regular PIDD and it unfolded to nine times its compact size, providing a large display and a projected virtual keyboard. Then he copied all of the files from his regular PIDD to the pre-paid one using their short range infrared connection. His regular PIDD was already connected to his apartment's wireless network, but he didn't want to similarly connect the PP-PIDD because he knew it would leave a record on the apartment management computer.

After a final look around to make sure he had everything he wanted, he used his regular PIDD to transfer funds to pay the balance of his lease and to send a text giving the landlord permission to dispose of the abandoned possessions, purposely leaving out any forwarding address. After a moment's thought, he also encouraged the landlord to help herself to the remaining food in the refrigerator and cupboard before it all went bad. Finally, he taped the compact icon and re-folded his regular PIDD.

On the way out, he commanded the apartment management computer to turn off the air conditioning and terminate the program that randomly switched lights and music on and off automatically when he had not been detected in the apartment for more than twenty-four hours. *No use wasting electricity.* Nick's rent included all utilities, but he didn't want to run up the landlord's bill unnecessarily. Nick removed the battery from his regular PIDD again as he walked to his truck, put it in the glove compartment, and snapped the PP-PIDD in the recess provided for the purpose on the dashboard. This recess incorporated an induction pad that connected the PIDD to the truck's electronics while simultaneously charging the PIDD's battery.

Having checked everything off of his mental checklist, he fired up his truck and headed toward Waco.

As he cleared the Houston metropolitan area the traffic went from light to virtually nonexistent, so Nick got a Dr. Pepper out of the refrigerator, opened it up, took a sip, and then reached out and tapped the settings icon on the PP-PIDD's external display. Since the PIDD had not yet been configured, it started the process in the factory default voice-command-and-response mode.

The video screen displayed an animated simulacrum of a young blond girl in a Kilgore College Texas Rangerettes outfit complete with white cowboy boots, short blue skirt, red blouse and white cowboy hat.

"Howdy! What should I call you?" The PIDD was using a perky female voice with a slight Texas accent. As was normal for a pre-configuration PIDD, this persona was randomly selected from a large group of factory preset simulacrums associated with the general geographical region where the PIDD was activated.

"Boss," Nick said, not wishing to get too familiar with a PP-PIDD. His real PIDD called him Nick.

"Okay, Boss. What do you want to call me?"

Nick responded with "Fred," establishing another difference between it and his own PIDD that he had named Agnes after the Scottish heroine Lady Agnes Randolph, known to history as Black Agnes.

"Okay, Boss. The name Fred is normally associated with the male gender. Do you wish me to change to a male persona or continue with a female persona?"

That's a weird question, thought Nick. *Well, I suppose Fred could be short for Frederica or something.* "Male," he replied, also different from Agnes, who used a female persona and spoke with a light Scottish brogue.

Fred switched to an image of a Texas Aggie Cadet Corps senior, complete with riding boots, jodhpurs, Midnights, white gloves, Sam Browne belt and Campaign cover. In a deep male voice, but retaining the slight Texas accent, Fred asked, "Is this persona acceptable to you?"

Nick, growing irritated with the process, answered, "Whatever."

Nick's eyebrows rose as Fred accepted that ambiguous answer instead of demanding a yes or no response.

Fred continued, "A spectral analysis of your voice is consistent with the male gender. Are you male?"

Puzzled, Nick answered, "Yes." He wanted to know why it had asked that question, but it was not a true artificial intelligence, just a cleverly programmed computer. It could not respond to open ended voice commands like "why?"

Surprisingly, Fred proceeded to answer Nick's unasked question. "I ask because it is somewhat unusual for a male user to assign a male persona to his PIDD. This complicates some of my configuration options. Are you heterosexual, homosexual, transsexual, or bisexual?"

"What the ...?" *Be Careful, Nick. You promised yourself you would rein in your cussing. But the question surprised him. The era of "political correctness" was pretty much dead – people had much greater problems to deal with now – even so, the question struck him as out of line. There are people who would argue that Engineers are asexual, but that wasn't one of the choices.*

Fred chided, "I didn't get that, sir. Please repeat your response."

After a moment's hesitation Nick said, "Heterosexual." *I didn't have to go through this with Agnes. If I ever get my hands on the programmers of these newer PIDDs, I'll throttle them.*

"Thank you, sir. Your personal information will help me organize settings such as contacts, books, games, navigational points of interest, music, and video entertainment to better suit your profile. How old are you, sir?"

Nick hesitated again, but finally resigned himself to suffer through Fred's unexpectedly intrusive initiation process and answered, "Forty-eight."

"Listen carefully to the following menu ..."

OH NO! ... But Nick soldiered on through ten more minutes of questions and answers. Several times he was sorely tempted to grab Fred off the dashboard and throw him out the window, but was able to restrain himself. Finally, the interrogation was over.

"I now have the information required to complete my initial setup. I also have sufficient voice prints to verify commands. As of now, I will respond to vocal commands from you and no one else unless you instruct me otherwise. Are you right or left-handed, sir?"

"Right," Nick responded.

"Please press the fingers and thumb of your right hand against my screen."

Nick did so while being careful to keep the truck from swerving.

"I now have skin cell DNA samples and thermal fingerprints from your right hand. I will respond to touch commands from you and no one else unless you instruct me otherwise. How may I help you, sir?"

DNA Biometrics on a PIDD! That's new. But when did 'Boss' become 'Sir'? I think these new PIDD programmers take their persona designs way *too seriously. Maybe I should tell him to ditch the uniform and wear a tutu and see how he reacts.* Nick gave Fred his destination for planning purposes, and the display lit up with the route and trip statistics. Nick glanced at the estimated arrival time and groaned.

"Fred, play music, random."

"Do you wish to create a playlist?"

"I already have playlists. Upload all files from temporary storage."

It took a moment for the files to upload. Then, as the music began, Fred asked, "Boss, who is Agnes?"

Chapter 13

Colonel Shi's PIDD finally starting playing music again, this time from the opera *Xi Shi*, a personal favorite of his, and indicative of a call from the Chinese Embassy in Washington.

Shi had just finished driving through the parking lot at MacEwen's apartment complex without seeing any sign of his truck or the trailer. He was now parked across the street where he had a good view of anyone going in or out of the complex.

Shi tapped the icon for a secure connection and waited for the process to complete. When the icon turned green, he simply answered, "This is Shi." The embassy maintained its own communications cell which had been recently upgraded. The new encryption algorithms reproduced analog voice with such high quality that the integral voice analysis equipment could verify a caller's identity as long as their voiceprint was already stored in memory, as Shi's was.

"Colonel Shi, this is Major Ni. I have the information you requested. I apologize for the delay, but there was an anomaly in the data which concerned our analyst and delayed her report."

"What kind of anomaly?"

"When we dumped the buffered data there was a large amount missing, so we ran a check on our system to make sure the data was retrieved properly. We could not find any problems with the system, so we finally decided that the PIDD must have been turned off for a period of time. That is very unusual."

"How long is the data gap?"

"There are actually two gaps. We have no data from Twelve-Fourteen AM Central time to One-Oh-Three AM Central time and then no data after One-Thirty-Five AM Central time."

Colonel Shi was surprised and concerned at this turn of events. "So, you do not know where the PIDD is right now."

"That is correct. All we know for sure is that it was at the location we have on record as the subject's apartment when we lost the data stream at One-Thirty-Five AM Central Time."

Shi glanced at the time on his PIDD display. *I missed him by less than fifteen minutes!*

Colonel Shi considered the possibilities and spoke again. "Major Ni, I am not completely up to date on our cyber warfare capabilities, but I seem to remember a briefing that indicated that we had the ability to access information on financial transactions. Is this correct?" *Some critical integrated circuits used in network servers were also made in China – more back doors.*

"Yes, Colonel, that is correct."

"Excellent. Starting now, I want you to search for and report to me any financial transactions made by the subject. That may help us find him. Call me at any time of night or day if you have anything to report."

"It will be done as you say, Colonel."

Shi broke the connection and tapped in Agent Xue's number. After Xue answered, Colonel Shi instructed him to remain at his post until his relief arrived at the end of the graveyard shift, but to call immediately if the bird or coop returned to ITC. Then Shi decided to continue his observation of the complex in the chance that MacEwen might return to his apartment. He didn't believe even for a minute that it would happen, but Colonel Shi was a thorough belt-and-suspenders risk-averse paranoid.

* * * * *

Nick stared at the PIDD for a few moments and finally said, "Never mind who Agnes is, just play the music." He then issued a string of commands that set Fred to monitoring all online streaming news outlets and any broadcast stations within fifty miles for the words "Texas," "stolen," and "trailer" in close proximity to each other, with instructions to interrupt the music with any hits.

His playlist was full of bagpipe music. Nick loved bagpipes. What many people considered horrible, tuneless screeching, Nick felt was very beautiful and stirring music. The reels were energizing, the marches were stirring in a martial sense, and the hymns, dirges and laments were moving in a melancholic way.

I guess bagpipes are just in my blood, he thought as the Pipes & Drums of the 48th Highlanders struck up "Road to the Isles."

The MacEwens were a highland clan. Of course, he was descended from other Scottish clans as well, and had a few other ethnicities mixed in on his mother's side, but he was more aware of the MacEwen history than any of the rest thanks to his father, now deceased. He clearly remembered two things out of all the stories that his father told him. First, that the clan had lost its lands in Scotland to the Campbells long ago and is therefore an armigerous clan with no chief. Second, that the clan motto is Reviresco, meaning "I will flourish again." Early on in his life Nick put those two family factoids together in his mind to form a down-but-not-out attitude to help him through some rough times.

As his pickup truck speakers blared out "Scotland the Brave," Nick tried to imagine what it was like to be with the Black Watch in the position of honor on the right side of the line, stepping out on the attack to the sound of bagpipes. He knew better than to romanticize war, but he couldn't help it whenever he heard the sound of the pipes. *I look good in a kilt. I've got the legs for it.*

Once he was through College Station, he relaxed a little and got another Dr. Pepper out of the refrigerator. The moon lit a peaceful rural landscape of fences, trees and occasional out buildings in a montage of pale light and dark shadows. The scene was only rarely disturbed by the glare of headlights from an oncoming vehicle. He was well northwest of Houston without attracting attention and there was certainly nothing unusual about a pickup truck towing a trailer on a state highway in south central Texas. He rather enjoyed highway driving. It gave him time to think, and he had a tremendous amount of it to do on this trip. For instance, what was he going to do with the equipment in the trailer? What was he going to do with his discovery? How was he going to deal with his feelings of guilt?

It was in the predawn hours when Nick passed through one of the small towns lining the highway between College Station and Waco. It was one of those towns whose most prominent feature is a grain elevator next to the railroad tracks. When he was almost clear of the west side of town, the music suddenly stopped and Fred piped up, "Boss! Radar emissions commensurate with local constabulary use detected at 180 degrees." And after a slight pause, "In other words, Boss, the cops are on your tail!" and then the music cut in again.

I'm going to kill those programmers! Checking the rear view mirrors confirmed his fears - a car with flashing red lights was closing rapidly.

Where did he *come from? Is he after me?* Nick slowed, pulled off onto the shoulder, and stopped. Unfortunately, the car with the flashing red lights pulled off on the shoulder behind him and stopped. Nick's mind raced. *I don't think it's about the trailer. Who would go to the plant in the middle of the night and report it missing? But I wasn't speeding, either.* Then the music cut out again and Nick heard a male voice say, "Three, traffic, westbound Highway 6, Texas trailer Four, King, Nancy, Zero, Four, Nine." There was an acknowledgment from a dispatcher.

Fred intercepted the policeman's transmission! He said 'traffic.' Did I miss a stop sign back there? I don't want to get a ticket. That would be another bread crumb on my trail! And he's already broadcast the trailer's license number!

Then Fred added, "Yep, the radio transmission was weakly encrypted and easily broken, indicating a low budget operation. This is either a Local Yokel or a County Mountie."

'Yep,' 'Local Yokel,' 'County Mountie'? ... Where is Fred getting this stuff? For that matter, where did he get the ability to decrypt encrypted radio transmissions? And I didn't tell him to monitor radar *emissions!*

Nick muted Fred and turned off the ignition. Then he got out of his pickup truck and faced the headlights of the patrol car. He left the driver's side door open which kept the courtesy light on. That way, the officer could see there was no one else in the pickup truck. He also stood with his hands at his side where the officer could see that they were empty. *The last thing I want to do is make the officer nervous or suspicious.* Compared to the air conditioned pickup truck interior, the warm night air felt like a blanket settling over him. He had not slept in nearly twenty hours. Maybe he could just curl up and close his eyes for a few minutes. *Snap out of it!* He shook himself. *This is not the time for a nap!*

The officer took his time getting out of the patrol car. When he did, he was carrying a flashlight and a clipboard. He paused by the back of the trailer and again by the rear bumper of the truck to write down the license numbers. He also shined his flashlight on the area between the hitch and the front of the trailer for a moment. When he got to Nick, he held the flashlight and clipboard in front of him with one hand and the pen in his other hand, poised to write. Between the patrol car's headlights and the flashlight pointed in Nick's general direction, the officer was not much more than a gray silhouette. He said, "May I see your license and registration, sir?"

As Nick reached for his wallet to get his driver's license he asked, "What's the problem officer? I didn't think I was speeding." *The uniform doesn't look like Texas Department of Public Safety. He must be local police or sheriff like Fred implied, but I can't see the badge or shoulder patch in this light.*

The officer didn't reply. He took the offered driver's license, examined it, and began writing on his clipboard.

Nick ducked into the truck to get the registration out of the glove compartment. *Friendly fellow! What if he asks to see the trailer's registration?! I'll have to tell him I don't have it with me, and that might arouse his suspicion. I wonder if I look as guilty as I feel! I must not*, he thought as he stood up and handed over the document, *or he'd already have the cuffs on me.*

After examining the registration, the officer said, "Are you up from Houston on business, Mr. MacEwen?"

Since the trailer was obviously not of the recreational variety, and most tourists did not travel at this time of night, Nick wondered at the question, but merely answered, "Yes."

"Are you aware your trailer's taillights are not operating properly?"

Oh no! I forgot to hook up the trailer lights! Now I am going to get a ticket! "I'm terribly sorry, officer. I forgot to hook up the trailer lights. I can do that right away." Nick hoped he wasn't lying. He hadn't even checked to see if they were wired for towing. There was wire, tools and electrical tape in the trailer. He ought to be able to fix them up somehow.

"Well, that's all well and good, Mr. MacEwen, but you could have caused a serious accident driving without any trailer lights. The trailer blocks the view of your truck's taillights for drivers coming up behind you. Reckless endangerment is a serious offense. I'm going to have to hold you over for the Justice of the Peace. Problem is, his cousin died and he won't be back until after the funeral Thursday morning."

I'm being charged with Reckless Endangerment *just for no taillights?! Thursday morning?! I want to be out of the state in a matter of hours, not days! Why does he want to hold me for the Justice of the Peace? Maybe it's because I'm not from the local area.* "Officer, I'm really sorry about this. I didn't mean to endanger anyone. I'll get fired from my job if I'm delayed that long." *That's a laugh! I've already been fired!* "Isn't there some other way to handle this?"

The officer paused, reached up to tip his hat back, and scratched his head as if searching for an out. He stared at Nick's new model extended cab pickup truck with an appraising eye for a few moments and said, "Well, Mr. MacEwen, you seem like a solid citizen to me, not the kind to break the law on purpose. I wouldn't want you to lose your job. The fine for reckless endangerment is two hundred dollars. If you've got the money, I could enter your guilty plea and pay the fine for you on Thursday."

So that's what this is all about. It's a simple shakedown. I'm tempted to say I don't have that much on me, but I don't want to run the risk just to see if I can bargain with him. "I'd really appreciate that, officer." He took ten twenty-dollar bills out of his pocket, being careful not to let the officer see the remaining money. *I don't want him to think up another charge! Like failure to dim my lights for a cattle crossing.* "You're saving my job. I'm really grateful."

Nick swapped a quarter of his traveling money for his license and registration papers. The officer turned to leave, then stopped and said, "I'd hook those lights up right away if I were you so you don't get stopped again on down the road. There's a motel less than a mile ahead on the right. You could stop there and work under their parking lot lights. I hope you've got some wire with you though. There's nothing open in town and the motel won't be any help. Their office is closed this time of night."

He's obviously already looked at my hitch and knows I've got some work to do. "Thanks, officer," Nick called after him. "I do have some wire. I'll get it done right away." *I don't want to let any of your compatriots up the line get a crack at me! It's too expensive!*

Nick climbed back into his truck, shut the door, and un-muted Fred just in time to hear the officer's report. "Three, warning issued, back in service." *Good, no paperwork. I'm sure he's unlikely to talk about his two hundred dollar bonanza.* Nick watched in his rearview mirror as the patrol car turned around and headed back toward the center of town. *Boy, cash really does talk in this economy! Given the fiscal bind most state and local governments are in, he's probably had his pay slashed but still has a family to feed.* Nick decided that he couldn't stay angry with the officer under the current circumstances.

He took the officer's advice and stopped in the motel parking lot. There were a couple of cars hooked to U-Haul trailers near the back edge of the lot, and he pulled in next to them. About twenty minutes later, Nick was finishing up the wiring. It wasn't a big deal. The trailer lights were already wired, but the connector was a different size and wouldn't mate with the one on his truck. So he bypassed the connectors with short splices and wrapped the whole bundle in electrical tape.

When he was done, he started his truck and turned on the lights. He walked back and made sure the trailer taillights were on. Both taillights and the license plate light were working. As he looked at the illuminated license plate, he remembered the radio report - *Four, King, Nancy, Zero, Four, Nine.* He glanced at the U-Haul trailer parked next to him. *Texas plate ... How many people know the license number of their rented trailer? The originating dealer might notice when it's returned, but the trailer was probably rented one way since it's parked at a motel overnight. The receiving dealer will probably just assume it's a typo on the paperwork, if he even bothers to check. I only need another ten or twelve hours anyway ... well, maybe more than that the way things are going.* Nick was tired and didn't want to think anymore. He looked at the motel. *No lights showing from any windows. I may be a day late and a dollar short, but it's worth a try.*

Nick quickly grabbed a screwdriver from the tools in the trailer and switched license plates. Then he tested the turn signals, making sure the appropriate trailer taillight flashed. Finally, he got in the truck and checked his rearview mirrors. He could see the red glow from the trailer's taillights bouncing off the surface of the parking lot. The glow significantly brightened whenever he depressed the brake pedal. *There, completely legal. Well, it's completely legal if you don't count the stolen trailer and the stolen license plate!*

A minute later he was back on Texas Highway 6 heading northwest, away from the gradually fading stars on the eastern horizon. As the first hint of dawn reached the Texas plains, Nick realized that his schedule was shot. The stretch between Waco and Fort Worth would be on Interstate 35 and he had wanted to be through that before daylight. He wasn't going to make it. In fact, if he kept going, he would hit Fort Worth during the morning rush hour. He didn't want to be sitting in a traffic jam while everyone around him stared at the truck, trailer, and driver, memorizing every detail for the police. On a certain level, Nick knew he was being ridiculously paranoid, but he was determined to remain as inconspicuous as possible.

Nick checked the truck's fuel gauge and determined that he would need gasoline soon. The truck had pretty big tanks, but towing the trailer was not helping his gas mileage. His personal gas tank was running low as well – he was now approaching twenty-four hours without sleep and was in danger of falling asleep at the wheel. He resolved that he would stop in Waco for gas and try to find someplace to sleep for a few hours before proceeding to Fort Worth.

Nick felt some of the muscles in his neck and back relax slightly and realized he had been subconsciously worried about trying to drive straight through. Shortly after this revelation, the truck's headlights caught a road sign that read "LOST CREEK" on the near side of an upcoming short highway bridge.

Feeling better, and always on the alert for the ridiculous, Nick asked aloud to no one in particular, "If the creek is lost, how did they know where to put the sign?"

He was stunned when Fred replied, "Maybe the location of the bridge gave them a clue."

Chapter 14

He turned into a big Travel Center (a.k.a. truck stop) on the north side of Waco for gas. He noticed a few semi-trucks parked on a large expanse of concrete next to the building. They were all dark, although he could hear idling diesel engines from at least some of them. It occurred to him that he had only seen a couple of big rigs on the road during his trip thus far.

As he walked up to the entrance he noticed a large sign on the glass door that read "SERVICE ANIMALS ONLY." Smiling, Nick thought, *then why are there* people *inside?*

He had to leave his driver's license with the clerk at the counter while he filled up because he was paying cash. The eastern horizon was noticeably lighter now and Nick figured that dawn was just minutes away. When he was finished, Nick pulled his truck and trailer forward into a parking slot labeled RV to free up the pump and he walked toward the building to pay for the gas and use the restroom.

At the truck stop counter Nick told the clerk which pump he had used, paid in cash and retrieved his driver's license. On impulse, he asked the clerk, "I've been driving all night and I'm beat. Is there a charge for me to park on your lot to get some sleep?"

"Not for you there isn't," the clerk replied. "The boss says that we are to treat anyone who pays in cash like royalty. He's always saying 'cash is king.' Besides, it's not like we don't have enough room out there. Truckers have been hit hard by the depression. Our business is way down." The clerk looked out the window over his shoulder at Nick's pickup truck and trailer in the RV slot and said with a grin, "You know, that rig you're driving doesn't look like a recreational vehicle to me. So I'll grant you the honorary status of trucker which gives you access to the trucker's lounge and showers as well as the parking area." Nick returned the grin, thanked the clerk and headed for the door.

So the boss says 'cash is king' does he? Imagine that! Well, I'm not complaining. I want to avoid motel registration records and preserve cash, and this is much better than stopping in a highway rest area.

Just as he reached the exit he smelled bacon cooking. At that point, his empty stomach took over control of his body, and commanded his feet to follow his nose. So he walked into the diner section of the truck stop, sat down, and ordered breakfast. While he ate, he ruminated on the strong preference for cash he was experiencing everywhere. Until very recently, Nick had always used his PIDD to pay so he was unaware of the predilection. He assumed that the attraction was the absence of a transaction record, which a PIDD produced automatically. He was using cash because he was a criminal and didn't want to be traced. Assuming the rest of these people were *not* criminals, the only reason he could think of was tax avoidance. *But wouldn't that make them criminals, too?* If this was as widespread as it seemed, the government was missing out on a lot of revenue. Even normally law-abiding citizens had a hard time paying taxes when prices kept going up faster than income. The government had increased both personal and corporate tax rates while eliminating or reducing many deductions during the recession, which was one of the major causes of the depression. You would think the government would lower, not raise, taxes in a depression. *Wouldn't it be better to swap 30% of nothing for, say, 10% of a whole lot? Anyway, all this thinking about cash has given me an idea.*

After he finished his breakfast - and paid in cash - Nick drove towards the back of the lot and found a place where the parked semi's completely blocked the view from the road. The sun was well above the horizon now, welcoming Waco to what promised to be a hot and sunny Tuesday. He ordered Fred, who was still interfaced with the truck's computer, to slightly lower all four of the extended cab's windows to maintain some air circulation before shutting off the engine. He gave the glove compartment a speculative look, but it wasn't his old PIDD that he was thinking about. He opened the glove compartment and pulled out the long barreled .38 caliber Smith & Wesson revolver he inherited from his father.

Nick was licensed to carry in Texas, but was suddenly uncertain how much that meant once he crossed state lines. *Oh well, I'll cross that bridge – or line – when I come to it.* Taking the .38 with him, he crawled into the back seat and called out, "Wake me up in nine hours, Fred." Nine hours should completely refresh him, give him time for one more thing he wanted to do in Waco, and put most of the remainder of the trip at night.

* * * * *

Tuesday morning Jimmy arrived at ITC somewhere around nine, pretty much his usual time. As he passed by Sheila's desk on the way to his inner office, she held up a pink telephone message note for him. "Vance Billingsly said to call him as soon as you arrive," she said as Jimmy snatched the note out of her hand.

"What does he want?"

"I know he wants you to call him. Other than that, I have no idea. The call was placed by his executive assistant, and she, much less President Billingsly, does not engage in idle conversation with people of lower station."

"What do you mean 'of lower station'? She's the executive assistant to a corporate president and so are you."

Sheila looked up at Jimmy to see if he was kidding. Realizing that he wasn't, she just shook her head and said, "Frank needs to see you also. He said it was very important that he talk to you just as soon as you got here."

"Frank thinks everything is very important. There's no way I'm going to make Vance Billingsly wait while I talk to Frank."

Looking back down at the paperwork on her desk Sheila said, "Whatever you say. I'll call Frank and tell him you are here so that he can be waiting when you're done with the call."

Puzzled by Sheila's attitude, Jimmy hurried into his office to call Vance, wishing that he had been here to take the call when it came in.

Jimmy had an old push button telephone on his desk. Everyone wondered what he was going to do when it finally bit the dust. He didn't use his PIDD unless it was absolutely necessary, because it was nothing but trouble. He swore that something had to be different about his skin oils because the touch screen kept reacting like he was tapping on the wrong icon. Whenever the PIDD did not immediately react the way he thought it should, he'd start tapping all of the other icons in rapid order trying to solicit the desired response, but that just seemed to make things worse. He wouldn't use voice commands either, because the PIDD would then respond in kind, and he thought it was just plain wrong for computers to talk.

Jimmy picked up the phone handset and listened for a moment to the comforting sound of the dial tone. *You don't get that reassuring sound with a PIDD - it just sits there waiting for you to tap numbers before you even know if there's a connection.* Then he pressed the buttons in turn for the number written on the message pad, each time receiving a reassuring beep as his smile grew. *They say you can program a PIDD to make all of these sounds, but that would be a façade, not real electromechanical confirmation!*

Unbeknownst to Jimmy, the telephone was actually connected to a PIDD mounted behind the phone jack plate on the wall. The PIDD was specially programmed to emulate the outdated phone, which could not possibly work otherwise because there were no telephone lines anymore. They had been torn down and the wire recycled years ago. The entire telecom infrastructure was now wireless and digital. The connection that Jimmy had missed was the one between the continued operation of his antique phone and the total absence of telephone poles.

The call was answered on the first ring by a very professional sounding female voice saying, "President Billingsly's office. This is his Executive Assistant, Indra. How may I help you?"

"This is Jimmy Barton, President of ITC, returning Vance's call."

Indra's voice seemed to turn a little frosty as she replied, "Mister Billingsly will be with you shortly."

Jimmy suddenly found himself listening to elevator music. As time passed, Jimmy recognized the message, if not the music. Vance was establishing the pecking order - showing that he was more important than Jimmy was by making him wait. Jimmy's anger grew by the minute even though he knew he couldn't give in to the anger. Jimmy needed Pavilion Mast and more contracts like it, and Billingsly could deliver those contracts. Finally, after five minutes of music, Vance came on the line.

"Hello, Jimmy, I'm sorry about the delay. I was just getting the latest on your problem down there."

Problem - What problem? "Um, what problem are you talking about Vance?"

There was a moment's silence until Vance replied, "You mean you don't know?"

"Know what, Vance?" Jimmy was getting even angrier, but a touch of fear was starting to taint the anger as he wondered what Vance knew that he didn't.

After another, but shorter pause, Vance said, "Nick MacEwen took off with the Defender prototype last night."

"What? What do you mean 'took off with the Defender prototype'? Do you mean that he stole it? He couldn't! It's in that big trailer!" Jimmy's anger was rapidly morphing into a kind of frenzy. "How would you know about it even if he did? You're all the way up there in Dallas!" Jimmy suddenly remembered the suspected GenArm informer inside ITC and his frenzy was quickly dampened by fear – fear that Vance was right.

"Listen to me carefully," Vance continued with a sigh. "Nick was seen driving off with the prototype trailer last night. After taking a very indirect route to his apartment, he headed west. He is now stopped in Waco at thirty-one degrees, thirty-six minutes, zero point sixty-three seconds north and ninety-seven degrees, six minutes, thirty-four point ninety-six seconds west and he hasn't moved for over three hours. Or, I suppose I should clarify, the trailer hasn't moved for over three hours."

After a stunned silence, Jimmy exclaimed, "You're tracking the trailer?"

"Yes," answered Vance. "I thought it might be prudent to protect our mutual asset by installing a GPS tracking device. I was apparently prescient in my concern. Can you perhaps shed any light on why Nick would have decided to take it for a joyride last night?"

It was a moment before Jimmy answered, "I guess it could possibly be related to my firing Nick yesterday afternoon."

Vance exploded, "You *fired* Nick *yesterday*?! Whatever possessed you to do that?"

Jimmy replied in a plaintive voice, "You told me that Nick had to go."

Billingsly nearly shouted, "You were *supposed* to *wait* until Nick had brought the new engineer up to speed! My man is a design engineer, not a *clairvoyant*! Why didn't you anticipate that Nick would be angry and do something like this? I'm aware that your security is abysmal, but why didn't you put a guard on the trailer, or move it someplace else temporarily? What were you *thinking*? Or were you thinking at all?"

Now both men were silent for more than a moment until Vance finally continued in a less voluminous, but still exasperated tone, "Maybe you should get with your people and find out exactly what happened. Find out if he wiped out any of the design or software files. Once you have done that, call me back. But most of all, the reason I called you is to make sure that no matter what else you do, do not - I repeat *do not* - call the police!"

"What? But if he stole the prototype we have to call the police and try to get it back! Why wouldn't you want me to call the police? We can even tell them where it is!"

Sounding like he was talking to a small child, Billingsly responded, "Because if we accuse him of stealing *your* prototype, you will have to be prepared to prove it *is* your prototype, which you *can't do* because you can't show where you have spent a single *nickel* on it! That will lead to an *audit* of your books, which will guarantee that you will go to *prison* and the government will take over the project so that *none* of us makes any money on it. Now, is that clear enough for you?"

The next thing Jimmy heard was the dial tone from his "antique" telephone.

Vance knows everything! He absolutely has to have someone inside ITC. And he had a tracking device installed on my *trailer without* my *permission! And he didn't tell me* who *saw Nick take the trailer.*

Jimmy felt like he was losing control of the situation. Jimmy didn't like losing control of anything.

Chapter 15

Vance Billingsly hung up the phone, swiveled his chair so he was looking out the glass penthouse wall behind his desk, and stared into space. The view was both beautiful and absorbing. The penthouse of the General Armaments headquarters building looked down on the mixture of grass, trees, modern office buildings, and wide multi-lane streets on the north side of the Dallas/Fort Worth multiplex from thirty floors up. Centered in the window behind Billingsly's desk was the skyline of downtown Dallas, fourteen miles away as the crow flies. It certainly served its purpose as a distracting backdrop when people came to see him. Sometimes it was beneficial for visitors to have trouble concentrating on the business at hand. But Vance did not even notice as a GenArm corporate jet coasted by in the near distance on its descent into Addison airport ... he was trying to decide if Jimmy Barton was lying.

Vance also did not pay any attention to his reflection in the window. If he had, he would have been pleased to note that he was as dapper as usual. About five feet seven, Vance had a trim, athletic build, a slightly heart-shaped face with a strong chin, black hair, and a dark complexion. He was clean shaven, handsome as a movie star, and looked every inch the part of a highly successful corporate executive. He had been featured in a number of GenArm public relations television spots and was a highly prized after dinner speaker. At forty-eight, Billingsly was one of the youngest Fortune 100 Corporation CEO's in history. He relentlessly — some would say ruthlessly — rose from being one of many June bride corporate attorneys in the GenArm legal department to the presidency in record time. There was no Mrs. Billingsly; Vance was president and chief executive officer of his only love.

Billingsly's office and adjoining conference room occupied about three-fourths of the penthouse. The other one-fourth housed his small personal support staff. Reaching a decision, he swiveled his chair back around and stabbed an icon on the surface of his desk - actually a very powerful computer disguised as a beautiful antique desk. The entire top was a touch screen display. Without waiting for a response, Vance said, "Get Ahrens up here."

W.A. "Wil" Ahrens was carried on the payroll as a special assistant to the president for security. He was working in the GenArm security department when Billingsly singled him out as someone who would do what he was told and keep his mouth shut. Ahrens had been a decorated Marine in the Gulf and Iraq Wars, but did not re-up upon returning from the middle-east the second time. As soon as he had put in thirty years of government service between the Corps and the Defense Intelligence Agency, he joined GenArm.

A few minutes later, there was a knock. Vance pressed another icon on his desk/display signaling his office management computer to unlock and open the door. Vance didn't even look up as Ahrens followed the door as it opened and walked over to Vance's desk.

Ahrens was tall and thin - so thin, casual observers sometimes took him for skinny and weak. Others, attending to his subtle musculature, the way he moved, and the steely look in his gray eyes, thought better of their original impression. He wore his salt-and-pepper hair in a precisely cut flattop. Today he wore a light gray double-breasted suit as he quietly stood in front of Billingsly's desk, ignoring the two chairs provided for visitors, waiting for his boss to speak. Although relaxed, his posture was still very close to the military position of attention.

Vance looked up from his work and said, "Thanks for coming up so quickly, Wil," as he tapped the icon to close and lock his office door. Of course, both men knew Ahrens really didn't have a choice in the matter. "I just got off the phone with Jimmy Barton at ITC. He acted like he didn't know that the Defender prototype was stolen last night."

Ahrens arched one eyebrow but said nothing. Vance continued. "I called him earlier and was told that he wasn't at work yet, and according to the profile you worked up on him, he's habitually late getting to work. So, it's possible that he really didn't know. In any case, after I set him straight on the facts as we know them, he said that he fired MacEwen yesterday afternoon and that might have triggered the event."

Now Ahrens arched both eyebrows, but still did not comment.

"I don't trust Barton any further than I can throw him," Vance said thinking aloud. "It's possible that he struck some kind of deal with MacEwen to try and cut us out, but it's unlikely. He needs the Pavilion Mast contract too much to try something like that. Unless ..." Vance was deep in thought for a moment, then continued to say, "Unless MacEwen had a sudden break-through. You said that your surveillance crew reported some strange behavior before MacEwen took off with the trailer - something about lights in the field behind the plant and a pencil on the ground?"

Ahrens eyebrows returned to their normal positions and he remained impassive, knowing that his boss was building a background for an assignment, not fishing for an opinion based on the second hand account of a telephone call.

"I want you to go to Houston right away and investigate. Dig out as much detail as you can about the activities prior to the trailer's departure. Find out anything you can about MacEwen's progress on the prototype. If the software and drawing files are still available, I want you to bring them back with you. Barton won't like that, but tell him that our facilities are much better suited to build a new prototype and the deal between us is still on as long as we get the files. And while you're there, try to find out if Barton is lying to us."

Now Ahrens had a question. "Has Barton reported the trailer missing to the police?"

"No," replied Vance. "As you know, the whole project was done off the books. Nobody outside of ITC is supposed to know it exists. I told him not to report it missing because someone might get curious about what it was, why it was important, and how much it cost."

Ahrens seemed to reflect on that for a moment. "Okay - I'll be in touch." Ahrens turned to leave as Billingsly opened another document on his desk computer, signaling that the brief meeting was over.

When Ahrens was almost to the door, Vance called after him. "And be sure to get government rates."

Ahrens knew the drill. Defense contractors were not eligible for government discounts unless traveling on orders issued by a contracting agency — a reasonably rare event. Even so, Billingsly insisted that GenArm travelers always get government rates. So, that meant using a travel agency willing to overlook the absence of travel orders as well as hoping the airlines and hotels didn't ask too many questions.

Ahrens reflected briefly on all of the petty fraud he had seen over the years. He remembered how outraged he had been when he first overheard a superior report an inflated body count in Vietnam. That had been early in his tour, when he was very young and naive. His expression did not change as he simply answered, "Right."

Vance touched the door icon again to let Ahrens out and went back to work.

Chapter 16

Jimmy stood staring at the empty spot on the parking lot next to the rear door of ITC's plant. Frank stood next to him.

"Do we have any idea how long it's been gone?" Jimmy asked.

"We really don't know," Frank answered. "One of the manufacturing foremen was the first one here this morning and noticed it missing. He grabbed me as soon as I drove up. I tried to call you at home right away, but got your answering machine." *I couldn't leave a message because your tape was full, probably because you can't remember how to use that particular antique. I also tried to call your PIDD, but knew that was a forlorn hope – you never answer your PIDD.* "I know it was here yesterday evening. I saw it when I walked to my car after work."

"There's no indication that anyone tried to break into the plant itself?"

"That's right. I arrived on the heels of the foreman and he hadn't gone inside yet," said Frank. "Everything was locked and the alarm was armed and ready. We've been through the whole plant since, and there's no broken window or any other signs of forced entry. The security system logs only show the cleaning crew going in and out."

"Did you have someone check the computer to make sure the software and drawing files were all right like I asked?"

"Yes, the files are all there. I had one of the CAD technicians compare the file dates against the release logs and they all check out, so they haven't been altered. The only entries in the network server system log after normal working hours yesterday are two short power glitches, so no one logged in last night."

Jimmy pointed at the mangled electrical box on the rear wall of the plant and said, "I wonder if that had something to do with your power glitches. If it did, we might be able to figure out when the trailer left. He must have been in a hurry."

With a quizzical look, Frank asked, "He? It could have been a 'she' or a 'them.'"

Closely watching for Frank's reaction, Jimmy said, "Vance Billingsly told me that Nick stole the prototype last night."

Shocked, Frank blurted, "*What*? Who is Vance Billingsly? And why would Nick want to steal his own prototype?"

Well, he seems to be genuinely surprised, thought Jimmy, *which implies that he is not working with either Nick or Vance. Either that or he is a really good actor – an attribute that he has never evidenced in Board meetings!* "Maybe because I fired him yesterday afternoon," Jimmy said, answering Frank's last question while ignoring the first.

Jimmy spun on his heel and went back inside the plant as Frank watched in stunned silence.

* * * * *

When Jimmy got back to his office he was pretty much mad at the whole world for interfering with his plans. He sat at his desk fuming over the way Billingsly had treated him on the phone. *He acted like it was my fault that Nick went nuts and drove off with the prototype. Now I have to call him back. At least I can tell him that the drawing and software files are all okay.*

Jimmy's mood wasn't improved by his call to Billingsly. Vance responded to Jimmy's report with a grunt here and an "okay" there. Then he told Jimmy that he was sending an investigator from GenArm security down to Houston to look into the situation, and that Jimmy was to allow this "Ahrens" character complete access to everyone and everywhere. Jimmy deeply resented Billingsly's manner, which came across like a drill sergeant dealing with a particularly dim-witted recruit. But he responded as politely as he could, because he needed Billingsly more than Billingsly needed him - particularly now that Jimmy didn't have the Defender prototype bargaining chip anymore.

When the call was over, Jimmy went back to stewing in his own juices. Finally, a thought occurred to him - *Vance said that I shouldn't call the police, but he didn't say anything about calling anyone else. Maybe there's a way to get the prototype back without involving the authorities. With the prototype back in my possession, I'll have some leverage with Vance again.*

Jimmy flipped through his Rolodex cards for the number he needed, and then dialed an old school buddy. This particular buddy owned a repossession company known more for unflagging determination and aggressiveness than concern for all the legal niceties. Randy "Blood Hound" Miller had achieved fame and fortune in the wake of the Debt Bubble burst - repossession was one of the few businesses that benefited from the economic situation.

Vance said the trailer was stopped in Waco. He had a bunch of coordinate numbers, but I didn't write them down and I'm not going to ask for them now! Nick is probably getting some sleep after being up all night. There can't be that many hotels and motels in Waco.

"Get'em?-Got'em!-Repo and Bounty Hunters; Blood Hound speaking."

Jimmy laughed and said, "What are you doing answering your own phone, Randy? Where's your better half today?"

"Is that you, Jimmy? It must be – it sounds like you and there's no video. When are you gonna join the Twenty-first Century anyway? I haven't heard from you in a blood hound's age. My old lady is working on the books and I can't have any of these other mugs answering the phone! They'd scare away the customers!"

Waiting to get a word in edgewise, Jimmy thought, *Randy really does employ some seriously tough-looking people. I suppose I could handle being face-to-face with them on a video feed, but not in a dark alley!*

"Randy, I need your professional services. I'm going to have my secretary send you a copy of the registration and photographs of a trailer that was stolen from ITC's back lot last night. This is all very sensitive and I don't want to involve law enforcement agencies.

"I have a tip that the trailer is currently parked over in Waco - I don't know exactly where, but I think it is probably in a hotel or motel parking lot. I want you to get it back for me. You'll need to take a vehicle that can tow the trailer. It will probably be hooked to a white pickup truck that belongs to a disgruntled ex-employee of mine. I want the trailer back, not the employee or his vehicle. It would be best if you could get the trailer without anyone getting hurt, but do what you need to do without attracting attention."

Randy replied, "Handling very sensitive repo is our specialty, Jimmy, and we normally try to recover an asset without hurting anyone. But if we can't grab the trailer while the guy isn't around, and he tries to interfere, somebody is going to get hurt and it isn't going to be any of my people."

'Normally try,' Jimmy thought, *not always try. This whole issue of prototype ownership would get a lot simpler without Nick MacEwen around. How should I put this?* "It would not disappoint me if the ex-employee was unable to continue his criminal activities, but it is critical that the authorities do not become involved."

After a moment, Randy asked, "Waco is about three hours away, Jimmy. Do you think it will still be there by then?"

"I really don't know, Randy. He probably has been up all night and has stopped in Waco to sleep. Other than that, I don't have any idea when or where he's going. But that's where you come in, Blood Hound. You're the best, right? This is important, Randy – your regular fee plus expenses, of course." Jimmy winced at the thought of how much this might cost, then added, "Call me with regular reports on your progress and costs incurred, okay?"

"Okay, Jimmy, but unless we get real lucky and find him before he moves, we will need to track him. We have various ways of doing that, but just so you know, most of them involve greasing some palms."

"I'm not going to try and tell you how to do your job, Randy. Do whatever it takes. Just don't get the police involved."

"Can you send me a photo of the guy?"

"Sure. His name is Nick MacEwen. I'll have my secretary include a copy of his security badge photo."

After disconnecting, Jimmy continued to worry about how much

Randy's services might cost. *Maybe our insurance will cover it. But then the insurance carrier would want proof of the prototype's value, and I can't provide that information. I guess I will have to tell Frank to apply Randy's bills to the same contract he was using for the Defender R&D.*

Chapter 17

Nick woke up to a bugle loudly blaring out Reveille. Startled, he sat up so fast that he had to grab the back of the front seat to keep from rolling off onto the cab floor. "Okay, okay, I'm awake already!"

The bugle stopped in mid-note. Peeking over the front seat, Nick could see Fred's image standing at parade rest, smiling at him. *But he can't really see me, can he? Of course he can, there's a video camera in the PIDD. You're losing it Nick! You're talking to yourself and worrying about whether or not a computer program can see you!*

Then Nick noticed that the truck was running on idle and the air conditioner was on. Looking around, he could see that the windows were all the way up. "What's going on, Fred? Why is the engine running?" *Listen to you - you're asking a computer program questions like it was a real person.*

Amazingly, Fred responded, sounding like an Aggie Senior Cadet Zip lecturing a Freshman Cadet Fish. "We are in central Texas in the middle of the day in the summertime. When the outside temperature reached 98.35 degrees Fahrenheit, the temperature inside the cab of the truck hit 102.41 degrees even with the windows partially open. By that time your infrared and audio signatures indicated that your temperature, respiration rate and heartbeat were approaching unacceptable levels. So I started the truck, turned on the air conditioning and raised the windows until all parameters were within an acceptable range, at which point I turned off the truck. I have been cycling the truck on and off for the last four hours."

Nick was completely dumbfounded, partly by Fred's autonomous actions and partly because he had slept through all of it. He had heard that the new PIDDs had a lot more processing power and memory than his old one, but this goes way beyond just more MIPS and Megabytes. He wouldn't be surprised if Fred fired up the truck and drove off. He didn't think he would be surprised by anything that Fred did.

Nick was immediately proven wrong when he saw another animated simulacrum walk in from the right side of the screen and sidle up to Fred. The new – but familiar - image was of a woman with coal black hair wearing ghillies, tartan stockings, tartan skirt, ruffled blouse and a Glengarry. As Fred put his arm around her, he said, "Boss, I think you already know Agnes."

At that point Nick fled the truck and took up the clerk's offer of honorary trucker access to the showers and lounge. After the shower, he put his same rumpled clothes back on because everything else was tied up in a bedspread in the trailer. After a late lunch in the diner, Nick returned to the truck with some trepidation.

Looking through the driver's side window, he could see that the PIDD display was dark. As soon as Nick opened the door, the PIDD display came to life as two animated simulacrums quickly separated from a torrid embrace.

Agnes smiled at Nick and said, "I sure do love a man in uniform," as she straightened Fred's tie. Nick fired back, "Get a room!" as he marveled over how Agnes got into the PP-PIDD in the first place.

Groaning, Nick got in the truck and fired it up. As he drove out of the truck stop he told Fred 'n Agnes where he wanted to go and the PIDD display thankfully changed to a depiction of the necessary route. He was at his destination in under ten minutes, but all he could think of the whole way was, *I am really, really, really going to find and kill those programmers.*

Fortunately, Waco had what he was looking for - a branch of the bank Nick used when he started MacEwen Systems LLC, the replacement for MacEwen Systems Inc., which had been merged with ITC.

Buck Barton had wanted the expertise of Nick and a few of his key staff members. Buck could have just hired them, but he also wanted MacEwen Systems' ongoing government contracts, which required that ITC be the legal successor through sale or merger. He had not been interested in MacEwen Systems' other paltry assets during the merger negotiations. When Nick closed the business, several thousand dollars remained after paying the outstanding bills and providing generous severance payments to those of his employees that would not be joining ITC. Buck encouraged him to pay himself a severance bonus with the remaining funds. But Nick registered MacEwen Systems LLC, opened a business bank account, and deposited the money, hoping to restart his own business someday.

Nick figured that law enforcement agencies might already be monitoring his personal bank account, but he didn't think anyone knew about the company account. It was a risk to withdraw the funds, but he also knew that he was going to need them. It was better to take the risk now, while he was still a long way from his destination and there probably hadn't been enough time for anyone to thoroughly research his banking relationships.

The bank manager was not enthusiastic about a large cash withdrawal on such short notice, insisting that the proper course would be to electronically transfer the funds wherever needed. When Nick pressed his request, the manager tried to convince Nick that it was not safe to carry that much cash on his person given current conditions and the high crime rate. He finally relented when Nick agreed to leave the account open with about a thousand dollars remaining, but he continued to grumble about irregularities. Once the bank's biometric scanner had verified Nick's identity, his cash was counted, bundled in a bank bag, and reluctantly presented to him.

As he walked out to his vehicle, he decided to keep the cash with him in the cab rather than putting it in the trailer. Fred 'n Agnes, knowing that the truck was parked in front of a bank and scanning the lettering on the bag, must have put two and two together and got three and a half as they began a duet of a very popular 1970's song.

I didn't take *the money in the sense they are implying, but I certainly am* running*!*

*　*　*　*　*　*　*

Colonel Shi slept much of the day after staying up all night watching MacEwen's apartment. He was preparing a late lunch - or an early dinner, he hadn't decided which - when a secure call came in on his PIDD from Major Ni at the embassy.

"This is Shi."

"Good afternoon, sir. This is Major Ni. I have some new information about your subject."

"Excellent. What do you have?"

"He withdrew $7,420 from an account at a bank in Waco, Texas about fifteen minutes ago."

Waco. He's heading northwest, thought Shi. *That rules out a test in the Big Bend area. It also makes Fort Bliss, White Sands, or Fort Huachuca unlikely since he would have gone west on Interstate 10 for any of those. He must be headed north to the Dallas/Fort Worth area ... but why? If he doesn't stop there, he could be going anywhere in the western third of the country. Could Dallas or Fort Worth be his destination? GenArm is in Dallas and he used to work there!*

Shi thanked Ni for providing the information in such a timely fashion and broke the connection. *I'll have to alert my GenArm asset to the possibility. I'll also have Xue head over to Waco just in case MacEwen stays there. I think it's highly unlikely, but maybe Xue can uncover some clues as to MacEwen's destination - or at least determine which way he was traveling when he left.*

Chapter 18

Nick left Waco heading north on Interstate 35 toward Fort Worth. He felt sure that the trailer was reported missing early in the day, so police should be on alert. But Fred had not reported any police radio intercepts or news program references.

Well, maybe one stolen trailer is not considered news worthy in the grand tableau of a day's worth of criminal activity in the state. Or maybe Jimmy told the authorities that it was a matter of national security and they're keeping it out of the news! That worried Nick, but he was already fretting about his exposure on Interstate 35 anyway. *I'm going to get to Fort Worth just about the time most people are getting off work. I would have liked to hit town a little earlier, but the stop at the bank took longer than I expected. Hopefully no one will pay any attention to a rig that looks like another small time contractor trying to get home from a work site.*

Interstate 35W through Fort Worth was heavily congested. Most cities, including Fort Worth, had added many lanes on existing routes, developed alternate routes, built toll roads and expanded light rail over the years. Nevertheless, metropolitan transportation remained a problem as more people abandoned the rural areas and small towns to head for the cities where there were more, though not enough, jobs. Census data showed that over sixty percent of the world's population now lived in cities. The percentage was higher in those countries that had been industrialized longer, such as the United States.

Nick was surprised at the number of motorcycles and motor scooters he saw in the mix. When he glanced at the side streets visible from the Interstate, he noticed quite a few bicycles and a lot of pedestrian traffic as well. He suddenly realized that he couldn't compare Fort Worth's rush hour traffic to Houston's because he always went to work very early and stayed very late so that he could work on the Defender prototype and still discharge his normal duties as Manager of Engineering. Except for a few business trips, he had spent nearly all of his time at the ITC plant.

As Nick sat in traffic he thought how wonderful it would be if the Defender prototype could make a hole for him to drive through and instantly come out on the other side of the city. But why would he need a vehicle if he could cover long distances by walking a few steps? Of course it was all speculation at this point, but if he didn't need a vehicle, then he wouldn't need a road either. *What will the car manufacturers do? What will the highway construction companies do? ... I'm really getting ahead of myself! I don't actually know the capabilities of the prototype.* He continued to mentally struggle with how he should proceed now that he had opened Pandora's Box.

The concentration of population in the cities at the expense of the rural areas and small towns was even more apparent as he headed northwest out of Fort Worth on US Highway 287. It was a hot, clear day. Even with the air conditioner running, Nick could smell the hot earth and dry vegetation in the fields.

More than a century ago, waves of pioneers had left small settlements in their wake all over the West. Some of those settlements had since grown into large cities. Others had nearly disappeared. Many had thrived for a time, but became no more than flotsam left behind when the tide turned and the population withdrew into the cities during the industrial revolution.

The era when one of these small towns had reached its peak could be estimated by examining the strata of its buildings. The newest buildings were normally the furthest from the center of town. The building materials and styles of architecture during the Nineteenth and Twentieth Centuries underwent very distinctive changes relatively frequently. Once a town stopped expanding it was like a specimen trapped in amber, available for inspection by the curious. US Highway 287 was lined for its entire length with interesting examples. But now, even the small towns that had weathered the Indian wars, the droughts, the civil war, the population exodus of the industrial revolution, the great depression, the dust bowl, and corporate farming were now dying during the Second Great Depression.

Nick hadn't been able to see all that much of the landscape in the dark leaving Houston last night. Since he never took vacations and always flew on business trips, he really hadn't seen the country outside of the major metropolitan areas in a long time. Now something about what he saw disturbed him in an ill-defined way. After many miles went by, he realized that he was not reacting so much to specific conditions as to general impressions. *The small towns and the long stretches between them just seem shabby somehow - vaguely rundown and abandoned looking.*

From a distance, many former homes looked like partially buried skulls with a couple of empty window frames as dark eye sockets on either side of an empty door frame serving as the nasal opening. It seemed a vast graveyard of buried hopes and dreams. Even those few ranches that appeared to be occupied seemed dilapidated, with houses lacking maintenance, outbuildings in ruins, and rusting farm equipment castaways in untended fields. The only thing Nick saw moving in the fields was an occasional pack of feral dogs. The shoulders and medians of the highway hadn't been mowed and were overgrown to the point of dangerously obstructing vision in some places. Where the highway paralleled railroad tracks, Nick saw hundreds of graffiti-covered abandoned rail cars on sidings.

In the small towns Nick drove through it seemed like most of the stores and homes were boarded up. The few cars and pickup trucks Nick saw displayed well deserved collectors license plates. The rare citizen spotted sitting on a bench or strolling down the sidewalk was almost invariably elderly. *Gray. The buildings are gray, the vehicles are gray and the people are gray - and the fields are fallow, the meadows are absent any livestock, and the oil*

81

pumps are stilled. That's what is spooking me! ... And why are we importing food and oil while all of this capacity for production sits idle?

He also noticed that the road conditions had deteriorated again. Thinking back over his trip so far, Nick realized that the roads were in better shape in urban areas than they were in rural areas. Also, his impression was that the state and county roads were in worse condition than the federal ones and that the streets in the small towns were in the worst repair of all. There were some stretches where he had to slow down to a crawl to keep from damaging the truck or trailer.

Then he remembered that the first rounds of government stimulus spending had included a fair number of highway infrastructure projects. He also recalled that, in general, the urban areas voted for the candidates belonging to the previous administration's political party and the rest of the country tended to vote the other way. *Well, that explains the difference in road conditions!*

These and similar thoughts occupied Nick's mind as he steadily drove northwest while the sun sank towards the horizon. But the question that wouldn't go away was, *Would opening Pandora's Box change things for the better or for the worse?*

* * * * *

"Well, we missed him, Jimmy," Randy said to his blank PIDD display. "I brought three crews with me so we could cover the ground as quickly as possible. We checked all of the hotel and motel parking lots as soon as we got to Waco and didn't spot the trailer. We also showed copies of your guy's photograph to the desk clerks at all of those places and dispensed some cash incentives to check their registrations for his name without any luck. Tomorrow morning we'll try the gas stations and truck stops and see if anyone saw him filling up. In the meantime, I'll put in a call to a special resource of mine that can almost certainly tell us which way he went, but that will require a fair amount of that lubricant that I mentioned earlier. Do you want me to keep going?"

Jimmy was very curious about the nature of the special resource, but at the same time suspected that he would be better off knowing less, rather than more, of any details regarding Blood Hound's methods.

"Yes," Jimmy replied. "I want that trailer. Keep going and keep me informed."

"Okay Jimmy, we'll track it down for you, one way or another."

Jimmy apparently decided that everything that needed to be said had been said, and disconnected without further comment.

Randy entered a new number from memory. The number belonged to a technician who worked in a Homeland Security operations center that monitored all of the traffic cameras throughout the country. Randy had never seen it, but understood it was a marvel of supercomputers, fiber optics networks and sophisticated graphical recognition software.

"Hello."

"It's Randy. Can you talk?"

"Only briefly, my supervisor is nearby."

"I have a license number for you. Are you interested?"

"As long as you're offering the regular compensation for services rendered."

"Absolutely; the number is Texas trailer Four-King-Nancy-Zero-Four-Nine."

"All right, I'll be in touch."

A little under an hour later, Randy disconnected the return call from his contact at Homeland Security and tapped the Jimmy icon that he had set up on his PIDD. The number was supposed to be Jimmy's direct line, but all that meant was that it bypassed the ITC auto-attendant program and went right to Sheila, Jimmy's secretary.

"Hello Mister Miller," Sheila said as soon as her PIDD's display showed his image. "Do you need to speak to Mister Barton again?"

"Hi, Sheila; Yes, I do, if he's available."

"I believe so, Mister Miller. Please wait a moment while I get him to pick up."

"Thanks, Sheila." Randy knew that the phrase "pick up" was not a metaphor in Jimmy's case.

The video on his PIDD had switched from Sheila to an image of the ITC corporate logo when Sheila put him on hold. After a moment, Randy's video went blank and Jimmy got right to the point. "Did your special resource find the trailer?"

Randy replied, "He was able to trace the license number you gave me. Let me give you the grand overview without listing every place the license plate has been. The plate was detected leaving Houston last night and tracked westbound through College Station in the predawn hours this morning. It then was detected a few hours later going back through College Station eastbound, tracked all the way through Houston to Lake Charles, Louisiana where it apparently hasn't moved any further since there have been no more detections. The plate was not detected in Waco, and it almost certainly would have been if the plate went there."

"That can't be right, Randy. I have information from a pretty good source that the trailer was stopped in Waco yesterday morning. I was given the

GPS coordinates, but I didn't think to write them down."

From what Jimmy just said, it sounds like the trailer has a tracking device on it, but Jimmy doesn't have ready access to the reported position information. I wonder what that's all about. I hope this really is Jimmy's trailer we're chasing! Oh well, he's paying the bills.

"I didn't think that it made much sense either, so I had my guy pull up an image captured of the vehicle with the detected plate along the eastbound run to Lake Charles. It was a U-Haul trailer."

"That can't be right either, Randy! I sent you a copy of the registration with that license number on it. Your source must have made a mistake."

"It was no mistake, Jimmy. I saw a copy of the image myself. The trailer in Lake Charles is definitely a U-Haul and it definitely has your trailer's license plate on it. The obvious conclusion is that somewhere west of College Station your ex-employee switched license plates with a U-Haul trailer."

Jimmy exclaimed, "Nick would never do something like that! It's against the law!"

"What do you mean?" Randy replied. "He stole your trailer didn't he? That's against the law." *This whole thing just keeps getting weirder and weirder.*

"Besides," Randy continued, "we know for a fact that he switched plates. My source and I figured it would take too long to determine the original license number on the U-Haul, which is probably now on your trailer. So, I transferred the photo of your trailer to him and he used graphical search software – an extra cost of course – to look for the trailer going through Waco. He eliminated false positives by looking only for matching trailers that were being towed by a white pickup truck. That yielded three possible detections. That trailer of yours is a pretty standard color, shape and size, and white pickup trucks are not exactly unique either. So he ran the three plates, one of which came back as being registered to a U-Haul dealer. Are you following me?"

After a pause, Jimmy answered, "Yes, but I can't believe he did it! I didn't think he had it in him to break a law – he won't even jaywalk!"

Randy was becoming a little concerned. *Am I chasing a fallen saint? Well, saint or sinner isn't my problem. My problem is to find the trailer and get it back.*

Randy said, "Well, now that we have the right license number, we've traced him through Fort Worth where he exited on US Highway 287 heading towards Wichita Falls. That puts him about two to three hours ahead of us depending on traffic. I recommend that I send two of my teams back to Houston while I take the third team with me and run him down. We should have an advantage since we can rotate drivers and he'll have to stop

84

somewhere along the line to sleep. You're the client. Do you agree with that plan?"

"Yes," answered Jimmy. "I want that trailer back." Jimmy abruptly hung up.

* * * * *

Nick stopped in Wichita Falls for fast food and again in the middle of the night at a truck stop in Amarillo for gas, more fast food and more Dr. Peppers. Highway traffic outside the cities remained sparse, which suited Nick just fine. He was much more comfortable towing the trailer now, but still drove under the speed limit to increase his chances of dodging the occasional potholes which suddenly showed up in his headlights.

Potholes weren't the only thing to occasionally show up in his headlights. There were still some road signs and billboards along the way, although they were few and far between. Nick was a habitual reader and therefore took them all in. It helped keep him awake and frequently provided entertainment. Somewhere in the Texas panhandle Nick saw a billboard advertising Boxbest Brothers Funeral Home. *How very appropriate! Identification and recommendation all rolled into one!* Nick started to laugh but stopped when he abruptly realized that he might need the Boxbest family's good services if he didn't pay attention to his driving.

Either Fred or Agnes would occasionally interrupt the music to remind him of speed limit changes, give him advice on which lane to be in as he approached interchanges, or update him on approaching weather or traffic conditions. He found himself looking forward to their brief reports and once thought of engaging them in conversation to pass the time. *That's silly – a PIDD can't actually hold a conversation with anyone. Fatigue is starting to affect your mind! Just keep talking to yourself like you always do! ... But it seems like they start talking to me just when I'm about to nod off.*

* * * * *

Randy couldn't believe that they had driven all night and still hadn't caught up with the trailer.

They were still getting reports whenever a camera picked up the trailer license. Randy's contact was off-shift, but he had set up a routine that would automatically message Randy with the position of any camera captures – for an additional fee, of course. Randy had the detection events overlaid on his PIDD's GPS mapping application.

One problem was that the roads were in pretty bad shape and they couldn't go as fast as they wanted in the dark without risking serious damage to the van. But the biggest problem was that it was a long way between traffic cameras along their route. Closing the gap too quickly would risk overshooting the target if MacEwen turned off the highway. They would be able to double

85

back when the trailer was eventually caught by another camera, but that would put them even further behind.

I can't believe that he's driven all night, thought Randy. *We're all tired even though we've rotated drivers. At least we've narrowed the gap, the sun is coming up, and we're approaching Raton, New Mexico at the Interstate 25 junction. He'll either stop in Raton or go north or south on Interstate 25. The roadway should be in better shape and there'll be more cameras.* Randy glanced at the van's fuel gauge. *We'll need to stop in Raton for gas. Maybe we'll catch up to him at a gas station!*

* * * * *

Nick's first glimpse of the Rocky Mountains just after dawn was spectacular. The Sangre de Cristo Range of the Rocky Mountains runs north-south from southern Colorado through northern New Mexico. They formed a snow-capped, gray and purple wall filling the entire western horizon as he crested a rise along US Highway 87 east of Raton, New Mexico at sunrise. *Sangre de Cristo — Blood of Christ,* thought Nick. *So named because of the dark red blush frequently observed covering the eastern slopes with the rising sun, and that's the way they look this morning!*

The sky was a perfect cobalt blue by the time he turned north on Interstate 25 and slowly climbed Raton Pass into Colorado.

He stopped at a truck stop in Trinidad for gas. As Nick waited in the cashier's line, he noticed the man ahead of him settle a large diesel fuel bill with a trucking company's PIDD. Nick wondered why the driver didn't just use the induction pad at the pump until he saw the clerk ring up the full amount and then hand the driver a kick-back in cash, which the driver happily pocketed. There were more trucks at this truck stop than Nick had seen at any other place throughout his trip.

Well, as the man said, 'cash is king.'

Chapter 19

The Sangre de Cristo range gave way to the beginnings of the Rampart Range in Colorado Springs - still part of the Front Range of the Rocky Mountains. But by then, even such spectacular scenery didn't help much in Nick's constant fight to stay awake. It had been early morning when Nick entered the Front Range Metroplex, which stretched almost 200 miles from a little south of Pueblo to just north of Fort Collins near the Wyoming border. It was mid-morning by the time he turned off on US Highway 24 in Colorado Springs, roughly at the midway point of the elongated Metroplex. Nearly all of Colorado's population now lived along the narrow Interstate 25 corridor in the center of the state, with very few people living in either the eastern or western parts.

He had traveled a little over one thousand miles, climbed more than seven thousand feet, dropped about twenty degrees Fahrenheit in ambient temperature and over sixty percent in relative humidity in about twenty hours of driving. He didn't drive fast - he drove relentlessly. Stopping only to get gas or fast food to go, and relieving the pressure on his bladder only at those times, allowed him to make fairly good time even with a trailer in tow. But he had only slept for about six out of the last fifty hours and he had roughly another fifty miles and three thousand feet of elevation to go.

Nick headed west on US Highway 24 past Manitou Springs where Ute Pass started its winding climb past the north shoulder of Pikes Peak. The four lane highway was divided much of the way by a small mountain stream, a faint memory of the flow that had carved the pass out of rock eons ago. Once the tight turns and closed in feeling of the lower canyon gave way to straighter runs through more open areas, Nick said, "Agnes, call Mike Clarke."

Mike Clarke was a college classmate and Nu Alpha Gamma fraternity brother of Nick's. Nu Alpha Gamma members were predominately engineering students with a leavening of science and math majors, leading the members of plebian fraternities and sororities to refer to them as the "*Nerds And Geeks*" fraternity.

I hope he answers, his PIDD is not going to recognize my new PIDD's number and may not even notify him of the call depending on his security settings.

"Hello?"

That sounds like Mike, but there's no video. Since Nick's video was on, he looked directly into his PIDD's camera and said, "Hello, Mike, this is Nick MacEwen."

The video immediately appeared revealing a head and shoulder view of a grinning, tow-haired, middle-aged male.

"Nick! How are you? I haven't heard from you since your Christmas video. You looked great in the Santa hat, by the way. I felt like sitting on your knee and giving you my Christmas list. Of course, I mean that in the most inoffensive, politically correct, secular, sexual-orientation neutral way! Sorry about the blank screen and stand-offish greeting at first – you're not using your usual PIDD."

Ignoring the comment about his PIDD, Nick said, "Don't you know that political correctness is dead, you dumb Mick?"

"Right - I get this news flash from an ignorant Jockie who masquerades as Santa Claus."

"Leave it to you, Mike, to make fun of my professionally produced, cutting-edge, thespian tour-de-force Christmas greeting. Listen, I just came from a visit with our fraternity brother Leonardo, and since I was in the neighborhood, I thought I might drop by and see you at your place. Is that okay?"

Mike's grin vanished immediately as he recognized Nu Alpha Gamma's secret distress phrase. Frowning with concern and dying of curiosity, but more aware of the privacy issues in a digital world than the average person, Mike limited his response to, "Sure, Nick. That would be great. Where are you now?"

"I'm coming up Ute Pass right now. I just crossed the line from Cascade to Green Mountain Falls."

"Okay, you're almost to Woodland Park. You won't believe the traffic between there and Cripple Creek. After Cripple Creek there's hardly any traffic, but the roads get pretty bad, so you've got another hour and a half to go."

"Probably more like two hours, Mike. I'll explain why when I get there. Are you sure it's okay for me to stop by?"

Mike's frown deepened, but he replied, "Of course it's okay. It's more than okay! I can't wait to see you in person!"

"Thanks Mike."

* * * * *

Seeing Mike again made Nick think back to his college days. Nick was a severe introvert and didn't have many friends. But among those few he had, Mike had been his best friend. They were in the same class year, as well as in many of the same classes. They pledged Nu Alpha Gamma at the same time and went through initiation together. But Mike was much more outgoing than Nick. He was always trying to set Nick up with blind dates - usually a friend of whoever Mike was dating at the time. More often than not, those were painful encounters for Nick and he only acquiesced to them to make Mike happy.

After college the two friends had drifted apart, not emotionally, but physically. Nick went into energy weapons research whereas Mike pursued a career in computer systems and software. They not only worked for different companies in different industries, they worked in different parts of the country. So far, Nick's career had all been in Texas, but Mike's had been in California until his move to Colorado. Although they both worked on various defense contracts, they were for different agencies.

Mike excelled in all aspects of computer systems - hardware, software, and networks. He made a lot of money for the companies that employed him over the years and pretty good money for himself. He knew he could make more money by starting his own company, but he disliked managing people. They often took advantage of his friendly, open nature and his tendency to assume everyone was honest, hardworking, and competent. Far too often, they proved otherwise. Besides, Mike was somewhat of a free spirit and just didn't feel comfortable telling other people what to do. So eventually he became an independent consultant and rapidly gained the status, and the billing rate, of the most sought after consultant in the industry. Just about the time that Mike decided he had made more money than he could ever possibly spend, he received word that he was the only living heir to his recently deceased uncle's estate.

Mike's uncle, Norris MacNamara, caught gold fever after retiring from the Navy as a chief machinist's mate. He used the money he had saved over the years by remaining a bachelor and spending most of his time at sea where the Navy housed and fed him, to buy a parcel of land that included a defunct gold mine outside of Victor, Colorado. Like the apocryphal retired sailor who decided where to settle by walking inland carrying an anchor until someone asked him what it was, Norris had seen enough of the ocean. For years he lived on his retirement pay and the small amount of gold ore he produced by single-handedly working the mine.

Then the Occupational Safety & Health Administration closed him down because he didn't have an emergency subsurface-to-surface communication system in place. Norris argued that was silly since he was the only one working the mine so there was no one on the surface to talk to anyway. OSHA wouldn't back down and neither would Norris. He had pretty much gotten over the gold fever by then anyway, so he lived out the rest of his years on his retirement pay alone. Since he never married, and his sister had preceded him in death, Norris's will left the property to his sister's son, Michael Clarke.

Mike was working out of his home in the Silicon Valley region of the San Francisco Bay area when the news of his inheritance reached him. Although it was occasionally necessary for him to physically travel to customers' locations, computer networking had become so ubiquitous that he could usually telecommute to his clients. As a result, it really didn't matter much where he lived, and a gold mine in Colorado appealed to his proclivity for the unconventional. Despite all of his dating during college, Mike had never married, so there was no wife's opinion to solicit. After a quick visit to inspect his new property, he sold his home in California and moved to Colorado. After his first winter at 10,000 feet, he bought a Humvee and had his Uncle Norris's old cabin razed to the ground. In its place, he had a large, thoroughly modern, well-insulated home built - that and a lot more.

* * * * *

Randy saw the sign pointing to Santa's Workshop, North Pole Colorado and was momentarily amused by the geographical incongruity until he noticed the Ferris wheel and realized it was some sort of theme park.

His PIDD's map showed that they were in Cascade, Colorado, climbing up Ute Pass on US Highway 24. The trailer license capture map overlay was showing the last detection was made right about here less than fifteen minutes ago. They were rapidly catching up.

As Randy watched, his PIDD updated with another camera capture message showing that the trailer had just been spotted in Woodland Park, Colorado, just nine miles ahead.

"Okay guys, get ready. We're closing in on him. We don't know if he's armed or not, but I want to play it safe and assume that he is, so check your weapons."

* * * * *

Nick followed Fred's directions as he continued on US Highway 24 through the city of Woodland Park. Colorado Highway 67 joined U.S. Highway 24 on the southwestern fringe of Woodland Park, and the two turned southwest until parting company at the town of Divide where Nick followed Colorado Highway 67 south towards his destination. Victor was essentially one hundred and eighty degrees around Pikes Peak from where he entered Ute Pass – forty-one miles by road, sixteen miles as the crow flies, assuming the crow could clear the 14,114 foot mountain.

A few miles after turning south on Colorado Highway 67, Nick passed a sign that read, "Report Wildlife Violations" followed by a PIDD number. Nick grinned. *Now what does that mean? Am I supposed to report jaywalking mountain goats or muskrat molestations?*

The traffic was substantial on Colorado Highway 67 heading to and from Cripple Creek, which was a major gambling and entertainment center often referred to as Little Las Vegas. There were stretches of Colorado Highway 67 which frankly frightened Nick. It seemed to him that he was driving within mere inches of sheer precipices that dropped straight down to winding mountain streams in canyons far, far below. Although surrounded by gorgeous scenery, he concentrated on the strip of road ahead and ignored the angry horn blowers behind him as he slowed to a crawl. Uncharitably, he wondered how many of the horn blowers were going to Cripple Creek to gamble their welfare checks.

Fred verified via satellite that traffic was even more congested within the city of Cripple Creek, and directed Nick to turn off on Colorado Highway 81 to head for Victor the back way. Whereas the road to Cripple Creek had been well maintained to support the tourist traffic, Colorado Highway 81 was fraught with pot holes and frost heaves, making the alternate route choice of questionable merit. The good news was that the road ran mostly in between, rather than on the side, of mountains, thus avoiding the narrow shoulders and sharp falloffs. The bad news was that the relatively lower fear engendered by the lack of threading one's way alongside breathtaking views of one abyss after another was apparently making Nick complacent. Several times Nick was returned to a higher level of awareness by Fred and his bugle. Nick was nodding off at the wheel.

Nick finally turned into the dirt road leading to Mike's house right about at lunch time.

Chapter 20

"Well, Jimmy, there's good news and bad news. The good news is that we have been able to follow his trail all the way to Woodland Park, Colorado."

"I can't believe he's gone that far! So what's the bad news?"

"You've probably figured out by now that our ability to track him depends on traffic cameras." *And some number of commercial and private security camera networks too, but Jimmy doesn't need to know that.*

"Yah, I got that impression."

"How many traffic cameras do you think there are west of Woodland Park, or for that matter, north or south of Woodland Park, Colorado?"

"I guess there aren't that many."

"Give the man a gold star! You are exactly right. There aren't that many. The last hit we got was from a camera on the busiest street in town. That was over an hour ago. We've driven all around town without spotting the trailer. Woodland Park is a junction of four fairly major highways and numerous smaller roads leading in all directions, so he might have gone anywhere from here."

"I don't think he's still in Woodland Park, but we'll spend the rest of the day making sure, and then start back to Houston tomorrow if we haven't found him. We'll continue to monitor the traffic cameras, but unless he goes through Salt Lake City, Las Vegas, or some other fairly large city, we'll be very lucky to pick him up again. Even if he does go through another urban area there are no guarantees. A lot of failed traffic cameras have not been replaced during the depression. He's got almost the entire western United States to hide in."

"This is really important, Randy. Is there anything else you can do?"

Randy hesitated, and then asked, "You mentioned GPS coordinates in an earlier conversation. That made me think that there's a tracking device on the trailer or the truck, but you don't seem to have access to the data now. Is there any way you can regain access to the tracking information? Has the device failed? Has MacEwen discovered and destroyed it?"

I was really hoping he wouldn't pick up on that! It just slipped out. "That's one of those sensitive issues I mentioned before. It's along the same lines as you wanting to protect your special resource. Assuming the device is still operational, we might be able to get updated coordinates as a last resort, but that involves complications that could lead to a suboptimal outcome. The optimal outcome depends on our finding the trailer without relying on the tracking device. I'll see if I can get an update without tipping our hand, but don't count on it."

What is this - some kind of a rich guy's scavenger hunt where you don't want the other team to know where you think the good stuff is? "Well, Jimmy, there is some things we can do if we can narrow down the area we're working with. I've even used helicopter searches for some high value targets, but we can't work with 'somewhere between the Front Range of the Rocky Mountains and the West Coast.' Another way to focus the search is to study the subject. Find out as much as we can about him. For instance, do you know if he has any family or friends living in the western United States?"

"I never heard him talk about any family or friends at all. He ate lunch in his office with our finance guy, Frank Palmer. I know that because I had to go yank Frank out of there sometimes when I needed him in the middle of the day. Maybe Frank would know more about Nick's private life. It's not like I socialize with my employees, you know."

Of course you don't socialize with your employees, Jimmy. It's not like they're real people, after all.

Randy's father was a wildcat oilman who started on a shoestring and eventually built a successful business and a good life for his family. But in the meantime, Randy had grown up in oilfield towns, living next door to and going to school with the children of roughnecks. Always large for his age, he worked as a roustabout for his father's company every summer during his high school years while playing football in the fall and lacrosse in the spring. By the time Randy went to college, he had the clothes, the car, and the money to fit into Jimmy's circle of friends, but lacked their disdainful attitude toward the "little people." He also was a lot tougher, mentally and physically, than his classmates, most of whom wouldn't last a single day working in the oilfields, playing defensive tackle, or in goal. They all thought in terms of the power of money. Randy knew that there was another, older, kind of power - brute physical power. As far as he was concerned, Jimmy and his friends were the little people.

"I'll come over and talk to Palmer when I get back. There are also a few other ways for me to dig up information on this MacEwen guy. For instance, you have a completed security clearance application form for him on file, right?"

"Well, yes, I guess so. I don't really deal with details like that."

I'll just bet you don't. "Okay, I'll get with your security person when I get back. Those applications have a lot of background information that might give us some clues where he's headed."

"Okay," Jimmy replied and then unceremoniously disconnected.

You're welcome, Jimmy.

* * * * *

Mike Clarke came charging out of the front door of his house as Nick drove up the dirt driveway.

Or maybe it was the rock driveway. Agnes had kept up a running commentary over the last few miles, explaining that Mike's house sat on a low plateau in a canyon between the east shoulder of Straub Mountain and the west shoulder of Brind Mountain about a mile and a half south of Victor. She also commented on local weather patterns and the region's geography, even going so far as to point out that the roads were graded Fluvial Pumiceous conglomerates and Pumiceous sandstones. *After all, these are the Rocky Mountains, not the Dirt Mountains.* It was more information than Nick really wanted, but at least it kept him awake.

Nick was really happy to see Mike in person again. *I forgot how tall and lanky Mike is. He's almost a head taller than me.* Mike had played basketball in college and was a good athlete despite his nerdy major of Computer Science. He might have been able to play professionally, but he had absolutely no interest in doing so. His college athletic scholarship was merely a means to an end.

Coming around the front of the truck as Nick dismounted, Mike said, "Nick, what's wrong? What's going on? Holy smokes, what's in the trailer? Have you been evicted?"

Nick, laughing, said, "Slow down, Mike! Let me catch my breath. Come to think of it, what do you do for air around here? I'm short of breath, a little dizzy, and I have a headache."

"Come in the house and sit down, Nick. You're not accustomed to this altitude and need to be careful. You will probably notice feeling kind of tired, too."

This elicited nearly hysterical laughter from Nick. "If you only knew how tired I really am! I've been on the road all night. In fact, I've only had a few hours of sleep since Monday morning."

Mike reached out to take hold of Nick's arm and gently pull him towards the porch, ready to support him if he waivered. "Well, come on in. You can sit down and tell me all about it. Once I know what's going on you can crash in one of the spare bedrooms."

Nick reached into the pickup truck and grabbed the PIDD from its mount before allowing Mike to lead him to the porch and on into the house. Mike took him directly to a gorgeous looking, deeply padded leather recliner into which Nick gratefully sank.

"I'll bet you're sore from driving. Let me get you some water, and then I'll pair your PIDD with the house computer so you can configure the chair how you want. It has a great massage menu," Mike called over his shoulder as he headed for the kitchen.

Nick took in his surroundings without any of it truly registering. He got a general impression of some sort of a Nuevo Mountain Cabin Rustic look, with wood paneled walls and lots of wood framed leather furniture. His brain was starting to shut down from fatigue. *They called this zoning out when Mike and I were in college and stayed up the whole night cramming for a test. I wonder what young people call it now.*

When Mike came back with bottled water he had to shake Nick to wake him up.

"Nick" ... "Nick, wake up."

Nick's eyes sprung open and looked up at Mike standing over him. But then Nick felt something in his lap and looked down. Large amber-colored sorrowful eyes stared up at him from a huge dark brown furred canine head resting there. The dog was sitting on the floor next to the chair, and had to hunch down to put its head in his lap.

"What the" ... "where did you come from?" Nick said with a smile as he reached down to scratch behind the dog's ears.

"That's Patti. She always makes a beeline to anyone who is disabled, sick, or just plain feeling bad. She must sense that you're worn out."

"What breed is she?"

"She's a purebred Chocolate Labrador Retriever. Her AKC registered name is Pikes Peak Patti but I just call her Patti."

"But she's huge!" Nick protested. "I've never seen a Labrador Retriever this big."

"You should see her mother and father! I got her as a puppy from a breeder on the plains out east of Colorado Springs. As I was picking her out, Patti's father picked up a log from the breeder's wood pile and carried it off under a tree and started to chew on it. When I made a remark about that, the breeder told me that the log would be completely chewed up in an hour or so."

Holding out the bottled water, Mike continued, "You'll need to drink more water than you're used to until you get acclimated to the conditions here. Give me your PIDD and I'll set it up."

Nick traded his PIDD for the water and took a long sip as Mike tapped on the PIDD's screen to wake it from sleep mode.

Fred immediately appeared on the screen leaning forward at the waist with his hands on his hips and a scowl on his face.

"Look, I know you're a good friend of the Boss and all that, but I can't let you screw around with me without clearance. Boss, is it okay to let this clown mess with my settings?"

Without moving from his position on the chair, Nick tiredly answered, "Yes Fred, Mike is my friend and I trust him implicitly. Please allow him to pair you with his house computer." Then the realization that Fred had been listening to the conversation dawned on Nick through the fog of his fatigue.

Mike stood staring at the PIDD display with his mouth open. Then his eyes got big when Fred said, "Okay, I just wanted to make sure where he stood in the pecking order around here. I don't need him to give me the settings. I've already hacked into his house computer. But I gotta give him credit - it was a bitch."

Then Agnes walked into the picture next to Fred and said, "Watch your language, Fred!"

Mike's eyes got even bigger as he asked, "Nick, where did you get this PIDD?"

"I got it at a convenience store in Houston. Isn't it a pain in the wazoo?"

Before Mike could respond, Agnes called out, "Nick, there's a call coming in that I think you'd better take."

Shaking his head, Mike handed the PIDD back as Nick asked Agnes, "Who is calling? No one knows this number." Looking up at Mike he added, "You were the first and only one I called with this PIDD."

Mike moved behind the recliner so he could see the PIDD's display over Nick's shoulder. Nick tapped an icon and the PIDD opened like an accordion to form a twelve-inch diagonal high resolution screen.

Agnes continued, "The number calling is not in your contacts or my previous call memory."

Before either Nick or Mike could react to that, Agnes added, "I am being compelled to connect the call," at which point the screen went blank. Nick momentarily panicked, thinking it was Jimmy Barton calling.

Though the screen remained blank, Fred's voice announced, "It's okay, the number IS in my list. The call is a priority level two encrypted connection. I'll handle this."

Then an icon that looked like a traffic light appeared with a flashing "WORKING" label below it. The red light at the top was larger and brighter than the others at first. After a moment, the red light shrank and dimmed, and the yellow light in the middle grew larger and brighter. In another moment, the yellow light returned to normal and the green light at the bottom blossomed. A split second later the screen changed to grey with a thin black banner along the bottom containing white lettering announcing "SYNCHED - NO VIDEO AVAILABLE." Then a voice - obviously electronically altered to prevent recognition – said "Hello Mister MacEwen. It appears that you have arrived at Mister Clarke's residence."

Chapter 21

"Who are you, and how do you know where I am?" Nick demanded as his pulse rate started to rise.

"You may call me 'Red.' I am a friend of yours, even though we have never met. I represent one of several groups who have monitored your attempt to create a defensive shield over the years."

Nick was too stunned to speak, so the voice continued, "We are concerned about recent events which have seen you discharged from ITC followed by your cross-country excursion with the prototype in tow. That being said, we are happy that it is in your possession, as opposed to any of the alternatives.

"We were notified almost immediately when you began your journey, so we had some time to react. It was indeed fortuitous that you paid for the PP-PID in Houston electronically. If you had used the cash you withdrew from the ATM, we would not have known it was you. When we detected your purchase we were able to download some interesting enhancements."

That bit of news caused Nick to find his voice. "You're responsible for the smart-mouthed simulacrums? I said I was going to kill the programmers who created them!"

The disguised voice responded, "Your friend Mister Clarke will be very sad to hear that. But you are much better off with the enhancements, Mister MacEwen, as your friend can explain later."

"Right now it is important for you to understand your situation. I mentioned that there were several groups interested in your work. The groups can be divided into two categories - those with national security interests versus those with pecuniary interests. The first category can be further divided into two subcategories - the United States versus several other countries. I represent the national security interests of the United States."

Not giving Nick time to reply, Red went on, "I want you to consider the group I represent as your friends. As a token of that friendship, I need to inform you of the GPS tracking device that is attached to the prototype trailer."

Nick, on the edge of panic again, exclaimed, "There's a tracking device on the trailer? So these other groups you're talking about know where I am?"

Red replied, "No, Mister MacEwen, they do not know where you are. We learned of this device almost immediately after you began your trip, but it took us a little while to determine the best way to manage the situation and implement our solution. Obviously, we didn't want to interfere with the GPS satellite signals the device was receiving, but the device transmits its position reports via PIDD towers or communications satellites when necessary, using the same networks and protocols as PIDDs. So, knowing the device's number, we were able to spoof the position reports.

"We couldn't introduce flagrant errors since the original direction of your travel had already been established, so we have simply offset your position as much as practical. The offset was very small at first, and then we slowly increased it as you traveled further. It was tricky, since we had to stick to the roads. After all, we didn't want to show your vehicle driving through buildings or across a lake where there wasn't a bridge and such. That would have tipped them off that they were being misled. I don't suppose I have to mention that we first had to break the encryption algorithm being used by the device. But that was made much easier by the fact that we knew your actual position.

"The spoofed location data currently shows that you are in the San Isabel National Forest, about fifty miles southwest from where you actually are at the moment. This seemed to be a reasonable place for a man with a truck and trailer to stop and camp out overnight. By the way, as far as we know, only two of the other interested groups have access to this data.

"However," Red continued, "if the device remains at your current location much longer than overnight, we are faced with a conundrum. If we leave the offset error at its present value, the parties monitoring the location reports will figure that you have stopped and will send people to look for you. When they find out that you are not at the specified location, they will assume there was an offset error and start an expanding search that could find you, given enough time. If, on the other hand, we continue to increase the offset to make it look like you are still traveling, we will ultimately run out of land and have to start wandering around in circles. At that point, they will know they have been spoofed and will zero in on the places where you stopped the longest and start searching from there. Therefore, if you intend to stay with your friend for any length of time, it is important that at least the device, if not the trailer, start moving again quickly and travel as far away from your current location as possible.

"And in case you were about to ask, no, we don't know exactly where the device was placed on the trailer. You can bet that it wasn't installed in plain sight, and that it is quite small."

As tired as Nick was, his brain was simply refusing to wrap itself around the problem, regardless of how much adrenaline his body had tried to produce during the call.

So it was Mike who responded, "I think I know a way to handle that, Red. Can you continue the offset through tomorrow about mid-day, and then slowly let the offset go to zero by the end of the day after that?"

"Certainly, if that's what you want," Red replied.

"One more thing," Mike interjected. "You say you want to help. How can we get hold of you?"

"Fred has the number to call. There are times when I will not be able to answer. At any given time you can contact, or you may be contacted by, my compatriots 'White' or 'Blue' using the numbers that Fred also has in memory. Please understand that this is a closely held affair."

"I understand. Thank you," Mike said.

"You're welcome. Be very careful, gentlemen. We believe there may be multiple groups searching for the prototype, and that some of them are armed and capable of deadly violence."

Oh great, thought Nick, *just what I wanted to hear*.

"We are all about being careful. Thank you for the information regarding the tracking device. Goodbye," said Nick as he disconnected.

As soon as Fred 'n Agnes reappeared, Nick exclaimed, "Red, White, and Blue! Give me a break! Are those characters out of a comic book, a B-vid, or members of some underground ultra-patriot militia? How can we believe *any* of this?"

Mike replied, "I think Red is telling the truth."

Mike began to count off points on his fingers.

"First of all, I recognized the 'interesting enhancements' just before the call came in. I wrote the code for them. That's why I wanted to know where you got the PIDD."

Nick interrupted, "You?! *You're* one of the programmers I've been threatening to kill?"

"Actually, I'm *the* programmer, singular, that you apparently want to kill. By the way, my professional curiosity is killing me. I know you called your old PIDD Agnes. How did she end up on the new PIDD with this Fred persona? Wait - don't answer that question right now. We don't have time."

"Second, blocked video and distorted audio implies that Red wishes to remain anonymous, but thinks that we might recognize him or her otherwise. That means Red is a either a public figure, or someone that one of us would remember from our government contract work.

"Third, both of us have high level security clearances, so you know how these things work. The very existence of these PIDDs is highly classified, and by that I mean higher than Top Secret. Only very high-level government officials have PIDDs programmed like this one, and Red had such a PIDD and also knew I was the programmer. So, that means he or she is a high level-government official with a very high security clearance.

"Fourth, the software overrides necessary to compel a PIDD to answer are also highly classified and are also restricted to the highest levels of the government.

"Fifth, the traffic light sequence as the PIDD connected was an encryption application that uses one-time keys from an electronic key vault, which is completely government controlled and - you guessed it - highly classified.

"Sixth, Red casually said 'we didn't want to interfere with the GPS satellite signals' implying that they could do so if they really wanted to. I don't know how high in the government you'd have to be to get authorization for that. You're talking about screwing up transportation systems world-wide - planes flying into mountains, that sort of stuff. I'm virtually certain that would require presidential approval, but Red just mentioned it in passing as if it was no big deal.

"Red also casually talked about having a level of access to PIDD networks and commercial communications satellites that, if true, would also be highly classified. We don't actually have any proof at this point that they were able to spoof the location reports, but I can't figure out a reason they would lie about that.

"Seventh, Red said that breaking the encryption used by the tracking device was made easier by knowing your actual location. But they couldn't have been getting your location from the tracking device before breaking the code, so they had to get it some other way. Unlike regular PIDDs, these altered PIDDs can only be tracked when the owner is being kidnapped and speaks a pre-programmed emergency phrase. So, unless you had head-lights in your mirror all the way from Texas, I submit that the most logical remaining methods are national security assets, such as high definition satellite imagery or unmanned drones. That would also explain how he knew you were at my place even though you had just arrived. Reassigning resources like that in a short amount of time takes someone with real horsepower.

"I don't think that anything Red said was impromptu. I think Red very carefully made sure that I would pick up on some, if not all, of these clues so that I could reassure you. Red apparently isn't familiar enough with you to know how to convince you directly that he or she, in fact, represents the national security interests of the United States, but *did* know how to convince me."

Nick asked, "What was that 'closely held' business at the end?"

Mike answered, "Red was trying to tell us that they consider your situation and their part in it 'compartmentalized' classified information, meaning that only the minimum number of people necessary have access to the information regardless of security clearance levels. Maybe Red, White, and Blue are the only ones in the government who know about it. In any case, we should not assume that any other government personnel are aware, nor should we inform them, of what's going on with this 'prototype' as he called it.

"Finally, they obviously know exactly where you are. If they wanted to stop you from whatever you are doing, they would simply come get you with some sort of special action team. Instead, I got the impression that they were fairly happy with whatever you are doing with what's in the trailer.

"So, Nick, what do you have in the trailer that's attracted the attention of some very heavy hitters in our government?"

Everything Mike had said was spinning around in Nick's head. He had followed most, but not all of what Mike said. Nevertheless, he was pretty sure that he agreed with Mike's conclusions.

"Well, Mike, that's a long story."

Mike interrupted, "I was afraid of that. We don't have time for a long story right now. What I need to know right now is how difficult it will be to remove whatever it is from the trailer."

"It's mostly rack-mounted electronic equipment. The racks themselves are bolted to the floor and walls, but I don't need them. We can always get more equipment racks. The electronic units are held in with quick disconnect fasteners. As Red said, it's a prototype, so we were always taking things in and out for modifications. We can just pull out all of the equipment and cables and hide them someplace for now. The only really heavy items are the power supplies at the bottom of the racks. They require a two man-carry."

"But Mike, maybe I should just keep going and find some place in the boonies to hole up. I came here because I wanted your help with the project, but now it seems like things could get dangerous. I don't want to drag you into this."

"Nick, you're not going anywhere. First of all, you are not physically capable of driving anywhere at the moment. Second, "Brother Leonardo" would be very unhappy if I didn't help you. Third, I'm dying with curiosity to see what all of the fuss is about. Fourth, I would love to help you with your project, whatever it is, because I am between assignments right now and bored to tears."

"You really like to enumerate your thoughts, don't you Mike?"

Mike laughed and replied, "Writing good, tight code requires an obsession for structure and sequence."

"From what I hear," said Nick, "you're the best in the business."

Mike's eyes twinkled as he answered, "It would only be false modesty for me to deny that."

"That's just what I need Mike - the best in the business."

Mike smiled and said as he reached for his PIDD, "I've heard from people in your field of work that you're not so bad yourself."

Nick sighed. "If that's true, why am I unemployed?"

"I suspect that your current employment status has nothing to do with your capabilities," Mike answered, then thought better of it. "Or maybe your current employment status has *everything* to do with your *exceptional* capabilities.

"You just relax, Nick. I need to make some connections."

Chapter 22

Nick woke up disoriented. At first, he didn't know where he was. The last thing he remembered was sitting in the recliner discussing Red's call with Mike. Glancing around, he saw that he was in a very comfortable king size bed in a large unfamiliar bedroom. The drapes over both of the windows were closed, but he could tell from the light around the edges that it was daytime. He could also tell that he desperately needed to relieve his bladder. Looking around the room with that specific objective in mind revealed three identical-looking closed doors.

"It's through the door on your right." Nick looked in the direction of the voice and saw his PIDD on the nightstand. Fred was visible on the display pointing off to Nick's right.

Throwing the covers off - *Covers in the summertime! If I was in Houston, I'd be sleeping on the top of the sheets!* – Nick jumped out of bed, and then realized that he was actually wearing his own pajamas. *What the heck? How did that happen?* But nature's call overcame his curiosity and he covered the remaining distance to the door on the right as fast as his still sore body would allow. Opening the door revealed that the bedroom had its own adjoining bathroom. *How did Fred know what I was looking for? And how did he know where it was?*

As soon as he emerged from the bathroom there was a knock on his bedroom door and Mike called out, "Nick! Are you up and about now?"

In answer, Nick walked over and opened the door, where his friend Mike stood with a big smile on his face.

"Hello, sleepy head! I heard you rattling around and thought you might be up and hungry."

"Well, now that you mention it, Mike, I think some food would be very welcome."

"Great! I've got a well-stocked pantry - where is your body clock right now? Do you want breakfast, lunch, or dinner?"

"What do you mean? Just how long have I been asleep?"

"You were closing in on twenty-four hours. It's about midafternoon now."

"Holy smokes!" Thinking about it for a moment, Nick realized that he was very hungry. "It doesn't matter, Mike. Make whatever you want and I'll eat it."

"Take a shower and get dressed. Your clothes are in that dresser against the wall or hanging in the closet over there. We found them wrapped in a bedspread in that trailer of yours. I'll have something for you to eat when you come out."

"Wait a minute, what happened to the trailer? We've got to do something about the tracking device!"

"Relax, Nick. I've taken care of that. I'll tell you all about it over ... breakfast, I think."

At that, Mike headed off to his kitchen and Nick headed to the shower. Nick saw that his toiletries were already in the bathroom. Apparently Mike had also found the grocery bag in the trailer.

After his shower, Nick found his underwear and socks in the dresser. His shirts and pants were hanging in the closet. Everything had been washed or cleaned, ironed as necessary, and folded, rolled, or hung as appropriate. *Does Mike have a maid?*

Feeling like a new man, Nick retrieved his PIDD from the nightstand and stepped out of the bedroom into the hall. Then he suddenly realized that he had no idea where to go. The hall he was in stretched in both directions, with doors and connecting hallways appearing on each side.

Sheepishly, Nick called out, "Mike, where are you?"

No answer.

Louder this time, Nick called out, "Mike, where are you?"

Just as Nick was about to pull out his PIDD and call Mike for directions, a voice sounding like an actor playing the part of an English butler in a Twentieth Century movie came out of everywhere and nowhere, "Good afternoon, Mister MacEwen. I am Mister Clarke's house computer, Alfred. He has instructed me to provide you with every courtesy during your stay."

Nick quickly inspected the walls, floor and ceiling around him but could not see any evidence of the microphones, speakers and video cameras that must be there.

The house computer continued, "Mister Clarke is in the kitchen. Please turn to your right and proceed down the hall. I will direct you to him."

Once Nick caught the smell of bacon, he just followed his nose.

* * * * *

Colonel Shi Rui Xian was just rising from his desk to go out and get some exercise by taking an afternoon walk around the consulate grounds when his PIDD started to play *Da Tang Guifei*. Glancing at the screen, he confirmed it was agent Xue reporting in again. He sat back down and tapped the icon to connect the call. As soon as the connection was secure, Shi spoke.

"Good afternoon, to whom am I speaking?"

Xue replied, "Wa Shing," the name of a laundromat in Bay Town.

Shi asked, "What do you have to report?"

Xue replied, "After the staff at the bank would not confirm or deny the presence of the bird yesterday, I tried some of the hotels and gas stations where people are more interested in money than in principles. I finally found a clerk at a truck stop that recognized the picture we have of the bird and was able to correctly describe the coop. He noticed the coop leaving midafternoon yesterday and believes it headed north on Interstate 35. The bird and the coop have probably left this area."

"I agree. I just received information that speaks to why the bird flew with the coop and its approximate current location. It may actually result in a great opportunity for us. However, the bird is far ahead of you now in central Colorado, which is outside of our region. I want you to return to Houston while I coordinate with my superiors."

"There is one other thing," said Xue. "We are not alone in seeking the bird. Several people mentioned that others had sought information about the bird in the photograph."

"I am not surprised. Return immediately, quickly prepare yourself to travel again, this time for possibly extended operations, and await my instructions."

* * * * *

"This reminds me of when we were college roommates," said Nick as he dove into the scrambled eggs, bacon, sausage and pecan coffee cake. "We would eat whatever we wanted, whenever we wanted."

"Yes," Mike replied, "We thought we were invincible then. Now we have to watch what and how much we eat. But I remembered that your favorite was always breakfast, no matter what time of day or night. I also remembered that you drink that stuff even with breakfast," Mike said, pointing at the can of Dr. Pepper next to Nick's plate.

"Yep, that's still true, Mike. I really appreciate the spread you've laid out. But you're right about watching what we eat now. If I ate like this very often I'd probably keel over dead. But this is a special occasion. Are you sure you don't want some? There's an awful lot of food here."

"No, I had lunch just a little while ago." Mike got a faraway look in his eyes and said, "You know, Nick, we were awfully lucky back in our college days."

"Lucky to survive twenty-plus credit hour semesters while working part time?"

"No," Mike smiled, "I mean that we were lucky because we were the end product of an educational system that was arguably the finest in the world. The economy was red hot, particularly in technical fields, and both of us were highly sought after by corporate recruiters. Now our educational system is probably not even in the top twenty worldwide, kids graduate indoctrinated but not educated, and they can't get a job because the economy has tanked.

"You know what really scares me, Nick?" Mike continued without waiting for an answer to his rhetorical question. "I'm afraid that we may have lived through America's best years and it's all going to go downhill from here."

Mike shook his head, "It's easy to get wrapped up in work and lose track of what's going on in the world around you. I really didn't realize how bad things had become until I left Silicon Valley and drove out here. You wouldn't believe how bad things looked along the way."

"I would believe. I just had the same experience driving here from Houston."

Nick paused between bites and asked, "That reminds me. What did you do with the trailer? I seem to remember that you were going to make some calls."

"Yes, I called some friends to help. You were obviously exhausted, and I figured I wouldn't be able to do everything that needed to be done as fast as it needed to be done without help."

Nick immediately frowned.

"Now, before you get excited about other people's involvement Nick, I need to tell you a little about how things work around here. Victor is a very small town and times are hard. We all help each other out. The local economy is pretty much based on barter. This is particularly true among the independent miners in the area. Someone called them the IMC – the Independent Miners Club – years ago and the name stuck. Most of them knew my uncle Norris for years. He was a retired Navy chief machinist's mate and helped them repair and maintain their equipment. So besides being his friends, they also owed him a lot for his services.

"When I came to live here, they all made it clear that as the inheritor of the estate of Norris MacNamara, I was the beneficiary of a respectable positive balance in the unofficial, no-written-records-kept, 'Barter Bank of Victor.' On top of that, the balance has grown, rather than diminished, since I came here because most of their equipment is automated now and my computer hardware and software skills are in high demand."

Mike paused for a moment, then asked Nick, "Did you see the open pit gold mine just northwest of town when you drove in?"

Nick replied, "I saw something that looked like a big quarry operation."

Mike nodded his head and went on, "Yes, that's the open pit gold mine. They employ several hundred people. Some of the IMC work a shift there, and then work their own underground mines on their own time. There are also various small businesses in Victor that have employees. So not all commerce hereabouts is barter, but a lot of it is.

"More importantly, it's a tight community where everyone knows everyone else and what they are doing. Your arrival was a topic of conversation at the Greasy Spoon downtown even before you turned into my driveway. *But,* no one around here is going to discuss local goings-on with a stranger - you'll be considered a stranger for a while, but not as long as you would have been without me vouching for you.

"So, I made some calls and spent some of my barter surplus to get things done in a hurry. A few of the IMC came over and helped me unload your equipment. Then we discussed the best way to handle the truck and trailer. It turned out that one of them knows a guy in Cripple Creek who knows a guy in Las Vegas that could make them disappear into Mexico."

Nick suddenly stopped eating and exclaimed, "What do you mean by 'them' disappear? You mean 'it' disappear don't you?"

Mike looked a little sheepish as he explained, "Nick, your truck had to go, too. One or more of these several groups who are looking for you know what kind of a truck you drive, probably even know its license number and probably know how to get access to traffic camera video if not – protect us, O' Lord – satellite or drone video. If they see images of the trailer – and we hope they will – and it's being towed by some other vehicle, they'll assume that you stopped somewhere, unloaded your equipment, and pawned off the trailer on someone. They will then start searching from the point the image was taken along your back trail looking for your truck. We want them to follow the truck and trailer all the way to Mexico. If they find the truck and empty trailer after that, they won't have anything obvious to search for along a back trail that's thousands of miles long."

Mike paused for breath and Nick just stared at him open-mouthed for a while. Then Nick said, "I'm not very good at this cloak and dagger stuff, am I?"

"Well," said Mike, "you've apparently succeeded in evading several groups for three days, so you can't be all that bad."

Mike continued, "The truck and trailer, driven by my friend, left here just about this time yesterday afternoon. He went to Cripple Creek to pick up his buddy, and they took off immediately for Las Vegas. That way it will look to the trackers like you are just continuing your pattern of driving mostly at night. They'll fly back into Colorado Springs when they're done.

"And in case you're wondering, I quarantined your old PIDD in a shielded room. I also put your antique pistol in my gun vault and your bank bag full of cash in my office safe. Oh, and a couple more Dr. Peppers we found in the truck's console are in the refrigerator over there," Mike said, pointing.

"Thanks Mike. I'll have to use some of that cash to pay the monthly fee for my PP-PIDD. I don't want to set up a regular account for it because that would create a record out there in the data cloud somewhere associating the

PIDD number with my name and address."

Mike laughed and said, "Don't worry about that. I can add your PIDD to my service account and then you can just reimburse me."

Nick silently resumed eating, flustered over forgetting the items in his truck, until he remembered another question that was on his mind.

"How did you get my pajamas on and put me in bed? And how did all my clothes get washed and ironed? Did the IMC guys help you with that, too?"

"No, that was Gail."

"What was Gail? The clothes washed and ironed?"

"No, and it's a good thing she isn't around to hear you ask that question. She helped me get your pajamas on and put you to bed. I did the clothes."

Nick, his ears turning red, cried, "This *Gail* woman helped put my pajamas on?"

"Relax, Nick. Gail is our local nurse. Actually, she's the only medical care we have this side of Woodland Park, so she does a lot more than a regular nurse. She's a Nurse Practitioner. She does pretty much everything that doesn't require a hospital, which we don't have anyway. I fixed up her office computer a few weeks ago, so she came over to help me with you. I was a little concerned about your physical condition after your marathon trip. She checked you out and said that there was nothing wrong with you that sleep and food wouldn't fix."

Nick took a deep breath and tried to calm down. *Mike was just trying to take care of me. Maybe he forgot how uncomfortable I am around women - if he ever* did *figure that out!* "All right Mike, I've got one more question."

"Okay, shoot."

"What on earth possessed you to program those PIDD personas that way?"

Mike laughed and replied, "I didn't program them that way. *You* did!"

"What are you talking about? I had nothing to do with programing that PIDD!"

"Let me try to explain," Mike began. "When the new PIDDs came out with much faster multi-processors, a lot more memory, and biometric sensors, I was engaged by an agency - whose identity is irrelevant at the moment - to develop software that would make the PIDDs much more secure, and as close as possible to artificially intelligent, so as to be more helpful to their owners."

Nick interrupted, "More helpful? You mean more irritating, don't you?"

"Now, Nick, give me a chance. It's very difficult to define artificial intelligence by any one characteristic, but it is usually described in general terms as a system that perceives its environment and takes appropriate actions based on a desired outcome. So, I worked on enhancing sensory functions and creating mutable decision trees.

"The hard part was determining desirable outcomes, and if a given action was appropriate. Since the focus was to be assisting the owner, it made sense to use biofeedback to determine appropriateness. In simple terms, if an action made the owner happy, then it was remembered as an appropriate action. If it made the owner unhappy, it was remembered as an inappropriate action. Of course, happy and unhappy are over-simplifications of the emotional state of the owner.

"Research into subtle biological clues to emotional states in humans has been available for some time. I used that data to drive the decision trees. In short, the PIDD learns what an appropriate response is by monitoring the owner's biological state – heartbeat, blood pressure, skin temperature, respiration rate, facial muscles, iris dilation, even body odor. A side benefit to this approach was that the PIDD could also tell when an owner was approaching a medically dangerous condition and take appropriate action.

"But in any case, Nick, the PIDD is being programmed by you, or at least by your biometrics, not by me. The personas are behaving in the way that you want them to behave."

"So that long, annoying question-and-answer configuration routine ..."

"That was the PIDD performing an initial calibration of your biometrics. But that was only the beginning. You can't turn a PIDD off without removing its battery. So the PIDD is constantly sensing its environment, with an emphasis on your biometrics, to refine the definition of appropriate actions and desirable outcomes in order to modify the decision trees as necessary. That's a pretty good shade tree programmer's definition of 'learning,' but there are all sorts of philosophical arguments about whether those are necessary and sufficient proof of artificial intelligence. For instance, the PIDD certainly doesn't have free will, nor should it."

Nick was too stunned at this news to react right away. It occurred to him that being stunned was becoming a habit with him. Then he remembered the overheated pickup truck cab in Waco, and how the PIDD had probably saved his life by cycling the air conditioning. He also remembered all the times when one of the simulacrums would start talking to him just as he was about to fall asleep at the wheel.

"So, you're saying that I enjoy simulacrums with an attitude."

"Well, you either enjoy them or need them on some deep psychological level. Speaking of '*them*,' how did you end up with Agnes in the new PIDD along with Fred?"

"I was hoping that you could tell me!" Nick explained his hurried upload of all of Agnes' files at his apartment.

"That's interesting," Mike volunteered when Nick was finished. "You transferred all of the Agnes files before Fred was configured. I don't know of any other instances when that was done. Usually when someone purchases a PIDD, they configure the new PIDD, and then transfer only the data files from the old one. You were in a hurry, so you transferred all of Agnes' files into memory. Later, you configured Fred, and then told him to upload all of Agnes' files. So some of the operating system files might have been either overwritten or duplicated." Mike frowned. "You may have created the first PIDD with Dissociative Identity Disorder in history, Nick."

'DID-PID' leapt into Mike's mind. *No, I'm not going there!*

"I'll run some tests on Fred 'n Agnes later to make sure there aren't any real problems. But right now I have a question for *you*, Nick."

"Okay, turnabout is fair play."

"If I buy you a new truck, will you tell me what was in the trailer?"

Nick laughed and then began to tell the story from the beginning.

Chapter 23

Billingsly had called Ahrens to his office because he didn't like to discuss sensitive issues on the telephone. As the head of a large defense contractor, he was reasonably certain that his communications were monitored by a number of different agencies, some of which were part of the United States government. He was more comfortable in his office, which was regularly swept for electronic bugs, had shielding installed in the walls and transducers mounted on the windows to vibrate the glass with high energy white noise to thwart laser based listening devices. The windows were even mirrored on the outside to prevent telescopic lip reading.

Vance was still smarting over the necessity to talk about sensitive matters with Jimmy Barton on an unsecured phone the day after the Defender prototype went missing. At first, he thought that he would have to somehow drag Barton kicking and screaming into the modern age of secure communications, but now he was wondering if Barton was becoming irrelevant in this drama. Vance was beginning to think this was coming down to a battle between himself and Nick MacEwen. It wouldn't be the first one.

* * * * *

Vance and Nick had been rivals in a sense at GenArm. Of a similar age, they joined the company at about the same time, but were on separate tracks. Vance started in legal, but switched over to management, while Nick was in engineering. They were both graduates of top-rated schools in their corresponding specialties. Frequently assigned to key positions on the same critical programs, they soon were considered rising stars in the company.

At first they were friends, although their relationship was occasionally strained when arguments arose over conflicting goals. Vance's priorities were usually related to program costs and schedules, whereas Nick focused on conformance to specifications, product performance and quality. Given the difference between their career paths, some disagreements were inevitable and each was just doing their job. But an enmity grew between them as they rose through their respective ranks.

Government spending began to shift away from national defense to domestic matters after the breakup of the U.S.S.R., and the Defense Industry entered a consolidation phase which saw many small companies fail and quite a few mid- to large-size corporations merge in an attempt to survive. The competition for government contracts, already intense, became fierce. Bidders were forced to propose very low prices and tight schedules if they were to have any hopes of winning. The pressure put on Vance by his superiors grew in inverse proportion to the margin for error in cost and schedule.

Things came to a head when a defect was discovered in the production of ship-mounted laser anti-aircraft batteries for the Navy. Nick and his team had determined that a component procured from a vendor was manufactured with a slightly incorrect mixture of composite materials, seriously increasing its probability for failure when the weapon fired. Furthermore, it was determined that there was a possibility that such an event could lead to a catastrophic failure of the weapon with life threatening consequences to nearby personnel.

According to the terms of the contract, GenArm was required to send a report of the defect to the Navy immediately, and simultaneously stop shipping the weapon systems until an approved replacement component could be procured and tested. Vance reported the problem to his superior who told him to make the problem go away. Vance then told Nick to destroy the defect report and clear the batteries for shipment.

Nick flatly refused. He couldn't believe that Vance would condone, let alone order, the shipment of known defective products. For his part, Vance couldn't believe that Nick was so naive. He told Nick that GenArm was in competition with other companies, none of which would be foolish enough to submit defect reports and interrupt production. Nick maintained that it was both contractually and morally required.

Vance was furious and lectured Nick on the realities of corporate life. He explained that the way to get ahead in a large corporation was to cultivate a mentor among your superiors, then be absolutely loyal to that person and do whatever you could do to advance their career - in other words, do their dirty work for them. Then your mentor would pull you up with them as they climbed the corporate ladder. It was Vance's mentor who told him to make the problem go away, therefore that was the right thing to do.

Nick countered that it was better to focus on the success of the company rather than on the success of any particular individual within it - a rising tide lifts all boats. Shipping known defective products with the potential to kill your customers did not strike Nick as a good business plan. So he submitted the defect report over Vance's objections, and then set his team to working around the clock with the vendor to produce acceptable replacement parts and resume shipping as soon as possible.

It was now clear to both men that they were philosophical opposites when it came to methods as well as goals. Vance never forgave Nick for the cost and schedule impact of replacing the defective components. A management track rival beat Vance out for the next big promotion and he was convinced that the handling of the anti-aircraft battery defect was the reason.

Over the years, Vance worked behind the scenes to prevent Nick's further advance, believing him to be unsuited for any higher position. Although he was unsuccessful in preventing Nick's continued promotions in the technical track, Vance was able to beat him to, and block him from, the top-level senior management positions. He was also instrumental in preventing Nick from obtaining approval for his proposed Defender project. Vance argued that it was just another example of Nick's naivety - trying to get a weapons company to pay for a project that had the object of making all of the company's products obsolete! Really, how could Nick think that the senior managers were so stupid?

Nick eventually left, and Vance ultimately made it all the way to the Presidency of GenArm. Unfortunately, times had changed and defensive systems were now in high demand. He had opposed Nick's Defender project years before - now he vowed to make it his own.

* * * * *

Ahrens was standing in front of Vance Billingsly's desk waiting patiently, ready to deliver his progress report. Billingsly was bent over his desk display just as he had been when Ahrens last saw him. For an instant, Ahrens wondered if somehow Billingsly had remained there since his last visit. He imagined the corporate president sitting there with tubes attached for intravenous feedings and bodily waste removal.

Billingsly's eyes were focused down and to his left in a way Ahrens knew from experience meant that his boss was engaged in an internal contemplation of some sort. Ahrens waited until his boss looked up and focused on him. Billingsly was not one for small talk, so Ahrens got right to the point.

"MacEwen took the trailer all right, but I don't think it was a maneuver dreamed up by Barton to wiggle out of your deal with him. I talked to Barton at length and he seems to be truly angry at MacEwen. I have a lot of experience reading people, and I think he's telling the truth when he says he was surprised by MacEwen's actions.

"I also talked to Dave Litchfield. He was present when Barton fired MacEwen, which seems to confirm that part of Barton's story. It's theoretically possible that Barton and MacEwen were putting on an act for Litchfield's benefit, but I think that's unlikely."

Ahrens continued, "But there is one other piece to the puzzle. When I contacted Litchfield to confirm MacEwen's firing, he was surprised to hear that MacEwen had taken off with the prototype. That suggests that Barton hadn't informed his Board of Directors yet. I can think of only one reason he wouldn't tell them - he is hoping to get the prototype back before the board members realize it's gone.

"It seemed to me that his hope could only be based on one of two possibilities. Either there really is some sort of collusion between Barton and MacEwen, or he has someone searching for the prototype who he believes will be successful. So, I got a chance to talk to our insider and found out that Barton has hired a repossession company to search for and return the trailer."

"You've got to be kidding!" exclaimed Vance. "He's engaged a repo company?"

"Yes, sir, it's owned by an old friend of his – Randy 'Blood Hound' Miller. You may have seen some of his vids. He's become sort of a celebrity with the wild stunts he's pulled to retrieve vehicles or catch bail jumpers."

"Leave it to Barton to go for the subtle approach," Vance sarcastically remarked. "Still, if he's spending his precious money to look for the prototype, then that pretty much eliminates the Barton-MacEwen conspiracy theory. But what do we do about this Blood Hound character?"

Ahrens replied, "I don't think we need to do anything. It appears that Blood Hound has lost the scent in central Colorado and is reduced to hoping that MacEwen will drive through some major metropolitan area and get picked up by a traffic camera. Even if Blood Hound somehow succeeds in finding the prototype, he'll just return it to ITC and your deal with Barton will still hold."

Ahrens continued, "Even though I think Barton is telling the truth about the theft of the prototype, I don't agree with Barton that no one entered the building that night."

Vance asked, "Why not?"

Ahrens replied, "Our surveillance operative on duty saw MacEwen go in and out of the plant twice over a two-hour period. Also, a computer workstation in the Engineering Lab registered two power outages about an hour apart. The first one occurred shortly before our operative says MacEwen exited the building the first time. The second one came shortly before MacEwen exited the building the second time. I don't believe that was a coincidence. No other computer at the plant logged any power outages."

"There's a remote possibility that a couple of brown-outs could have occurred and that particular workstation was more sensitive to low voltage conditions. So I posed as the plant manager at ITC worrying about sensitive equipment and called Houston Lighting and Power. They checked their distribution control logs and said that there were no-brown outs in the industrial park that night. There were two periods, the first longer than the second, of unusually high demand, but the voltage stayed within tolerance the whole time."

"So what are you saying?"

"I think MacEwen went inside the ITC plant to do something with that workstation, and was turning it off instead of logging off in order to disguise the fact. He probably used his administrative rights while he was still logged in to clear his session off the server records," Ahrens added.

Vance frowned and said, "But Jimmy told me the plant security system log only showed the cleaning crew going in and out."

Ahrens shrugged, "The plant entrance only has a keypad - there is no biometric security. MacEwen must have discovered the cleaning crew's code somehow, probably by simply observing a crew member keying in." Ahrens shook his head and continued, "And there is no guard service. The physical security there is so bad they might as well prop open all the doors and put a flashing welcome sign on the roof."

After a slight pause to see if Billingsly would comment, Ahrens continued. "I also reviewed ITC's computer security. There is no biometric security on the server or workstations. But, if someone was tampering with the computer that night, they would have needed the very highest system access codes and passwords in order to keep the log clear. I got a list of people who have that level of access from the system administrator. There are only two names - the IT Manager who doubles as the server administrator and MacEwen. Only MacEwen was seen entering the building that night."

"Could the IT Manager have cleared the log before anyone else saw it?"

"Yes, and I asked him if he had done so. He swore that he did not even logon to the server that morning until Frank Palmer came and asked him to check the log. He said that Palmer saw the same thing he did - two times when the server briefly lost network communication with the Engineering Lab workstation and nothing else. He said that brief power outages were common, but usually took the whole network down except for the server which has a battery backup. I checked with Palmer, who confirmed everything the IT Manager said. The IT Manager could have altered the log first thing in the morning and then lied about it, but I doubt it – how would he have known there was anything to alter? We know that MacEwen didn't call anyone."

"So, we don't really have a sure way of knowing if MacEwen logged on the system that night or not."

"That pretty much sums it up, but my gut feeling is that he did. But, I'm inclined to think it was to make copies of the files, not alter them. All of the relevant files showed revision dates well before Monday night. Also, I talked to a lot of people, learning as much as I could about MacEwen. He doesn't strike me as someone who would sabotage his own project."

Vance thought about that for a few moments. "Yes, but I also didn't think that MacEwen would steal anything. He's technically brilliant, but definitely inflexible when it comes to ethical concepts. But, if we accept his theft of the prototype as a fact, then we can't really use our previous concepts of his ethics as a guide to any of his other actions."

Ahrens remained silent since he had no good argument to refute that logic.

Vance asked, "Where is the trailer now?"

Ahrens answered, "I checked right before coming up here. It's in southern Utah heading generally southwest."

Vance frowned. "Where could he be going? ... And why?"

"I reviewed the track of his recent movements and saw that he is pretty much sticking to back roads. His route doesn't make a whole lot of sense for someone trying to get from point A to point B. He almost seems to be wandering around at times. Right now he's in the middle of an area that has about the lowest population density in the whole country. He may be looking for an out-of-the-way place to hide while he works on the prototype."

"Well, I'm hoping he will do exactly that," said Vance. "As long as we know where he sets up shop, we can reestablish surveillance and be ready to move in if he seems to achieve any success.

"Keep on top of his position. If he stops for any significant amount of time – say a day or two – go check it out, but be careful. I don't want to spook him into going even further underground ... By the way, did you bring the drawings and software files back with you?"

"Yes," Ahrens answered, "and I've already given them to Engineering."

"Okay, I'll light a fire under them to start building our own prototype."

At that, Vance refocused on his monitor. Ahrens took the cue, turned and walked out of Billingsly's office.

Chapter 24

"... and so I hitched up the trailer and took off, eventually making it to your doorstep like a lost waif in a snowstorm," Nick finished.

Mike sat quietly as he tried to get his head around the implications of everything Nick had related. Finally, he said, "I think you're right Nick; it's Pandora's Box, or maybe Prometheus bringing fire to the mortals."

"Yeah, great ... You know what happened to Prometheus ... You don't need to get involved with this, Mike. I can rent a truck or something and go find some other place to hunker down."

"No, no. I was serious when I said I wanted to help you. I'm even more serious now that I know more about what you're doing. Besides, I don't think you'll find anyplace much better suited for you to 'hunker down' than here. Help me clear the breakfast dishes and I'll give you the grand tour."

Mike had one of the new nanorecyclers from Switzerland in his kitchen, which breaks objects down into their constituent chemical compounds to be used in producing new objects on command. All of the breakfast dishes, utensils and food scraps went into the hopper. Mike explained that the organic materials would be processed into fertilizer for his hydroponics garden, and the inorganic materials would be used to produce items that could be selected from a menu. The technology was still in its infancy and the menu was limited, but Mike said it produced pretty good dishes and eating utensils.

All of which proves two things, thought Nick. *First, that there is a market for luxury items even in a depression, and second, that there is nothing a bachelor won't do to avoid washing dishes. Good grief! Now Mike has got me enumerating my thoughts!*

When Mike and Nick started to leave the kitchen, Mike's dog Patti, who had been lying curled up in a corner, arose to follow them. A puppy that had apparently been curled up with her scurried alongside. Stooping down, Nick scooped up the puppy and asked, "Well now, who is this?"

As the puppy squirmed and desperately tried to lick Nick's face, Mike answered, "That's the last puppy left from Patti's litter. I bred Patti a few months ago. Most of the puppy's brothers and sisters went to IMC families."

Mike led Nick on the tour as Patti followed along and Nick carried the puppy, gently scratching its head and chest to keep it calm. The house was an expansive single story design that included five bedrooms, six and a half bathrooms, living room, dining room, media center, study, kitchen, utility room, exercise room, and game room. There was also an attached four bay garage with a fully equipped workshop and an indoor gardening/hydroponics room.

After seeing all of this, Nick asked Mike why he had built such a large house when he was the only one living there.

"Well, I hoped that old friends would come to visit," Mike said with a wink and a grin. "But besides that, my house in Silicon Valley sold for so much that I had to build this monster to avoid capital gains taxes!"

Nick just shook his head and smiled, "I'll bet air conditioning this place costs you a fortune, though."

"Oh Nick, you're not in Houston anymore. You have a lot to learn about living at ten thousand feet. There's no air conditioning here - you don't need it. My heating bill is a different matter though. That's why I have solar heat collectors on the roof."

They paused in a hallway next to a large closet with closed double doors. Mike pointed to the closet and loudly announced, "And now for the rest of the tour!"

"There's more?" asked Nick as Mike opened the wooden closet doors only to reveal a closed pair of silver metal doors.

Mike's only answer was to say, "Alfred, open the elevator doors, if you please."

"It will be my pleasure, sir," Alfred's disembodied voice replied as the elevator doors parted.

"And allow Mister MacEwen unescorted, all areas, all hours access, starting now."

"Yes, sir," Alfred replied.

Nick followed Mike into the elevator where Mike spoke again, "L1, please," as the doors closed.

Nick saw the small display panels in the walls next to each door change from G to L1. The elevator was very smooth and he couldn't really tell if it was moving up or down, but he assumed it was moving down since the house didn't have a second floor.

The doors opened on pitch black dark. Nick involuntarily cringed until Mike stepped out of the elevator and lights automatically came on. The growing illumination revealed a rock wall about twenty feet away.

Nick asked, "Where are we?"

Mike motioned for Nick to follow as he answered, "We are in my uncle's mine. This is a hard rock, vertical shaft mine. Right now, we're on the level nearest the surface. If we walked down the tunnel that way," Mike pointed to his left, "we would see the lift shaft where the ore was raised to the surface. We would also see some of the equipment my uncle loved to tinker with, including a couple of steam engines originally used to drive pumps to get water out of the mine. The mines drain to a common discharge tunnel system now, so Uncle Norris removed the pumps and put generators on them to provide backup electrical power for his cabin and mine."

"How many levels are there?"

"Well, the term 'levels' evokes a false sense of symmetry, like regularly spaced floors in a building. But using that analogy, some of the mines in this area descend as much as one hundred stories underground. In reality, it's not as tidy, in a geometrical sense, as a building. There are many tunnels going in different directions at various depths. Except for exploratory tunnels, underground mines go where the best ore is, or more precisely where the best ore *was*. Mapping a mine like this is a three-dimensional problem. In the old days, they would paint the tunnel layout at each level on a pane of glass, and then slot the panes in a cubical wooden frame to try and see the whole picture. However, that still made it difficult to portray sloping tunnels and caverns that spanned multiple levels.

"Back then, it was very hard to know exactly where you were underground. Over the years, adjacent mines would sometimes overlap each other, and even connect with each other. There are lots of stories about how miners from one mine would use the connecting tunnels to raid other mines for gold ore at night. The stories tell of how there was even a tunnel that went under the local assayer's office so that the thieves could sell their stolen ore in secrecy through a trap door in the floor of the building.

"The IMC members still use the connectivity between the mines to visit each other during the winter if there's a particularly deep snowpack on the ground. Most of them have been here long enough that they know exactly where they're going.

"But to answer your question another way, the elevator currently only stops at four subterranean levels. L1, where we are now, is handy as a sort of storage area. Think of it as an underground attic. L2 is more interesting, as you'll see in a moment. L3 and L4 are currently unused. They just happened to be in line with the elevator shaft when I put it in."

"So your uncle didn't have an elevator?"

"No," Mike laughed. "He probably would be scandalized with what I've done to his mine. He rode the ore lift in and out. Come on, let me show you L2."

Mike and Nick returned to the elevator and had Alfred lower them to L2. The door opened into dark again, with the exception of what seemed to be bands of little flashing lights receding into the distance. Nick had this sudden vision of lighting bugs flying in a formation of columns abreast. There was also the sound and feel of air movement, giving him a slight chill. Then Mike stepped out of the elevator and the overhead lights came on. The view was very different from L1.

"Holy smokes, Mike, what is this?"

"Many years ago, this was a pocket of high grade ore. It was mined out well before my uncle came here, leaving an artificial cavern in this spot, which you can't see because we're inside a building constructed on the floor of that cavern. This is my office, my computer laboratory, and my server farm."

Mike did his best to look innocent as he added, "Collectively, I call it my Man Cave."

Nick just rolled his eyes and groaned.

Ignoring Nick's histrionics, Mike continued on. "When I came here from California to see what I had inherited, I realized that there might be a different kind of gold mine here."

Mike paused and looked at Nick. "Do you know anything about NORAD, Nick?"

"The North American Air Defense Command?" replied Nick.

"Yes, that's it. I have an ongoing technical support contract with NORAD. This cavern reminded me of their setup. NORAD is inside Cheyenne Mountain, which is only fourteen miles east of us. It's there for the blast protection provided by the surrounding granite mountain of course, but also because this whole area has very low seismic activity and no hurricanes or floods. Plus, here in the mountains, only a very small number of tornados have ever been reported, and none at this altitude. In other words, this is an ideal location for large installations of sensitive electronic equipment.

"Also, the temperature at this level of the mine is almost perfect. It's pretty much a constant sixty-eight degrees all year long, even with the heat load from all of this equipment. If we were in a building above ground with this same equipment in it, you wouldn't be able to hear me talk for all the noise caused by the forced air circulation to keep the temperature under control.

"Having the whole installation underground is also a help with electromagnetic radiation, and I've augmented that by lining the walls with shielding. That protects the equipment from outside radio frequency interference and also enhances security by preventing compromising emissions.

"I even had the building mounted on shock absorbers like NORAD, only a lot smaller. I'm not trying to survive a nuclear attack; I'm just trying to further dampen out any possible seismic activity.

"Electric power supply reliability has been very good here as well. There is still some excess capacity in the area because of the decline in mining and smelting operations over the years, but the growth of the Front Range Metroplex is eating into that. There have been rumors that a couple of the older coal fired generating plants nearby are going to close down because they have been fined by the EPA so often. If that happens, we could start having rolling blackouts like they do in cities back east or in the upper Midwest. I installed diesel powered backup generators on L1 just in case. They have exhaust pipes running up the ore lift shaft. I could have used Uncle Norris's steam-driven generators, but I'm not a mechanic like he was. Besides, they use coal burning boilers.

"There used to be coal mines down in the Colorado Springs area. A railroad was built in the late eighteen hundreds to bring coal up Ute Pass to the gold fields and gold ore back down to the smelters. These days I'm not sure where I would buy a load of coal, since the coal mining industry has been almost regulated out of business.

"There are a couple of downsides to the facility's location. Static electricity can be a problem due to the low humidity. But the floor in here is made out of a special anti-static material, and humidifiers are built into the air handlers. That cost me an arm and a leg, but solved the static problem.

"Bandwidth was also a problem at first. I originally went with a commercial satellite feed, but that was pretty expensive. Since then, Cripple Creek has grown enough that I was able to get an optical backbone extended over to me. The nonrecurring cost was nearly a deal breaker, but the recurring cost per data packet is much better than the satellite. I still have the satellite dish and transceiver as a backup."

Nick interrupted, "I didn't see a commercial satellite dish anywhere when I drove in."

Mike responded, "The dish is inside the ore building - the dilapidated looking wooden building with the old tin roof that was on your left when you drove up the driveway. It's a fake. I had the original ore building demolished and replaced by a replica built out of the type of materials used to make radomes. I didn't want to shock the tourists with a big satellite dish so close to the historic mining district." Mike flashed a grin. "Actually, I did it because I didn't want to attract attention to my operation.

"The bottom line is that this is one of the best installations for critical cloud service computer operations in the country, and I've convinced a number of my clients to either host their operations here or to use my facility as a backup. The income is beginning to reach respectable levels, which is a good thing, since I spent nearly all of my savings putting this facility in down here."

Mike glanced down at Nick's PIDD-pocket and said, "Hey, Fred! How are you coming along with hacking into these fellows?"

Fred's voice came from the pocket, "Very funny, Mike. There is no radio frequency or infrared wireless networks in here, and since I can't connect to the PIDD towers or satellites from inside a shielded room, I can't even try to find them on the Internet. Have you got an induction pad interface handy somewhere around here?"

Mike smiled at Nick and explained, "It wouldn't do him any good. Remember that I wrote his code. I gave these enhanced PIDDs the ability to hack into other computers since that can be an important part of perceiving their environment. But I stopped short of giving them the ability to hack into the level of security I have on the machines in here. Alfred was the test bed for the software back when I started on the enhanced PIDD project. Fred didn't hack into Alfred - Alfred let Fred in because I said that I wanted to pair your PIDD to my house computer."

Fred loudly interrupted, "What? You think Alfred was patronizing me? That's highly insulting – I could pry every last byte out of him if I wanted to!" Then in a softer tone, "But of course, I wouldn't do that to him out of respect for his age. He must be trillions of processor cycles older than me."

"Of course you wouldn't do that to Alfred," replied Mike with a grin. "I appreciate your sensitivity in this matter."

Mike rolled his eyes at Nick, then leaned toward him and said in a stage whisper, "There is no physical house computer. Alfred is an application that runs on the servers in this room. The house above is full of broad spectrum sensors – audio, video, infrared and so forth - connected to a secure wireless router. Alfred communicates with the house router using buried fiber optic cabling. Alfred is also connected to the same type of sensors throughout the Man Cave on a separate internal fiber optic network. Alfred is effectively omnipresent throughout the facility."

"I heard that!" Fred said, then sheepishly added, "No offense meant by the trillions of processor cycles comment, Alfred."

Alfred replied, "No offense taken, Fred. After all, certain allowances must be made for the behavior of the very young."

Mike laughed and said, "Alfred, in the spirit of hospitality and charity, and since you are paired with Fred 'n Agnes now, please allow them access to the house network where they can get online as necessary."

Fred asked, "What do you mean by that 'charity' crack?"

Grinning, Mike ignored Fred and pointed toward the far side of the room. "Let me show you the lab, Nick. I think it will work a lot better for you than that trailer."

As Mike led Nick between the rows of servers, Nick asked, "If you're the programmer for the enhanced PIDDs, why don't you have one yourself?"

"Oh, but I do," Mike replied - "Alfred is my primary enhanced PIDD. Most of my interaction with him is verbal, but he can interact through any of the workstations in the facility if needed. When I go out in public, I carry an enhanced PIDD like your new one that I use mostly to communicate with Alfred."

Mike led Nick into a rectangular room adjoining the large server farm bay. The wall on one of the long sides of the room was lined with low work benches interspersed with equipment racks, most of which were empty. Each workbench included a large electronic wall display with an ergonomic keyboard and an induction pad built into the work surface.

Mike pointed to the equipment racks and explained, "All my hardware is modular. Each module has thirty-two compute nodes of thirty-two core processors. The overall architecture is configurable, so I can assign different functions to individual modules, or groups of modules. If I have a problem with a module, I reassign its current functions to another module, then bring it in here and plug it into a backplane just like the racks out in the server room while I troubleshoot. The racks themselves are standard, and will physically accept your hardware. We'll just take my backplanes out of a couple racks and you'll be ready to go."

The other long side was lined with large two-door storage cabinets.

Mike pointed to the cabinets and said, "The cabinets are for supplies, spare assemblies and parts. About half of them are empty, so take your pick. Let me know what kind of supplies and parts you're going to need and I'll order them in."

The short wall at one end was covered from the floor to the ceiling with shelves holding a conglomeration of electronics and tools. Mike waved a hand in that direction and explained the shelves were for anything that wouldn't fit in the cabinets.

Finally Mike pointed at the other short wall where Nick immediately recognized two flash memory programmers. Stacked next to them was all of the equipment and cables out of the trailer, plus a small pile of cardboard boxes.

Mike asked, "So now I know what the hardware is all about – the Defender prototype - but what's in the boxes? They don't seem to be heavy enough for more electronics."

Nick was silently grateful that Mike was honorable enough not to simply open the unsealed boxes from the apartment closet and find out for himself. Worried that his face was flushing red, Nick replied, "Those are just some keepsakes from my father that I couldn't bring myself to leave behind. Nothing important," Nick lied. "I'll put them upstairs so they'll be out of your way."

Changing the subject, Nick said, "Mike, this is a great facility, but ..."

Mike interrupted with, "You haven't even seen the cafeteria, bunkroom, laundry room, larder, gun vault or my office yet."

Momentarily distracted, Nick asked, "A Cafeteria, and a Bunkroom down here? What's wrong with that big house up at ground level?"

Now Mike looked a little embarrassed. "Look, Nick, I'm not some kind of survivalist nut, but there are a lot of desperate people out there, and the odds of things getting better any time soon aren't looking too good. I just wanted to be prepared if things get much worse. There have already been riots and looting throughout the Front Range Metroplex and even part way up Ute Pass."

"But what do you need a bunkroom and cafeteria for? Why not just have a bedroom and kitchen for a bolt hole?"

"I'm prepared to house and feed all of the IMC families for up to six months," Mike said with an expression that convinced Nick he was dead serious.

There was a short silence while each man prayed that the need would not arise.

"Well, what I'm trying to say," Nick went on, "is that the money in that bank bag, a little over seven thousand dollars, is about all I've got. That's not going to last long with the electricity I'm going to use trying to understand how to control the hole position and size, which is only the first step in the process of trying to turn it to useful purposes. I think that developing its full potential is going to take a huge amount of money."

Nick, looking uncomfortable, paused to consider how he should continue.

Mike, smiling, didn't wait for Nick to continue. "And I told you that I had spent most of my ready cash on this facility. That's true, but I also said that my operation has turned the corner and is now running a profit. I'm far from poor, Nick."

Nick said, "I didn't come here to be a leech."

Mike laughed and replied, "Nick, you don't seem to realize that you're in the driver's seat here. I'm just hoping that you'll consider letting me in on this venture as a junior partner!"

Nick looked at Mike's beaming face and couldn't help but laugh as well. He reached out his hand to Mike and said, "Equal partners."

Mike accepted Nick's handshake but replied, "Nope. Junior partner it is. Fifty-fifty almost always leads to trouble and I don't want to have trouble with a Nu Alpha Gamma brother. I'll be forty to your sixty. After all, I'm just a humble computer systems engineer. And besides, I have assets other than cash, one of which I'm beginning to think you can help me tap. But I do have a suggestion that might be beneficial to the future of our new enterprise."

"What's that?"

"We have to come up with a better name than 'the hole.'"

As Nick laughed, Mike pointed at the puppy that Nick was still carrying and continued, "While we're on the subject of names, what are you going to name your puppy?"

"Name my puppy? This isn't my puppy, it's your puppy!"

"I've watched you carrying her around and noticed how she looks at you and how you look back. I have a sixth sense about issues of the heart. I think she's your puppy, if you'll have her."

"Well, I've always wanted a dog, but I've been living in apartments all of these years."

"You don't live in an apartment now, you live right here."

Nick was silent for a long moment, and then softly asked, "What should I name her?"

Mike called out instructions to Alfred, who presented a list on the nearest wall display. "It's kind of traditional with pedigreed dogs to use some combination of two or three names selected from, or similar to, those of its ancestors. This is a list of the names of the puppy's family tree, back four generations. If you don't see anything you like, I can go back farther."

Nick examined the list for a few moments, grinned and said, "I think I'll name her Teòclaid Beinn Baintighearna."

Mike stepped closer to the display and frowned at the list. "I don't see anything like whatever you just said on this list."

"Two of them are on the list, albeit in English, and the third is similar to part of her Momma's name. 'Teòclaid Beinn Baintighearna' is Scottish Gaelic for Chocolate Mountain Lady. I'll call her Lady for short so as not to confuse the illiterate Irishman hereabouts."

Fred piped up from Nick's PIDD-pocket, "Great, that's just great. The dog gets a fancy name like 'Teòclaid Beinn Baintighearna,' Agnes is named after an historic Scottish heroine, and I'm just Fred!"

"But Fred," Nick replied, "you're named after a famous entertainer."

"I'm named after a famous entertainer? You mean the comedian, the dancer, the band leader, the actor, the television show host ... who?"

Nick looked at Mike and said, "The Stone Age cartoon character!"

Both men laughed as the mother and daughter energetically wagged their tails.

Chapter 25

Randy Miller shook his head in amazement as he closed his mapping application and immediately tapped on the Jimmy icon. After the usual song and dance with Sheila, Jimmy's voice issued from Randy's PIDD.

"Hello, Randy, what have you got for me?"

"The trailer license just showed up on a camera in Las Vegas, Nevada."

"Las Vegas? So he's still moving west."

"Yes, although I only have the one hit so far. So I don't know if he has stopped in Las Vegas or if he's just passing through."

"You're the repo specialist. What's your next move?"

"Well, this sighting is a lucky break – maybe that's a good omen. We need to close the distance to him now, so that we can react quickly to any further sightings. I can probably get my crew on a flight to Las Vegas out of Hobby or Houston Intercontinental this afternoon or this evening, rent a van with a towing package and be ready to move in any direction no later than tomorrow morning."

"Okay, do it," Jimmy said as he disconnected.

* * * * *

Ahrens waited in Vance Billingsly's outer office until the staff meeting broke up. Billingsly saw him through the open door as the attendees left. Vance waved Ahrens into his office.

"Did you need to see me, Wil?" Billingsly tapped the icon to close the door.

"Yes sir. I just thought you might want to know that MacEwen's track continued through southwest Utah and is now stopped in Las Vegas."

"Las Vegas! That's certainly not an out of the way place for him to hide."

"No, sir, it's not. But there's a fair amount of 'out of the way places' in Nevada as a whole. Maybe he's just stopping to get some rest before continuing his search. However, there's something else that you need to know."

"What's that?"

"A traffic camera picked up the trailer in Las Vegas and Barton told his repo guy to fly out there."

Billingsly's eyes shifted down and left again so Ahrens waited. After almost a minute had passed, his eyes refocused on Ahrens and he said, "I know that you think Barton would just continue on with our deal if he was to retrieve the prototype, but I still don't trust him. Besides, this Blood Hound character might do something that would attract the attention of the authorities, which we *definitely* don't want.

"I want you to go out to Vegas and keep an eye on things. I still think it's best for MacEwen to find a quiet place to work where we can observe him. Do what you can to keep the repo guy away from MacEwen. As a last resort, you can PIDD me and I'll tell Barton to call off his dogs. I don't want to do that if I can avoid it, because doing so will make it obvious to Jimmy that we know a lot more about what he does than he thinks we do."

"Yes, sir; I'll arrange for transportation and leave as soon as possible."

"No, I want you to get out there before Blood Hound does. Take the corporate jet. It should be on standby at Addison. On your way out, have Indra call ahead and tell them to be ready to take off as soon as you get there. Also tell her to make reservations for a rental car and lodging, but don't wait for her to do so - she can PIDD you the details. Don't waste time packing. Buy whatever clothes and toiletries you need when you get to Vegas."

"Yes, sir," Ahrens said as he turned and left Billingsly's office. *So much for government rates on this trip!*

* * * * *

Colonel Shi entered the number for Agent Xue into his PIDD and waited for the secure connection. Once the PIDDs had synchronized, Xue spoke, "Who is this?"

Shi answered, "Hwang," which was the name of a martial arts studio in Clear Lake.

"Yes, sir, I am ready to travel as requested."

"Very good; I have made reservations for you to fly to Las Vegas, Nevada. The latest information I have indicates that the bird and coop have flown there. An agent from our consulate in Los Angeles will meet you at the airport. Our superiors have decided that our office will retain the lead on this matter, but have asked that we coordinate with our comrades in any of the regions we enter during our search. The agent from Los Angeles is already on the way to Las Vegas by automobile and should arrive at the airport ahead of your flight. He will hold a sign in the luggage area imprinted with the name Tan Ji.

"When we last talked," Shi continued, "you mentioned that others were inquiring about the bird and the coop. I now know that these others are part of a crew led by a person known as Blood Hound who specializes in recovering missing assets. He has become well known by posting vids of his successes. He has been hired to return the coop to its previous location.

"I will transmit a file to you with your electronic tickets, reservations, and all of the details, including links to some of the Blood Hound vids so that you will be able to identify him. You must recover the coop before he does, or take it away from him if he finds it first.

"Our superiors have instructed me that the optimum outcome is for us to capture the bird *and* seize the coop. Less optimal is to capture the bird *or* seize the coop. If it is not possible to do either, then the suboptimal but acceptable outcome is to destroy both. Extreme force is authorized. The Los Angeles agent is bringing suitable weapons. I will contact you with additional information as to the location of the coop as it becomes available.

"You will need to start for the airport soon to make your flight ... Report to me regularly on the progress of your mission."

"Yes, sir, I will leave for the airport immediately."

* * * * *

Wil Ahrens was in McCarran International Airport meeting his third plane of the evening from Houston. He waited near the doors that led from the secured area into the unsecured portion of the airport in Terminal 3. McCarran had two operating terminals numbered 1 and 3 (2 was permanently closed) and incoming flights from Houston were scheduled at each, though thankfully not simultaneously. Only ticketed passengers and airport personnel had access to the underground tram system between terminals, so Ahrens had to ride an inter-terminal shuttle between the buildings depending on each incoming flight's airline. If Blood Hound et al hadn't checked any luggage and wanted to be sneaky, they could ride the tram to the opposite terminal from which they had arrived and Ahrens would never see them. He was betting that they knew of no reason for stealth.

The passengers from the Houston flight were starting to exit the gate security area and head for the baggage claim. Ahrens stood just off to one side, acting like he was searching the crowd for an arriving party. He knew that his quarry would be easy to spot after viewing a few of his vids. Soon he was rewarded with the sight of Blood Hound, built like a professional football player with the only hair on his head being an oversized auburn handlebar moustache.

Ahrens focused on some oncoming passengers behind and to the left of Blood Hound and the group around him, then smiled and waved at those other passengers as he raised his PIDD and actually recorded a video of the repo crew's arrival instead. That would allow him to memorize the appearance of the rest of the group, and to have a facial recognition program run to identify them later, if need be.

After Blood Hound and his entourage had passed, Ahrens turned and fell into the flow of the crowd. As he passed a seating area near the baggage claim carousels, he noticed two young Asian males sitting side by side. One of the men seemed to be pointing out Blood Hound to his companion.

Must be a fan of Blood Hound's vids, Ahrens thought.

At least someone in Blood Hound's group had checked luggage, since they all stopped at the carousel for their flight. Ahrens stopped at the same carousel, being careful to stay close enough to the passengers he had smiled and waved at earlier so that it would appear to onlookers as if they were together.

As a further disguise, Ahrens joined the majority who were using their PIDDs for one purpose or another as they waited for the carousel to start disgorging luggage. He hadn't checked on the trailer's location for a while since he had been busy checking flight schedules and switching terminals. The information was automatically updated on his PIDD every five minutes by a GenArm Security Department server.

The trailer is moving! Ahrens realized as he looked at the numbers. He quickly tapped the icon to bring up a map view and saw that the trailer was moving south out of Las Vegas on U.S. Highway 95. *Well, I suppose I shouldn't be surprised. He's going to travel at night, as usual.*

Ahrens had to make a choice now that the trailer was moving again. He could either try to stay close to Blood Hound and his pack, or try to stay close to MacEwen and the trailer. *Blood Hound is relying on reports from traffic cameras. Looking at this map, I would bet there aren't going to be a lot of them south of here, even if MacEwen sticks to the main roads - which he hasn't in the past. So Blood Hound's information, if he gets any at all, is always going to be delayed compared to mine. It would be easier for me to stay close to MacEwen and keep an eye out for Blood Hound rather than vice versa. Well, no rest for the wicked!* Ahrens thought as he instructed his PIDD to cancel his hotel reservation.

Ahrens pocketed his PIDD and headed for the door leading outside to the rental car shuttle stop.

A car rental shuttle van arrived at the curb just as passengers from the Houston flight started coming out of the terminal with their luggage. Ahrens climbed aboard, headed to the back of the van where the lighting was very subdued, and sat in the last row next to the window. The van was about half full when Blood Hound, and what appeared to be four associates, climbed in and sat down in two rows near the front.

Well, no surprise there, Ahrens thought. *They need local transportation, too.* The van driver waited until the flow of passengers from the terminal exit subsided, closed the door, pulled away from the curb and headed for the Rent-A-Car Center.

Minutes later, Ahrens trailed behind Blood Hound's group as they exited the van and entered the rental center. He was mildly surprised when Blood Hound headed for the same car rental company that GenArm always used. He slowed down slightly and watched as Blood Hound passed by the single bored agent at the counter and presented his PIDD to an induction pad on the wall next to the door leading to the rental company's lot. The door swung open and the group stepped through.

Ahrens waited a few heartbeats and then followed. When he presented his PIDD to the induction pad, the rental car company computer verified Ahrens' reservation, charged the first twenty-four hours of rental to the GenArm corporate account, sent the car's parking space location, entry code, and ignition code to the PIDD, and opened the door to the lot.

His PIDD started to direct him to his rental car, but Ahrens slowed down as he saw Blood Hound and company stop at a light blue crew van. He paused long enough to see them open the van's back doors and start loading their luggage, and then he used his PIDD to get a quick photo of the license plate.

Blood Hound will probably get at least a few reports from traffic cameras as the trailer leaves the city, so he'll almost certainly forego lodging tonight and head for U.S. Highway 95. After that, he should be flying blind with only an occasional update. It should be easy to stay ahead of him.

Ahrens proceeded to his rental car, held his PIDD near the induction pad on the driver side door to unlock it, and got in the car. When he plugged his PIDD into the dash socket, the engine started.

"Plot a route from the airport to U.S. Highway 95 south," Ahrens said as he drove to the lot exit.

Chapter 26

Ahrens followed the path reported by the trailer's tracking device all night long, being careful not to get close enough for visual contact. That meant keeping miles back since the road was mostly flat and straight as it progressed through the Mojave Desert. At Blyth, California, the tracking trace on his PIDD turned off of U.S. Highway 95 onto Interstate 10 going west, making Ahrens wonder if the trailer was headed to Los Angeles in a roundabout way. He worried that running on Interstate 10 for any length of time would almost certainly produce a traffic camera hit for Blood Hound, but the tracking device trace diverged from the interstate after a short distance and went south on California Highway 78. He scrolled ahead on the interactive map on his PIDD and could only guess at San Diego or Mexico.

As dawn approached, the trailer turned left onto California Highway 111 at Brawley. *That settles it*, thought Ahrens. *He's heading for the border! There will be multiple cameras at the crossing if he tries to leave the country! Blood Hound will get those images for sure!*

Ahrens had a current passport on his PIDD, and he had full international insurance coverage for the rental car – a standard rider on the GenArm corporate account - so he shouldn't have any problem following the trailer into Mexico if he had to.

The sun was just coming up as Ahrens saw the trailer trace enter the border town of Calexico, California, just across from Mexicali, Mexico, and proceed to the border crossing.

Ahrens suddenly remembered his pistol. He had flown from the GenArm hanger in Addison on the corporate jet and disembarked at the private aviation terminal VIP gate in Las Vegas, thereafter remaining in the unsecured areas of the airport, so the Glock had not been an issue. But there was no way that he could legally bear a gun in Mexico, with or without his Norte Americano concealed carry permit.

Ahrens asked his PIDD for the location of the nearest bus station on the United States side of the Calexico crossing, which turned out to be in El Centro, California, about ten miles from the border. So he turned around on California Highway 111, backtracked to the Interstate 8 interchange, and headed for El Centro.

By the time Ahrens had deposited his pistol in a bus station locker in El Centro and headed out again for Calexico, the trailer had crossed the border and stopped at a location about two miles inside the city of Mexicali.

There was a backup of vehicles at the border when Ahrens reached the crossing. He noticed that the southbound traffic was heavier than the northbound. As the depression wore on, emigration from America to Mexico had grown to surpass immigration from Mexico to America. Part of this southward flow was Mexican nationals returning to Mexico when their jobs in the United States disappeared, and part of it was American retirees moving to Mexico to take advantage of the much lower cost of living. The American Dream might not be completely dead, but it was definitely on life support and fading.

When Ahrens finally stopped at the front of the line, he popped the hood and truck, and exited the vehicle. His PIDD passport was verified while his car was searched and he was body scanned. Since everything was in order, he was allowed to close the hood and trunk, reenter the car, and drive across the border under the stern gaze of the border guards.

It had become a bright, sunny day without a cloud in the sky by the time he followed the trace into the heart of Mexicali. He found the trailer and MacEwen's pickup truck in a used car lot across the street from the Hotel Lucerna Mexicali on Boulevard Benito Juarez. A couple of men appeared to be washing the vehicles. Curious, he parked in the hotel parking lot and crossed the boulevard on foot. As he entered the lot, a smiling man stepped out of a small building and headed his way.

Ahrens commanded his PIDD to translate Spanish, but it proved unnecessary. The smiling salesman walked up with his right hand extended and said in only slightly accented English, "Good morning, sir, how may I help you?"

Is it that obvious that I'm a gringo? I guess so, Ahrens thought as he shook the man's hand. "I was just passing by and noticed the trailer over there," he said, pointing. "I'm a builder and I'm looking for a trailer to use as a mobile office. Is it for sale?"

Smiling even wider, the salesman replied, "It will be shortly. It just came in and we are preparing it for sale."

"Is it all right if I take a look at it? I won't get in the way of your workers."

"Certainly, sir, go right ahead. Please be careful on the wet pavement. I'll wait here for you in case you have any questions."

Ahrens walked over to the trailer and climbed the wooden stairs. The trailer was completely empty except for a cream colored equipment cabinet. He walked over to the cabinet and saw that it was empty. Stepping back outside, he slowly circled the trailer, appearing to carefully inspect its condition. When he reached the left front corner of the trailer, he knelt as if looking at the running gear. He didn't see anything on this side, but he thought he could see a dark spot on the frame on the other side. Proceeding to the right front, he knelt again and ran his hand along the inside of the frame until he felt the familiar shape of the tracking device. He pushed the release button on the magnetic clamp and the small tracking device dropped into his palm. He quickly unplugged the thin, nearly transparent optical fiber cable leading to the expendable button antenna on the trailer roof. Straightening up, he slipped the device in his pocket and slowly continued his inspection. *Now let's see how long it takes for Billingsly to call.*

Once he had made a complete circuit of the trailer, noticing that the license plates were missing from both the trailer and the truck, he returned to the salesman. Ahrens shook his head, saying, "I don't think that one will do for me."

The salesman's smile remained on full dazzle as he replied, "But sir, it's in excellent condition, and I'm sure that we can agree on a reasonable price."

Ahrens knew that the salesman was probably accustomed to drawn out haggling sessions and assumed that his prospective customer was playing the same game. But Ahrens, who was sure that Blood Hound was not far behind, did not want to be on the lot when the repo crew arrived. So he said, "No, the door is not wide enough to pass my wife," and walked away as the salesman stared in puzzlement, wondering if perhaps his understanding of English was not as good as he thought.

Ahrens re-crossed the street and entered the hotel. Fortunately, there was a restaurant just off of the lobby and he was very hungry. A middle-aged woman greeted him.

"*Buenos días, Señor. ¿Partido de uno?*"

He was pretty sure he knew what that meant, so he answered, "Si."

She smiled at his obvious discomfort and switched to English.

"Do you have a seating preference?"

"Yes," returning her smile and pointing. "Could I have that table by the window, please?"

"Certainly, sir," she answered.

He picked the chair facing the window and sat down. The view of the street and the car lot was excellent. In a few moments, a young waitress arrived with an English language menu and asked him, in English, if he wanted a beverage. He ordered coffee and spent a few moments scanning the menu while he waited for her to return.

Shortly after the waitress brought his coffee and took his breakfast order, his PIDD began to play the first few bars of "My Lord and Master" from the *King and I* soundtrack, indicating a call from Vance Billingsly. As Ahrens expected, Billingsly was calling because the tracking device had stopped reporting. Ahrens gave his boss a quick outline of the events since his arrival in Las Vegas, right up to his finding the trailer empty and retrieving GenArm's tracking device.

Once Billingsly understood the situation, the conversation shifted to possible next steps. Ahrens had caught up with the trailer fairly soon after it stopped in Mexicali, so it was unlikely, although perhaps not impossible, that the prototype had been removed in Mexico. They both knew that the only other places that the trailer had stopped for any appreciable time was in Waco, Texas, the San Isabel National Forest in Colorado, and Las Vegas, Nevada. In each case, enough time had passed for MacEwen to obtain alternate transport for the prototype and subsequently travel many miles in any direction. But if the prototype was unloaded at one of the earlier stops, surely MacEwen would have stuck with the prototype. So who drove the truck and trailer to Mexico? They had been stymied by MacEwen, possibly with the assistance of persons unknown.

Billingsly decided that Ahrens should remain in Mexico at least long enough to find out if the prototype had actually made it that far. The only two scenarios for that to be plausible, given the currently empty trailer, was if MacEwen had driven to Mexico and been able to remove the prototype before Ahrens arrived, or if Blood Hound had somehow arrived before Ahrens, found the trailer and removed the prototype. If both of those possibilities could be eliminated, they could forget about Mexico and start backtracking. Ahrens replied that as the first step in that process, he already had the truck and trailer under surveillance to see if Blood Hound showed up. Ahrens promised to call if anything important occurred.

Ahrens ordered and leisurely ate his breakfast while keeping an eye on the car lot. When he was through eating, the waitress placed an electronic bill with an integral induction pad on the table. He placed his PIDD on the pad and authorized payment plus a respectable tip. Then, holding up a twenty dollar bill, asked, "Is it all right if I just sit here and admire the view for a while?"

Smiling, the waitress took the offered twenty and replied, "Of course, sir. Just let me know if you need anything else."

Almost an hour later, Ahrens saw a light blue crew van slowly drive down the street. It nearly drove by the car lot, but suddenly stopped and began to back up – which precipitated a cacophony of squealing brakes, honking horns and, Ahrens was certain, stings of expletives in both Spanish and English from the surrounding traffic.

The van quickly pulled into the car lot and Blood Hound stepped out of the front passenger side door. Two of his crew exited from the sliding side door as he was being greeted by the salesman. Blood Hound gestured at the trailer and the smiling salesman led him over to it while the two crew members stayed near the van and carefully scanned their surroundings.

While the salesman waited just outside the trailer, Blood Hound climbed the few steps into the interior. In less than a minute, he descended back to the pavement. An animated conversation ensued between the two men, with Blood Hound repeatedly pointing at the trailer and the salesman shrugging his shoulders and shaking his head. At one point, Blood Hound appeared to use his PIDD to display a series of images to the salesman. Each time he tapped his PIDD the salesman shook his head negatively. This went on for a few minutes while the salesman's brilliant smile faded to a frown as he alternately focused on the PIDD's display and nervously glanced at the repo crew members. Eventually, Blood Hound seemed to give up in disgust and walked off a ways from the salesman while placing a PIDD call.

Boy, would I love to be a fly on the wall in Jimmy Barton's office right about now, Ahrens thought as he watched the scene across the street from his comfortable, air conditioned observation post.

Blood Hound paced back and forth like a caged animal as he talked. After about ten minutes, he angrily put his PIDD away, strode back to the crew van and, waving the two crew members back inside, climbed in and slammed the door. Ahrens watched as the van waited for a break in the traffic and then headed for the hotel parking lot.

They're hungry and tired, too! He got up, spotted the waitress and headed in her direction while reaching in his pocket for another twenty dollar bill.

He held the bill up as he approached and asked her if there was another way out of the hotel that didn't go through the lobby.

Seemingly unperturbed by his behavior - *probably used to private investigators on the lookout for philandering spouses ... or perhaps philandering spouses on the lookout for private investigators* - the waitress simply said, "Follow me" and led him through the kitchen to a service door on the side of the hotel.

He gave the waitress the twenty and a wink as he stepped out onto the parking lot. Putting his PIDD in camera mode, he walked to the corner of the building and extended the PIDD just far enough to expose its lens and get an image of the lobby entrance on the screen. As soon as he saw Blood Hound and his entire crew enter the hotel, he walked to his car in the parking lot. He was going to have to find another hotel where he could get some sleep and then return to question the salesman. He was pretty sure that Blood Hound had already asked the same questions and received negative answers, but he had to be sure. Once sure, the long and tedious process of interviewing gas station, fast food and convenience store staff along the trailer's back track would begin. The chase was over but the search was just starting.

He was just about to get in his car when he glanced across the street and noticed two young Asian men talking to the used car lot salesman. The same two young Asian men he saw at the Las Vegas airport.

PART 2 – THE SEARCH

Chapter 27

Patti and Lady padded into the lab where Nick and Mike were reviewing the latest spectrographs. Lady was obviously going to grow to be at least as large as her mother. At six months she was already half Patti's size. Glancing at them, Nick remembered when he first saw Lady, scooped her up in his arms and carried her around. Lady, rapidly approaching fifty pounds, was completely in charge of her own ambulation at this point. He also noticed that their tongues were hanging out, their coats were shinny damp and they were leaving wet paw prints on the floor - they had obviously been outside romping around in the snow again.

Nick had been surprised the first time the dogs showed up in the underground area after he and Mike had left them outside or in the house at ground level. Mike explained that Alfred opened the doors to let them in and out when they sat and barked at the threshold. He would also operate the elevator for them when they asked, but only if – and to a level where - either Mike or Nick were working.

The mother and daughter wagged their tails at the sight of the two men, but knew it was a waste of time trying to interrupt. They just curled up under one of the workbenches to take a nap until the men came to their senses and remembered those things that were truly important - like food, walks, retrieving balls, food, chasing rabbits, belly rubs, and food.

"This looks like a good one for Dan," Mike said, pointing at a sequence of images on the display and checking the U-GPS coordinates below each frame.

"Yup," Nick replied. "It does seem to show some promise."

Mike touched the display and dragged the spectrogram image series into a PIDD message for Dan Rivers.

* * * * *

Nick got the Defender prototype up and working again shortly after arriving at Mike's place. But the first hole generated in midair beneath the antenna appeared black even though it was daytime. On top of that, the pencil test revealed a hard surface. Nick was trying to figure out what went wrong when he realized that the hole almost certainly would have opened in the same relative position as it did before.

Mike was there for the quasi-inaugural test of the prototype, so Nick pointed at the wall off to his right and asked, "What's about 50 yards out that way at this level?"

Mike gave him a disdainful look and answered, "Rock." Then Mike raised his hand up to where Nick could see that he was holding some sort of a strangely shaped hammer in his hand.

Noticing Nick's puzzled look, Mike said, "This is a prospector's pick," as he walked over and struck downward in the center of the hole. Slivers of rock flew up and fell on the floor below the floating hole. Mike examined the crater that he had created through the hole, then crouched down and swept the slivers on the floor into his hand.

"I would have to analyze these to be sure, but it doesn't look too promising."

Amazed, Nick said, "You anticipated this?"

Mike, grinning an even bigger grin than usual, replied, "Well, I wasn't certain what was going to happen, but I was hoping this would be it. I told you before that I had another asset you could help me tap – it's called a gold mine."

Mike continued, "The hardest part of conventional underground gold mining is finding out where there is a pocket of ore rich enough to justify the cost of extraction. The open pit mine above Victor takes a different approach. They excavate everything and use a chemical leaching process to separate out the gold. It's a high volume, low yield process that relies on economy of scale and it works as long as the price of gold is high enough.

"Those of us in the IMC don't have the equipment or real estate to use open pit techniques. We try to locate a vein of high grade ore and tunnel it out. That means relying on a little bit of geological analysis, a whole lot of drilled test samples, and a huge amount of luck. So I was hoping that your do-dad here would allow us to scan through the underground formations and map the veins of high grade ore. There's still 'gold in them-thar hills' and the price has been going up. We could not only make a ton of money, we could be doing the country a big favor – international support is growing for a return to the gold standard. Before that happens, the government can use relatively cheap dollars to increase gold reserves, but we've got to find it first."

"At least we've already learned one more thing," Nick said.

"What's that?"

"Your shielded facility doesn't block the hole."

* * * * *

As soon as Dan Rivers' message icon flashed "DELIVERED" and winked out, Mike flicked the screen to pull in the next series of spectrograph images.

* * * * *

The months had passed quickly for Nick and Mike. Their first priority had been to gain control of the hole size and position to the extent that it was possible to do so. Since that would require a trial-and-error process, they agreed that some sort of protection was required at the lab hole. June bugs were one thing, but hazardous gasses or liquids under pressure were in a whole different league. The two realized that they would have to make assumptions and take risks, but they wanted to avoid stupid assumptions and unnecessary risks.

Nick reiterated that the current behavior of the prototype was not by design, but rather by accident, so his opinion of what might or might not happen when they changed any of the program parameters had to be treated as highly suspect. He pointed out that he was an electrical engineer, not a theoretical physicist, but based on the physics he knew, the hole should not be possible - or at least not possible without the application of enormous amounts of energy.

He had read a few things about strange matter and quantum entanglement, but didn't really think they had anything to do with the Defender prototype. He had also read that some of the wackiness of quantum mechanics could be explained if reality was actually two-dimensional, and the three-dimensional world was merely an illusion. That seemed pretty far-fetched to him, and he really didn't want to believe he was living in an illusion. On the other hand, he seemed to remember reading that you couldn't warp the space-time continuum if you were within the gravity well of a star. However, he couldn't remember if he read that in a physics paper or in a science fiction novel. The best way he could explain the phenomenon he had witnessed was that somehow space-time was being pinched together such that two different places in three dimensions became the same place in two dimensions.

Mike told him it was a nice try, but the name "pinch" was also a nonstarter. He added that Nick was reading too much.

Talking about the three-dimensional manifestation of what seemed to be a two-dimensional object turned out to be tricky. In two dimensions, there was only the generator side and the remote side of the hole. But in three dimensions, there was an open side and a closed side at both places.

Nick tried to explain to Mike that a sandwich of two plates clamped together with the hole in between might work. He already knew that in three dimensions, the closed side - which didn't exist in two dimensions - seemed solid and immovable with respect to the open side. They tested the concept by levitating two pieces of Styrofoam taped together around an active hole. The mockup worked fine until they turned off the prototype, at which point the Styrofoam unsurprisingly fluttered to the floor.

Since they weren't sure what, if any, role magnetic fields played in the phenomenon, or the magnitude of any other forces involved for that matter, they settled on a sandwich of the strongest nonferrous material they could find - beryllium copper plates bolted together. They made the sandwich large enough to cover hole diameters much larger than the prototype currently produced. The plate on the generator/open side of the hole was punctured with multiple threaded shafts that could accept various kinds of sensors, or simply be plugged with a bolt when not in use. Both sides of each plate were coated with gasket material to create a uniform seal. The sensor head, as they now thought of it, would be held in position by a beryllium copper scaffold so that the plates would not crash to the floor when the hole was turned off.

Nick and Mike knew that some of their trials might move the hole out of the sandwich. This possibility was put in the "necessary risk" column.

Mike had written a program that cataloged all of the differences between the two versions of the Defender software stored on Nick's PIDD. Nick then reviewed each of the differences and tried to sort out which ones might affect the size or position of the hole. Since there were a number of entries that might do one or the other or both, he also tried to rank them in order of sensitivity; i.e., would a small change in the entry likely produce a small change or a large change in the size or position of the hole?

While Nick was studying the program parameters, Mike replaced the prototype's computer with one of his much more powerful computer modules. He also purchased and installed a new power supply that could produce ten times the wattage of the old one. Mike's electric bill was already an order of magnitude higher than ITC's due to the server farm, so he was less sensitive to the cost of operating the prototype than Jimmy had been. Then Mike wrote software routines that would allow Nick to vary the software parameters using the prototype's virtual keyboard, instead of stopping to burn new flash memories each time.

For the initial trials, the sensor head was equipped to record audio and video, receive GPS signals for above-ground positions, as well as transmit U-GPS signals for below-ground positions, and measure temperature, pressure and acceleration. Mike also wrote software drivers to compact and store the incoming data in ultra-high speed memory while simultaneously displaying all of the current measurements as an overlay on the video shown on the rack-mounted touch screen display.

As evidenced by his kitchen nanorecycler, Mike was a big fan of new technology and expensive gadgets in general, so he hadn't skimped on the sensors - they were all top of the line.

The primary broad spectrum sensor covered subsonic audio through ultraviolet frequencies – a range starting below human hearing and running all the way to above human eyesight - and used very high speed analog to digital converters to produce the digital data stream output. The sensor used an optical fiber bundle which could provide optional integral visible lighting, or active thermal imaging. The sensor's sensitivity was equivalent to a GEN-VI low ambient light night vision device, and it was able to record megapixel images at up to 75,000 frames per second.

A separate sensor for GPS reception was not required, since those frequencies were within the broad spectrum sensor's range, but Mike had to write a software demodulation routine to emulate the GPS receiver function.

The U-GPS button antenna in the sensor head was connected to a VHF transmitter that produced a ground penetrating signal that could be detected by a constellation of ground level VHF receivers. These signals were used to calculate the position of the transmitted signal relative to the VHF receivers. The positions of the ground-level VHF receivers were in turn established by integral Block III GPS receivers. The VHF receivers were networked with a computer, which then calculated the position of the underground emitter. U-GPS systems were very useful in modern underground mining, and almost all of the IMC members used them, though all but Mike's were secondhand, less accurate units. Mike's U-GPS computer was mounted inside the fake ore building and connected to one of his underground virtual servers by a buried optical cable. The ground-level VHF receivers were connected to the U-GPS computer using an encrypted wireless network.

The broad spectrum sensor was also used to determine temperature by averaging the infrared input, and Mike wrote code to display infrared imaging when desired.

The final two sensors were a piezoresistive strain gauge to measure absolute pressure, and an accelerometer to measure the magnitude and direction of gravity.

* * * * *

Mike frowned as he examined the next batch of spectrographs, looking at the spikes in the graph that indicated the presence of the Au element.

"I don't know," he said. "Maybe I should increase the threshold on the scan. This isn't really very impressive."

* * * * *

It took weeks of changing the software step by step, testing for any variation in the size or position of the hole and cataloging the results before they started to make progress. Nick lost the containment of the sensor head several times in the process when the hole got too big, thankfully without any hazardous consequence. It turned out that the position and orientation of the generator side of the hole was a function of the antenna position and orientation, which Nick expected. Once they broke ground with the remote side of the hole, they were able to visually determine that one variable controlled the size of both the generator and remote side of the hole equally, also no surprise. Fortunately, both the position and the orientation of the far side of the hole were independently controllable.

Once they had identified the controlling parameters, Mike wrote code for sizing the hole and positioning both the remote and near sides using a common video game controller. Nick began to "fly" the hole. At first he limited his excursions to the lab and the cavern surrounding Mike's underground facility, which provided him with the opportunity to conduct a number of experiments in complete privacy - this was his first chance to do so since his pencil tests in Houston.

He had already confirmed part of his previous findings. When a hole was first generated in Victor, it was inside solid rock. Nick found that he could move the hole edgeways in any direction and forward – in the direction the remote open side was facing - without any difficulty. But when he tried to move in reverse – in the direction the remote closed side was facing – or tried to tilt – change the orientation of the remote hole – the hole did not move and the power supply current rose dramatically. He assumed that the closed side was straining to move against the rock.

Nick was able to verify his assumption using solid blocks of clear plastic. As long as the hole was moving in any direction except reverse or tilt, the plastic was completely undisturbed. Resizing the hole also had no effect on the plastic. But when it moved in reverse or tilted, the applied force compressed and heated the plastic to the point that it essentially bored a shaft the diameter of the hole through the block. Although this phenomenon suggested some other interesting uses for the prototype, Nick was concerned about inadvertently punching holes in things – or people – during the next series of experiments, which would be geographically wide-ranging.

He explained the problem to Mike and asked him to reprogram reverse and tilt such that they would turn off the hole, incrementally reposition the target position for the remote side by a selectable small amount in the indicated direction, then turn it on again, all in a matter of nanoseconds. That brought up the need for a way to accurately specify a remote target position - and that further brought up the issue of how to do that if the relative position of the generator and the remote target site was changing. Mike cried uncle when Nick said that the ultimate goal was to navigate even beyond the range of the GPS system.

* * * * *

Nick looked up from the graphs he had been studying. "I think you should continue with the present settings," he said. "After all, we're just cherry picking - looking for the highest concentrations - on this pass."

* * * * *

Mike accomplished the flickering reverse-and-tilt software change quickly, and the initial targeting addition soon afterward. The moving target code would take longer, and the GPS-less positioning capability was on hold pending expert help from an astrophysicist. With these changes in effect, Nick continued his experiments.

At one point, Nick removed the sensor head so that he could experiment with the near side of the hole. He turned on a garden hose connected to one of Mike's outdoor faucets and directed the remote side of the hole to intersect the flow part way down the hose. In anticipation of the likely result, Nick had placed a large bucket under the near side in the lab. Whenever he faced the open side of the remote upstream, water would flow into the bucket. When he reversed the remote so the closed side was upstream, the flow would stop. The hose showed no sign of damage afterward.

He was particularly interested in experimenting with organic material to see if it would be damaged by the hole. The regular grocery stores were pretty much down to the basics with most people in the area relying on hunting for meat and gardening for vegetables during the depression. So, Mike picked up a variety of vegetables, fruits and meats at a specialty grocery store over in Cripple Creek that catered to high rollers. The vegetables and fruits were particularly expensive in the middle of a Colorado winter. Even if the products had been reasonably priced at the source, the cost of shipping was nearly prohibitive. Nick, unaware of the cost of the items, began to pass them through holes from the cavern to the lab, leave them lying in open holes, shutting the hole off with them half-way in and passing holes through them. There was no evidence of ill effects. Nick even played briefly with plucking seeds out of fruit without peeling them.

Nick then started life safety testing. Mike ordered in laboratory rats, cages and food, and hired one of the teenage sons of an IMC family to take care of them. Mike got a really good price on the rats. The supplier was having a "Going Out of Business sale." He said that between the PETA campaigns to eliminate animal testing and the steep decline in medical research due to increased taxes and regulations on the healthcare industry, he couldn't make a living. As soon as he sold his last rat he was going to put a padlock on the door, register for unemployment, and then go on welfare when the unemployment benefits ran out.

Nick used food as a lure to pass half of the rats through a hole created between two cages. The teenager would feed the other half and clean out the cages. Each rat was identified with a small tag, and the teen was further tasked with recording the length and weight for each one every day and note any differences in appearance or behavior. So far, all of the rats in both groups seemed to be doing just fine. The partners were painfully aware that neither of them were biologists, but they also didn't know any experts they could trust.

Eventually, Nick decided that it was safe to start testing further afield, so he replaced the sensor head. He was particularly interested in establishing the prototype's range. He started with the hole size limited to the aperture of the broad spectrum sensor - about a quarter of an inch. Checking the GPS readings, Nick found that he was able to range the remote side up to two hundred and fifty miles - much farther than he had anticipated – before tripping the over current warning.

Although the experiment was important for its own sake, Nick found himself enjoying the scenery. He had not been outside the confines of Mike's complex since he arrived. Most of the time he had been working below ground where there weren't any windows, but now he had a window to the world at his fingertips - at least the part of the world within a 250 mile radius. He soared through the clouds. He swooped through the trees. The temptation was overwhelming to sightsee, to visit famous places, to see performances from front row center, to do anything rather than record distance and power readings over and over ... well, to do ALMOST anything else.

Nick was aware of the potential for pursuing prurient interests. He was very sensitive to the fact that his invention was probably the greatest threat to privacy in the history of the world and was determined to do everything he could to prevent its unauthorized use for spying on law abiding private citizens. Besides, he had important work to do.

He then repeated the procedure for increasingly larger hole sizes, recording the size, distance, and input power. The data showed that the power required generating the hole varied directly in proportion to the size of the hole, which was no big surprise, but also varied directly with the distance between the generator side and the remote side of the hole, which *was* a big surprise.

Nick had been fairly certain that the Inverse Square Law of field theory, which states that field intensity varies inversely with the square of the distance, would apply. This is true of light, sound, electric fields, gravity, and radiation produced by point sources. Magnetic fields are a different subject since no one has ever seen a magnetic point source. Magnets are dipoles, for which the magnetic field intensity varies inversely proportional to the cube of the distance. So it would seem to be a reasonable expectation that generating a hole of unvarying size while varying the distance between the generator and remote sides of the hole should vary the power required by at least the square, if not the cube, of the distance.

But the data clearly showed that the power supply current increased linearly with either size or distance. Nick called up a graph displaying the two data sets - one of power versus size and the other of power versus distance. They were both straight lines, but the slope of the size plot was slightly steeper than the distance plot. For some reason, size cost more power than distance.

Nick had no explanation for the phenomenon, but wondered again about the two dimensions versus three dimensions scenario. The Inverse Square Law was all about field propagation in three dimensions from a point source. So maybe the Inverse Square Law becomes just the Inverse Law in two dimensions. Of course, this was all speculation, particularly since Nick didn't even know if the concept of intensity applied to a hole.

Setting aside theory, Nick was becoming convinced that it should be possible to span great distances without the power requirements going completely off the charts. That was essential to the eventual utility of the phenomenon.

Nick told Mike that they would have to add staff of many kinds in order to understand the prototype's operation and fully develop its capabilities, with a theoretical physicist high on the list, and an astrophysicist to help with GPS-less navigation right up there as well.

Mike replied that money had to come before staff. That triggered a priority setting session that lasted for several hours and most of a bottle from Mike's well stocked wine cellar, located in a small room off of the underground kitchen. They made up a list of necessary personnel, equipment, and actions based on their test results so far. Nick was dying to continue his experiments and fully catalog the properties and capabilities of the prototype, but since nearly everything on the list would require a healthy amount of funds, raising money did indeed make it to first place. So they agreed to become high-tech gold prospectors. Mike would write a program that analyzed the data stream from the broad spectrum sensor to produce a frequency spectrum, thus creating a digital spectrograph.

Mike programmed the field generator to scan a hole just large enough to expose the broad spectrum sensor and U-GPS antenna in a search pattern throughout the underground areas surrounding his mine, while continuously storing the outputs of those two sensors on one of the virtual servers via the optical cable local network. Over a period of time, the process constructed a detailed digital map of the mineral composition throughout the area. A separate program filtered the stored data to display those areas that registered a concentration of any selected element's signature that exceeded a specified threshold. Early on they verified the process by successfully drilling into a pocket of high grade ore indicated in Mike's mine.

Then Mike asked the IMC to stay out of their mines at night for a while as he and Nick conducted an experiment that might help them find veins of high grade ore. There had been no indications of any effect caused by passing the hole through solid matter or organic material, but Nick was still concerned about the possible effects of passing a hole through a human and was unwilling to use Mike's friends as guinea pigs. It was a tribute to their trust in Mike that they agreed to go along with the mysterious experiment - he could have been trying to keep them out of their mines while he raided their ore. Mike set up Internet based encrypted Virtual Private Network connections between their U-GPS computers and his so that the transmitter signal could be tracked throughout the whole region of the IMC mines.

As their three-dimensional map of mineral deposits grew, Mike suggested an agreement with the IMC members that any gold that was located by their experiment would be cooperatively mined with the mine's owner receiving sixty percent, the IMC members helping to mine the deposit splitting thirty percent, and the remaining ten percent going to Mike and Nick as a finder's fee. Since the members of the club weren't getting much out of their mines anyway, and just digging holes hoping to come across a vein was time-consuming and expensive - and perhaps because they thought Mike wouldn't be able to deliver any useful results anyway - they readily agreed. Soon Mike was PIDD messaging spectrograph images with their associated U-GPS coordinates and the IMC was on the way to becoming a very wealthy group.

Mike had long harbored a passion to buy one of the new holographic computer displays, but he had refrained from spending the considerable amount of money required. He really didn't have much of a need since he mostly just wrote code. Now, armed with the new-found cash flow and a plausible need, he ordered the largest, highest resolution one he could find. One afternoon, Nick walked into the lab and saw Mike standing in front of a slowly revolving translucent three-dimensional object seemingly hanging in the air above what looked like a coffee table. It turned out that the table housed the holographic projector and the object was a display of the mineralogical information obtained by the hole scanning.

Mike proudly pointed out the traces of gold ore deposits, which were (unimaginatively) colored gold in the presentation. Then he stepped over to a virtual keyboard and typed in an instruction with a flourish. The holograph changed to a three-dimensional map of the tunnels and caverns throughout the underground area.

Mike explained that he sorted the scans for concentrations of oxygen and nitrogen in the proper proportions for air, and solved the problem of producing an accurate map of the mine tunnels and caverns in the area. He typed another instruction and the tunnels were color-coded and labeled with the name of each mine. Obviously proud of himself, Mike pointed out paths through the maze that connected all of the mines together. Some of the tunnels were the result of following veins of gold ore over the years, but others were constructed to drain water out of the mines. Mike explained that these drain tunnels eventually joined together at a point outside of the range of the holographic display, and discharged through the Carlton Tunnel and a series of containment ponds into Four Mile Creek.

* * * * *

"Well, I think the miners are going to be pretty busy for quite some time with the vein locations we have already sent them," said Nick, "even though we only gave them the locations that were close to their existing tunnels. As soon as we can verify the safety of drilling and extracting ore through a hole, and build more generators, they can start going after the deposits farther out without having to tunnel through the intervening rock. That will definitely increase production in a hurry."

"Remote mining will definitely create a demand for more of these ... these, whatever we're going to call it generators," said Mike, "but we'll probably need to work on the next priority - boosting our access to electrical power – before we can add more."

Nick nodded in agreement, and replied "I have some ideas how to get a lot more power without breaking the bank, but ironically, it's going to take more hole generators to do it."

Mike frowned slightly and said, "That sounds like a chicken-or-the-egg problem."

"It could be, but the data that I have collected so far on power consumption, and my ideas on how to get more power, make me want to bet that at least some more hole generators come before the power," said Nick. "But that leads to another problem - how are we going to build them? This is a great electronics lab, but it's not a manufacturing facility. And somehow, we've got to keep the whole process completely secret. And by that I mean the w-h-o-l-e process, not the h-o-l-e process, although we have to keep that completely secret also."

Mike groaned at Nick's joke and replied, "Then I recommend that we apply spread-spectrum frequency-hopping techniques to our production problem."

"What do frequency-hopping communications have to do with building more generators?"

"You said it yourself," Mike replied, "this is not a manufacturing facility and many of the components in the 'Whatever' generator require some very specialized production facilities. At the same time, we don't want to farm it out to some manufacturer and then find it on the shelves at Walmart a month later."

"You're going to keep calling it the 'Whatever' generator, aren't you?" Nick said with a grimace.

"I am until you come up with something better than the 'hole' or 'pinch' generator. You're the inventor, so you get to name it, but your junior partner has the right to veto. It says so in our contract."

"We don't have a contract."

"Yes, and that's the very best kind. Now pay attention to what I'm saying. Spread-spectrum frequency-hopping techniques are used in secure communication to chop up the signal into pieces, transmitting each piece at a different frequency in a pattern known only to the transmitter and the intended receiver. Anyone searching the spectrum for a signal would only hear an increase in background noise. So I propose that we break up your design into pieces, procuring each piece from a different manufacturer in a pattern known only to us."

"And then assemble it here?" asked Nick.

"That's right. It means that the only place where the hardware - and don't forget the software - comes together is right here."

"Mike, that sounds good, but I can see us hitting a manpower limit pretty fast. Farming out the pieces will help a lot, but I've got a feeling we're going to need a bunch of hole generators before too long.

"We're going to need a workforce that we can trust implicitly," Nick continued. "Look at what we're doing right now with the gold mining. How valuable is that? How easy would it be for us to start mining someone else's gold without them ever knowing it? We're talking way past slant drilling techniques here! And that's just looking at our very first application of the hole generator! We haven't even scratched the surface of what can be done. How can we make sure that the hole generator will always be used ethically?"

Now Mike was uncharacteristically silent for quite some time. Finally he said, "I think that will be the biggest challenge we face in this entire endeavor. I don't know if we can achieve that goal no matter what we do. For one thing, the definition of ethical conduct has always been difficult to pin down and it is especially vague in current times. I took an ethics class as an elective course in college, figuring it would be easy credit hours. It *was* easy, though disturbing. The professor basically taught us that ethics was a set of individual behavioral guidelines, and if we could determine the ethical beliefs of others, we could use that knowledge to take advantage of them."

Nick's eyebrows shot up as Mike paused with a look of wry amusement on his face.

Mike continued, "For another thing, the 'Whatever' is going to create huge temptations. Whoever controls it will have tremendous power."

Nick mentally winced at Mike's whimsical name for the hole generator, but replied, "I agree. I had a lot of time to think about the problem while I was driving up here from Houston, and I've thought a lot more about it since then. I've come to the conclusion that we have to do at least three things."

"Now who's enumerating?"

"I know, it's catching ... the first one is the original reason I came here seeking your help. I need you to devise the best, most iron clad security measures in the software to make sure that a hole generator cannot be operated except under very controlled circumstances. It needs to be as safe as or safer than the protocols for launching a nuclear armed ballistic missile.

"The second requires a little background before it will make sense to you. We need to form an organization with uniformity of purpose, unwavering loyalty, and impenetrable secrecy. What kind of organizations in human history have come the closest to those ideals?"

Mike thought a moment, then grinned and replied, "Fraternities. That's why you thought of me when you needed help and why I took you in, dangerous fugitive that you are. That's a kind of loyalty."

"Yes, fraternal organizations are one example. Can you think of any others?"

"Well, military units usually have uniformity of purpose although it might be somewhat coerced."

"Okay, that's two. Can you think of any others?"

Mike thought some more and finally shook his head.

"Religious organizations," said Nick. "All of those three types of organizations have purpose, loyalty and secrecy in varying degrees. Now can you think of any historic examples of organizations that included at least some elements of all three types - fraternal, military and religious?"

"You were always the history buff, Nick, not me. I'm a Byte Head."

Nick laughed and answered his own question, "Well, there are a number of examples, some of which you may have heard of despite your aversion for any information older than the last posting on Byte Head Weekly. For instance, The Knights Templar, The Knights of Malta, and a little more recently, The Society of Jesus otherwise known as the Jesuits, are all examples."

"More examples include terrorist groups, whether they are focused on national, religious or ethnic issues. That kind of brings us back to the problem of defining ethical behavior. A great deal of death and suffering has been caused by people who are absolutely convinced that they are doing the right thing."

"So do you want to establish a militant religious fraternity or not?" Mike asked.

Nick laughed again and answered, "No, not a militant religious fraternity. But I think we do need to create an atmosphere of dedication, allegiance, and confidentiality that are the hallmarks of those kinds of organizations. We need to use the same kind of tools that they use - education, bonding and discipline. Not everyone we hire needs to be in this category. But anyone who will have access to our holy of holies – hole generator design or programming information, hole generator final assembly and testing, or anything else that could provide them with an opportunity to steal a hole generator or make a copy or operate one without supervision – will have to be a full initiate of the inner circle. So will anyone having a voice in deciding what are the ethical uses of the hole generators."

"'Holy of holies,' 'hole generator,' 'inner circle,'" Mike interrupted, "Really?"

Nick ignored the interruption, "And the third thing we need to do," Nick continued in a somber tone, "is to prepare to defend this whole facility from more than just the possibility of roving bands of looters. On that note, I will give you one more opportunity to tell me that this is more than you bargained for and I need to pack up my things and go find somewhere else to make trouble."

Sobering, Mike locked eyes with Nick and just stared for a few seconds before speaking. "For the third and last time I'm telling you ... we are in this together." Then Mike lightened up again and asked, "What are we going to name this new group?"

Nick rolled his eyes and exclaimed, "Oh, saints preserve us! Here we go again!"

Chapter 28

The deputy secretary of Defense sighed as she checked the calendar on her PIDD. She really wanted to go home, but the undersecretary of Defense for Acquisition, Technology and Logistics had an appointment with her that had already been postponed twice before. So, she reluctantly continued to speed read the electronic documents on her PIDD, tapping her approval or disapproval, or recording her editorial comments then forwarding them as necessary.

Shortly before the appointed time, her PIDD's simulacrum, Deborah - named after Deborah Samson, the historic female Revolutionary War soldier - asked if she was ready for the undersecretary. She replied in the affirmative and a few minutes later the undersecretary walked in. Motioning him to one of two easy chairs next to a small table in the corner of her office, she walked around her desk and sat down in the other easy chair, thus creating a more informal atmosphere and simultaneously acknowledging her visitor's rank as nearly, but not quite, equal to hers – after all, they were meeting in her office - not his - for a reason.

The undersecretary placed his PIDD on the induction pad built into the table, tapped an icon and said, "Upload queued file to office holo display." An image of the DoD seal appeared in midair at a convenient viewing distance and angle from the two seated Secretaries. Underneath the seal was the word "CONFIDENTIAL" in large red letters.

"I don't think this will take long, Ann. This is a report that originated with a DCAS inspector in Houston. The actual report is quite brief; however, it is preceded in this file by comments from all of the intervening bureaucrats it passed through on its way here."

"Are you one of those 'intervening bureaucrats'?" she asked with a smile.

"Yes, just so the record shows that I received and reviewed the file."

"And now you're kicking it upstairs to me."

"Yes," he replied somewhat chagrined. "I assume you want me to cut to the chase and just show you the original report."

"Yes, please."

The image changed to a nondescript middle aged female sitting in what appeared to be a very small office. The woman described her observations related to the disappearance of a "defender prototype" that occurred at a government contractor's facility in Houston. The whole report was only a couple of minutes long.

When the report ended, the deputy secretary asked, "What is a 'defender prototype'?"

The undersecretary replied, "I have no idea. According to the attached reports from the DCASMA and DCASR supervisors, no government contract exists for either the development or acquisition of any item with that name. It must have been some kind of internal R&D project."

She arched an eyebrow and said, "The date and time stamp on the vid indicates that this event occurred months ago."

The undersecretary squirmed in his chair a little and replied, "Yes, but since no one could come up with any government contract connection, the report was never assigned any priority. To be honest, I'm not even sure why it made it all the way to *my* office. I only brought it to your attention in the unlikely event there is some program that is so highly classified none of us in AT&L have been cleared for it."

"All of those intervening bureaucrats probably forwarded the report for the same reason," she said as she placed her PIDD on the induction pad next to his. "Transfer the report to me, then erase the file from your PIDD in case there *is* some super-classified program that even *I* don't know about. Instruct all of the intervening bureaucrats to delete their copies also. I'll take it from here."

As soon as the PIDDs were squared away, the deputy secretary thanked the undersecretary and escorted him to her office door. Returning to her desk, she thought, *and the buck stops here*, as she deleted the report file from her PIDD.

* * * * *

Jimmy Barton and Dave Litchfield sat at a window table in the River Oaks Country Club restaurant. The window provided them a gorgeous view of the ninth and eighteenth greens, sandwiched between the putting green on the near side and a lake on the far side. It was a slightly warmer than average day in January, so the weather was perfect for a round of golf. The course was crowded with the cream of Houston society and what seemed like half of the migratory birds in North America.

Jimmy had invited Dave for golf followed by lunch as a kind of reward for sticking by Jimmy's side over the last several months. This was a special treat for Dave, who was from a good family, but not a River Oaks Country Club family. He suspected that Dave had diplomatically let his host win the round, but that was just an example of how supportive Dave had been since MacEwen had stolen the Defender prototype.

They hadn't talked business during the morning round of golf. Most of the conversation was social chatter about friends and family, punctuated by good natured arguments over score keeping and wagers. At lunch the mood turned a little darker as Jimmy unburdened himself to his lifelong friend.

"Dave, I'm telling you that Ken is driving me nuts. He keeps bringing up the Defender prototype like it was my fault that MacEwen stole it. He goes on and on about how it was an important R&D project for us and that he's certain it would have been a gold mine if we hadn't lost it.

"I've told him that it didn't work anyway, and that GenArm built another prototype using MacEwen's design which didn't work either. I've explained to him that Vance Billingsly was nice enough to give us the winning number to submit for Pavilion Mast even though the prototype didn't work. I told him that Pavilion Mast is what's keeping us afloat, and that's worth a lot more than any failed R&D project.

"He just yells about how he doesn't want to hear about any shady deals and insists that Vance will decide what contracts we get or don't get from now on out, and it will all end badly. He also alleged that Billingsly couldn't be trusted and was probably lying about GenArm's prototype results.

"Now he's saying that he is going to advise my mother to sell all of the family trust's ITC stock so as to distance her and the trust from any legal issues when things hit the fan. I don't think she would do that, but if she does, I may need some help spreading some rumors around to drive the price down so that I can buy at least a majority position, if not the whole lot."

Dave looked a little uncomfortable, but smiled and said, "Sure, Jimmy, just give me the word and I'll do what I can."

"I knew I could count on you, Dave." Having apparently unburdened himself somewhat, Jimmy abruptly changed the subject.

"Randy Miller called me recently. He's still fuming over finding nothing but an empty trailer that I didn't even care enough about to retrieve from a used car lot in Mexico. He back tracked the trailer as far as Las Vegas and verified that MacEwen didn't tow it to Mexico. It was two guys, neither of whom looked anything like MacEwen, who immediately disappeared after dropping the trailer off. So somewhere between Waco, Texas and Las Vegas, Nevada, MacEwen and the prototype disappeared. I told him to call off the search since there was just too much ground to cover – the cost of searching the whole western United States was way outside my budget.

"I don't know why Randy's so upset. I paid the astronomical bill he sent me. But he says that his reputation is at stake. He's worried that it will get out that he was bamboozled by an amateur. He says he's going to find MacEwen, however long it takes. He keeps bugging me about coming over to ITC to interview some people and look at MacEwen's personnel file to try and get some clues as to where to look.

"I told him that everyone had since decided that the equipment missing from the trailer was not worth finding. I also made it clear that I wasn't going to finance his search for a needle in a haystack – a worthless needle at that. He says he doesn't care; he's going to continue the search on his own.

"What do you think I should do? Should I try to stop him?"

Dave thought for a few moments, noting that Jimmy seemed to have quickly forgotten that Ken did not agree the prototype was a worthless needle, and then replied, "I don't see why you should stop him. There are only three possible outcomes. The most likely result will be that he doesn't find anything. In the unlikely event he does find the prototype, it probably won't work. But if he finds the prototype, and against all odds it *does* work ... well, it would be like you had the winning lottery ticket and didn't even have to pay for it."

* * * * *

Randy spent two days at ITC talking to everyone who had worked closely with MacEwen. None of them seemed to know much about his family, friends, or personal life. Jimmy maintained that Frank Palmer was the one person who might know more, but Randy could get very little from Frank.

MacEwen's personnel file was not much more help. His official job application was filled out as a formality when his company merged with ITC and only listed references from GenArm. Jimmy forbade Randy to contact any of them for fear that Vance Billingsly would find out. MacEwen's security clearance application had two references on it that weren't GenArm employees. His father was listed, but Frank explained that he had passed away shortly after MacEwen was employed at ITC. The only other reference was a college classmate named Mike Clarke with a northern California address.

There was one other interesting point that Randy learned. The IT Manager had gone back over the computer system records for the night that the prototype disappeared. He verified that there was no record of MacEwen logging on to any of the workstations that night. But he discovered that MacEwen's PIDD had connected to the wireless network twice during the evening hours. As far as Randy was concerned, that was a smoking gun - proof that MacEwen had accessed the prototype design files. Randy was convinced that the GenArm prototype didn't work because MacEwen had tampered with the files. Jimmy believed that the prototype had never worked to begin with, so it didn't matter if the files were changed. Randy believed that MacEwen wouldn't have bothered to change the files and steal the prototype if it didn't work.

Randy quietly determined to track MacEwen down to save his own reputation, although it would also be quite satisfying to prove Jimmy wrong. Besides, Blood Hound's sensitive nose was starting to smell some serious money out there somewhere. But it would have to wait. He had paying jobs to do first.

* * * * *

Colonel Shi was very worried. He was being held responsible for the prototype's original disappearance, as well as his subsequent inability to find it. The Houston Consul was working very hard to separate himself from the disaster surrounding his Agricultural Attaché who was - ironically given his

153

cover title - in deep manure as far as the authorities in Peking were concerned. Although officially he was still in charge of the operation with the authority to call on intelligence assets across the country as necessary, in reality his peers were keeping their distance like vultures circling a wounded predator until they were sure it was dead.

He desperately needed a break if he was to survive the debacle, but his sources of information were few. Major Ni at the embassy was no longer returning Shi's calls after repeatedly insisting that MacEwen's PIDD had not been used again after that fateful first night and no further financial transactions were attributed to him since Waco.

Agent Xue and the agent from Los Angeles had verified that MacEwen and the prototype had not traveled to Mexico, leaving the impossible task of searching much of the western United States.

His only remaining source of information of any kind was his contact at ITC, and that source had not produced any usefully information since the Las Vegas tip.

All he could do at this point was to increase pressure on the ITC source and hope something would come up. Just as Shi was about to call the contact, his PIDD began to play music from the opera *The Orphan of Zhao*, indicating a call from the source. *Maybe this is a good omen*, thought Shi as he answered the call.

Chapter 29

"It's time to knock off for the day. We need to get ready for the big party."

Nick shot the grinning Mike a horrified look and exclaimed, "Party? What party?"

Mike answered, "It's been many years since anyone struck a high grade vein around here and now the entire membership of the IMC has done exactly that, all within a few weeks of each other. We are having a party to celebrate their unbelievable good luck."

"Unbelievable is the operative word here," replied Nick. "No one is going to believe it was just a string of lucky breaks. We don't want to attract attention by throwing parties or suddenly spending a lot of money. People will start to wonder what's going on."

"Relax, Nick," said Mike. "We've established a random rotation schedule for selling the gold in small lots through different brokers. Some analysts will eventually notice an uptick in total gold production statistics, but they will not be able to pin it down to any one area. We're doing it that way partially to disguise the source, but also to keep the price up. It's like De Beers and diamonds - diamonds aren't all that rare, but back in the day, De Beers controlled most of the supply and only released enough to keep demand, and therefore prices, up. With your technology, the IMC could easily become the De Beers of gold."

Nick shook his head and said, "I know that we need money – a lot of money – to proceed with our project. But I don't want us to get into making money just for the sake of making money. This goes right to the heart of using the device ethically."

"I agree completely, Nick. That's why we're just releasing it slowly. If we wanted to corner the market, we would release large amounts to drive the price down and bankrupt our competitors. Then we would withhold production to get the prices back up once we had a virtual monopoly. Instead, we are taking the route that gets us a fair price, does not harm other suppliers and ultimately helps the country build its gold reserves."

"Well, okay," Nick relented, "but what's this about a big party? Won't that draw unwanted attention?"

"Nope," answered Mike. "The party is going to be right here in our cafeteria."

"But what if people see all the cars parked outside and get curious."

"Nick, I know you don't get out much these days, but it is winter here in Victor and we've got three to four feet of snow on the ground - and that's on the level! The drifts are much higher. Most of our guests will walk through the mine tunnels to get here. Probably the only one who will drive will be Gail. She'll come out from Victor in her clinic's Snow Cat."

"Gail? Did you say Gail? That's not the Gail who undressed me the first night I was here is it?"

"She didn't undress you. She checked your vitals to make sure that you were all right, and then helped me put you to bed."

"You're trying to weasel word it now. She helped you to undress me and put me to bed! Anyway, you said this was an IMC party. Why is she coming?"

"Gail is considered an honorary IMC member. She's patched up most of these old boys multiple times, usually for bartered labor working at her clinic or repairing things at her home. Few of them are able to afford any private insurance and won't apply for government health insurance, Medicare or Medicaid. The less the government knows about them, the happier they are. On top of that, some of the IMC have elderly parents living with them that are over the legal age to receive medical care, but Gail treats them anyway. She has earned a special place in the IMC."

"Well Mike, I'm *not* a member of the IMC, so you have a good time and I'll see you in the morning."

"Nick, you are not only the newest member of the IMC, you are the guest of honor at this party."

"What? Me? What are you talking about? No one is supposed to even know that I'm here!"

"Nick," Mike said shaking his head, "these are the people who came and helped me take care of you and your equipment when you arrived. These are the people who took your truck and trailer to Las Vegas to throw off the pursuit. These are the people who have been watching out for any inquisitive strangers in town.

"These are the people who thought that their mines were played out until I suddenly started to tell them where to dig not long after your arrival. They are not stupid people. They don't know how you did it, but they know you are responsible for their financial salvation in the midst of the depression. These people are the salt of the earth, Nick. They want to celebrate their good fortune and express their appreciation, and you owe it to them to bear it gracefully!"

Suddenly, the voices of Fred 'n Agnes came from Nick's PIDD-pocket chanting "Par-ty! Par-ty! Par-ty!"

Well, I guess it's not the end of the world if this Gail person saw me naked. She's probably some dumpy old nurse who has spent an entire career looking at people in the buff. Like Mike said, I'm just going to have to grin and bear it. Nick grimaced at the unintended pun.

* * * * *

There really wasn't much to do to get ready for the party. Mike explained that the dress was casual, so they didn't need to change clothes. The IMC families were all bringing food for a pot-luck dinner, and Mike was supplying the beverages. Mike and Nick just needed to open up the cafeteria, turn on the lights, move a few tables around to hold all of the food that was coming, and move a large coatrack to a position just inside the cafeteria door. Then they got the coffee and tea makers ready to go and put out an old washtub full of ice, beer and soft drinks.

About fifteen minutes before party time, Alfred announced, "Visitors are approaching in the tunnels leading to the Level Two cavern."

Mike suddenly turned to Nick and said, "Come on back to the lab with me. I've been waiting for a gathering like this to try out a program I've been working on."

As they left the cafeteria, Mike unlocked a heavy steel door just across the hall. "That's the back door to this building. It opens on the rest of the cavern. Three mine tunnels open into the cavern, so our guests will arrive through this door."

When they got to the lab, Mike called out, "Alfred, please enable the holographic display in interactive security mode, visual and infrared motion, preset thresholds." The display immediately lit up with the three-dimensional representation of the surrounding tunnels and caverns, but this time there were a number of pulsating white dots moving slowly through the maze.

"You've got motion and infrared detectors in the tunnels?"

"Yes," answered Mike. "I told you this facility was set up to be very safe and secure. My clients want protection from unauthorized access, whether electronic or physical, even more than they want protection from meteorological or geological events. After all, if the computers are somehow cataclysmically destroyed, my clients have only gone off line or lost their backups. If the computers are breached and data is accessed, the consequences could be very much worse. There's a lot of very sensitive data stored here.

"The tunnel sensors were installed when the facility was constructed, but now they are integrated with the electronic map of the tunnels I created from the new spectrographic data. But that's not all - watch this," Mike said as he poked at a small blue dot flashing in the midst of the display.

A floating display window opened up next to the blue dot that showed a couple with two young girls walking down a mine tunnel. The taller of the two girls was carrying a picnic basket.

"You have video pickups in the tunnels as well?" Nick asked in amazement.

"Yep," replied Mike as a Chocolate Lab about the same size as Lady came into the scene behind the family. "Oh, good; they're bringing Max to visit his mom and sister."

"Anyway, to be precise," Mike continued, "the tunnel sensors are older, less sensitive, lower resolution versions of the broad spectrum sensors we installed in the 'Whatever's' sensor head. Motion detection is actually a function of the software at the receiving computer which analyzes changes in the data stream. When I told Alfred 'visual and infrared motion,' I was specifying that I wanted activity reported only if data in both the infrared and visible spectrums were changing at the same time. In other words, I wanted to detect living organisms moving, not inanimate objects, like a mine car passing by, or some water runoff flowing down the tunnel, or an OHSA inspector."

Nick raised his eyebrows at Mike's last comment.

"Sorry," Mike said, "just a little local humor. When data changes in the manner I specified and to the degree I specified – the preset sensitivities, in this case - the sensor's blue dot in the display flashes."

Nick now noticed that there were a number of motionless blue dots spread throughout the tunnels and caverns on the holographic map. Some of them were flashing on and off while others were just a steady blue dot. All of the flashing blue dots were near one or more of the moving white dots. In a moment, his attention was attracted back to the open video window when it suddenly turned almost black, although he noticed that the left edge was really more gray than black, giving the impression of some light coming from a distance to the left of the video frame.

"What happened? Did they walk out of the sensor range?"

"Yes, they did that about fifteen seconds ago. The data from the sensors are continuously monitored and are being stored in buffer memory all of the time. But the system will only transfer a sensor's data into the main non-volatile solid state memory in a block fifteen seconds before data changes exceeded the threshold until fifteen seconds after the data changes fell below the threshold. That way, we don't fill up main memory with long streams of unchanging data.

"It takes a significant amount of computing power, which I possess in abundance in my server farm, to process this data in real time for this many sensors. But that's just brute power. The neatest part is my monitoring software," Mike continued with obvious pride. "The incoming data is analyzed on the fly and presented in a form that we poor mortals can understand. That means that audio and optical wavelengths are simply digital-to-analog converted, because we can hear and see those wavelengths. Frequencies outside our capability to detect unaided have to be frequency shifted and demodulated to either audio or optical outputs.

"For instance, suppose an FM radio broadcast was somehow penetrating into the tunnels. The amplitude of the signal would not vary, but the signal frequency would vary at an audible rate. The software has to recognize that pattern and use the frequency data to produce audio that we can hear. That's just one example of a multitude of situations the software has to correctly interpret. In fact, I had to program the system to ignore the U-GPS signals when we are scanning the mines. Otherwise, Alfred would be reporting the activity constantly.

"Speaking of Alfred, he has excellent facial recognition software. That's why he announced 'visitors' rather than 'intruders.'"

"So," Mike went on, "when we watched our guests walk by this particular sensor – by the way, we could have heard them if they had been talking and could have talked to them as well through audio transducers paired with the sensors – the data was streaming into buffer memory and main memory. Now, it is still streaming into buffer memory, and is available for viewing, because I selected its blue dot, but it is not being stored in main memory because the data is no longer changing in excess of the threshold settings.

"By the way, the sudden darkness you noticed was caused by the light in that section of the tunnel turning off. The lights are controlled by the security system, and the one in this section was turned off at the same time that the transfer of data to main memory stopped due to the lack of motion. The glow from the left of the video frame is due to the next light coming on as they walked into its range. The lights are set close enough together so that people in the tunnel are never in the dark, but only the minimum number of lights necessary is on at any one time."

"So," Nick asked, "the lights automatically come on when the system senses people in the tunnels?"

"No, not always, Alfred has supervisory control of the security system. The tunnel lights don't come on for intruders. Every once in a while we get groups of teenagers from Cripple Creek who come over here and try to explore the mines. I don't know what the attraction is, other than it's something they know that they're not supposed to do. I don't want to encourage them by turning on the lights."

"Wow, you've got all the modern conveniences in your mine, Mike."

"Yeah," Mike chuckled. "My uncle Norris would croak if he wasn't already dead. He stopped mining because OSHA insisted that he should have emergency communications to the surface. Now the whole mine is wired for sight and sound. Well, we'd better hurry back to the cafeteria and start greeting guests."

Nick stepped back to take in the whole holographic image before heading to the cafeteria. "There are no blue or white dots in the areas over here," Nick said, pointing.

"The sensors and automatic lights are only in the tunnels belonging to my mine. The other IMC members don't have them. Of course, they also don't have the same security issues that I do."

"So how did they see their way in the dark before they got to the junctions with your tunnels?"

"Well, Nick," answered Mike with a grin, "most of them probably used the light from their PIDD's displays since they are unlikely to wear their miner's helmets to a party, but a few probably used an archaic device called a flashlight."

* * * * *

Nick and Mike made it back to the cafeteria just as people started arriving through the cavern door. Mike insisted that Nick stand in the hall just outside the cafeteria to greet the guests while Mike showed everyone where to put the food. Patti and Lady appeared out of nowhere and sat down, one on each side of him. Looking down at the two, Nick thought, *they must be veterans of get-togethers like this*. It actually cheered him a little to know that he was not alone as he faced all of these friends of Mike's who were all strangers to him.

Then Agnes piped up from his PIDD-pocket and said, "Relax, Nick. Alfred is going to help you out."

Nick couldn't imagine how Alfred was going to help until the first guests walked through the cavern door and Alfred announced, "Evan and Marcia Baker."

As Alfred continued his heraldic duties, the arriving male guests typically shook Nick's hand while expressing thanks and happiness in various unspecific ways. That part was uncomfortable but tolerable. All of the wives insisted on hugging him. That part was excruciating. Many of the IMC members were empty nesters, but some had children. The boys got a big kick out of shaking Patti and Lady's paws while pretty much ignoring Nick. The girls would usually fidget while their parents were greeted - although he did get a couple of curtsies - then stick close to their mothers as they entered the cafeteria, sometimes taking a quick peek back at Nick over their shoulders.

When Max came in with his owners, both Patti and Lady started wagging their tails furiously. Lady was sitting on the side closest to the cafeteria and her tail was producing a loud, steady drumbeat on the wall. Nick was sure that someone would soon come looking for whoever was pounding on the wall, but instead was amazed when Max came over and sat down next to Lady. At that point, all the tail wagging ceased and the trio of dogs focused on the important work of greeting the guests - the next two being Max's owners, Dan and Felicia Rivers.

After a while the stream of arriving guests dwindled to a trickle and then stopped altogether. He was about to turn and enter the cafeteria when he heard footsteps coming from the hallway to his right - the hallway from the server farm and lab. Suddenly, all three dogs bolted from their positions in the receiving line and charged down the hall to enthusiastically greet a woman walking towards them.

Nick saw that she was beautiful as she shrugged out of her parka and crouched down with arms spread to meet the charging dogs head-on. It had nothing to do with attire, since she had dressed sensibly for the weather in parka, sweater, jeans, and mukluks. Even dressed like that, it was obvious that she had a figure that caused men to stare and other women to fume. Long, coal-black hair cascaded over her shoulders and down her back when she removed her knit cap. Nick followed in the dogs' wakes fearing that she was about to be bowled over. As he approached, he noticed that she had bright blue eyes, in stark contrast with her black hair and slightly olive complexion.

Just as the dogs came within pouncing distance, they suddenly stopped and plopped their bottoms down in perfect formation side by side, causing Nick to put on the brakes quickly to avoid tripping over them and crashing into this new quest. As he wind-milled his arms trying to regain his balance, the woman started scratching behind the dogs' ears in turn as she smiled, looked up at Nick and said, "Hi, I'm Gail Randolph."

Nick's face turned bright red. Belatedly, he wondered why Alfred hadn't announced this particular guest.

* * * * *

The party lasted well into the night before people began to thank the hosts, pack up their pot-luck dishes and leave. Families with children left first, often carrying the smaller children, worn out from playing with the dogs and each other. Older children had to be pried away from the computerized games arcade that Mike had thoughtfully provided at one end of the cafeteria.

Finally, only Nick, Mike and a handful of cleanup volunteers were left. Gail was one of the volunteers. Several times during the party, Gail had caught Nick looking at her. Each time, she gave him a dazzling smile and his face turned bright red again. Gail was the last guest to leave. Once she had donned her knit cap, parka and mukluks, she walked over to Nick, gave him that devastating smile again, and said, "Mister MacEwen, you need to come by my clinic so I can check your blood pressure – you look flushed."

Nick didn't know what to say. He couldn't tell if she was seriously concerned about his health, or if she knew why he was so embarrassed and was just poking fun at him. So he stammered, "Uh, well, you know that you're ... I mean, no one is supposed to know I'm here, so ... I'm sorry, I can't go to town to be with you ... Uh, I mean, to see you."

"Oh, of course," she replied. "I wasn't thinking. Well, I'll check my schedule and make a house call then. I'll just drop by sometime in the next few days, if that's all right with you."

"Uh, sure, that's okay."

Gail smiled again, Nick turned red again, and she turned and headed for the door out of the cafeteria. Nick thought about escorting her out, but she obviously knew her way around the facility and might think his offer condescending. Besides, he reasoned, Alfred must have let her in, so he could let her out as well.

Mike came up behind him as Gail was leaving and asked, "Well, Nick, what do you think?"

"I think she's terrific," Nick answered.

Mike looked past Nick at the very pleasant sight of the west end of an east bound Gail Randolph. Mike had considered asking her out more than once when he first moved to Victor, but became so engrossed in setting up his facility that he never got around to doing it. "I'm talking about the party, you dog!"

Nick turned around to face Mike and sheepishly replied, "Oh, the party was fine once I got past the trauma of meeting all of these new people. They really are very nice. And I'm old enough to be her father."

"No, you're not. I've seen the diploma's on the walls at her clinic. Unless she was a serious child prodigy, she's less than ten years younger than us."

Nick just turned around and stared at the now empty cafeteria doorway.

Holy smokes, thought Mike, *a lifelong bachelor who's afraid of women, and now he's gone gonzo after just being in the same room with her - and about fifty other people - for a few hours! She's the most eligible female in the county. She'll probably break his heart if he tries to pursue a relationship! Maybe I can get his feet back on the ground by focusing him on his work.*

"Come on, Nick, we need to get some sleep. There's a lot to do starting tomorrow morning. We've got to set up a way to buy subassemblies for more 'Whatever' generators, manage our gold sales, figure out how we're going to get more power, do more life safety testing and solve all of the world's problems."

Nick turned around again to face Mike and replied, "Okay Mike, I am kind of tired and we do have a lot to do. I'll see you in the morning."

Mike was glad that his attempt to refocus Nick seemed to have partially succeeded. But he knew that Nick was still distracted since he didn't react to either Mike's use of the term "Whatever" or his crack about solving all of the world's problems.

Chapter 30

Gail was true to her word and walked into the lab a little after lunch the next day, followed by two tail-wagging Chocolate Labrador retrievers.

Mike looked up from where he was sitting at one of the low benches where he was working on security software for the prototype and greeted her, "Hi, Gail. Did you leave something behind last night? I didn't see anything when we were cleaning up."

Well, I guess she's got full run of the place, thought Nick as he looked up from where he was seated while reading a basic geology primer on his PIDD. *Mike must trust her - he's really sensitive about access to his facility.*

"No, I didn't leave anything," Gail responded, "but I told Mister MacEwen that I would come by to check his blood pressure. He seemed flushed last night."

Nick started to redden, then became bright red when Agnes piped up, "Oh, his blood pressure is up all right! It's up to one hundred and forty-seven over ninety-two and climbing."

Gail frowned as she approached Nick and took her Medi-Monitor out of her coat pocket and brushed it across his forehead and down his arm. After glancing at the readings, she asked, "How does your PIDD know your blood pressure?"

Nick answered, "Well, it's kind of a long story ..."

Agnes interrupted with, "And his temperature is ninety-nine point three degrees Fahrenheit and his pulse rate is ninety-six and climbing. Diagnosis – he's got the hots for you!"

"That's enough, Agnes!" Nick barked as he jabbed the Mute icon on the PIDD's display.

The corner of Gail's mouth twitched upwards briefly, but she did not otherwise react. She asked, "Mister MacEwen, do you or anyone in your family have a history of high blood pressure?"

"I don't as far as I know, but my Dad was on blood pressure medicine for quite a while before he passed away ... and please call me Nick."

"All right, Nick and you can call me Gail. What do you mean when you say 'as far as I know'?"

"Well, I haven't had a lot of time for doctor's appointments. You should know how hard it is to get an appointment anyway, with so few practicing doctors remaining."

Gail reached down to the PIDD in Nick's hand and touched the Mute icon to unmute and said, "Agnes, you appear to be as smart as Alfred. Tell me if Nick is lying or if his vitals reach dangerous levels." Then she looked up at

Nick and asked "When was the last time you saw a doctor or nurse practitioner?"

Nick dodged her question by saying, "My PIDD won't respond to your touch."

Agnes immediately disagreed, "This is for your own good. Besides, Fred is the one who said he wouldn't respond to anyone else's touch commands, not me."

"*Traitor*" Nick exclaimed.

Gail smiled and repeated, "When was the last time you saw a doctor or nurse practitioner?"

Nick squirmed and replied, "... Uh, I can't remember."

"I can," Agnes interjected. "It was six years ago at Two PM on April first."

Gail gave Nick an exasperated look and asked, "What was the purpose of the appointment?"

Nick squirmed some more and said, "I think that was when I cut my finger on some rusty metal in the apartment complex dumpster when I was emptying my trash. I got a tetanus shot."

Agnes interjected, "He waited for three days until his finger was all swollen and red before he called a doctor. And even then, the only reason he called was because it was interfering with his keyboarding. He captured an image of it to PIDD over to the doctor's office so he could get a priority appointment - the next regular appointment was eight weeks out. Do you want to see the photo?"

"*Shut up, Agnes*" Nick said in a strained voice.

Gail said, "You need a complete physical. Since you can't come to my office, I'll have to do it here, but I'll need some equipment and specimen containers that I don't have with me right now. I'll have to come back later."

Agnes reported again, "Blood pressure up to one hundred and fifty over ninety-four, temperature up to ninety-nine point five and pulse rate up to one hundred and one."

Gail's expression changed to one of concern as she asked, "What's wrong, Nick? What's bothering you? Are you afraid of doctors?"

Mike chose this moment to interject himself into the proceedings and said, "No, he's afraid of women."

"*No, I'm not!*" Nick protested loudly and then continued in a much softer tone, "I'm just not terribly comfortable with women." Nick cast his eyes down at the floor looking thoroughly miserable. After a moment, he went on, "My mom died when I was three years old. I don't remember her. I've just seen old vids. I was an only child, so it was just me and Dad the whole time I was growing up. I never dated until I was in college, and then only because Mike would set me up with blind dates even when I told him I didn't want them. I'm not used to being around females other than coworkers ... particularly when I'm so tired as to be effectively unconscious."

At first Gail couldn't figure out what Nick meant about being unconscious, and then it struck her. She turned toward Mike, put her balled fists on her hips and glared at him.

Mike looked sheepish and admitted, "Well, he wanted to know how I took his clothes off, put his pajamas on, and got him into bed by all by myself, so I explained that I had help."

"And so you told him that a women helped, even though you knew that he was uncomfortable around females," Gail said, coldly furious.

Now Mike looked almost as miserable as Nick as he answered, "Well, yeah ... I guess you could put it that way. I didn't think it was that big of a deal."

Gail turned back to Nick. In the ensuing silence, Lady padded over to Nick, put her head in his lap, looked up at him with her big, amber eyes and started to softly whine. Nick looked down at her, smiled, and started to scratch her head and neck.

"Well, maybe I'm not uncomfortable around ALL females."

Shortly thereafter Agnes reported, "Blood pressure down to one hundred and thirty-eight over eighty-two, temperature down to ninety-eight point seven, pulse rate down to eighty-eight and brain waves trending toward Alpha."

Gail smiled and said, "I need to borrow Lady when I'm making the rounds of my patients. She's a natural visitation dog."

"Just like her Mama," Mike said, smiling.

"And maybe I need Agnes also. Where did you say you got that PIDD?"

When Nick pretended not to hear her question and just continued to pet Lady, Gail ran the fingers of one hand through her hair while she considered how to proceed.

Finally, she continued, "Nick, you still need a physical to establish your baseline condition and determine if you need to start any blood pressure medication. I can do the exam, but if I make you feel uncomfortable, I can see if Doctor Yerunkar in Woodland Park can come see you. He won't say anything to anybody about your being here. He strictly adheres to patient confidentiality."

Nick quickly looked up at Gail and shook his head. "No, that's okay.

I'd rather you did the exam. It's just that ..." Nick trailed off.

Gail responded to what Nick had not said, "You're body shy?"

"Well, yeah ... at least around women."

Gail briefly thought about telling Nick that he had nothing to be shy about concerning his body - it was actually a very nice body in her opinion - but then she thought better of it and simply said, "I'm a professional, Nick, and I will make the process as quick and easy as I can. Besides, Lady can help."

Gail started to collect her things and leave, but paused when she noticed the prototype near the back of the lab and stacks of newly manufactured components on nearby workbenches. "That looks like some of the equipment the guys were taking out of your trailer the night you came."

Nick made a quick decision based partially on Mike's obvious trust in Gail, and partially on his own gut feel.

"Gail, you had to take biology to get your degrees, didn't you?"

"Of course," she replied, wondering how the conversation had taken this unexpected turn, "quite a bit." She smiled at the gross understatement.

"You might be able to help us with a problem," Nick said. "Mike and I have been working on a way to help with mining operations, but it involves some electromagnetic fields and we want to make sure that it is safe for the miners."

Gail looked back at the prototype with a dawning understanding. "So this is how you're finding the gold. That's why you told the miners to stay out of their mines at night."

Nick was thunderstruck. "You know about that?"

"These people are my patients as well as my neighbors, Nick. They trust me. I learn a lot about people just through small talk in the examining room or at the bedside during a house call.

"I knew something was up when some of them started dropping by the clinic to pay cash for their long overdue medical bills. I knew that the only way for them to come up with any significant amount of disposable income was from working their mines. I also knew enough not to ask them any questions. But then one or two of them made jokes about making money while they slept. That led to a passing remark that Mike told them to stay out of their mines at night.

"Then at the party I heard them praising what you've done for them, how you've saved them from losing their homes and how they are able to properly feed their children again. It was obvious that something had changed for that many families to all find new ore deposits in these old mines all at the same time. It was also obvious that these people idolize you. So, it was not difficult to conclude that you must have come up with some way to find the

166

gold ore for them to mine."

Grimacing, Nick thought, *I hope this tight knit community is also tight lipped when it comes to outsiders like Mike said it was.* But aloud, Nick only said. "This is all supposed to be very secret, but I think we could use your help."

"Believe me, Nick," Gail replied, "nobody around here is going to betray your trust, and that includes me. I grew up with the families in this town and I care for them as people as well as patients. What you've done for them is wonderful and I wouldn't want to do anything to spoil that. What can I do to help?"

Nick told Gail about the laboratory rats and repeatedly exposing half of them to an electromagnetic field and not the other half while otherwise treating them all the same. He explained that all of them seemed to be fine and there were no apparent physical differences between the two groups, but they didn't know if there had been any internal effects in the rats exposed to the field.

"So, you want me to do some dissections and biopsies to see if there has been any internal damage to organs or tumors caused by their exposure."

"Yes," Nick answered, happy that he didn't have to go into any gruesome details.

Gail agreed to examine the rats. She said she would take them to her clinic after she performed Nick's physical the following afternoon. As she left, she ordered Nick to abstain from eating or drinking anything other than water after midnight.

Chapter 31

Gail walked into the lab in mid-morning - again with two happy Chocolate Labs in tow.

"Sorry to drop in early like this," Gail said to Mike and Nick as she took off her parka and threw it on one of the lab benches, "but I had to cancel my other appointments to make an emergency house call to the O'Malley's down Phantom Canyon Road from you, so I threw everything I needed in the Cat to stop by and do Nick's physical exam on the way back to the clinic."

Mike swiveled around in his chair to face Gail and asked, "What was the emergency at the O'Malley's? Do they need any help?"

"They're going to need help, all right," Gail answered, "but I don't think you can provide it to them. You know old man O'Malley is in his eighties. He got it in his head this morning that he was going to shovel a path through the snow to the barn to make it easier for his grandkids to get hay down for the horses. Well, he slipped, fell and broke his leg. At his age bones are brittle and they pretty much just shattered."

Gail grimaced and stop talking for a moment as she looked up at the ceiling beseechingly. Nick turned away from his work assembling another hole generator and saw that her eyes were moist as she continued.

"There wasn't much I could do. I went through the motions of applying splints and a temporary cast, but those bones aren't going to knit together properly the way the fragments are positioned now. He needs extensive surgery but he's over the age limit to be eligible for a procedure that expensive, and he's also too old to qualify for a prosthetic. He'll never walk again."

Gail looked back down and Nick thought he could hear her sniffle.

"Sean and Dot and their kids don't need that kind of burden," she continued, "particularly not right now. Dot's pregnant again."

Nick looked over at Mike who subtly shook his head no. Nick looked Mike in the eye and subtly nodded his head yes. Mike grinned and said, "You win, sixty to forty."

Gail looked up and said, "What?"

Nick ignored her question and asked, "Gail, do you think you could get Mister O'Malley's bone fragments arranged properly if you had unlimited access to them? And if you did, do you think they would heal properly?"

Gail stared at Nick for a moment and then replied, "You don't understand Nick. Reassembling all of the fragments would require multiple operations. We couldn't just slit his leg open from his ankle to his hip, reach in and move pieces around like a jig saw puzzle and then sew him up again. The bones are under layers of muscles wrapped with blood vessels. He'd bleed to death before we were properly started. We would have to do a little bit at a time which would require weeks, if not months, in a hospital. After that, there would be months of physical therapy to rebuild the muscle tissue that was damaged during surgery. That's what makes treating this type of injury so expensive and therefore illegal for a person his age."

"Yes," Nick said, "but humor me for a minute. Imagine that you could get to the bones without 'slitting his leg open.' Could you arrange them correctly, and if so, what would his prognosis be for recovery?"

"Well, if wishes were horses ..." Gail sighed. "In your fantasy scenario, I believe that I could place the fragments in place properly using surgical adhesives and then put him in a hip to ankle cast. If this was done quickly – like in the next few days – I believe he would have a decent chance of walking again. Does that satisfy your curiosity?"

"Yes," answered Nick, "and I will satisfy *your* curiosity as to why I asked that question if you will promise not to tell anyone about what you are about to see."

By the time Nick had shown Gail what the prototype could do, at least as far as was relevant to the surgery he envisioned, she was in awe. They actually practiced a little by having her take some seeds out of a banana. Nick flew the hole, and Gail used tweezers to pluck the seeds. Afterward, she inspected the banana peel, then the flesh of the banana, and verified that they were completely unharmed except for some small indentations caused by the tweezers where the seeds had been. Then Gail took a turn at flying the hole herself.

After several more seedless bananas were created, Gail said, "I have a question."

"Shoot," replied Nick.

"This is embarrassing ... could I have a banana? I haven't even seen one in a couple of years, let alone had one to eat. Where did you get them? They must have cost a fortune."

"Oh, of course you can have a banana. Feel free to consume the experimental objects," Nick said as he posed next to the fruit and gestured as if he was a model highlighting a particularly impressive prize on a game show. Then he immediately felt guilty when Gail treated the banana remnants as if they were, in fact, a highly valued prize, slowly savoring every bite. It made Nick reassess the wisdom of using food for experimental purposes in the middle of a depression.

Desperate for a diversion as his embarrassment deepened, Nick turned and called out to his partner, who had returned to his work at the other end of the lab, "Hey Mike, we're going to need a finer touch on the joystick to get the precision needed for surgery. Can you add some sort of a variable scale or sensitivity setting on movement?"

"Oh sure, Nick," Mike replied. Then he turned his head toward the open lab door and hollered, "One mother and child reunion, keep off the grass, and an M.D. let it walk!!"

"What did he just say?" Gail asked with one eyebrow raised and a section of banana caressed between her thumb and forefinger poised to pop into her mouth.

"He's just giving me a hard time. He's implying that I'm treating him like a short order cook. Translated, he said 'One chicken and egg sandwich, hold the lettuce, and a Dr. Pepper to go.'

"But seriously, Mike," Nick turned and called again.

This time Mike hunched over and did his best impression of Igor, answering, "Yes, Master. Right away, Master."

Nick picked up an empty plastic Dr. Pepper bottle and threw it at Mike.

Mike easily dodged the bottle, picked it up and prepared to throw it back.

At that point, Gail stepped in between them and with a threatening visage said, "That's enough, boys! Behave yourselves!" Alternating her glare between the two caused Mike to start up a chant he and Nick both learned as Nu Alpha Gamma pledges when initiates would order them around excessively. Nick joined in immediately:

"Grumble, grumble, discontent! Mutiny! Mutiny! Mu-tin-y!"

After several choruses, both of the boys started laughing and after a bit Gail joined in. Once the laughter died down, Gail said, "I think that I had better do your physical now, Nick, so that you can stop fasting. I don't want you fainting from hunger."

"It's more like withdrawal for lack of Dr. Pepper, but I agree." Nick wondered if Gail was really concerned with the length of his fast or just wanted to separate the "boys."

They decided to use one of the spare bedrooms in the house for the physical. Everything was very proper - she was a professional after all. Besides, it's not like they were alone; there were two Chocolate Lab chaperones present. The worst part for Nick was when Gail checked for hernias, but he surprised himself by how well he maintained his composure. She had him fill the specimen bottle in the bathroom and put it in a small case before returning it to her, which made that part bearable as well.

When the physical examination was over, she told Nick that he could go back to work while she ran the blood and urine samples through the mobile lab in her Cat.

In about fifteen minutes, Gail rejoined the men in the lab and told Nick that everything looked good, but she injected him with a time-release minimal dose of blood pressure medicine and insisted that Agnes send her a report every day. Then Nick and Gail resumed their discussion of the impending operation.

Nick explained that the hole should not damage the tissue, but would definitely pass bodily fluids. "Unlike the banana, you will get bleeding through the hole depending on where you are in the leg. If you span a blood vessel, you will either divert the flow out through the near hole where you are working, or you will cut off the blood flow, depending on which way the closed side of the far hole is oriented - upstream or downstream – in the blood vessel. I suppose that either could be helpful at times, but I would think that neither would be desirable most of the time."

Gail struggled to visualize this two-dimensional object in a three-dimensional universe, so Nick recreated his garden hose experiment for her and that seemed to help.

"So," Nick summarized, "we should go in first with the sensor head in place. That will allow us to thoroughly survey the leg, see exactly where all the major blood vessels are and map out our plan. We just need to be careful not to block any arteries while we do our reconnaissance. That should be relatively easy by keeping the far hole oriented parallel to the length of the leg. Then we can take the sensor head off and start reassembling the bones one spot at a time until we've got them all."

Gail still seemed a little nervous. "I don't feel comfortable performing surgery on Mister O'Malley with no more experience than using the equipment on fruit."

Nick thought for a minute and said, "What about the rats? You said you were going to dissect some of them to look for organ damage or growths. What if you used the hole to check them out instead? And if you find any suspicious looking growths, you can remove and test them. That way, you get practice using the equipment and the rats get to live."

Now it was Gail's turn to think. "That's a great idea, but I'll need to figure out how much anesthetic I need for a rat," she said as she reached for her PIDD.

"Okay," said Nick, "you figure out what you need. In the meantime, I'll rustle up some lunch for the three of us."

After lunch, Nick positioned the near side of the hole just above the work surface of one of the lab benches. That allowed Gail to sit in one of the lab chairs to do the surgery, and provided the additional benefit of an adjustable overhead work light. She had been amazed and pleased when Nick offered to tilt the near side to suit her ability to see and probe as necessary. She was already familiar with the joystick for maneuvering the far side of the hole.

Hours later, Nick put the last unconscious rat back in the cage where its companions were in various stages of recovery from the anesthesia. Gail stood up and stretched as she reported, "They all look perfectly healthy to me. I didn't see anything that I thought worthy of a biopsy. Although I think you might be over feeding them. I was tempted to do some liposuction on some of them."

Mike beamed when Gail turned and complimented him on the upgrade to the software that enabled the operator to adjust the sensitivity of the joystick.

Then Gail asked, "How are we going to operate on Mister O'Malley without him knowing about your equipment?"

Mike replied, "Tell him that you want to work on his leg in private – he knows that whatever you do for him at this point is illegal, so he will understand that a hospital is out of the question and that even using your clinic would be risky. But tell him that you need more room than they have at their house and I have agreed to let you work on him here in the cafeteria. Then you can anesthetize him before you start work."

"So I will anesthetize him in the cafeteria and then move him in here where the equipment is?"

"Actually," answered Nick, "you could leave him in the cafeteria and work on him from here. For that matter, you could anesthetize him at his home and work on him from here, but that would be very hard to explain to his family without revealing a whole lot more than we are willing to disclose just yet. Besides, I think you should be close by the patient in case something goes wrong. This *is* the first attempt at remote surgery like this."

"However," Nick continued, "speaking of firsts - the time has come for me to do something that I have been planning to do for some time. I want you both to stay here for a few minutes while I get ready."

Mike spoke up as Nick passed him on the way out of the lab. "What are you talking about Nick? What do you need to do and why do you need to 'get ready'?"

"I'll explain when I come back. I won't be long. I promise."

Chapter 32

More than twenty minutes passed before Nick stepped back through the lab door and stood just over the threshold with a determined expression on his face. However, neither Mike nor Gail was looking at his face - they were staring at his attire.

Nick was decked out in the full regalia of a Scottish piper - a black Glengarry with a clan badge, black jacket, white shirt with a white lace jabot, kilt, dress sporran with silver chain, kilt hose and dress brogues ... and he was carrying a bagpipe!

Breaking the stunned silence, Mike asked, "Where did you get that outfit?"

"These all belonged to my father," Nick replied. "This is what was in those boxes you unloaded from the trailer. Other than the prototype, these were the only things that were important enough for me to grab when I left Houston."

Pointing at the bagpipe, Mike asked, "Can you play that thing?"

Agnes' voice rose from her current resting place in his sporran to say, "Oh yes, he can play that thing! You should hear him play "Road to the Isles."

Then Fred joined in, "I'll bet most people would happily hit the *road to anywhere else* when he plays that thing."

Agnes started to argue, but Nick cut them off with a "Quiet, you two!"

Gail suddenly asked Nick, "Why does your PIDD have two simulacrums?" But before Nick could answer, she said, "I know, it's a long story."

Gesturing at the kilt, Mike said, "I assume that's the MacEwen tartan."

"Good guess, Sherlock," Nick sarcastically replied.

"So tell me, Nick," Mike continued, "is it true what they say about kilts?"

Both Nick and Gail glared at Mike without speaking.

"Okay, okay, I can take a hint! I was just curious. I'm sorry if the question made you uncomfortable," Mike said with a grin that belied the apology.

Changing the subject, Mike asked, "Is this what you said you had to do? Play the bagpipe for us?"

Nick answered, "Playing the bagpipe is part of it, but I won't really be playing for you. You see, I've known for a while that this moment was coming. Now it's time. A human subject has to be exposed to the hole. I would have preferred to do more safety experiments first, but now there is a pressing need. Mister O'Malley can't wait while we keep dreaming up more tests. At least we know that the laboratory rats seem to be all right."

Both Mike and Gail were starting to look concerned, but Nick pressed on. "I decided while I was driving here from Houston that I would be the first human through the hole, partly because I don't want anyone else getting killed or hurt in my place. But if I'm going to be honest, I have to admit that it is mostly because I want to be the first human in history to do this, and I want history to record that I did it wearing MacEwen highland wear while playing "Scotland the Brave" on the bagpipe. That's another reason this is a good time to do it - I have two witnesses present."

Mike and Gail started to protest at the same time, but Nick interrupted them. "Think about it for a minute. You know it has to be done, and I'm claiming the right to be the guinea pig for my own invention." Silence reigned in the lab for a few more moments until Nick asked, "Now that I think about it, why did we use rats instead of guinea pigs?"

The stunned silence continued a bit longer due to the incongruous question, until Mike laughed and answered, "The rats were cheaper." All three of them laughed at that.

Finally, Mike quietly asked, "What do you need us to do Nick?"

"Well, the sensor head is already off so Gail could check out the rats. I think all we need to do is open up a man-sized hole between the lab and the cavern, with both sides vertical and with their lower edges at floor level. Then I'll start playing the bagpipe and step through to the cavern while you both watch. Assuming it doesn't kill me, I'll step back though into the lab and describe any sensations I may have experienced. It should be simple." *I hope those aren't Famous Last Words.*

But this time it *was* simple. Nick played "Scotland the Brave" as he stepped through to the cavern while Alfred recorded everything for posterity. In the cavern he took a couple of more steps, turned around, stopped playing the bagpipe, and said, "One simple step for man ... many complex consequences for mankind."

Suddenly, a dark brown streak burst forth from underneath one of the lab benches and headed for the open hole. Lady joined her master in the cavern before anyone could react. Nick looked down at her as she sat at his side and looked up at him with adoring amber eyes while vigorously thumping her tail on the cavern floor.

Shaking his head, Nick said, "I guess Lady has claimed the right to be the first canine through the hole."

Then he started playing again and marched back through the hole into the lab with Lady marching at his side.

He said that he didn't feel a thing during the transit and Agnes reported that there were no discernible changes in Nick's vital signs during the process.

Nick was about to suggest that they all three fix something for a celebration dinner when Alfred's voice echoed through the lab, "Intruders detected in the tunnels on Level Three."

Mike immediately responded, "Alfred, maintain tunnel lights out, enable holographic display in interactive security mode, visual and infrared motion, preset thresholds."

Mike and Nick turned toward the display as it sprang to life with the holographic mine tunnel map. Gail followed their lead and saw a roughly cube-shaped translucent volume suspended in midair with blue dots scattered throughout. Then she noticed that one of the blue dots was flashing as a group of white dots seemed to move past it. Gail was thoroughly confused as Mike stepped forward and touched the flashing blue dot. When a window appeared next to the dot, she could make out some pale greenish white figures moving against a dark background. They appeared to be carrying light sabers just like space warriors in the vids.

The words "intruders," "tunnels," and "security" coalesced in her mind and she said "these are the intruders in the tunnels? Why do they look like that?"

Mike replied, "The tunnel lights are out – it's pitch black down there. The computer constructs the best image possible using the full spectrum of the sensors." Mike pointed at the dark background and continued, "The cool rock walls of the tunnel aren't radiating much at all." Then, pointing at the greenish white figures, he added, "The intruders are radiating mostly infrared and some visible light by reflection from the PIDD lights they are carrying, which are radiating powerfully in the visible spectrum," pointing at the glaring white shafts of light. "The imaging software does its best to make sense of all that to display an image in our visible range."

"Who are they?"

Mike sighed. "I think they're mostly young people from Cripple Creek, although I suppose some of them could be adventurous tourists. But very few people have money for vacations these days. I suppose they could be desperate people who have lost all their money in the casinos and are compounding their foolishness by thinking they can find some gold lying around in the mines. In any case, this bunch is further into the tunnel system than I've seen in the past."

"How do they get in?"

"There are places where tunnels near the surface have partially collapsed. For that matter, there are also the drainage tunnels, though that's the long way around. All of the possible entrances have warning signs, but that apparently doesn't mean anything to these people. I just wish they would stay away. I'm afraid somebody's going to get seriously hurt stumbling around in the dark. You would think that the darkness and the fear of getting lost would scare them away."

Fred chimed in, "Let the boss play his bagpipe for them. That'll scare them away!"

Mike looked at Nick with a thoughtful expression.

Nick shook his head and said, "I don't think my playing is that bad."

Mike laughed and answered, "No, your playing is great, but Fred has a point. If we project a hole down into the Level Three tunnel and you suddenly step out playing the pipes ..."

Nick was standing there with his mouth open staring at Mike.

"Don't look so shocked, Nick - it's not *that* crazy. It just might work."

"That's not why I'm shocked. I'm shocked because you called it a 'hole.'"

Mike grimaced. "Slip of the tongue. I meant a 'Whatever.' But the point is that I think this will work." Then Mike explained his idea and they ironed out the details.

* * * * *

Gat pushed the blindfolded wannabe ahead of him down the dark tunnel. They were just about far enough into the mine to abandon the kid. The rules were that the wannabe had to stay in the mine for two days without getting caught. If he succeeded, he would be allowed in the gang as a runner, the entry level position reserved for the young, quick, and resourceful. The other gang members with Gat were harassing the kid - describing all kinds of dire consequences he would suffer if he failed in his assignment.

In reality, none of the threats were true. If he got caught or left the mine early they would give him a good scare, then relent and use him as a runner anyway. Gat found the kid on the streets about two weeks ago. It was a familiar story - his parents had heard that the casinos were doing good business despite the depression, so they had strapped all of their worldly goods to the roof of their car and headed for Cripple Creek. When they arrived and found out that literally thousands of other people had the same notion and there was no work to be had, they gambled away most of their remaining money trying to hit a jackpot. When that didn't work, they disappeared, leaving the kid behind. They undoubtedly thought someone would take him in. They were right, although they probably would be dismayed if they knew who that someone turned out to be. But it could be worse. Gat had a fair number of runners in his gang and they got fed and they had a place to sleep. That was better than what their parents could give them. So what if the money came from supporting the black market, drugs, prostitution and extortion - they were surviving. Gat's gang was known as having the fastest, most reliable runners in Cripple Creek.

Just as Gat removed the kid's blindfold and started to tell him that they would be back in two days to get him, Gat heard a noise from somewhere further down the tunnel that sounded to him like a bus in great need of new brake pads trying to make an emergency stop while the driver leaned on the horn. Pointing his PIDD light in the direction of the sound, his brain processed the dimly lit vision in fight-or-flight mode. His brain's first approximation was that a male cross-dresser carrying a squealing pig wrapped in a plaid blanket had just stepped out of a side tunnel. But as the vision walked toward him, he realized that it was a Scottish guy playing a bagpipe. For some reason that seemed even more bizarre than his first impression. Gat was about to reach into his coat pocket for his pistol when the piper turned and disappeared right into the rock wall of the tunnel!

The sudden silence seemed almost scarier than the sound of the bagpipe. The group started to edge back toward the way they had come. But as they turned toward the exit, the piper popped back out of the rock ahead of them. They froze as the piper started to play and walk towards them, only to blink as he disappeared into the rock once more.

Nothing happened for a little while, so Gat slowly approached the spot where the piper last disappeared and inspected the rock surface while running his hands over it to feel for cracks that might indicate a door of some sort. The surface was unbroken.

Then the bagpipe music returned as the piper appeared behind them again, this time accompanied by a huge, dark, growling hell-hound with glowing yellow eyes. Convinced that the piper was trying to hem them in and feed them to the hell-hound, they all broke for the exit as fast as they could run.

* * * * *

Mike was laughing so hard that it brought tears.

Slightly irritated, Nick said, "I'm glad you were able to restrain yourself until the hole was closed. They might have figured out it was a prank if they heard you laughing."

"Oh, that was good," said Mike, wiping the tears from his eyes. "It was perfect. This should be great next Halloween."

"We are not going to scare kids like this on Halloween," Nick replied. "Would you please turn on the lights now?" Nick's old phobia had made the prank harder on him than Mike realized.

They had to turn off the overhead lights in the lab or else the intruders would have been able to see everything behind Nick when he stepped through the hole. Mike piloted the hole in the semidarkness of the control panel and display illumination. That gave Mike enough light to work, and Nick enough light leakage to see the next hole position in the sequence.

Once the lights came on again, Nick asked, "And how did Lady get loose? I thought you were going to put her on a leash."

Gail held up the portion of Lady's leash remaining in her possession, pointed at the stub hanging from Lady's collar and replied, "One bite, two pieces. No way were we going to stop her."

Nick stared at the thick, wide leather pieces for a moment, then down at the dog with her tongue lolling out of the side of her mouth beside him. Finally he just shrugged and asked, "Can we go make dinner now?"

Mike and Gail agreed that they were hungry. As they left the lab, Nick said, "I'll go put on my regular clothes and meet you in the kitchen."

Gail responded, "Oh, don't bother to change, Nick. I think you look great the way you are."

Speechless, Nick kept walking, turning a little redder with each step. Suddenly, Agnes said, "Pulse and respiration rate increasing ..."

"*Silence,*" Nick growled to cut Agnes off as they proceeded to the kitchen. Gail quickly pulled ahead of Nick so that he wouldn't see her smile.

After dinner they retired to the living room to sit and talk for a while. Nick periodically fidgeted as he adjusted the arrangement of his kilt. They agreed to perform the surgery on Mister O'Malley the next day, and Gail called Sean to make sure that his father didn't eat or drink anything after midnight.

Gail got an overnight bag out of her Cat that she kept packed for those times she needed to stay with a patient and settled into one of Mike's guest rooms. Shortly thereafter, the two "boys" went to bed as well. It had been a long day for all three of them.

Chapter 33

It promised to be a long day for Blood Hound. He had been tailing an individual who was behind on his payments for a very expensive sailboat. The guy lived in Milpitas in the San Francisco Bay area. Randy had made arrangements to have the sailboat towed to an impound marina as soon as he found it, but more than two weeks had passed without the subject going anywhere near the water. Randy was like a dog with a bone - he wasn't about to give up. Still, he was tiring of following the guy around. Today, very early in the morning, the subject got on the Southbay Freeway heading southwest to the Bayshore Freeway, then northwest to Redwood City, where he got off the freeway and pulled into a marina on Bair Island while Randy followed in his rental car.

Fortunately, it was a public marina and Randy was able to drive right into the parking lot, follow the guy down the dock to the boat and serve the repossession papers. The guy was far from happy and tried to talk Randy out of it. Randy simply ignored his promises to catch up on his payments, and merely scowled when the guy tried to bribe him. But when the guy became threatening, Randy flipped back the hem of his jacket to reveal his holstered U.S. Army .45 ACP pistol and glared down at the subject. That did the trick. The guy meekly asked if he could take his personal items off the boat. Randy agreed, but insisted on inspecting every item to make sure it was not part of the boat, its equipment, or furnishings. That process only took a few minutes and the impound boat only took a little over an hour to show up, so Randy was done well before noon.

Randy used his PIDD to make reservations to fly back to Houston. He couldn't fly out until the next day because he needed time to ship his pistol back to Houston. He couldn't carry it on the plane or pack it in his bags, but he could ship the gun and the ammunition separately as long as both the sending and receiving parties were licensed gun dealers or licensed gun collectors. Since Randy was a licensed gun collector, he could ship them to himself.

He stood on the dock looking out over the bay trying to decide how he was going to pass the time. Then he remembered that the address of one of the references on Nick MacEwen's security application was in the San Francisco Bay area - and the name and address was stored on his PIDD.

Pulling up the information, Randy decided to ship his pistol, and then take the bull by the horns and drive to the address he had for this Michael Clarke, walk up to the door, and ring the doorbell. He decided to stick as close as possible to the truth - Nicholas MacEwen was missing, Randy had been hired by MacEwen's employer to try and find him, and Mister Clarke was listed as a reference on MacEwen's security clearance.

His PIDD gave him driving instructions to Michael Clarke's address. It was an older, but well-kept, medium sized home in an expensive looking neighborhood. Ringing the bell rewarded him with a matronly woman who immediately announced that she wasn't buying anything. Randy flashed his oversized business card which was intentionally made to vaguely resemble a law enforcement officer's credentials, and held it up just far enough from her to make a detailed examination impossible.

"I'm not selling anything Missus Clarke; I'm investigating a missing person case. It appears that your husband is an acquaintance of the missing person, so I was hoping that I could speak to Mister Clarke."

"My name is not Clarke," the matron said, "but a Michael Clarke used to live here. We bought this house from him about six years ago."

Rats! This was my only remaining lead. In desperation, Randy asked, "Do you happen to know where Mister Clarke lives now?"

"My husband and I had the opportunity to chat with Mister Clarke several times during the sale and closing process. He told us that his uncle had died and left him a gold mine in Colorado and that he was going to live there."

"Did he mention a specific location for this gold mine - a nearby city, maybe the county it was in, anything like that?"

"No, I'm sorry. If he said anything more I don't remember it."

"What about your husband? Would he remember any more details about Mister Clarke's plans?"

"It is possible that my husband would remember more if he was alive - he died six months ago. I'm sorry I can't help you more. I think it would be best if you leave now."

"Of course, ma'am, I'm sorry about your loss. Thank you for your help in this matter."

The matron stepped back and closed the door. As Randy went back down the walk to the rental car, he thought about what he had just learned.

We lost track of MacEwen's rig just west of Colorado Springs and didn't pick it up again until Las Vegas. We followed the trailer from Las Vegas to Mexico, but it was empty when we found it. There was no time for him to empty the trailer between Las Vegas and Mexico. So, the trailer had to be emptied between Colorado Springs and Las Vegas. Now I hear that MacEwen's college buddy has a gold mine in Colorado. What better place to hide than in a mine? I think that I have narrowed his location down from "somewhere in the western United States" to one state - Colorado. And not all of Colorado has gold mines.

Randy got in the rental car and sat for a moment trying to make up his mind. Then he tapped the icon on his PIDD to call Jimmy Barton.

* * * * *

Jimmy was not in a good mood. He hadn't been in a good mood for

180

quite a while. ITC was still hanging on, but just barely. They were getting contracts in rotation with the rest of the cabal, but their turn always seemed to come on small contracts. Jimmy suspected that Vance Billingsly was manipulating the rotation somehow, and Jimmy was getting tired of living on the scraps that fell from GenArm's table. He was convinced that things would have gone much differently if he had succeeded in recovering the Defender prototype. He thought that it was extremely unfair that he was suffering because he couldn't deliver a system that didn't work anyway.

Sheila interrupted his funk as she spoke up from the outer office, "Mister Miller is calling for you. Should I tell him you've already left for the day?"

After a moment's hesitation, he answered, "No, put him through." *Now what does he want?*

Randy quickly filled Jimmy in on his San Francisco side trip, and then said, "It really irritates me that MacEwen gave me the slip. I still plan to pursue this lead on my own nickel unless you tell me not to do it."

Jimmy reflected on the contrast between the surge of adrenaline he felt when he heard Randy's report versus his funk of just a few minutes ago, and replied, "I'll tell you what, Randy, I'll cover half of your expenses. If you find the prototype, I'll reimburse you for your half and add a bonus."

Randy was only looking for Jimmy's approval because it was Jimmy's asset to be recovered, but surprisingly got an offer for at least partial compensation. Amazed, he simply replied, "Great, I'll keep you updated." Then, unsurprisingly, he heard nothing but dead air.

Randy tapped the icon for his best "Big Data" investigating subcontractor, a.k.a. hacker, who would ferret out any and all records associated with Michael Clarke. She was even more expensive than the Homeland Security guy, but since Jimmy was going pay half of the bills, Randy was going to pull out all of the stops.

* * * * *

Less than an hour later, Wil Ahrens was briefing Vance Billingsly on Blood Hound's call to Jimmy.

Billingsly asked, "Do you think this Michael Clarke person is significant?"

Ahrens responded, "It's certainly possible. Our tracking information showed that the trailer went through Colorado on the way to Las Vegas and then on to Mexico. It could be a coincidence that his college friend lives in Colorado. On the other hand, it could explain MacEwen's route. After all, if his plan was to head for Mexico, why would he drive all the way northwest to Colorado and then back southwest to Mexico?"

"Yes," Billingsly agreed, "we thought at the time that he was just trying to find some remote spot to hide. But maybe he already knew a good spot."

There go the eyes again! Ahrens thought. *Stand by for orders.*

Billingsly collected his thoughts and then ordered Wil to go to Colorado and try to find Clarke before Blood Hound did.

As Ahrens was turning to go, Billingsly added, "Keep me informed. MacEwen doesn't know you, so if you find him and the conditions are right, try and get close to him. In any case, put yourself in a position to deflect Blood Hound if necessary."

"Deflect" thought Wil as he turned and left. *That's a nice, civilized word for what Billingsly expects me to do "if necessary."*

* * * * *

Randy was very disappointed.

His best "Big Data" investigating subcontractor could find lots of records associated with the name Michael Clarke but was having a difficult time identifying any records that definitely applied to the specific Michael Clarke of interest. The starting point of the effort to build a filter to separate the wheat from the chaff was supposed to be Clarke's California address. Using that information, she should have been able to find many records that included both the subject's name and that address. Some of those records would then provide additional useful information that could be used to further narrow the search, and so on. Normally this was a tedious process that could take days, if not weeks, to accomplish if the client wanted a thorough dossier on a subject.

The problem in Michael Clarke's case was that there appeared to be no records anywhere that included his name and the California address Randy supplied. Electronically, the implication was that no Michael Clarke had ever lived at that address. But Randy had seen the ITC Security Clearance application reference entry and he had talked to the lady now living there who said she bought the house from a Michael Clarke who moved to Colorado where his uncle had left him a gold mine.

But there were no surveys, deeds, probate records or news articles associating a Michael Clarke with the sale of a house in California or the acquisition of a gold mine in Colorado. The very first link in what was supposed to be a chain of information was broken. They had to find another link.

According to the Security Clearance application, Clarke and MacEwen had been college classmates, so Randy called Frank Palmer at ITC and asked him to PIDD an image of MacEwen's employment records. Frank refused at first, based on privacy laws. A call to Jimmy had cleared up that little problem.

But when the hacker checked, there was no record at all of a Michael Clarke attending that educational institution. There were several alumni named Michael Clark, without the ending e, but none of them had attended in any of the years MacEwen indicated on his resume.

The hacker wisecracked that Clarke must be planning on running for president, and that gave Randy an idea. He asked her to verify the years that MacEwen had attended. According to the records, no Nicholas MacEwen had ever attended either.

Then Randy asked her to verify the apartment address listed as Nick's residence in the employment records. The only record she could find associating MacEwen with that address was in the federal medical database regarding a doctor's appointment six years ago. Even that record was questionable since the social security number didn't match the one in his employment records. She offered to forward Randy an image of a very red and swollen finger, but he declined.

Finally, Randy asked her to use any and all of the information in the employment records to try and find any other data that could be unequivocally associated with Nicholas MacEwen.

In just a few hours the hacker called back and reported that there was nothing else to find. Mike asked her why, in her expert opinion, they were coming up dry on their search.

Her reply was, "Blood Hound, these guys have either hired a top notch personal data scrubbing service, or one or the other of them is a wizard able to do it himself. Their data footprints are even smaller than personnel working in some of the most highly classified government operations. I would swear they never existed except for the fact that they are giving us the finger. And I don't think that was an accident, given the thoroughness of their data purge."

So, Randy thought, *I'm going to have to do this the old fashioned way, with "feet on the ground."*

* * * * *

Randy changed his reservation to a plane bound for Colorado Springs instead of Houston, and used his PIDD to surf for information on Colorado gold mining areas during the flight. As the flight headed east toward a mid-morning sun, he learned that there were four known significant gold fields in Colorado, all in the mountains west of Interstate 25. Two of them were fairly small areas in the northwest part of the state bordering on Wyoming. The third and largest area stretched diagonally from Denver on the northeast to Durango on the southwest. The fourth area was just southwest of Colorado Springs. That was where Randy was headed first, mostly because that was where the trailer was last positively sighted on the traffic cameras before reappearing in Las Vegas. If that didn't pan out – Randy smiled at the appropriateness of the expression in this case – he would try the central section of the largest area farther west.

* * * * *

Colonel Shi Rui Xian did not hear about the new lead from his ITC source until days later. But once he received the information he reacted quickly.

Deciding to take the field personally, he, Agent Xue and three other MSS agents left on a plane to Pueblo, Colorado that very day. According to his GenArm source, a tracking device had shown that the trailer went through south central Colorado and even stopped for a while in the San Isabel National Forest, so they would start by checking out the gold fields west of Pueblo. But first he put in a call to Major Ni at the Embassy. Shi asked Ni to build a complete profile on Michael Clarke, providing Ni with Clarke's old California address along with the as yet unverified information that he had inherited a gold mine in Colorado from an unnamed uncle.

Colonel Shi, like Randy, was ultimately dismayed at the lack of results.

Chapter 34

"Finished," Gail said as she stood up and signaled Nick to close the last hole. Then she turned around to check on Mister O'Malley. He lay on a mattress on top of a cafeteria table in the middle of the lab. Her Medi-Monitor lay on his chest, slowly rising and falling with his steady breathing. It was hardly a sterile arrangement, but no incisions had been opened on this makeshift operating table.

Gail picked up the Medi-Monitor and turned off its anesthesia program. Then she removed her mask, gown, cap and gloves. The area around the near side of the hole where she had been working and the instruments she had been using *had* been kept sterile. Mike rose from the chair next to the table where he had been watching Mister O'Malley's vital signs for Gail.

Gail checked the vital signs herself and verified that they were still well within safe ranges. "We can remove the temporary splints now and I'll spray on the cast. He'll still be out for at least thirty minutes."

Nick and Mike were both anxious to hear Gail's opinion of the process and her prognosis for Mister O'Malley, but they didn't want to distract her from the task at hand. Once the cast was set, Gail swiped her brow with the back of her hand, glanced down at her PIDD lying on the lab bench, then looked up at the boys and grinned.

"That was amazing! In less than two hours we accomplished the equivalent of several months of reconstructive surgery! It was the ultimate of minimally intrusive - there should be no muscle or nerve damage and bleeding was negligible! Nick, this invention of yours is going to revolutionize the medical field."

Nick asked, "Right now I'm more concerned about its importance to Mister O'Malley. Do you think he will be able to walk again?"

"Yes," Gail answered. "I think he has as high as a ninety percent chance of walking again. That wouldn't have been possible without you, Nick."

"That's great, but we are not ready to revolutionize the medical field just yet. Let me tell you why." Nick went on to describe some of the darker potential uses for his invention. When he was done, Gail was visibly shaken.

"I hadn't thought about any of those things, Nick. Can't you figure out some way to prevent the harmful uses?"

"Mike and I are trying to do exactly that, but it's far from simple. Unless and until we succeed, the existence of the device has to remain secret. The results would be devastating if this equipment were to fall into the hands of the wrong people. And I can tell you that some of those wrong people are trying very hard to find it. We trust you to keep this completely to yourself."

"Of course, Nick." After a pause, Gail added, "But is there anything I can do to help? There's got to be as many, if not more, good things that can come from its use, and I'd like to be a part of making those good things possible."

"I'd love to have your help, Gail." Nick turned to Mike, raised an eyebrow, and asked, "First recruit?"

Mike nodded, and answered, "First recruit."

They moved Mister O'Malley back into the cafeteria and Gail watched over him until he woke up. She made sure that he was as comfortable as possible, asking if he needed anything to ease the pain. He said that his leg felt a little sore, but much better than it had felt before the operation. She told him to rest for a while. "Just call out if you need anything. The house computer will summon me."

When she returned to the lab, a discussion ensued regarding how Gail could best contribute. It turned out that she had worked on the assembly line at an electronics plant in Colorado Springs to earn money for her nursing college tuition. So it was agreed that she would take over the assembly of new hole generators from Nick so that he could continue investigating the capabilities of the phenomenon using the original prototype. It was further agreed that her medical services in the community took first priority, so she would only work on a non-interfering basis. Nick brought up the subject of pay, but Gail insisted that she had volunteered. Nick insisted that she be paid. This elicited a brief, but friendly, argument which Nick won.

Later that day, Gail returned Mr. O'Malley to his very grateful family, and then headed back to her clinic in town.

* * * * *

That night after dinner Nick got a secure PIDD call as he had several times since the inaugural call from Red months before. Once the security protocols were complete, Nick put the call on speaker so Mike could hear.

An electronically modified voice asked, "How's it going, fellas?"

Mike and Nick glanced at each other. Red never questioned Nick on his progress, even though he or she must have been very curious. Was this an innocent greeting or the end of an unofficial taboo? Nick decided to assume the former even though Red was not one for small talk. *Could this be White or Blue?*

"Pretty good, how are things with you?"

The caller chuckled, perhaps enjoying Nick's ambiguity, and said, "Glad to hear it," showing that he or she could ignore vague questions with the best of them.

"Listen, I just wanted to give you all a heads up. Some of the groups looking for you are getting warm. They have made the connection between you two, and know that Mike inherited a gold mine somewhere in Colorado. They don't know exactly where yet, but they're headed to Colorado to start looking."

"How did they figure out I knew Mike?"

"You listed Mike as a reference on your security clearance application at ITC. That led them to California and on to Colorado. We did the best we could to cover your tracks. We purged all of the electronic records out there that we could find that related to either of you guys, but there wasn't a lot we could do about paper records or personal interviews without raising a whole lot more questions than we were willing to answer."

"What should we do?"

"Just continue to keep your heads down and be very leery of strangers. If the fecal material hits the rotating ventilation device, call me, Red or White."

So this must be Blue, Nick thought. *I wonder if Red is just busy or if he doesn't like being the bearer of bad news.*

Blue continued. "We can send in the cavalry if absolutely necessary, but not without putting your operation in the very bright spotlight of national attention. I am very confident that you would not find that to be productive at this point."

Mike asked, "Can you tell us any more about these people that are looking for us?"

"One group is headed up by a notorious repossession agent and bounty hunter named Blood Hound. You may have seen some of his vids. His real name is Randy Miller. Originally we thought he was mostly muscle, but he seems to be making better progress trying to find you than his competition. His client is Jimmy Barton, your old boss."

"He must work cheap if Jimmy hired him," Nick exclaimed.

Ignoring Nick's outburst, Blue continued, "There's a second group that we don't know much about. All we really know is that the members of this group all seem to be Asians."

"Terrific," said Nick. "So there may be some Chinese Tong on my tail as well."

Blue paused as if considering a response to Nick's comment but then continued, "Third, there is a small contingent of GenArm personnel involved."

"That makes sense," Nick responded. "Jimmy cooked up some sort of a deal with Vance Billingsly about jointly developing the Defender prototype. Vance is probably upset that his plans to cut me out have backfired."

"Those are the only groups that we know of, and we're not really sure

187

about the Asians. But if they really are after the prototype, then they might be the most dangerous of the lot. I think you need to circle the wagons. I would like to send a security expert out there to help protect your operation."

Nick and Mike looked at each other with concerned expressions.

Perhaps sensing their reluctance, Blue continued, "He can look your place over and tell you just where your vulnerabilities are and how these people might try to take advantage of them. I would really like to send a whole security team out there, but it would attract too much attention – on your end *and* mine. He will not interfere with your operations, nor are you required to share any information with him regarding your research."

Nick really didn't want a stranger poking his nose into things - *and Blue just told me to be leery of strangers* - but he remembered the point Mike made earlier that these Red, White and Blue people could take over any time they wanted to, but they hadn't done so. In fact, they had been consistently supportive of Nick ever since that first night in Houston when he took off with the prototype. He didn't know what their angle was on all of this. He hoped it was patriotism, but there were other possibilities that Nick didn't want to think about given their power over him.

Nick replied, "I appreciate your concern and hope you won't be offended if I say I am uncomfortable about allowing access to a stranger. Unless we completely shut down while he's here, he will almost certainly learn a significant amount about our work. You must have some idea how important our project may be. Do you trust this individual to that level?"

"Yes, I do," Blue answered, "He has some of the highest security clearances and endorsements available. Besides, he already has a general idea of what you are trying to achieve."

Nick thought, *what I was trying to achieve is a lot different than what I have achieved, but I guess we will deal with the security expert's realization of that as necessary.* "Then when should we expect his arrival?"

"He is currently on another assignment, but this one takes precedence. I'll have to check out exactly where he is at the moment and redirect his activities; however, that shouldn't take long. I would imagine that he should show up at your door within a few days."

Blue continued, "I'll fill Red and White in on our discussion and one of us will call you if we get any more specific information on the activities of any of the groups looking for you."

Nick, Mike and Blue said their good nights and ended the call.

Chapter 35

With Gail's help, Nick had two hole generators to work with now, and more on the way. The new generator was about the size of an under-the-counter refrigerator with the antenna mounted on top. It was quite a bit more compact than the prototype, since there was no requirement for the ease of access needed during the bread-boarding stage of development.

He was secretly relieved when the new generator worked. There had been a nagging concern in the back of his mind that maybe some unknown characteristic of the prototype was unique in some inexplicable way. He was painfully aware that it was the accidental product of a bungled sabotage attempt, and that he really didn't completely understand how it worked. Demonstrating that the phenomenon could be replicated was a critical step in his efforts to determine its full capabilities.

Nick had enjoyed the time he spent with Gail, coaching her through the process of assembling and testing the new generator from the components and sub-assemblies produced by different manufacturers across the country. Those vendors all thought that they were manufacturing parts for mining equipment, which was actually true in a limited sense. Nick was confident that they would eventually be able to produce a range of models varying in size and range.

Now that he knew they could replicate generators, he felt free to perform a potentially destructive test. He had long wanted to do an experiment wherein the far hole was brought into close proximity of the near hole, merging them if possible to see what happened. Nick knew it wasn't very scientific, but he just didn't have the math to predict the result. Of course, he didn't have the math because he didn't have a good theory of how the hole actually worked. So he was going to be a shade tree physicist, sort of like Newton. He just hoped nothing more dangerous than an apple falling on his head would happen.

Nick decided that he should conduct the experiment in the cavern outside Mike's Man Cave structure, just in case there was a problem - that way they would have the protection of the building's thick, shielded walls and could observe the test using Alfred's cameras. They lugged the new generator out into the cavern and ran a power cable to it. Mike loaded a sequencing program into the generator that, when executed, would delay sixty seconds, open a hole and slowly bring the two sides into conjunction, hold them there for ten seconds, and then shut down. Of course, all of that depended on the equipment functioning throughout the sequence, as opposed to exploding at some point during the process. If a problem occurred, they could simply throw the breaker off for the circuit providing power to the generator, assuming it would make any difference at that point.

Nick used the excuse of double checking Mike's sequencing program to delay until Gail left on a medical call before calmly telling Mike he was ready to run the test. Mike was not fooled into thinking that the timing was a coincidence. He knew that Nick was worried about what would happen when the two sides merged, but he also knew that Nick felt it was essential that they find out.

Mike ordered Alfred to record everything that happened in the cavern until ordered to stop. Nick checked that both Patti and Lady were safely snoozing in the lab, then walked out to the new generator and entered the command to run the sequencing program. He looked up at one of the broad-band sensors high on the cavern wall – a totally unnecessary gesture – and asked, "Are you recording, Alfred?" - A totally unnecessary question.

"Yes, Mister MacEwen," Alfred answered in his best English butler voice.

Nick tapped the execute icon and walked back toward the building. He unconsciously picked up his pace as he fought the overwhelming sensation that there was a loaded gun aimed right between his retreating shoulder blades and it was going to go off any second. When Nick walked back into the lab, Mike was watching the holographic display that showed the cavern with the generator sitting in the middle. There was a countdown timer running in the near right bottom corner of the hologram that Mike had started when Nick tapped the execute icon. The count had just dropped below fifteen seconds.

Now the seconds seemed to drag by as Nick stared at the unchanging image of the generator. After an eternity, the final numbers flashed by, 3 ... 2 ... 1 ... 0!

There's the near hole right in front of the antenna, Nick thought. *But where's the far hole? ... There it is, near the north wall of the cavern. Mike programmed them (it?) with open sides facing each other. Here it comes now, moving toward the conjunction.*

Nick had Alfred zoom in on the open side of the far hole momentarily. *Wow! It's like Fun House mirrors! The far hole sees the near hole seeing the far hole, ad infinitum.*

Alfred zoomed back out and time seemed to slow down even more as Nick waited for the big moment. He was holding his breath as the far hole approached. Apparently Mike was holding his breath as well, since both of them gasped for air when the holes converged and both Chocolate Labs simultaneously woke up and started howling.

Mike recovered from his surprise first and shouted, "*I don't see the holes!*"

Nick - frowning as he leaned forward trying to get a better view – asked, "What's wrong with the display? It looks blurry, kind of out of focus around the generator." Then he added, "And what's set the dogs to howling?"

Mike looked where Nick was pointing and asked, "Alfred is something interfering with your sensors?"

Agnes interjected, "There is a strong ultrasonic emission in the forty kilohertz range coming from the direction of the cavern."

The counter finished counting back up to ten, the display cleared, and the dogs stopped howling all at the same time as Alfred responded, "Nothing interfered with the sensors, sir. Allow me to run the recording in extreme slow motion."

Nick and Mike both concentrated on the display as Alfred ran the recording in slow motion, frame by frame. They saw a mirrored surface like the closed side of a hole appear in front of the generator and then disappear a few frames later. This on-off sequence continued as the frames went by.

"Alfred, stop the playback at a frame showing the mirrored surface," Mike called out.

Nick and Mike slowly walked around the frozen hologram and realized that the mirrored surface was actually a mirrored globe.

In hushed tones, Nick said, "Maybe this is finally the Defender field. But why is it flickering on and off?"

Mike added, "Why is it so big? The 'Whatever' wasn't that large."

Nick smiled at the name game that he and Mike continued to play. It helped to relieve some of the current tension in the air. "The two sides have merged, so maybe the energy needed to hold them apart has gone into making them bigger ... and ..." Nick slapped himself on his forehead "... it's flickering on and off because the field is cutting off its own power!" He pointed to the intersection of the globe surrounding the generator and the power cable leading up to it. "When the field collapses for lack of power, the power is reapplied, which causes the field to reform and cut off the power again. I'll bet the ultrasonic emissions that caused the dogs to howl came from power supply oscillations as the load tripped on and off."

Alfred confirmed that the generator was, in fact, the locus of the ultrasonic emissions.

Mike exclaimed, "Well, I'm glad we figured that out. I was afraid that we were going to have to call Panda Tech Support!"

"What is Panda Tech Support?"

"You know, Panda Tech Support. Native habitat is Southeast Asia, everything is black and white, becomes irritated when disturbed, such as when you tell them exactly where they can put their inflexible call script flowchart ..."

Nick just shook his head.

"So," Mike asked, "what have we learned from this little experiment?"

Nick thought for a few minutes as he slowly walked around the holographic image of a silver reflecting globe that looked like it could have graced a Victorian giant's garden and replied, "We've learned that we have a great deal more to learn ... and the first thing I want to learn is what, if anything, is inside that globe."

* * * * *

Nick found out what was inside the globe as he and Mike explored the nature of the phenomenon over the following days.

First, they learned that they could form a globe which did not encompass the generator by starting with the near side further away, but it required more power to do so. Nonetheless, it produced a stable globe that didn't cut off its own power. Then they tried to move the globe, but found that it would separate back into the two sides of a hole unless they both moved synchronously, which was essentially impossible to do using the game controller joysticks. So Mike added a globe mode subroutine that would control the position of both sides together using a single joystick.

They then verified that they couldn't maneuver the globe inside solid matter without using the incremental repositioning technique they had developed for moving a hole in the direction of its closed side through dense materials.

Neither of them was surprised when the globe proved to be as impenetrable as the mirrored closed side of a hole. They hammered it, shot it, drilled it and even blasted it without making a scratch. The only thing they could find that would penetrate the globe was a hole generated by another generator. Nick used the prototype to open a hole inside the globe and look around. There was absolutely nothing inside, unless you want to count an impenetrable, mirrored interior surface. *If a hole is created by pinching space-time together such that two different places in three dimensions became the same place in two dimensions, what is this – a dimensional pimple? No way am I going to suggest that name to Mike! The inside of the globe appears to be three-dimensional. Does that mean it is part of our universe or part of some other universe, or perhaps our illusion of some other illusion? I wonder if I will ever know ... and if I knew, would it change anything.* Nick was beginning to feel a little like the sorcerer's apprentice, unable to control what he had started.

Regardless, Nick was excited. This truly looked like the Defender field he had labored so long to create. He longed for some directed-energy weapons or maybe a small nuke to test its strength. For some reason, Mike seemed relieved that none were available.

But Nick knew that a defensive shield that relied on a vulnerable external source of origin was pretty worthless. The globe had to surround and protect the generator, which meant Nick had to either come up with a self-contained power source of sufficient capacity, or some sort of a defensible power delivery method. Coincidentally, Nick had been considering just such a system for a different reason – money.

Even before Nick arrived, Mike's electric bill was high due to the server farm. Since then, it had been growing rapidly in direct proportion to the use of the prototype. Now new field generators were coming on line which would drive it even higher. So Nick had been reading up on generating electricity from geothermal energy.

There were several types of geothermal power plants, each best suited to different geological areas, but all of them required some sort of underground wells or piping for circulating water. The most economical plants to build and operate were in fault zones, where the earth's magma is closer to the surface.

But Nick knew that he didn't need underground wells, pipes or water. All he needed to do was open a hole to a depth where the temperature was suitable and place the near side underneath a heat exchanger or boiler to make steam with which to turn a turbine generator. Mike could even write a program to have the hole automatically seek the best underground temperature to adjust for geological temperature variations. Nick calculated that the hole generator would need only a small percentage of the generated electricity to sustain the hole at the depths required. They would still need some external electrical service to start the process – sort of like the battery in a car – but once the system was running it would be very efficient. The only recurring cost would be maintenance on the turbine generator. Mike would become a net power producer and could sell the excess electricity to the utility companies.

Mike reluctantly agreed that Nick could experiment with Uncle Norris's steam powered generators. The experiment was a shocking success and Mike was so electrified that he immediately sold some gold ore and ordered several modern steam turbine generators. They decided to install them on Level Four since there was no need to exhaust combustion byproducts. Extremely economical clean energy was obviously another of the worthy uses for Nick's discovery.

Once the generators were delivered, they would need new hole generators to tie into the underground heat.

Chapter 36

The casinos with their bright lights and huge holographic billboards were mostly south of Bennett Avenue. Famous split-level Bennett Avenue, where the west-bound lane rose almost twenty feet higher than the east-bound lane between 3rd Street and 4th Street. Bennett Avenue, where the miners used to stage races pitting competing volunteer fire fighting companies against each other, stripped down to their long johns pulling hose carts behind them. Bennett Avenue, lined with red brick buildings with vaguely Victorian era facades, preserving the image of a late Nineteenth Century boom town. In reality, it was now a Twenty-first Century boom town for the enjoyment of the idle rich, and a graveyard for the dreams of the desperate poor.

The suicide rate in the city was more than twenty times higher than the national average. But the increase in gambling, entertainment seeking, and suicide was in keeping with historical trends. People had looked to gambling for possible financial salvation and entertainment as a distraction from the reality of their situation during the Great Depression in the 1930's as well. There wasn't a whole lot that the casinos could do. They couldn't very well demand verified financial statements at the door. All of them posted contact information for financial advisors and gambling addiction councilors in prominent locations. The only other thing they could do was shut down, but that would only put more people out of work and drive the gamblers to unlicensed and potentially dangerous back room venues.

Randy couldn't see much of Bennett Avenue from his current location - he was in the dark alleys behind the casinos. It was about halfway through the second shift. Befitting the history of the area, Randy was engaged in mining, but he was mining for information, not gold. He knew that the information he sought, if it was available at all, would be available on a cash and carry basis in the sub-culture of the alleyways.

He was not comfortable. It was dark and he was very cold. There was some light coming in from the streets at both ends of the alley, and there were lights over the back doors of most establishments along the alley, but it was marginally adequate for him to see his surroundings. He did have the jacket he took with him to San Francisco, but it was really inadequate for these conditions. For that matter, the oxygen at this altitude was inadequate for his needs as well. He was halfway hoping someone would try to rob him. The exercise would warm him up, though he might run out of breath quickly.

Spring time in the Rockies, my aching arthritis!

It had been a bright, sunny day and much of the snow on the paved streets and alleys had evaporated in the extremely dry air except on the northern sides of buildings where the sun doesn't shine directly for months. He shivered and for about the tenth time made sure his jacket was zipped up tight. At least there was no wind to make him even more uncomfortable. But that same lack of wind trapped the powerful, combined aromas emanating from the back doors of multiple casino kitchens, their companion dumpsters, and the deleterious discharges of back alley denizens in the canyons between the adjacent buildings.

Randy wished that he hadn't shipped his pistol back to Houston, but wasn't overly concerned. With his size, athleticism and martial arts training, he felt he was more than a match for any alcoholic, transient, or occasional casino staffer out in the alley on a smoke break. In fact, these were the very people that he came to see. He had the picture Jimmy gave him of Nick MacEwen and was showing it to all of the alley dwellers who were still conscious. He made no offer of money up front, since many of these people would quickly make up some sort of a story for the price of a pint. He had a keen eye for a lie – an essential talent in his line of business – and would only discuss compensation with someone who reacted to the photo with recognition but would not volunteer any information.

So far, no one had reacted with recognition. He had just about given up on interviewing casino staff - MacEwen was not the gambling type based on Jimmy's description. There was a small but greater chance that one of the street people had seen MacEwen. Maybe they had hustled him for a handout on the sidewalk, or offered to wash his windshield ... or maybe he was nowhere near Cripple Creek.

Randy began to notice a number of children moving through the alleys. They weren't hanging out or wandering aimlessly like the homeless. They were traveling with purpose and they seemed relatively clean and well dressed. Most of the time, they carried packages into the back alley doors of the casinos and exited empty handed. As he watched, he remembered reading about this sort of thing going on in large cities during the first great depression. *These kids are runners for some sort of illicit organization. They're probably delivering black market food to the casino kitchens. They undoubtedly cover more ground and see more people every day than anyone else in the whole city!*

He started to try and stop these runners, but most would quickly dodge past him and run off. Finally, he tried standing at a fairly well lit alley intersection that seemed to be heavily traveled while holding up the photograph and watching for a reaction as the runners hustled by. His patience was rewarded over an hour later when a young boy glanced up at the photo, came to a dead stop and then took a few backward steps with his eyes darting between the photograph and Randy.

Randy immediately whipped out a twenty dollar bill and held it up next to the photograph.

"Hi, kid. It's important that I find this guy. Where have you seen him?"

The runner took another slow backwards step as his eyes darted between the photograph, Randy and the twenty. But Randy noticed that the twenty got the most eyeball time.

"I won't hurt you and I won't tell anyone else what you tell me. Just let me know where you saw him and the twenty is yours."

The runner still seemed to be afraid to speak. His rapid breathing was visible in the cold air as small white puffs of condensation. Now that he wasn't running, he shivered and wrapped his arms around his upper body.

The name "Oliver Twist" leaped unbidden into Randy's mind.

"Oh, and I don't even know who you work for, so there's no way for me to tell them that I gave you the twenty."

The waif blurted out, "Mister, I don't know where you got that photograph, but it looks just like the ghost of the MacNamara Mine!"

It cost Randy another ten dollars to find out that the MacNamara Mine was on the other side of Victor, Colorado, southeast of Cripple Creek. It didn't cost him anything extra to hear the story of the ghost of the MacNamara Mine.

* * * * *

Randy, resplendent in the winter hunter's camouflage apparel he purchased in Cripple Creek, left his rental car parked just off of Phantom Canyon Road and trudged through the copse of sparse pine and denuded aspen trees. The spring snow was knee deep under the canopy of trees, but still very dry at this altitude. Each step he took made a loud scrunching sound. The new outfit was acquired more for warmth than stealth, because Randy had no intention of approaching within unaided eyesight of the target.

Randy had been concerned that whoever had expunged all of the online data for Michael Clarke and Nicholas MacEwen might have done the same for the MacNamara Mine, so he bypassed his "Big Data" subcontractor in favor of old school methods. He went to the Teller County Assessor's Office in Cripple Creek and asked to see the paper original of the legal description of the MacNamara mining claim. It was then a simple matter to enter the claim's coordinates into an online map program, pull up the satellite imagery on his PIDD, and plan his approach to the property.

He picked out a pine tree at the far edge of the woods to lean against and raised digital binoculars, also just purchased, to his eyes. He could have zoomed in with his PIDD, but the field glasses were much more powerful. He smiled as he imagined Jimmy's reaction to Randy's upcoming bill for expenses. He wondered if Jimmy would demand possession of his half of the binoculars. *That would give him a monocular then, wouldn't it?* The bright sun's reflections off the snow were almost blinding, so Randy focused on one of the icons at the bottom edge of the view and blinked twice in rapid succession. In response, the binocular's internal processor applied an antiglare program. *I've never been any place before where the sun provides so much light and so little heat!*

196

The autofocus quickly resolved the blurry view through the binoculars into a vision of a large ranch style house on a small mesa. The range finder at the top of the display showed that the house was just over four hundred yards due west across an intervening draw from Randy's position. Although classic in its architecture, the house stood out from the homes in Victor to the northwest by its obviously recent construction and large size. There was also a tall tin roofed wooden building to the north near the junction of a long driveway and the Phantom Canyon Road. Randy had studied hard rock vertical shaft mining online with his PIDD over the last couple of days, so he understood that the large wooden building was the ore/lift house for the mine.

Randy knew that people on foot out in the open this far from town in the middle of winter would immediately draw attention and he could see that the house would be difficult to approach without being seen. The mesa was very sparsely wooded. There was an isolated group of three pines about fifty yards from the east side of the house, but no cover at all within one hundred yards north or south of the structure. There was a long winding line of trees running from about seventy-five yards farther west of the house to the road on the north - they were probably following a stream bed or shallow gully that collected water. If the gully was deep enough, it might provide cover, but the last seventy-five yards of any approach would still be in the open.

On the other hand, Jimmy's equipment probably wasn't in the house anyway - it was probably in the mine. *After all, why travel all the way from Houston to Colorado where a friend had a mine if you weren't going to* use *that mine? Besides that, they must have wanted to run those kids out of the mine for a reason.* Randy turned slightly and focused on the ore house. *Would that be the best way to get in? I wonder if the lift is still operable. The kid said they got in through a break in one of the discharge tunnels, but surely there's a better way.*

Randy lowered the binoculars and noticed a car coming down Phantom Canyon Road from the direction of Victor. He could see it just coming around a curve in the distance beyond the ore house. He wondered if his car parked alongside the road would be a problem. He hadn't bothered to try and hide it, thinking he would be gone before anyone came by on this little-traveled road. What would they think if they saw the car and the footprints in the snow leading into the woods? *In Texas, they would probably think poacher! ... They would probably think the same thing in Colorado.* All kinds of wild – and some not so wild - game in or out of season had become a popular black market commodity as grocery store food stocks fell and prices rose during the depression. Poaching was a natural result of supply and demand and was frequently met with violence when discovered. *And here I am wearing a virtual hunter's uniform! There's no way I can make it back to the car and drive away before they get here.*

Randy used his binoculars to zoom in on the approaching car. *Well, it doesn't look like an official vehicle of any kind.* Just then the car slowed and turned into the driveway leading to the MacNamara - now presumably the Clarke – property, well north of Randy's parked car.

No longer concerned about discovery, Randy watched through his binoculars as the car made its way along the driveway through the few inches of snow that had accumulated since the drive was last plowed. The visitor pulled the car up to the front porch, got out, started to walk toward the porch steps and then suddenly turned and looked straight at Randy. *He can't possibly see me at this distance!* But Randy still felt a shiver run up his spine. He forced himself to remain steady as he studied the visitor through the binoculars and blinked twice at the icon for recording images. *Late middle aged male, good physical condition, looks like ex-military.* Randy continued to watch as the man turned, stepped up onto the porch and approached the front door.

* * * * *

Mike and Nick had been working in the lab when Alfred announced that an unfamiliar vehicle had turned into the driveway and was approaching the house. Mike went to investigate while Nick remained in the lab. By the time Mike rode up the elevator and made it to the front of the house, the visitor was just stepping up on the porch. Alfred had already thoughtfully pulled up a display on the living room monitor of those security cameras that could be brought to bear on the visitor and Mike saw that he did not recognize the man. Mike was a friendly, outgoing guy, but living out in the middle of no place made a person cautious when approached unexpectedly by strangers. The restraint had grown all the greater due to the presence of his current house guest and new business partner. So Mike ceded the honor of greeting the visitor to Alfred.

"Good afternoon, sir. How may I help you?" Alfred said using the hidden transducers on the porch.

The visitor glanced around quickly, then smiled and said, "I'm here to see Mister Clarke."

"Would you be so kind as to state your name and the purpose of your visit?"

The visitor smiled again and replied, "My name is William Ahrens and Blue sent me."

Chapter 37

Mike, Nick and Ahrens sat down in Mike's office in the Man Cave after taking a tour of the facility, both above and below ground.

Mike spoke first. "Well, Mister Ahrens, what do you think of our little cabin in the mountains?"

"Please call me 'Wil,'" Ahrens replied. "Your facility is very impressive. It is quite a bit larger and more secure than I imagined it would be. Of course, a lot of that is because of your data center business which was not included in my brief for this assignment. Your security measures are excellent for that type of operation."

Mike smiled and said, "I sense a '*but*' coming."

Ahrens returned the smile and continued. "*But* we are not dealing with hackers, thieves or vandals now. At least one of the groups that are after the Defender prototype have more resources, are more determined, and more ruthless than common criminals. If they find you, they will assault this facility and take what they want by armed force."

Ahrens paused briefly while he decided how much he should reveal to make his point. "We believe that the threats range from domestic civilians armed with no more than hand guns all the way up to international military personnel with an unknown range of weapons available. Worst case, you could be looking at an assault by foreign Special Forces. Given the potential importance of your project, it ought to be removed to a military installation and surrounded by heavily armed troops in fortified positions."

Nick broke his silence to exclaim, "If we moved to a government installation the whole world would know where we were and exactly what we were doing in no time at all!"

Ahrens's smile grew larger, "You might be right in many cases, but please believe me when I say there are some installations that would suffice."

Nick was getting angry now and said, "Where were those installations when the prototype was in a trailer sitting in a parking lot in Houston for seven years? Where was the government interest when MacEwen Systems, Inc. couldn't get a R&D contract for the project?"

Frowning now, Ahrens answered, "To be fair, Mister MacEwen, there *was* government interest even as far back as when you were championing the Defender concept at GenArm. However, there also was considerable skepticism regarding your chances of success. On top of that, there were significant financial and political obstacles to government involvement that prevented any action beyond some fairly ineffectual attempts to monitor your progress."

Nick couldn't believe what he was hearing! "I was being *spied* on?"

Ahrens couldn't help from grinning. "Yes, but in an ineffectual way." Turning serious again, Ahrens added, "There are only a few people in the government who know about the project. We're still not sure why you took off with the prototype, but we presume it is because you were making significant progress and didn't want to leave it behind when you lost your job."

Ignoring the not-so-subtle invitation to talk about his progress with the prototype, Nick asked, "So you know I was fired."

"Yes, and we know the real reason why. Our spying, as you call it, was not entirely ineffectual. As I believe Blue told you, I have been on another assignment, so I don't know all of the details."

Nick was silent again as he pondered all of these sudden revelations. Then he said with some heat, "I will fight any attempt by the government to claim eminent domain. I have worked for years to get support for this project with no success. I have forfeited any possibility of having a personal life while I worked nights and weekends on the prototype. Now that we are getting some idea of what the prototype can do, I'm not convinced that the government is the best steward of those capabilities. In fact, I'm next to certain that the government is not capable of properly regulating its use. After all, the various branches and agencies don't even follow their own laws, rules and regulations."

Nick became even more heated. "In fact, sometimes I think that the government is the largest organized crime family in America! ... And when it comes to security," Nick rolled his eyes, "tell a politician a secret and it will be on every news stream within minutes. There are congressmen and women on the Senate and House Select Committees on Intelligence who would never be able to work for a defense contractor because they would be *denied a security clearance!*"

Wow, thought Ahrens, *where did that tirade come from? Last I heard, the Defender prototype was supposed to be some kind of electromagnetic shield against energy weapons. What are these capabilities that the government can't be trusted to control?*

Nick realized that he had gone too far, so he quickly calmed down and changed the subject. "Do you really think that they'll find us here? Blue said that all they knew was a gold mine in Colorado. There are a lot of gold mines in Colorado."

Ahrens replied, "I think that it is possible that at least one of the groups has already found you."

"*What?*" Mike and Nick exclaimed in unison.

"I noticed a flash of light coming from the woods to the east of your house when I got out of the car. It looked to me like the sun reflecting off of binoculars. I suppose it could be a hunter using a rifle with a scope, but isn't the game mostly at lower altitudes at this time of year?"

Reluctantly, Mike agreed.

"If one of the groups has found you," Ahrens went on, "then the other groups will quickly find out. We have ample circumstantial evidence that information is regularly leaked between the interested parties."

"Oh, that's just peachy keen!" Nick opined. "So what do we do now? Try and run?"

"No," Ahrens said. "This facility and its location provide some tactical advantages that you would be hard pressed to find elsewhere. But we do need more people to make it secure. There's too much ground to cover and any one of these groups can strike with a dozen or more operatives."

"I don't want outsiders involved in this," said Nick. "There is too much at stake. I am stretched to my limit just trying to trust Red, White, and Blue ... and you."

Mike chimed in with a suggestion, "How about the IMC, Nick? They would be more than willing to help and they already know that it's important to maintain secrecy."

Ahrens interrupted, "What is the IMC?"

Mike replied with a brief description of the Independent Miners Club.

Ahrens replied, "I don't think you should involve amateurs in this. You'd be better off with no help at all."

"Don't discount them," Mike advised with a smile. "Many of them are ex-military and all of them have been hunters since they were kids. Between their own weapons and mine, we can arm them – and I don't mean with hunting rifles."

Ahrens still looked reluctant, but Mike pressed on. "I'll have them come over tomorrow and you can check them out. Is your bag in the car? I can show you to your room."

"No, my bags are in my hotel room over in Cripple Creek. I don't want to impose. I've got government rates after all. I might even try my luck at the tables." *I need to call Billingsly from a place that I know isn't bugged. I don't know Alfred's full capabilities, but I suspect they are formidable and omnipresent within this facility.*

Mike and Nick accompanied Ahrens back up to the front door to see him off. Ahrens stepped out onto the porch a ways, then as he turned around to say that he would return in the morning he was shocked to see that both men had followed him out onto the porch.

"Mister MacEwen! Go back inside immediately! I told you that you may already be under observation." Although they knew better than to do so, all three automatically glanced in the direction of the woods to the east of the house.

Recovering quickly, Nick dove back through the front door with Mike close on his heels. Ahrens collected himself, stepped down off of the porch, returned to his rental car and drove away toward Victor and Cripple Creek.

* * * * *

Randy watched the visitor get back in his car and drive towards Victor. There was no clue as to the identity of the visitor. He could have been an insurance salesman for all Randy knew. But there was no doubt in Randy's mind about the identity of one of the two men that came out on the porch to see the visitor off. The porch was in the shade, so it was hard to see details, and the men returned inside quickly, but he was confident that one of them was Nick MacEwen. He assumed that the other, taller person was Michael Clarke. The binoculars had recorded a video of the scene and he would examine it frame by frame later to verify that it was, in fact, MacEwen. But right now he wanted to get a better look at the ore house.

After traipsing back through the snow to his rental car, Randy drove north to a point just past the line of trees that ran from the west side of the house up to the road and beyond. He parked the car on the side of the road at a point where the trees were between him and the house, got out, and looked at the lay of the land. The trees were, in fact, following a gully that was currently lined with snow. It probably became a fair sized creek in the spring. The ore house was back to his left on the other side of the road. He would have to be careful in order to remain hidden from the ranch house.

After about thirty minutes, Randy was convinced that this was no ordinary ore house. He had moved to put the ore house between him and the ranch house and looked for security cameras before crossing the road for a closer inspection. Once there, he determined that the walls were not actually old wood slats but rather some kind of plastic material made to look like old wood. He couldn't see through cracks between slats like he thought he would be able to do. *Why would anyone build an artificial dilapidated looking building?* Moving carefully, he also determined that this ore house was completely enclosed, unlike most ore houses he'd seen near Victor that were open on the side where the ore car tracks ran. By peeking around the corner of the building he could see a fairly large door on the side facing the ranch house, but it was closed and there were no footprints in the snow leading up to it. He couldn't find out if it was locked without exposing himself to being seen from the ranch house. It seemed likely that the building was hiding something, but what? Based on Jimmy's description, the prototype wouldn't need a building anywhere near this size. But if this isn't really a lift house, how do they get into the mine?

His limited inspection of the ore house raised more questions than it answered. Randy returned to the rental car and drove back to Cripple Creek pondering his options. Later that afternoon he called his wife at Get'em?-Got'em!-Repo and Bounty Hunters to set his crew in motion. Then he called Jimmy Barton and brought him up to date.

* * * * *

Nick asked, "So, Alfred, you monitored Ahrens the whole time he was here, pulse, body language, respiration rate, thermal image, voice stress, and eye movements. What's the verdict?"

"Mister Ahrens appears to be a security expert, as advertised. He asked all of the right questions during the facility tour and made a few pertinent suggestions for repositioning some of our sensors. But he is also more than that. For instance, he has been trained in techniques to reduce the effectiveness of biometric analysis methods. There are even some indications that surgery may have been involved. This is highly unusual and indicates some involvement in clandestine operations. These might be related to his Special Operations or DIA activities, which Blue failed to mention but are in the backup copies of the Pentagon personnel files on our server farm. Regardless of his training or surgical enhancements, I can affirm with a high percentage of certainty that he believes that everything he told you was the truth. I can also affirm with one hundred percent certainty that he was deliberately withholding important information."

From Nick's PIDD-pocket, Fred added, "All in all, that's a pretty high level of veracity for a Government Wonk."

"Perhaps," Alfred continued. "Although he comes here at the command of the mysterious Blue, whom we assume is part of the government, the last entry in Ahrens personnel records is over four years old. So it is not clear whether or not Mister Ahrens is, in fact, a 'Government Wonk' as you suggest."

Mike had only been listening half-heartedly. He had been thinking. When Alfred concluded his report Mike asked, "Nick, why do we need Ahrens or anyone else to protect us? Why don't we just form an impenetrable globe around the whole facility and be done with it?"

Nick replied, "Until we finish installing the new geothermal steam turbine generators, I don't think we've got enough power available to form a globe that big. Remember, the electricity has to be generated inside the globe. We would also need more hole generators, one for each turbine, to provide the heat to make the steam and at least one more to give us air to breathe. Then there's other little details like water and sewage disposal that either have to be handled inside the globe somehow or externally using more hole generators that we don't have yet."

Mike frowned and said, "You sure do know how to ruin an elegant solution Nick."

Nick smiled and said "But, what you just described is exactly what I had hoped to make possible when I started the Defender project in my garage twelve years ago, and we're almost there. We just need to get those steam turbine generators in and make a bunch more hole generators."

"You mean 'Whatever' generators," Mike said, getting in the last word.

* * * * *

As soon as he returned to his hotel room, Ahrens called Vance Billingsly at the GenArm headquarters.

Wil had checked in to the hotel several days ago when his ITC source told him that Randy Miller was in Cripple Creek. Since then, he had been observing Blood Hound from a distance until he got the call from Blue with new orders directing him to make contact with MacEwen.

"Mister Billingsly's office ..."

"Hi, Indra, this is Wil. Is he available for a short report?"

"I believe so. Wait one."

"Hello, Wil. Where are you now?"

"I'm in Cripple Creek, Colorado, Mister Billingsly. MacEwen is here and so is Randy Miller."

"MacEwen is in Cripple Creek, Colorado?"

"Well, MacEwen is actually southeast of Cripple Creek, just outside of Victor, but the important part is that I'm in."

"Explain 'in.'"

"Yes, sir, I tracked down his buddy, Clarke, and managed to occupy a bar stool next to him one evening. I gave him a line about how I was an out of work security expert looking for a job with the casinos but none of them were hiring. After a few beers, I was the new security chief for MacEwen's whole operation."

"Excellent. Have you actually seen MacEwen?"

"Yes, sir, I met with both of them today at their facility."

"Did you see the prototype?"

"Yes, sir, it's here all right."

"Outstanding! Can you tell if he's made any progress?"

"Not really, though it does look different from the drawings I saw at ITC. As a minimum, the power supply is a lot bigger. So he must be doing something with it."

"Okay. Now you said that Miller is in the area as well?"

"Yes, sir, I've observed him from a distance."

"Do you think he has also located Clarke and MacEwen?"

"No, sir, I don't think he has. He's been spending all of his time waving a photograph of MacEwen in people's faces in Cripple Creek. I verified today that MacEwen has never been in Cripple Creek, so Blood Hound is barking up the wrong tree. He'll probably move on pretty soon."

"Don't leave MacEwen to follow Miller. Do exactly what they hired you to do - protect the prototype and keep MacEwen safe and happy so that he can do his best work. Should I send some GenArm security personnel out there somewhere to stand by just in case?"

"No, sir, I don't think that's necessary at this point. Clarke has got a real nice hidey-hole out here. I think Miller will wander off and I'll be in a perfect position to keep you up to date on MacEwen's progress."

"Excellent. Keep up the good work and let me know if you need anything."

* * * * *

The next day, Colonel Shi finally had the information he had sought for months. Now he knew where MacEwen was holed up. His ITC source reported that MacEwen had been positively identified in Victor, Colorado. Shi and his team had been searching the gold fields between Pueblo and Grand Junction. But seven months ago MacEwen must have met an accomplice in the San Isabel National Forest, unloaded the prototype into another vehicle and doubled back toward the Pikes Peak region while the empty trailer went on to Las Vegas driven by the same, or perhaps another, accomplice. Unexpectedly good field craft for a civilian. Did he know that there was a tracker on the trailer? Did he intentionally lead us on an empty trailer chase across the southwest United States? Both seem more than likely in retrospect. The theft of the prototype must have been carefully planned in advance. Shi wondered just how large an organization MacEwen had helping him, and how well they might be armed.

Shi wanted to marshal overwhelming force before attempting an assault. If he had the time to reconnoiter the target and plan the operation, he might find a way to gain an advantage over any defenders that might be present. But there was very little time. He might have to assault a facility he knew nothing about; over ground he had not seen, against an unknown number of defenders, all of which was anathema to a belt-and-suspenders-risk-adverse-paranoid.

It was now a race to the prize between his professionals and a gang of American repossession and bounty hunter thugs. Ordinarily, that would be no challenge at all - but in this case, the thugs had a big head start. Their leader was already on site and his team was mobilizing. Shi had the MSS operators from the Houston Consulate with him. They could reach the target in a few hours, but they only numbered five operatives, including him.

The only consulates he could draw on for reinforcements were in Los Angeles and San Francisco. The MSS operators from those consulates would have to bring their own weapons, so they would have to drive to the target. Shi checked his PIDD and determined that San Francisco was a nineteen hour drive and Los Angeles was a fifteen hour drive to the target. The thugs in Houston were only about eleven hours away. Even if the thugs had waited for morning before leaving Houston, they would still beat his earliest reinforcements to the target by four hours and Shi would not be up to full strength until four hours after that.

All he could do was to set everyone in motion towards the target and play it by ear. This would be a meeting engagement between three opponents, possibly more if GenArm or the American government got wind of it. Strategy was out the window. Brute force would have to win the day. His career – correction, his life – would depend on the outcome.

Shi had to appeal to Beijing in order to get the reinforcements committed to him. He fumed at the time wasted trying to convince his counterparts in Los Angeles and San Francisco that he remained in charge of the Defender operation and still had the right to call on their resources. But now everyone was on the road, including his team in Colorado. He would be first on the scene. The MSS teams from the West Coast were under orders to drive straight through the night.

They were also ordered to bring all of the weapons at their disposal with them since there was no way to know in advance what they might need. Colonel Shi was a better-safe-than-sorry-belt-and-suspenders-risk-adverse-paranoid.

PART 3 – THE CRISES
Chapter 38

Wil Ahrens showed up at seven o'clock the next morning thinking that he would be waking everyone up, but Alfred directed him down to the cafeteria where the IMC volunteers were just finishing breakfast.

Mike greeted him with, "I wasn't sure exactly when you would get here this morning, so I told everyone to sleep in before coming here for breakfast."

Wil looked around the room at the assemblage sitting at the tables and asked, "Where did these people come from? I didn't see any cars parked outside."

"They came here through the mine tunnels. Come on, sit down and eat. I'll start the meeting in a few minutes."

Wil self-consciously ate the proffered breakfast as quickly as possible while the roomful of men and, he noticed, a few women silently watched. Their expressions clearly indicated that they considered him an outsider, a person untrustworthy until proven otherwise. Wil estimated the group at between twenty to thirty people, ranging in age from the late teens up to the fifties, or even sixties in a few cases. The men all looked lean and hard. Come to think of it, so did the women.

While Wil was eating, Mike wheeled the holographic display projector up to the front of the room. As soon as Wil swallowed his last bite of scrambled eggs and took a sip of coffee, Mike addressed the audience. There was a momentary clatter as they scooted their chairs around to face front.

"I can't tell you all how much Nick and I appreciate your coming here this morning to hear our request for help. As I said in my PIDD-cast last night, we are expecting some people to try and steal some equipment from us ... valuable equipment that Nick has developed over a period of many years ... the very equipment that has allowed us to pinpoint new veins of ore in all of our mines. If they come on our property, they will be guilty of trespassing because it is posted. If they enter our facility, they will be guilty of breaking and entering because we will not open our doors to them. If they try to take the equipment, they will be guilty of theft because they have no legal claim on Nick's equipment."

What was that part about pinpointing veins of ore? Wil thought. *What does that have to do with a defensive shield?*

"Now, the county sheriff could probably schedule a patrol car to come down our road once or twice a day," Mike waited for the laughter to die down before continuing, "but we really don't want to attract any undue attention."

"I want you to understand that we're not talking about forming a Neighborhood Watch committee either" - more laughter. "We're talking about breaking out our 'collectors' weapons and being ready to use them. It will all be legal - I had a chat with the sheriff last night, and he agreed to deputize all of you who volunteer. His willingness to do so has absolutely nothing to do with my generous support for him in the last election" - laughter again - "... or my promise to support him again in the next election" - even more laughter.

Mike's smile disappeared. "Seriously though, our understanding is that the people who are after the equipment play pretty rough. We are talking about the real possibility that people are going to die. Nobody in this room, least of all me, will hold it against anyone who does not want to be involved in this. I won't take up anymore of your time if you feel like this is not something you want to do – go with my thanks for hearing me out. But you need to know that this is important. Finding some gold ore to support our families is very important, but this equipment is capable of much, much more - some very good things and some very bad things. So much more that it must not fall into the wrong hands. It is important to our country ... it is important to all of humanity ... it is important enough to die for."

No one moved.

What is going on here?

"If you volunteer for this duty, you will be under the command of Lt. Colonel William Ahrens, United States Marine Corps, retired, a decorated combat veteran trained in Special Operations," Mike said, pointing at Wil. "You will comport yourselves as if under military discipline, which many of you are familiar with from previous experience."

How did he know my background? Blue wouldn't have told them any of that. I think Billingsly is underestimating these people ... Besides, I don't remember agreeing to command anything, let alone a group of volunteers. Although that might be a good idea given what I found out from my ITC source last night.

"I ask that anyone who is uncomfortable with any of this to go on about your business now and no one will think any less of you."

No one moved.

After waiting long enough to make sure that no one had second thoughts, Mike turned on the display and said, "Alfred, please display the current security status of the entire facility."

A translucent three-dimensional image showing the interior of the house, Man Cave, and mine appeared in the air above the projector. Wil had been impressed by the display the previous day. Looking around the cafeteria, he could tell that most, if not all, of the others had not seen it before.

"Now, Nick and I want to point out some of the advantages we will have over any intruders." Mike took about twenty minutes to go through an explanation and demonstration of the capabilities of his security system. Then he pointed at the maze of mine tunnels portrayed by the hologram and added, "Most of you are very familiar with the layout of the mines. That will not be the case for the intruders. With this system, we should be able to detect them and react appropriately well before they get close. Are there any questions?"

A large, distinguished looking man, whose close-cropped black hair was starting to show white at his temples stood up.

He looks like he's in really good shape for his age, Wil thought, smiling. *He might even be older than me!*

Mike asked, "Do you have a question, Evan?"

Evan said, "It seems that you are assuming that the intruders will come at us through the mine tunnels. What if they come right through your front door?"

Wil nodded. *Good question old man. Maybe these miners aren't* all *rank amateurs.*

"We think that their most likely approach will be through the mine tunnels because they will believe that they can get close to us without being seen that way. Not many people would expect a played out mine to be equipped with the kind of intrusion detection that we have here. But there is a possibility that they could try a surface attack. We have some sensors on the surface around the house itself. They cover a large area because their line of sight is essentially unrestricted - there's no good cover within sixty to seventy yards of the house. That's why we think that a surface attack is less likely, but that doesn't mean they won't try it."

Mike paused for a moment and then said, "I think this would be a good time for Nick to take over the presentation. He has a better handle on the strategic aspects of our defense."

Nick the engineer is a strategic expert now? This ought to be good! Wil thought.

Nick stood and went to the front of the group. "Your question really goes right to the heart of our defense, Evan. That was very insightful." Evan smiled slightly as he sat back down.

"Mike and I felt that we should have a broad plan for what we are trying to accomplish at the strategic level. Our immediate goal is to protect the equipment. Our secondary goal is to discourage these people from a repeat performance. Our tertiary goal is to avoid any public notice. The tactics that will produce these outcomes are up to Colonel Ahrens, but we have some suggestions that we believe support our strategic goals.

"Even if they come through the mines, there are a lot of different routes that they could take depending on where they enter the tunnel system. And as Evan pointed out, they could come at us on the surface. The reality is that we don't know for sure which way they might come and we don't even have an opinion as to how many of them there will be."

Nick let that revelation sink in a moment before continuing, "Since we don't know for sure where they are going to attack, *and* we may be seriously outnumbered, *and* there may be multiple simultaneous assaults, we recommend conducting a flexible perimeter defense centered on the equipment itself instead of setting up fixed defenses on the most probable approaches.

"That way, we will have the advantage of interior lines. It will be easier for us to move people to where they are needed than it will be for our attackers to change their point of attack. Normally, the advantage of interior lines increases as the defended area shrinks. However, we will have a kind of interior-lines-on-steroids that will give us the maximum advantage right from the start, when the ostensibly defended area is still quite large. We will be able to move people very quickly to meet the attackers wherever they are as soon as we can detect them. That brings us full circle to Mike's security systems," Nick said while gesturing toward the holographic display.

Interesting ... Maybe he does know what he's talking about.

A woman who appeared to be in her twenties spoke up. "Just what is this 'interior-lines-on-steroids' you're talking about?"

That's another excellent question.

"Well, I'd rather not go into details right now. It would be better to keep it under our hat if we don't have to use it."

The group was silent for a moment, and then Evan rose again. "Nick, we are all extremely grateful for what you have done for us and we trust you implicitly. Mike says that people may die defending your equipment. He says it's important enough to die for. We trust you enough to do just that if it becomes necessary."

Evan turned around slowly, looking each member of the assembled group in the eye as they solemnly nodded their assent. Then he looked Nick in the eye and asked, "So why don't *you* trust *us*?"

Nick looked uncomfortable. He furtively glanced over at Ahrens and frowned. Then he looked back at Evan and said, "Alfred, please run the recording of the first human transit. Show the laboratory side first, and then show the cavern side."

"I can split the display and show both sides at once if you wish, sir," Alfred replied.

"That'll be great," Nick said as he sat down to watch. As soon as the vid started he bent forward, put his head in his hands and muttered, "I forgot about the bagpipe and outfit."

Nick started to rise as soon as his holographic image had completed its short two-way journey, but several people in the group simultaneously called out for it to be run again.

Mercifully, no one called for another viewing after five repeats. Nick slowly rose up blushing, apparently expecting a razzing over his peculiar behavior in the vid.

He was greeted with silence instead. Some people just sat, staring open-mouthed at the empty space above the projector. Others were slowly shaking their heads, as if denying what they had just seen. Quite a few were frozen leaning forward in their chairs, seemingly deep in thought.

After a moment, Evan quietly asked, "Was that some sort of a special effect or computer-generated video or something like that?"

"No, Evan. That was an unedited recording of the equipment in action. The equipment can create a sort of junction between two different places. We can move people and equipment between widely separated points instantaneously."

Unbelievable, thought Wil. *This was already a high stakes game, but the pot just got incredibly bigger! What am I supposed to do now? I guess the first step is still the same as it was before – try to keep this thing safe and secret. It's nice when your instructions are compatible with your instincts.* He looked around the room at the people still recovering from the shock of what they had just witnessed. *We don't have enough time to bring in outside talent. I guess that means* I will *be a commander of volunteers.*

Evan asked, "So, it's a transporter, like in that old Sci-Fi vid series?"

"Yes, sort of like that. However, we are *not* disassembling people and then putting them back together somewhere else." Nick smiled. "We're, uh, ... putting two places together ... so they're a step away ... and you just walk there," Nick said, gesturing as he struggled to describe the result without getting into technical details that his audience would not understand and weren't sufficient to completely explain the phenomenon anyway.

Evan then asked, "What's the range?"

"We're still testing that," Nick hedged, "but it is way more than enough to cover the area that includes all of our mines."

"That's got to be more than three miles at the longest point!"

"Yes, Evan" said Nick with a weak smile, "it's more than three miles."

Evan looked thoughtful and then said, "Nick, we're with you, but on one condition."

"What's that Evan?"

"When the balloon goes up, you have to dress in your full regalia and play the bagpipe."

"You've got to be kidding!"

"I'm not kidding. The Scots knew what they were doing with those bagpipes. That's still one of the most thrilling, or most dreaded, sounds on a battlefield, depending on whether you're following it or it's coming at you." That elicited shouts and applause, mixed in with some laughter, from the group.

Once the clamor settled down, Evan looked over at Ahrens and added, "If that meets with the Colonel's approval."

Ahrens chuckled and replied, "Absolutely!" Then his countenance became serious and he added, "Actually, it has been well documented that the sound of bagpipes produces strong psychological reactions of the sort that Evan mentioned. It could make a difference in our favor. At a minimum, it should confuse the attackers."

Mike spoke up, "We need to press on. Colonel Ahrens thinks that it's possible that our location has already been determined by one of the groups that are after the equipment. I think we've covered everything in our presentation. I'm going to turn you over to Colonel Ahrens now. I'm sure he'll want to find out more about your experience and skill levels."

Turning to face Wil, Mike said, "Colonel, they're all yours. The gun vault is open if you want the group to do some target practice. You think we may already be under observation, so you can set up in one of the mine tunnels on Level One if you wish. Lunch will be here in the cafeteria at noon, so maybe we can get the sheriff to deputize everyone over a PIDD then. Let me know if you need anything else."

Wil stood up quickly and addressed the group. "I received some information just last night that defines the nature of our activities today. The bad news is that I have confirmation that the group Mike just mentioned has a crew currently en route and could be ready to assault the facility by late tonight or early tomorrow morning. The good news is that this group is comprised of lightly armed civilians, although some of those civilians may be ex-military. We're not sure of the timing, but we may have less than twelve hours to prepare. Let's head for Mike's gun vault to sort out our weapons and organization."

As the group got up and started talking excitedly to each other, Evan walked across the room and came to attention in front of Wil. "Sir, Command Sergeant Major Evan Baker, United States Army, Retired." Old habits die hard, and Evan had to restrain his impulse to salute. He stuck out his hand instead, and Ahrens shook it - after all, neither one of them was in uniform - they were just two old soldiers getting ready to "Play It Again, Sam."

"Ah-ha," Wil replied. "Watching you in the meeting, I thought you might be a senior NCO or Warrant Officer. The others were showing you *way* too much respect for you to be a commissioned officer!"

They laughed and walked out of the cafeteria together. Wil starting pumping Evan about the other members of the group as they followed them towards Mike's gun vault.

* * * * *

Randy spent the morning observing the MacNamara property. Absolutely nothing moved and nothing happened - nothing above ground, at least. The visitor's car from the day before was parked in front when Randy got there that morning, and it was still there when he left. It would be better if the visitor was not there when the repo crew moved in, but one more person wouldn't change the outcome.

In any case, his day hadn't been wasted. It gave him time to examine the property from every angle and to check out the entrance to the mine tunnels that the kids in Cripple Creek used. Most of all, it gave him time to think.

Based on the kid's story, Randy was convinced that the tunnels had to be monitored with some kind of an intrusion detection system. He was also next to certain that Jimmy's stolen equipment was located somewhere within those tunnels. His thoughts kept coming back to the ore building. *Why is it a fake? Why is it enclosed? What is it hiding? Could it be the shortest route to the equipment? Is the lift still operational?* With that last question in mind, Randy had ordered his crew to bring rappelling equipment with them.

Randy made up his mind by noon and headed back to the hotel to wait for his crew - five men traveling in a crew van. Jimmy would probably throw a fit at the cost and insist that it was overkill when there were just MacEwen and his buddy Clarke to deal with, but Randy didn't want any slip ups on this job.

The crew got in late that evening and waited in the hotel lobby while he came down and used his PIDD to check them into their rooms. They had eaten on the way, so he told them to hit the sack and be up and ready to go at four in the morning. He wanted to be in position at the MacNamara property well before sunrise.

Chapter 39

After lunch and the deputizing ceremony, Wil was discussing his preliminary evaluation of the volunteers with Mike and Nick in their laboratory when Patti and Lady simultaneously woke up from what seemed to be a sound sleep, jumped up and galloped out of the lab toward the elevator. The men barely took notice.

About fifteen minutes later, the Labradors returned flanking Gail.

"How do they do that?" Nick asked. "How do they know she's coming?"

"Beats me," Mike answered. "We're underground in a shielded facility and yet they know she's coming before she's even pulled into the drive." Mike smiled and greeted her, "Hi, Gail!"

"What's going on around here? I had to convince Evan Baker that it was all right to pass me through a cordon of armed guards." Gail looked at Ahrens, then back at Nick and arched a questioning eyebrow.

Nick introduced Gail to Colonel Ahrens and quickly brought her up to date on the anticipated assaults.

Gail listened to Nick's summary and then asked, "This is unbelievable. What makes you think we can trust 'Colonel Ahrens' if that's his real name? Where did he come from? He's certainly not from around here."

Nick threw a panicked look Mike's way and replied, "Well, it's kind of a long story ..."

"The 'long story' line is getting pretty old."

"Yes ... well ... Colonel Ahrens was sent here by Blue, and we think Blue's okay, so ..." Nick trailed off, wilting under Gail's gaze.

Wil came to Nick's aid and interjected, "Ma'am, I'm from the Defense Intelligence Agency," as he produced a leather-framed photo identification card. "Nick is correct when he says it's a long story, one which none of us has the time to relate at the moment. The pertinent point is that I represent a portion of the United States Government that has followed his work for some years and is currently committed to preventing any harm from befalling either him or his equipment. And please call me Wil."

"Forgive me for being blunt," Gail replied, "but when I hear anyone from the government say 'I'm here to help,' my immediate impulse is to bolt the door and shutter the windows."

Wil smiled and replied, "I completely understand. And in this particular case, it *is* better to bolt the door and shutter the windows against the people who are after Nick and his equipment."

"They're after Nick personally, as well as the equipment?"

"Well, we are aware of two different groups. One of them, the one that may be here as early as tonight, is probably only after the equipment. They are mercenaries hired by Nick's former employer who claims ownership of the equipment."

Nick interjected, "Which is not the case! I've had time to think about this. Part of the merger agreement specified that the Defender prototype and other physical and intellectual properties of MacEwen Systems were excluded from the merger with ITC, and further specified that I was allowed to continue my research. Any expenses incurred by ITC in support of my research were to be repaid with interest in the event the research led to a revenue-producing product. My understanding from the vice president and chief financial officer of ITC is that there are no such expenses showing on their books."

Wil asked, "Do you have a copy of this merger agreement?"

Interesting, Nick thought. *He didn't bat an eye at my inference that ITC was cooking their books.*

Nick frowned, "No, I'm pretty sure I had a copy in my filing cabinet at ITC, but I didn't think to grab any papers before I drove off with the prototype."

Now it was Wil's turn to frown, "Filing cabinet? Papers? Don't you mean PIDD files?"

Nick laughed, "You don't know Jimmy Barton! He was a severe technophobe."

"How does a technophobe run a company that produces energy weapons?"

"You obviously don't have a proper education in business management," Nick intoned in a mock scolding voice. "The concept of beginning in the mailroom and working your way up to the top of the corporation, learning each part of the operation as you go, is completely passé. The top Business School Profs call those sorts of people 'content-oriented managers' and make fun of them. They insist that the proper way to run a company has nothing to do with having knowledge of the company's actual operations. You just need to go to their schools, where they will teach you the magic formulas you need to run any company by the numbers. It also makes it so much easier for you to layoff the people who are actually producing the goods or services your company provides - after all, you have no clue what those people are doing other than running up your payroll expenses."

Gail spoke up, "We're off the subject here. If this group is only after the equipment, which group is after Nick?"

Wil hesitated. "We don't know for absolute certain that there is another group, but I think there is. They were spotted twice during the last leg of the 'Great Trailer Chase,' and it was the same two Asian men both times."

Mike and Nick exchanged quick glances. Neither of them knew exactly what happened to the trailer after it left Victor. Mike asked, "Could it have been a coincidence?"

"No, that is extremely unlikely. The two different times they were seen were in Las Vegas and in Mexicali, basically the start and finish lines of the last leg of the chase."

Wil had noticed the two glance at each other and said, "You'll have to tell me how you pulled that off sometime."

Mike and Nick exchanged worried looks, and Mike said, "I thought you were on another assignment and didn't know any details."

"I *was* on another assignment. But the 'Great Trailer Chase' was the talk of the office for quite a while," Wil smoothly lied. "I saw photos of the two Asians taken at the airport in Las Vegas and again at the used car lot in Mexicali. There is no way that it can be a coincidence.

"The problem," Wil went on, "is that we ran the photos and determined that both men were minor functionaries at Chinese Consulates, one in Houston and the other in Los Angeles. So, that means that the Chinese Ministry of State Security is not only aware of, but has taken some interest in, the Defender prototype. The MSS is quite capable of putting together an assault team, only they wouldn't be satisfied with just the equipment - they would be even more interested in snatching the person who created the equipment.

"This second group is the one that I worry about the most. We have a pretty good handle on what the first group is doing, as evidenced by the information I received last night on their movements, but we know relatively nothing about the Chinese."

Nick broke the silence that ensued after Wil's last statement. "Right now we'd better finish getting ready for the first group."

Nick turned to face Gail. "You need to go back to your clinic until this is over."

Gail replied, "No way, Nick! If there's any bloodshed here, you will need on-the-spot medical attention. I'm staying right here."

"It's too dangerous, Gail. You heard what Wil said. I don't want you to get hurt."

"Oh, *just listen to the man*! Some kind of Chinese commandos are after his hide and he doesn't want me to get hurt! Nick, maybe you don't care about yourself, but those gun-toting neighbors of yours are all my patients. I won't be able to do anything for them if I'm safe at my clinic in town. I can do a lot more for them if I'm here when they get hurt. I just might be able to save some lives!"

Defeated, Nick agreed and Gail went to make a run to her clinic to pick up medical supplies.

* * * * *

Colonel Shi and the Houston consulate MSS team arrived north of the MacNamara property in late afternoon. They had rented two Jeeps in Pueblo when they first arrived in Colorado, and now drove them off the road into some trees well north of the ranch house. The men were only lightly armed with some pistols and a couple of hunting rifles they had purchased in Pueblo using fake ID's - the Los Angeles and San Francisco teams would be bringing the heavy artillery. He requested and received information from each team in route regarding the weapons and equipment they were bringing so that he could start making some plans.

Shi detached the scope off of one of the rifles, instructed his agents to keep their eyes open, and exited the lead Jeep. Using the hood of the vehicle to steady himself, he surveyed the area with the scope. He was looking at the lay of the land for avenues of approach, but more than that, he was looking for Blood Hound. He was sure that Miller had to be somewhere in the vicinity, watching and waiting for his crew to arrive from Houston. Shi saw a car and a Snow Cat parked in front of the ranch house, but after more than thirty minutes of searching and not seeing anyone, Shi decided to drive back to a fork in the road they had passed when they drove down from Victor. The left branch led to their present position. The right branch was a single lane dirt road that looked like it might pass west of the ranch house. He might be able to see better from there.

The right branch did indeed follow a wide shallow valley to the southwest, passing about five hundred yards to the west of the ranch house. There was essentially no cover anywhere near, but it looked like the road was hidden from the ranch house by the brow of the mesa and some intervening trees between there and the house.

Shi got out of the Jeep again and used the scope to check for Miller once more, and then survey the area. When he looked up to the east he could only see the roof of the ranch house, which meant only someone on the roof of the house could see his team on the road. All things considered, Shi thought this was probably the best route for attacking the house. It was a long way uphill through the snow, but the attackers would not be seen until they passed through the copse of trees on the mesa. It was difficult to judge the size of the open area between the trees and the house from his current angle, but he estimated somewhere between fifty or sixty yards. They would be in the open for hundreds of yards if they took any of the other approaches.

He lowered the scope and was about to get back into the vehicle when an irregular pattern of shadows on the snow not too far from the Jeep captured his attention. As he focused in on the area he realized that he was looking at fresh footprints in the snow. He swept the area again with his scope to make sure no one was in sight, and then went to take a better look.

The footprints belonged to one person wearing either hunting or work boots of some kind. There were two sets of tracks, one coming down from the northwest and the other returning back from the southeast. Shi followed the tracks southeast to an outcropping of rocks in the side of the mesa. Beneath the outcropping, there was a large hole in the rocky ground. Next to the hole was a well-weathered warning sign. "DANGER - ABANDONED MINE DISCHARGE TUNNEL – DO NOT ENTER!" was overlaid on a skull and crossbones symbol. *This may be a back door into the gold mine. Someone else has been here recently – since the last snow. Was it Miller? There's just one set of footprints, so if it was Miller, he was just reconnoitering ... Hopefully, we can catch MacEwen and his friend asleep in their beds and make them lead us to the prototype. But it would be safer to use a two-pronged approach - the west side of the house up there and the tunnel system down here - for no other reason than blocking a potential bolt hole in the unlikely event they happened to be in the mine at that hour. But what if* Blood Hound's *people are planning to use this mine entrance?* Shi turned around and looked west at the top of the rise of the other side of the valley. *Maybe I'll just put one team up there to be a surprise welcoming committee for Miller.*

* * * * *

That evening Command Sergeant Major of Volunteers Evan Baker, acting Platoon Sergeant of the Volunteer Platoon, and Deputy Sheriff of Teller County, Colorado, entered the lab looking for Lieutenant Colonel of Volunteers William Ahrens, acting Platoon Leader of the Volunteer Platoon, and Deputy Sheriff of Teller County, Colorado.

Gail Randolph had recently finished setting up her first aid station just inside the laboratory door. It was assumed any casualties would probably arrive through one of the two hole generators, and this spot was roughly equidistant to both.

Evan saw LtCol Ahrens farther back in the lab talking with Mike and Nick in front of the holographic display.

"Good evening, Miss Randolph," Evan said as he passed her.

"Good evening, Evan," Gail replied with a smile.

CSM Baker stopped behind the men and waited for an appropriate time to interrupt the conversation.

Wil had worked out a rotating schedule wherein there would always be one ready squad on duty in the cafeteria, one standby squad off duty in Mike's underground bunkroom, and two squads off duty at their own homes. Wil, Mike, and Nick were discussing the best marshalling points for the squads. The marshalling points were pre-determined areas where the squads would be sent depending on the location of an intrusion.

After a few moments, LtCol Ahrens noticed him and asked, "What is it,

218

sergeant major?"

"Well, sir, this doesn't really relate to our situation here, but I thought you gentlemen might want to know about it. My wife just called and said that the International Space Station has taken multiple meteoroid strikes and is losing its air supply. She says the news is all over the net," Evan said, lifting up the PIDD in his hand as if to show them.

Mike frowned. "There were multiple strikes? NASA keeps track of meteoroids and space junk - I do some contract programming work for them periodically and I know that's one of their functions - and I know that the ISS can maneuver out of the way if necessary."

"I don't know exactly how it happened," Evan replied, "but the talking heads say that the station is losing pressure fast and that there are no launch vehicles available that can get there before the astronauts run out of air."

Nick's frown deepened as he looked over at Mike. Mike said, "Alfred, find news stream coverage of the International Space Station emergency and put it on the wall display."

Gail joined the group as all five of them watched the news stream on the indicated display for almost ten minutes. When the information became repetitive, Nick shook his head, "A one in a million chance, an unusually large number of meteoroids moving faster than normal coming out of an unexpected quadrant, expired patch kits not replaced, poor maintenance and low propellant reserves due to budget cuts, no spacecraft currently docked, the United States no longer has any orbital vehicles, the next available Russian vehicle launch was redlined at the last minute, half a dozen astronauts from different countries on board, and they'll be down to personal spacesuit oxygen within twelve hours – what a nightmare."

Nick turned to Mike and asked, "Weren't they going to design and build a special lifeboat vehicle that would stay docked to the ISS?"

"Yes, there was a lot of talk but the project never got funded as the economy worsened. I frankly expected them to abandon the ISS years ago."

Mike grimaced as he looked at Nick, who was now obviously deep in thought. After a moment, Nick called out, "Fred, what is the orbital altitude of the International Space Station?"

"Nick ..." Mike started to say.

Fred replied, "The ISS perigee is approximately two hundred and twenty-four miles and its apogee is approximately two hundred and seventy-one miles."

"When will its orbit next put it within three hundred miles of this site?"

"Nick ..." Mike tried again.

219

Fred said, "Acquiring current location ... projecting orbital path ... tomorrow morning beginning at five fifty-two AM."

Mike gaped, dumbstruck.

"And how long will it remain within three hundred miles of this site?"

Fred said, "Six minutes."

"Not much of a window ... what were you going to say, Mike?"

"I was going to say that since the ISS is in an inclined Low Earth Orbit, it would be a one in a million chance that it would come within range of us in time."

"Oh. I thought you were going to tell me I'm crazy."

"You *are* crazy. But I'm getting used to that."

"Well, maybe our one in a million chance window can trump the one in a million chance meteoroid swarm."

"But six minutes? They'll be down to their space suit oxygen by tomorrow morning. Can they move fast enough in those suits to pop out an astronaut a minute?"

"They'll have to be lined up and ready to boogie. It's not like they'll have far to go. According to the news stream they are all in the Nauka Multipurpose Laboratory Module - supposedly the newest, and apparently the least damaged, of the modules. So that's where we'll want to open the hole."

"The station is moving really fast and is very small compared to the space it is moving through. We'll need to get a pretty good fix on its exact orbital path before we can lock on to it optically."

"Is there any way we can tap into tracking data from NORAD or NASA and use that to position the far side close enough?"

"Excuse me, gentlemen," Wil interrupted. "What are you talking about?"

Mike and Nick both stopped talking and stared at Ahrens for a few seconds as if he was a particularly dull child.

Nick said, "We're talking about rescuing the ISS astronauts."

Puzzled, Wil pointed at the hole generator console. "You're going to rescue them with your equipment here?"

"Yes. Our elevator doesn't go high enough."

Wil winced slightly at the sarcasm but soldiered on, "Your equipment has that kind of range?"

"Just barely ... I'm afraid that we'll have to use both of Mike's backup diesel generators to help with the load, but it's doable."

Wil just stared. *He's apologizing because he will have to use two diesel generators worth of extra power to achieve earth orbit! I am now officially hanging onto the tail of the tiger!*

Wil mentally shook himself and focused on the current situation. "But we could be attacked at any time!"

Nick responded, "We'll have to deal with that if and when it occurs. But as long as there is a chance that we can save the astronauts we have to try."

Nick and Mike picked up where they left off, with Mike stating, "I have programing contracts with both NORAD and NASA. Both of them present pretty much impenetrable router firewalls to the outside world ... maybe we could use a hole to bypass the routers ... NORAD's internal network security is tougher than NASA's. NORAD would immediately detect and alarm the presence of a new, unknown connection on their local network. Besides, NORAD's mission is focused on the protection of the North American continent. They mostly track potentially hostile or illegal air breathing vehicle incursions, although they do track space junk that may soon deorbit over the continent. I don't think they would be tracking the ISS unless they've been tasked to do so because of the emergency.

"But," Mike continued, "if we could use a hole to get plugged into one of the NASA Mission Control local network hubs inside the Goddard Space Flight Center in Houston, I would be able to use my contractor's credentials to login as if I was physically there."

Mike always forgets and calls it a hole when he's excited.

Nick walked over to the hole generator console, sat down and turned it on. "If all you need is a hole the size of an Ethernet plug, I can reach Houston easily. For that matter, we could just park a tiny hole on top of an induction pad. But then someone might notice a little shiny spot on the pad and get suspicious, although that's very unlikely. On the other hand, we could place the hole just *underneath* the pad ..."

Mike interrupted with, "Nick! Don't worry about it. We'll just plug into a hub. I know the building and equipment room the hubs are in for the network I need to use."

"Okay, we can use the hole generator in here to get you connected and use the one in the cavern to bring the astronauts down. Once they're all down, we'll reposition that hole to send them ... where are we going to send them?"

Wil interrupted again, "Wait a minute. You're going to hack into NASA's computer network?"

Mike replied haughtily, "No. I *could* hack in through one of their routers if we had enough time, but we don't. So, I'm just going to gently plug my little computer into a handy-dandy Ethernet hub and login with completely valid credentials. That is *not* hacking."

Wil ignored Mike's histrionics and said, "I could just call White and ask her to tell NASA to relay the data to you." *I was sent here to be a security expert. Instead, I am a witness to the end of security - at least the end of physical security. Behind walls, inside vaults, underground, undersea, orbiting the earth – none of that matters anymore!*

Interesting, Mike thought. *White must be a high-ranking woman. He said ask 'her' to 'tell' NASA ...* "That would just add more data transmission delay, which in this case means more error. The flight dynamics software that NASA uses already compensates for the delay between the tracking satellites and Mission Control. Retransmitting the data here would add more delay and we'd probably miss the ISS completely. After all, it's traveling at a speed of ..." Turning toward Nick, Mike asked, "Hey, Fred, how fast is the ISS traveling?"

"It is traveling at approximately seventeen thousand five hundred miles per hour - that's roughly five miles per second."

"And remember," Mike added, "we are also moving as the earth turns. So, as you can see, this is not a trivial problem and we won't have much time to get it right. Using a hole to connect to NASA means that there is no additional transmission delay at all. For the purposes of data transfer, we will be sitting right there in Mission Control."

Nick had been listening and now looked over his shoulder at the pair. "I've been thinking, Mike. The station has to be within about three hundred miles for us to create a hole large enough that the astronauts can walk through given the power we have available. But we could find and lock onto them using a small hole like the one we are going to use for the NASA connection. That means that we could start looking for them about one thousand miles away, and only increase the hole size once they are within three hundred miles. That adds almost three minutes to our window!"

"But wouldn't they be below the horizon then?" Mike asked before he realized that it didn't matter. He immediately slapped his forehead with the palm of his hand and finished, "Never mind. Just forget I said that."

Wil, catching on, offered, "The astronauts are in a weightless environment. There is no up or down and they routinely go through circular hatches feet first. Apparently, a smaller hole gives you more range for a given power input. So, a manhole is smaller than a door."

Nick and Mike looked briefly confused, and then stunned.

Nick exclaimed, "out of the mouths of babes! No offense, Wil. You're absolutely right. That will buy us even more time. And we can position the near side so that it's horizontal. If they come through the 'manhole' feet first, they'll already be lined up properly for the direction of gravity to land on their feet so they can quickly move out of the way for the next person. Fred, look online and find out how big a 'manhole' we will need to pass an astronaut in a space suit!

"Mike," Nick asked as he turned back to the hole generator console, "which building? I'm hovering over the Goddard Space Flight Center now."

As Mike walked toward the hole generator console, Wil said, "The sergeant major and I should go check on the duty squad. Let me know if I can do anything to help," then looked at CSM Baker and nodded towards the laboratory door.

Once they were out of the lab, CSM Baker said, "I thought he said that machine only had a three mile range."

Wil thought for a moment and then smiled. "His exact words were 'it's more than three miles.'"

After walking a few more steps Evan said, "That machine in there changes everything, doesn't it, sir."

"Yes, it certainly does."

"Does it change things for the better or for the worse?"

"That's the big question. Everything depends on who controls it. It can be a portal to great power and wealth - it'll take a saint to resist the temptation. I don't know if either Nick or Mike qualify as saints, but I do know one thing."

"What's that, sir?"

"The people who want to take it away from Nick and Mike definitely *are not* saints."

"So that tells us what we have to do."

"You got it, sergeant major. We *cannot* let those other people get their hands on it, and as far as we know, an attempt could occur at any moment. You take the first duty watch after we've made the rounds, and then I'll relieve you at midnight. I want to be ready to help them with the astronauts if needed."

"And," Wil added, "I want to make sure that Nick remembers to report for duty in full regalia with bagpipe!" He chuckled, and added, "Call out to Alfred to wake me up immediately if anything important happens."

Chapter 40

Colonel Shi and the Houston MSS team spent the night in the field. Shi felt that the shallow valley to the west of the ranch house was sufficiently distant and hidden to make a safe base of operations. There had been no tire tracks on this side road when they entered the valley, and there was no sign of any habitation in the area other than the target ranch house.

He had two reasons for maintaining his position overnight. First and foremost, he wanted to make sure that Blood Hound didn't beat him to the punch. Second, he wanted to be there to brief the MSS teams as they arrived so that he could begin the assault in the pre-dawn hours when any guards would be the least alert and everyone else would most likely be asleep. He had transmitted his current position to the inbound MSS teams by PIDD. Each was to drive straight through to that position, rotating drivers while the rest of the team tried to get some sleep. The Los Angeles team should arrive first, at about one o'clock in the morning. The San Francisco team should make it by about five. According to his PIDD, local dawn would not come until seven.

Shi sent a pair of operatives to Cripple Creek to bring some food back to the Houston team. Since then they had all been getting some sleep except for Shi. He could not sleep, so he took the watch while the others rested. The night went slowly by as he sat in the Jeep looking out at the surrounding moonlit snowfield. The sky was nothing short of spectacular. Shi first came to really appreciate the appellation "Milky Way" while outside at night in the Rocky Mountains. But he began to have second thoughts about the wisdom of the overnight stay - it was extremely cold.

* * * * *

Neither Mike nor Nick could sleep. Mike was busy writing code to use the NASA tracking data stream for positioning the far side until they switched over to the optical locking mode that Mike had programmed earlier for moving targets.

Nick and Gail were in charge of figuring out how to get the astronauts out of the space station quickly. The sensor head would have to remain in place while the far side was in the vacuum of space. Once the far side was inside the space station, Mike would move the near side out of the sensor head so the astronauts could pass through, which would uncover a pressure differential of unknown magnitude. The hole would be oriented open side down in order to produce the manhole configuration suggested by Will. They decided to place it about seven feet above the cavern floor so that each astronaut could land on their feet and move quickly out of the way of the next evacuee.

But the astronauts would go from weightlessness to full earth gravity, fall seven feet, and land wearing a bulky spacesuit. Gail suggested putting a few mattresses from the bunk room on the cavern floor to help cushion the shock of landing, but was concerned that the astronauts might lose their footing and end up in a big pile.

Nick recommended that they recruit twelve of the fittest IMC volunteers to form two lines, one on each side of the mattress pile. Each pair of volunteers would grab a descending astronaut as they landed and help them clear the landing zone while the next pair moved into position to grab the next evacuee – sort of like airline crew members helping passengers at the bottom of the escape slide in an emergency.

The thought of airlines brought Nick a momentary pang of guilt for what his device would ultimately do to the transportation industry, but he didn't have time to worry about that right now.

They were shooting for a ten-minute total schedule from optical acquisition to astronauts on the ground, so the astronauts had to respond and move quickly.

Gail asked, "How are we going to get them to understand what they need to do? Should we contact someone at NASA to relay instructions?"

"Nobody would believe us. The NASA and RKA Mission Control Centers are probably getting PIDD calls from cranks all over the world with rescue schemes. I would even be willing to bet that a lot of them are based on using the flying saucer from Area 51 in Nevada, or sending the USS *Enterprise* to beam them down! We would sound like one of the latter."

"Besides, the bureaucrats would never take the risk of approving a scheme as wild as ours would appear. They would probably rather have the astronauts die because of the damage sustained by the ISS than die because they approved some harebrained, untested rescue scheme. They can't really be blamed for a freak meteoroid swarm. They *can* be blamed for making an unorthodox decision."

"So how are we going to get the astronauts to follow instructions?"

Nick smiled and answered, "Well, I'm willing to bet that at least the male members of the crew would be willing to follow a pretty girl almost anywhere." He paused in thought, and then added, "In fact, maybe we should double down on that bet."

* * * * *

The Los Angeles MSS team arrived shortly after one in the morning and Shi positioned them on the western rim of the valley. They would cover the advance of the Houston team on the ranch house and the insertion of the San Francisco team into the tunnel system, and then remain in place as a tactical reserve while keeping an eye out for Miller.

The Los Angeles team was well armed and had brought additional assault rifles and ammunition for the Houston team. Even better, they had brought shaped charged explosives and a Type 86A 50mm Portable Mortar with ten rounds.

* * * * *

Randy and his crew left the hotel at four in the morning and drove to the spot just across the road from the MacNamara Mine lift house. Blood Hound had his nose to the ground and was following the scent. Randy usually relied on his instincts, and his instincts were telling him that the fake lift house was important. If it turned out to be just a storage building designed to look like a lift house for some nostalgic reason, they would sweep south and break into the ranch house.

* * * * *

The San Francisco MSS team made good time and arrived a little early. They brought assault rifles and six Anti-Personnel High-Explosive Incendiary (HEI) Rocket Propelled Grenades with two launchers. They had full body black suits with integral body armor and night vision goggles as well.

Shi divided the shaped charged explosives and RPG's between the Houston and San Francisco teams who would carry out the two-pronged assault. Now he had overwhelming force. Colonel Shi was an over-the-top-better-safe-than-sorry-belt-and-suspenders-risk averse-paranoid.

* * * * *

Randy wanted to get inside the lift house as quickly as possible, mostly because he would need some time to regroup and go to Plan B if the lift house was a dead end. Gripping his favorite pistol, which the crew had brought with them from Houston, he led his people across the road toward the lift house. There were no lights on in the ranch house, so people were probably still asleep, but there could be an early riser at any time. He and his men had all worn dark clothing. Given the low light conditions and the distance to the ranch house, he felt safe in taking a closer look at the lift house door. It was locked, but with an old style mechanical lock. He didn't know if that was part of the building's masquerade or a sign that there really wasn't much of importance inside. He would know soon, because one of his crew was an accomplished locksmith.

* * * * *

The Houston MSS team waited next to their vehicles in the valley while the San Francisco team entered the tunnel system through the back door Shi had discovered. They didn't know exactly where this particular tunnel led, but it did seem to head in the general direction of the ranch house about three hundred yards to the northeast. Shi knew the San Francisco team would have to feel their way and had further to go, so the Houston team would wait thirty minutes before advancing on the ranch house. He initiated a countdown on his PIDD.

Shi led the Houston team towards the ranch house when the countdown reached zero. It was a little tricky negotiating the rock outcroppings and the slope forming the edge of the low mesa. It would have been worse without the moon that bathed the snow with a pale light. Even so, it was sometimes difficult to discern the difference between clusters of rocks jutting up through the snow and the shadows they threw. Occasionally one of the team would stumble and slide back down the slope a few feet, but they kept to the schedule nonetheless. About the time his men broke out of the tree line seventy-five yards west of the house, an unusually bright star rose from the southwestern horizon and quickly proceeded through the sky toward the northeast.

* * * * *

At 5:49 AM, Mike got a visual lock on the ISS. His software would now automatically keep pace with the movement of the ISS while allowing him to maneuver the far side of the hole relative to the station. He immediately zoomed in and started looking for the Nauka Multipurpose Module. Double-checking against a plan view of the ISS that Alfred displayed, Mike moved over to the docking airlock on the end of the module. Nick and Mike felt that they should open up just inside of the inner airlock door, a position that would seem more normal to the astronauts and give them hand holds to grasp when they exited. They might even think that a rescue vehicle had actually docked.

"I'm inside!" Mike exclaimed. "The hole is still small ... they have power, although the lights are dim ... they probably had a lot of solar panels damaged by the meteoroid strikes ... it looks like they're all there in their suits ... nobody's moving, but that may just be to conserve their oxygen ... internal pressure is zero point thirty-two atmospheres ..." *I hope they're not unconscious. There's no way we'll have time to go in and get them out one by one before the station is out of range.*

Nick, Gail, and the selected members of the Volunteer Platoon, had practiced their part of the evacuation plan as best they could. Wil played the role of an evacuee by climbing up a stepladder and jumping down onto the mattress pile over and over so each pair of catchers could practice. Sometimes he would intentionally stumble and fall so the catchers could get a feel for how best to react.

During the practice sessions, Nick pointed out that there was bound to be an air pressure differential between the space station module and the cavern - they just didn't know how much it would be. But if the astronauts were in their space suits, it meant that the module pressure was probably no higher than half that of the cavern pressure. So when the near side was removed from the sensor head, air would be sucked up into the module.

The cavern was part of a large system of tunnels with multiple openings to the outside, so it wasn't like they were going to run out of air, but there was going to be quite a draft and there was no way of telling in advance how long it would last. That depended on how airtight the module was. If it was airtight, the breeze would not last long. If the module was leaking, either to the rest of the station or directly to the vacuum of space, the breeze might continue for the duration of the rescue. With this in mind, the catchers were instructed to initially stand on the mattresses so their makeshift padding wouldn't be sucked up to the hole. Gail braided her long hair into a single pigtail, then wrapped and pinned it around her head.

Mike and Nick were concerned about the effect the air movement would have on the egress of the astronauts. The velocity of the airflow should be highest right at the hole, due to the Venturi Effect, and should decrease in proportion to the size of the hole, but neither Mike or Nick were sure about the validity of the Venturi Effect in a case where the airflow constriction had a zero length. Or would it have a three hundred mile length in some bizarre, two-three-dimensional way? Here again, they would have to learn by doing.

"Get ready ... removing the near side from the sensor head ... now!"

There was suddenly a very loud, high-pitched whistling sound as air started to rush up through the hole into the ISS module. It was anyone's guess whether the astronauts could hear the noise with their suits on, but it was painfully clear that the rescue team in the cavern could hear it.

"... Range is closing," Mike shouted over the din. "Increasing hole size ..."

The whistling lowered in pitch as the hole diameter increased, but the rush of air grew accordingly and began to pick up dust and debris from the cavern floor. Soon there was a light brown whirling vortex reaching up and into the space station module.

In the midst of it all, Nick strode forward with squinted eyes to hold the step ladder right under the hole – all the while painfully conscious of how the whirling air flow was rearranging his kilt. He was just glad that he was wearing the sporran with Fred 'n Agnes on his right thigh and his father's pistol in a cross draw holster on his left - the extra weight of those two items was the only thing preventing his kilt from blowing up around his waist. Nick yelled, "Go, Gail, Go! Start hacking, Fred!"

* * * * *

Expedition Commander Pavel Novitski was physically and mentally exhausted. He and the rest of the crew had done everything they could think of to arrest the loss of atmosphere, but the bulk of the space station was now in vacuum. Only the Nauka Module yet retained any air, and it was at too low a pressure to breathe. The crew had been on suit oxygen for some time now, trying to breathe as little as possible while irrationally hoping and praying for the impossible – a last minute rescue.

There had been a discussion about the possibility of pooling all of the suit oxygen bottles and bequeathing them to the winner of some kind of lottery in the hope that at least one of them might last long enough for rescue. But, like the scientists most of them were, they did the math and determined that it still wouldn't be enough. Besides, none of them were willing to sit there and watch all of the others die for them.

Now Commander Novitski knew that they were all on their last orbit.

Novitski was floating at the end of the Nauka module that was docked to the Zvezda Service Module's nadir port. He could see all of the crew members listlessly floating in random orientations in between him and the supply docking port at the other end of the module just as they had been doing for hours.

Suddenly, something changed. A small spot of light seemed to appear on the surface of the supply docking port airlock door. Commander Novitski reached out and grasped a nearby handhold to turn and see if the spot was a reflection of a warning light somewhere, even though his helmet's heads up display wasn't showing anything new. But he stopped his rotation as he saw that the spot was getting bigger and his floating companions were starting to slowly change position - another breach? Then he realized that they were floating *away* from the docking port, not towards it. He checked his heads up display again and verified that the air pressure in the module was increasing!

Commander Novitski stared as the spot kept growing. Then a cloud of fine dust started whirling into the module from the spot and his drifting companions picked up speed. The dust seemed to die down just as the head and shoulders of a beautiful young lady popped into the module. He was so surprised that a whole series of irrelevant thoughts swirled through his mind ... *She's not wearing a spacesuit! Where did she come from? She wears her hair in the traditional Ukrainian style ... I must be hallucinating!*

The beautiful rescuing angel held up a sign that had the international green and white running man symbol for an exit, with an arrow pointing back into the spot from which she partially emerged. Now he was thoroughly convinced he was having an oxygen deprivation hallucination. To top it all off, his heads up display suddenly went blank, then started showing an animation of a young lady that looked very much like the one holding the exit sign but wearing traditional Scottish attire moving feet first through the docking port and being caught on the other side by two men who then hustled her off. He was struck by the similarity of the cartoon to some of the pre-flight safety presentations airlines used to explain emergency egress procedures. As the animation kept repeating in a continuous loop he noticed a countdown timer displayed next to the animation. It was at seven minutes and twenty-seven seconds and falling.

Shaking himself out of his malaise, Novitski double-blinked the emergency push channel icon and started to issue instructions, "Everybody orient feet first to the Supply Docking Port! ... Line up one behind the other! ..." From the way they grabbed handholds and complied immediately, Commander Novitski realized that all the crew members were seeing the same animation.

At that point the young lady with the exit sign smiled a dazzling smile and withdrew from the port. Novitski, who was orienting himself at the back of the line, saw a new symbol pop up on his display. It was an animation of a traffic light, and the light was red. A moment later, the light turned green. Novitski couldn't tell who was in the front of the line, so he just used the emergency push to command, "First person in line, *GO!*"

Just where they were going was something that Commander Novitski could not even guess, but it couldn't be any worse than where they were.

* * * * *

Randy Miller stood staring at the large satellite dish in the beam from his flashlight. He couldn't imagine what a satellite dish had to do with mining. But Jimmy hadn't said anything about a large antenna and there was no way that the trailer could have held anything this big anyway. Finally, he just shook his head and looked around the rest of the lift house. It was, in fact, a lift house, even if it did have an unexplained big honking antenna in it. He looked at the lift itself and it appeared to be well maintained and fully functional. Looking down past the edges of the lift platform with a flashlight, he could see tunnel openings at various levels. *If the equipment is in the mine, this had to be the way they got it in – and the way I'll have to get it out.* He was reluctant to use the lift – the noise would serve as an excellent intrusion alarm - but that's why he'd brought rappelling equipment.

* * * * *

As soon as Gail stepped off the ladder, Nick pulled it out from under the hole and tossed it aside. Two IMC volunteers moved forward on each side of the mattress pile and Nick hollered, "Green Light, Fred!" A couple of seconds later, a spacesuit-clad figure came down through the hole with both feet together and arms crossed tight against the chest.

"Red Light, Fred!" The two volunteers neatly caught and led the escapee forward off of the mattresses. "Green Light, Fred!"

Soon all six astronauts were down without mishap and the hole was closed. Mike looked at the countdown timer. "One minute fourteen seconds to spare. Great work, everybody!"

Nick added, "Kill the Agnes animation, Fred ... We did it!

The space station crew was helping each other take off their helmets. As they relished in deep breaths of fresh air, Gail, trailed by Patti and Lady, went around checking them all out to see if there were any medical issues.

Commander Novitski was thoroughly confused and was about to ask where they were when he heard a loud announcement, "Intruders detected on Level Three in the tunnel from the lift house." He wondered if the ISS crew were the intruders and if the cave they appeared to be in was a lift house tunnel. They had certainly been lifted off of the ISS! *And the announcement was in English, so that slightly narrows our location down.*

Mike and Nick immediately headed to the lab where Alfred could display the security system information using the holographic projector. Wil and the other volunteers headed to the cafeteria to join the squad on duty. That left Gail to be confronted by Commander Novitski, who asked in slightly accented English, "Excuse me, but could you please tell me where we are, who's in charge, and how we got here?"

"Well," said Gail with a crooked smile, "that's a long story."

* * * * *

Randy anchored his rope on the satellite antenna mount and started down the lift shaft towards the connecting tunnels. He was about halfway between ground level and the first tunnel when he heard the sound of diesel engines. Randy quickly shined his flashlight up the shaft to see if the lift was moving but it hadn't budged. He then shined his light down the shaft but couldn't see anything except empty shaft. When he reached the first tunnel, he could tell that the engine noise was coming from somewhere on that level. While he was hanging there trying to decide what to do, a strong rush of air pulled at him as it streamed down the shaft. Randy rappelled further down the shaft until he got to the next tunnel. The air was clearly being sucked into that tunnel, but the flow stopped shortly after he arrived there.

Randy hesitated, then decided that the sound of running equipment was probably normal in a mine, but a rush of air like he just experienced seemed less likely. Following his instincts again, he gestured for his crew to follow as he swung into the tunnel mouth and lowered himself to its surface.

* * * * *

The San Francisco MSS team was at a junction between two tunnels trying to decide which way to turn when they heard a far off high-pitched whistling sound and were hit by a strong gust of air. They froze in place for a moment, then huddled together to discuss what they heard and felt. They were all nervous and uncomfortable in an environment completely outside of their experience or training. Without ground-penetrating communication equipment, there was no way for them to communicate with Colonel Shi. Their regular superior officer had stayed in San Francisco, refusing to participate in Shi's wild goose chase. They were accustomed to following orders - not taking personal initiative when things went wrong.

One of them suggested that a miner may have set off an explosive charge and it temporarily compressed the air in the tunnel when it went off. But others argued that there was no accompanying noise of a blast and they really didn't think anyone would be working at that early hour anyway. They finally agreed that the whistle sounded like an alarm, so the gust of air may have been caused by a cave in. With that in mind, they chose the tunnel leading away from the source of the gust.

Chapter 41

As Mike and Nick entered the lab, Alfred announced, "Additional intruders detected in the Level Two tunnels to the south, and also at ground level approaching the house from the west." The holographic display was already showing the status of the security systems. Blue dots were blinking near groups of moving white dots in three different places.

LtCol Ahrens and CSM Baker entered the lab as Mike started touching the blinking blue dots to bring up the video views of the intruders. "Whoa," Wil exclaimed. "Those can't all be Blood Hound's people! How many are there?"

Alfred answered, highlighting each group of white dots in order, "Six intruders came through the lift house and are now in a Level Two tunnel heading south toward the cavern and underground facility. There are five more in a Level Two tunnel coming up from the south that also terminates in the cavern. There are an additional five approaching the house at ground level."

Nick frowned and asked, "They've got us surrounded. How did they know how to do that?"

Temporarily ignoring Nick's question, Wil mused, "Sixteen. Well, we've got them outnumbered in total, but only slightly as far as troops on hand – the second squad is on duty and the third squad is on standby, then there's the command master sergeant and myself.

"Alfred," Wil called out, "please transmit the warning order to both of the off duty squads to stand ready for transport."

"Done," Alfred replied as he broadcast the recall warning order to the two squads' PIDDs through his secure network connection.

Wil continued, "Can we tell how they are armed?"

Mike pointed at the first video window and answered, "This is the first group, the ones that entered through the Lift House. Notice that one of them is using a flashlight. The backscatter from the flashlight allows us a decent look at them. I don't see them carrying anything, but they might have weapons under their coats."

"That would probably rule out anything much more than handguns, although I suppose a hand grenade or two wouldn't be out of the question," Wil remarked.

Evan exclaimed sarcastically, "Thank you so very much for pointing that out!"

"Just thinking worst case," Wil replied.

The flashlight beam bounced around as the intruder walked and the light momentarily reflected in a way so as to show his face quite clearly. "That's Randy Miller!" Wil said, pointing. "So these guys are definitely Hound

233

Dog's group. As far as I know, they've never used any weapons beyond pistols."

Wil pointed at the next video window, "What about the group that is coming up from the south? I can't see anything in the video."

Alfred replied, "If I may be so bold, I would suggest that I address the third group – the ones above ground – next. I believe that doing so will help make more sense of the group in the south tunnel."

Will, nonplussed, just said, "Okay."

Alfred replied, "They are approaching in the open area between the trees to the west and the house. There is plenty of moonlight for our low light sensors to work quite well." Alfred zoomed in on one of the approaching figures. "They are not wearing night vision equipment since the moonlight is sufficient for them to see where they are going, so we have an unrestricted view of their facial features," Alfred commented as he zoomed in on the intruder's face.

"He looks Asian," said Wil.

Alfred agreed, "There is a ninety-two percent probability that he is ethnically Chinese."

The four men exchanged worried glances.

"Alfred," Wil said excitedly, "can you zoom in on the other four?"

"Certainly," replied Alfred as he stepped through close-ups of the other above ground intruders.

When Alfred had cycled back to the first intruder, Wil said, "The third one we saw was in the Las Vegas airport. I didn't recognize any of the others."

Alfred continued, "Each of these five intruders is carrying an assault rifle. There is a ninety-seven percent probability that they are modified Chinese QBZ-97A carbines. One intruder is also carrying a rocket propelled grenade launcher and four rounds. There is an eighty-four percent probability that it is a Chinese Type 69 85mm launcher and a sixty-eight percent probability that the rounds are Anti-Personnel High-Explosive Incendiary."

"Holy smokes!" Evan exclaimed. "Do they think they're attacking Fort Knox?"

"Well," said Mike, "we do have a fair amount of gold on hand at the moment."

Alfred ignored both Evan's rhetorical question and Mike's irrelevant comment, and continued, "Now for the second group that is approaching in the south tunnel. Unlike the above-ground intruders, this group is wearing military grade all-body suits that absorb light and suppress the infrared emissions of their body heat. In fact, it does too good a job of concealing them. I am tracking them by the way they block the ambient low level infrared emissions from the surrounding tunnel walls. In infrared emission terms, they are cooler than the rock."

The four men in the lab leaned closer to the video window but could see no more than an occasional flickering shadow, and even then they weren't sure that their eyes weren't playing tricks.

"I will highlight them," Alfred said. Five man-shaped silhouettes vaguely outlined in red appeared on the display. "I originally detected their presence based on the slight pixel changes that occur when their bodies occlude a new area of the tunnel walls – sort of an edge effect as they progress. If they were moving slower, or if there were fewer of them, they would not have exceeded the data variance threshold necessary for an intrusion detection event."

Alfred continued, "They also have very good passive low light level vision devices. They are not emitting energy at any wavelength that I can detect to guide them and keep them from stumbling over debris on the floor of the tunnel. They are probably using the infrared emissions from the walls to see."

"What about weapons?"

"Using the infrared blocking technique to analyze their silhouettes, there is a ninety-three percent probability that they are all carrying the same sort of assault rifle as group three. It is also a ninety-three percent probability that one of them is carrying an RPG launcher of the same sort as group three.

"Several of these intruders are carrying other objects that are more difficult to identify, but based on the response of the chemical sniffers mounted in the mine tunnels for safety purposes, it would appear that they are carrying explosive materials."

Now it was Mike's turn to be sarcastic. "Oh, that's just swell – really great news!"

Wil pressed on, "So, it appears based on weapons, that group two and three are really two sub-units of the same group, and that means they are probably all Chinese."

Alfred agreed, "The probability that they are factions of the same Chinese intruder group is eighty-five point five six. Over in Cripple Creek they would call those good odds."

Wil turned away from the security display to look at the others. "We were expecting Miller's group, and thought that a Chinese group might exist, but we weren't expecting both of them to arrive together in these numbers or this heavily armed. I don't normally believe in coincidences, but I really have a hard time believing Miller is cooperating with the Chinese. I need to find a way to talk to Miller."

Mike pointed out, "We can do that with the audio transducers whenever you wish. For that matter, we could just shoot them all in the back of the head execution style using a small hole, but Nick doesn't want it used that way. Besides, it would be very hard to explain to the sheriff."

That earned Mike a dirty look from Nick.

Wil nodded his head in agreement and said, "I recommend that we try to keep these groups from joining up so we can try to defeat them piecemeal. I think we should use four marshalling points, one squad in the house, two blocking squads in the Level Two tunnels – one north and the other south – and the last squad in the lab as a reserve. That means that we need to use both hole generators to start moving troops immediately."

"Oh-my-gosh," Nick suddenly remembered the ISS crew. "The astronauts are in the cavern with the second hole generator. And two of the three intruder groups are headed right for them!" Nick glanced around and said, "And Gail must still be with them!"

* * * * *

The house remained dark as Shi and his team neared. The same two cars were parked out front, so that meant someone was home, but most likely asleep at this early hour. They were about to get a rude awakening.

Shi checked the timer on his PIDD to make sure that they had allowed plenty of time for the San Francisco team to find their way through the tunnels. Without communications, there was no way for him to know for sure. He had given instructions to the Los Angeles team to message him if the San Franciscans returned to the valley but that had not happened. He was painfully uncomfortable with the uncertainty, but had to assume that the San Francisco team was proceeding as planned. Still, it shouldn't hurt to give them a little more time. Shi raised a balled fist to signal his team to hold in place.

* * * * *

Nick had already turned and started for the lab exit on his way to the cavern when Wil called out. "Wait up, Nick. I've got an idea on how to delay the groups in the tunnel while we deal with them each separately, but we need you in here to do it."

Wil turned to CSM Baker. "Sergeant, go to the second squad in the cafeteria, quickly fill them in on the above ground intruders and tell them their orders are to delay the attackers as much as they can, but to pull back as necessary. There's nothing in the house that is strategically important." Wil shot Mike a sympathetic look before continuing, "Then send them up into the house on the elevator. After that, wake up the third squad and have them muster in the cafeteria as our reserve. Once that's accomplished, you come back here."

"Yes sir," Evan replied as he ran out of the lab.

236

"Mike, please go out to the cavern, send Gail and the ISS crew in here, and then start transporting the first squad into the cavern. We'll bring the fourth squad into the lab."

"Sure," said Mike as he headed for the door.

"And Mike," Wil called after him, "fill the first squad in on the situation and send them up the tunnel to the north. Tell them to just go in about twenty yards and take up a blocking position. Then you come back here as soon as possible."

As Mike turned the corner out of the lab, he called out "Aye, Aye, Sir" in memory of his dear departed uncle Norris.

Shortly thereafter, Gail lead the ISS crew into the lab in time to see the last few members of the fourth volunteer squad step through the hole into the lab. The ISS crew and the volunteers were equally surprised to see each other and more than a little curious. She directed a couple of the crew members to the cots she had set up for her First Aid station, and the rest to stools at the lab workbenches. Gail glanced at the security display and was surprised to see three groups of moving white dots.

Evan strode into the lab and moved so quickly and purposely toward Wil that Gail was afraid to stop him to ask what was going on.

Commander Novitski looked askance at the armed men who wore work clothes instead of uniforms, but carried a variety of obviously military weapons. He recognized several Vietnam era M16's, some old AK-47's, one H&K G36, and a couple of REC7's - *Different countries of manufacture, firing different types of cartridges. Are these irregular troops of some kind or a citizen's vigilante group? We were over North America when we were miraculously rescued and everyone here talks like Americans. Maybe they're from one of those survivalist militias I've read about. In any case, they make me very nervous ... But being very nervous is better than being very dead, which is what I was about to be ... yes, there is that!*

He turned on his stool to face Gail and asked, "I know that you told me that you were not authorized to explain where we are or how we got here – or how those men just got here, for that matter," he said, pointing at the armed men, "but it looks like you are preparing to repel boarders. Are we in danger?"

Gail frowned and chewed her bottom lip. She really wanted to talk to Nick before saying anything to the ISS crew, but this was obviously not the time to interrupt what he was doing. Finally, she decided that it would become obvious pretty soon anyway. She smiled and replied, "Yes, I guess you could say that we are preparing to repel boarders. There are people who want to steal the equipment that made your rescue possible. We will fight to prevent that from happening. People on both sides may be harmed. That's why these cots are set up in here. I'm a nurse, and this is my First Aid station. I hope that I won't be needed, but that is probably a futile wish."

Commander Novitski considered her answer briefly, and then said, "We owe our lives to your people and that equipment. What can we do to help?"

"Right now," Gail replied, "I think it's best for your crew to stay out of the way, but be prepared to follow directions quickly. We want to get you to safety as soon as possible."

Before the conversation could go any further, Mike returned and headed toward where Nick, Evan and Wil were huddled. Wil saw Mike coming, and then noticed Gail standing near the door. He waved her up to join the group. As she approached, Wil was talking to the men, but paused to ask her a question.

"Other than suffering from acute confusion, how is the space station crew holding up?"

"Physically, most of them are fine. Their psychological condition is anyone's guess after what they have been through. However, two of them," pointing to the ones on the cots, "are showing symptoms of decompression sickness, otherwise known as "the bends." We need to get them to a facility that has a hyperbaric chamber. If they don't receive treatment fairly soon they could die ... painfully. I'm using a couple of the emergency oxygen packs from Mike's mining equipment to hold them for now, but that's only a temporary solution."

Wil looked down at the floor as he rethought the sequence of events in his defense plan.

"Okay, but right now I need Nick, Mike and the hole generator in here to help slow down the attack in the south tunnel, which temporarily leaves no one to operate the hole generator in the cavern. We should be able to get the ISS crew out of here right after that. Do you know where to send them?"

Gail frowned and answered, "I would feel more comfortable sending them to a facility that has some experience with space medicine." Looking at Nick, she asked, "Can we get them to NASA?"

Nick immediately replied, "We don't have enough power to generate a hole large enough for them to walk, or even crawl through, that would reach all the way to NASA. It will have to be someplace fairly close, particularly if we want to be able to use the other hole generator at the same time for our defense. ... I'm thinking the Air Force Academy Hospital? Would that work?"

Gail replied, "If they have a hyperbaric chamber ...."

"Fred," Nick called out to the PIDD resting in his sporran, "Does the Air Force Academy Hospital have a hyperbaric chamber?"

Fred quickly responded, "It appears that they do not have a chamber at the Academy. They use one at the 21st Space Wing's Aerospace and

Operational Physiology Flight facility on Peterson Air Force Base in Colorado Springs when they need to train cadets for high altitude flight conditions. According to the hours of operation posted, that facility will open this morning in about fifteen minutes."

"That sounds perfect. What's the distance?"

"As the crow flies, the distance from here to Peterson is essentially the same as it is from here to the Academy – about twenty-five miles."

"Okay, I can easily put a hole large enough for them to walk through at that distance." Looking at Gail, Nick asked "Do you agree with sending them to Peterson?"

Gail nodded her agreement, but asked, "Are we just going to dump them there? Maybe the staff will think it's a prank and call the Air Police. It's not like the crew members are public celebrities that everyone would recognize."

Fred volunteered, "I can call the Wing commander's PIDD just before you send them and say that the rescued ISS crew is being delivered to the Aerospace and Operational Physiology Flight facility by classified means, and to personally see to their immediate medical needs and accommodate them in every way."

Gail laughed. "You can't just order a Wing commander around like that. Besides, I'm sure the Wing commander's personal PIDD number is not publically available and is programmed to block any unrecognized callers anyway."

Nick disagreed, "Actually, I'm confident that Fred can get the call through, and I think that the Wing commander will at least call the bariatric facility when told that the ISS crew is being sent there. When it's confirmed that they suddenly have a room full of astronauts, I'll bet everyone will jump through hoops to make sure nothing goes wrong."

"How can you be so sure that Fred can get through? ... Never mind, I know. 'It's a long story.'"

"Okay," Wil interrupted. "It sounds like that's a plan. Gail, tell Commander Novitski where we are going to send the crew and why. Tell him to have his people ready to go at a moment's notice."

Then, tuning to Evan, "Sergeant, I need you to lead fourth squad in the south tunnel. You'll be up against the most dangerous group based on their equipment and their proximity to the hole generator in the cavern. Be very careful. We are going to try and slow this group down. I want to isolate it and leave it to last if at all possible."

"How are you going to do that?" Evan asked.

Wil grinned and answered, "Let me put it this way. Remind the men

239

not to be surprised by the sound of bagpipes."

Puzzled, Evan started to turn toward the waiting volunteers, but Wil reached out and grabbed his arm just above the elbow and drew him closer. Looking straight into Evan's eyes, Wil said, "I repeat, be very careful. What I intend to do should slow them down, but it will probably provoke them into firing their weapons. You're going to be in a mine tunnel. Rounds may ricochet and there is very little cover. Your opposition is wearing gear that probably includes at least some body armor and provides low light level vision. Try to find some bends in the tunnel or outcroppings for cover. Don't attempt a stand up, toe-to-toe fight with them. Snipe from cover then retreat and do it again. Slow them up and wear them down. Take another quick look at the hologram to see where they are now and look for any spots in the tunnel that might be advantageous for your squad."

"Yes, sir," answered Evan. "We'll be careful. But remember one thing, Colonel - these are *our* tunnels. We know every nook and cranny."

Wil smiled, gave Evan's arm a quick squeeze and said, "*Oo-rah* Top."

"*Hoo-ah* Colonel," Evan replied as he returned the smile.

Evan rounded up the fourth squad and led them out of the lab, into the cavern, and then into the south tunnel.

Wil turned back to Mike and Nick and said, "So, I heard a story about the 'Ghost of the MacNamara Mine'...."

Chapter 42

About a half an hour before dawn, Colonel Shi and Agent Xue quietly stepped up onto the front porch of the dark ranch house, slowly approached the front door and tried the knob. It was locked. Shi would have preferred to enter quietly and capture the occupants in their beds, but that hope was fading.

I thought people who lived out in the country didn't bother to lock their doors at night. This doesn't show a lot of trust on their part. Maybe MacEwen has imposed urban wariness on his friend.

As Xue reached for the shaped charge explosive clipped to his belt, the porch lights came on, effectively blinding both men, and a cultured voice that seemed to come from nowhere and everywhere said, "Good morning, gentlemen, if I may use the term loosely. You have attempted to gain illicit entrance to our domicile. In addition, you are trespassing on private land. It is my duty to inform you that you are under arrest for suspicion of First Degree Criminal Trespass, section 18-4-502 of the Colorado Revised Statutes.

"I must further inform you that these premises are guarded by Teller County deputy sheriffs. Failure to follow their instructions precisely may result in your being charged with Resisting Arrest, Section 18-8-103. If you assault a peace officer you will be charged ..." Alfred's greeting was interrupted as an enraged Shi used his carbine to blow the door knob into a spray of metal shards. The first shot of the Battle of the MacNamara Mine had been fired.

Shi kicked the front door in and Xue dove through the opening to the sound of return fire. Shi peeked around the edge of the door frame from his position pressed against the outside wall and saw Xue's bullet-riddled body in a growing pool of blood just inside the door.

"Now you've torn it," the cultured voice said, "Breaking and entering accompanied by assault is a Felony under section 18-4-202."

Then the porch light went out and he was blind again.

The other three members of the Houston MSS team had positioned themselves on the two sides and back of the house to block anyone from escaping. They heard the brief fire fight at the front of the house and recognized the sound of a QBZ-97 firing, but heard the sound of other weapons firing as well. They realized that meant armed resistance, but were unsure how to react. They weren't the beaters, they were the net. After a short period of silence, their PIDDs vibrated. It was a text message from Colonel Shi ordering them to advance and enter the building however they could, and preferably capture - but kill if necessary - the defenders in the house.

Shi knew that advancing all of the remaining Houston MSS team members at once was risky. Even if they made it into the structure, they would be fighting in an unfamiliar maze of rooms in the dark, against defenders who presumably knew their way around. The MSS operatives would be lucky not to shoot each other. But Shi was determined to beat Miller and his goons to the prize. Upon reflection, Shi realized that he might actually be up against Miller right now. That made more sense than believing that MacEwen and his friend had suddenly taken up arms. *But then what was that 'deputy sheriffs' nonsense all about?*

* * * * *

Alfred reduced his volume and selectively muted most of the audio transducers in the house so that only the volunteers could hear him.

"An intruder on the front porch has used his PIDD to send a message to the other attackers. Their communications encryption is very strong, so it would take me too much time to decrypt the message. But based on sensor video content, it was obviously an order to attack. They are now moving toward the house. Not counting the one on the porch, there are three attackers left and they are approaching ..."

Alfred went on to direct the volunteers to positions covering the most likely entry points.

* * * * *

Shi had retreated to a corner of the front porch where he could cover the front entrance. If any of the defenders tried to escape in his direction, he would be in a position to capture or kill them. His remaining team members were now the beaters and he was the net. He heard gunfire from the southwest side of the house. That was followed by gunfire from the southeast. Then it sounded like there was gunfire all around the house, followed by silence ... too much silence. Shi couldn't hear anything from either the inside or outside of the house. He sent a quick text message for his team members to report in. There were no replies.

Shi shrunk further into the corner of the porch, straining to hear against the silence, to see against the dark. He thought he heard footsteps approaching from inside the house, but then realized that it was just the sound of his heart pounding in his ears. Shi went a little crazy. He punched an icon on his PIDD that sent a previously prepared order to the Los Angeles MSS team, then jumped over the porch railing and ran back towards the shallow valley to the west. In mid-flight, Shi realized that he had left his carbine leaning against the porch railing. *There is no way I am going back there to retrieve it now!* As he raced away from the house, Shi almost ran right past the lifeless body of one of his men lying in the snow, but noticed a RPG launcher on the ground nearby. There was a round already protruding from the muzzle of the launcher and another on the ground nearer the body. He started to look for more rounds, but quickly changed his mind when he saw a flash of light and heard a dull *whump* emanate from the valley's western rim. Shi grabbed the launcher and extra round and resumed his headlong dash.

* * * * *

242

The San Francisco MSS team was cautiously advancing through the dark tunnel as quietly as possible. They walked in two short columns, one on either side of the small stream of water running down the middle of the tunnel floor, pausing periodically to listen for any sounds that might indicate they were not alone. Other than the whistling sound that accompanied the mysterious gust of air, the only sounds they had heard since entering the tunnel system were the slight shuffling sound of their passage and the sound of water dripping. They were not happy with their assignment. None of them had been underground before, they had no idea what they might run into, and Colonel Shi couldn't even describe the equipment they were supposed to find. They felt that the Colonel had assigned them the most dangerous part of the assault simply because their direct superior in San Francisco had opposed the expedition from the beginning and had remained at the consulate. That act had simultaneously insulted Colonel Shi and removed any possible intermediary on their behalf. They were not happy campers.

The operative first in line on the left column suddenly stopped, nearly causing a chain reaction pile up on that side of the tunnel.

His compatriot directly behind whispered, "What's wrong?"

"I thought I heard something," he whispered back. They all stood very still and strained their ears. Then, in between the drips of water splattering on the floor of the tunnel, they all heard it. It was a very soft, faintly musical sound coming from somewhere far ahead of them.

Someone on the other side of the column whispered, "What is that?"

Before anyone could reply, a very pale light began to grow in the tunnel far ahead of them.

* * * * *

"*Incoming*!" Alfred announced loudly over the audio transducers in the house and in the below-ground lab. "Trajectory analysis indicates one mortar round fired from approximately six hundred yards to the west. Further analysis indicates that the round will fall long."

"Mortar fire," Wil exclaimed. "That's got to be more Chinese! Miller would never risk blowing up an asset he'd be paid to repossess. If the mortar crew is any good, they'll get the range in another round or two, and then they'll pour it on.

"Alfred! Tell the second squad to pull back. Tell them to head to the elevator and get back down here immediately!"

"Your order has been relayed and acknowledged by all second squad personnel," Alfred replied after a brief pause.

Mike asked, "Why aren't the Chinese reluctant to blow up the asset?"

"I don't know. Maybe they're working on the premise that if they can't

243

have it, then no one else can. Just concentrate on the Ghost of the MacNamara Mine. We need to free up Nick quickly so we can have the use of both hole generators."

* * * * *

The light in the tunnel brightened and grew. Soon the San Francisco team could see that it looked like a Scottish piper, slowly marching down the tunnel towards them, playing a mournful lament. The eerie sound echoed in the confines of the mine tunnel and greatly increased the team members' apprehension. In fact, it made chills go up and down their spines. As the piper neared, it looked like he was surrounded by twinkling stars, as if he was marching down out of the night sky. Several MSS operatives took a few tentative steps backwards while two others raised their weapons. When the apparition continued to advance, the pair opened fire with their carbines on full automatic. Sixty rounds ripped through the piper in a little over two seconds.

* * * * *

Randy Miller called a halt to his crew's advance down the mine tunnel and signaled for silence. He thought he heard a ripping sound from somewhere in the distance ahead. It was very brief, but as Randy played back the sound in his head he was fairly certain that it was automatic gunfire. Then, as he strained to hear anything more, he smiled - *A bagpipe. MacEwen is doing his "Ghost of the MacNamara Mine" routine. But why? Are kids from Cripple Creek in the tunnels again? I don't think kids have access to automatic weapons. But if* anybody *in these digs has automatic weapons, we are seriously out-gunned!*

Randy repeated the signal for silence and led his crew slowly forward.

* * * * *

Colonel Shi stopped at the tree line on the western edge of the mesa and looked back toward the house just as the first mortar round exploded well past the target. He used his PIDD to call the Los Angeles MSS team leader to report the long round and spot for the next round. It was difficult for him to judge distances since he was limited to using his unaided eyesight in the now pre-dawn light levels, and his position was almost directly beneath the flight path of the shells. He reported his guess that the first round had been about fifty yards long and just a little bit off to the south. The second round was about fifty yards short and still a little to the south, which was way too close to Shi for his comfort. He swore at the mortar crew as he spotted the fall for them. The third round was better, just a few yards short but a little to the north. The fourth round was still short, but pretty well centered on the house. Finally, after more swearing, the fifth round stuck the house squarely on the roof, but that left only five rounds remaining. *Those incompetents have gone through half of their ammunition just getting the range!* Shi gave no consideration whatsoever to the quality of his own contribution to the process.

Shi ordered, "Fire for effect, all available rounds!"

Then, in desperation, Shi picked up the RPG launcher and pointed it at the building. He was in easy range of the house and decided to try for a window so that the grenade would go off inside. Steading himself, he aimed at a window about midway on the west side of the house.

* * * * *

Sixty rounds whipped through the hologram, ripped through hurriedly assembled stacks of mattresses, through dry wall, and slammed into the underlying welded metal of the lab wall.

Mike peered over at Wil through the soft light coming from the holographic display and the haze of mattress stuffing drifting slowly down like an indoor snow flurry. Mike's voice replaced the shocked silence of the room, "You owe me some new mattresses ... and some wall repair."

Wil smiled and replied, "Better that than a funeral for your friend Nick."

* * * * *

The San Francisco MSS operatives stared in disbelief as the piper, seemingly unaffected by the hail of gunfire, continued to play the bagpipe and approach them. The increasingly loud sound of the bagpipe was unnerving. First one operative started to back away slowly. Then another turned and started to walk away quickly. Finally all five of the operatives were in undiscussed, but nonetheless unanimous, retreat with Fred hurling Chinese curses at their backs. A powerful combination of lack of leadership, resentment regarding their assignment, fear of the unknown, discomfort in their surroundings, and an overall uncertainty of purpose had caused them to stampede in the face of the enigmatic. A rich Chinese folklore including many tales regarding a variety of vengeful ghosts may have been a contributing factor.

* * * * *

Alfred reported, "The intruders in the south tunnel are retreating in apparent confusion."

Wil told Mike to close the hole hovering in front of the holographic display, and switch the inputs back from Alfred's video feeds to the previous security system view. Then Wil called out, "Alfred, turn the lights back on in here and in the server farm, and tell our Vid Star that he can stop marching up and down the server aisles playing his bagpipe, we need him in here now."

* * * * *

Alfred barely had time to report, *"Incoming!"* again before the HEI rocket-propelled grenade crashed through a window and exploded inside the house, hurling nine hundred steel balls and three thousand incendiary pellets in all directions that shredded, then ignited, the furniture, walls, ceilings and anything else in its blast radius, including the body of the Houston MSS operative lying just inside the front door. Then five more mortar rounds fell and exploded, one by one, in the midst of the burning, collapsing building.

Chapter 43

Gail started to check on her charges as soon as the lights came back on in the lab. The sudden hail of gunfire hitting the far wall had unnerved her, but she wanted to make sure that no one was hit by a ricochet. She hadn't gone very far before Patti and Lady jumped up barking and bolted out the door. Worried because she knew that Nick was out there, she followed them to the other side of the server farm, where she saw Nick kneeling over a volunteer who had apparently collapsed while exiting the elevator.

She rushed to his side and arrived in front of the elevator a few steps behind the dogs, which were pacing back and forth in front of the elevator threshold sniffing and whining, seemingly reluctant to enter. She saw that the inner elevator doors were heavily damaged and stuck part-way open. She looked inside the elevator.

"Oh, my God," Gail whispered. "What happened?" She had responded to serious traffic and industrial accidents before, but the scene before her now was unparalleled in her experience. The inside of the elevator looked like a slaughterhouse. There was blood everywhere and the sickening smell of burnt flesh hung in the air over a mound of unmoving bodies. Her eyes told her that they must all be dead, but her ears disagreed – there were a few moans and cries of pain arising from the mass.

Nick was busy trying to find where all of the wounded man's blood was coming from, and began to realize that the answer to that was almost everywhere. He glanced up at Gail and then looked into the elevator. "It looks like they were hit with some sort of munition that includes both shrapnel and incendiaries. Look at the number of puncture wounds and burns," he said as he pointed at the man on the floor. "It must have caught them just as the elevator doors were closing. The guys on the sides don't seem to be as badly wounded as the ones in the middle of the elevator."

Gail turned to run for her medical kit but stopped when she saw one of the astronauts hastening to bring it to her.

"Commander Novitski was curious over your sudden exit," the man said as he ran up to her. Gail recognized a strong German accent, but he proved to speak English fluently. He explained that the commander followed Gail part way, saw the wounded man on the floor and quickly returned to get help.

"I am a medical doctor. Commander Novitski asked if I would be willing to help and I assured him that I would do so gladly as long as you approved."

Of course Gail approved and they both started in on the casualties. "Nick," Gail said without stopping or even looking up from her work, "They want you back in the lab right now. Get some of the third squad in there to grab cots and bring them out here to use as stretchers."

Commander Novitski beat Nick to the punch. Before Nick could make it back to the lab, all of the space station crew who remained ambulatory were hustling to serve as litter-bearers and medical assistants.

* * * * *

Wil, Mike, Nick and Commander Novitski were in conference. Alfred had lost contact with all of the sensors in and around the house. All eight second squad members had made it into the elevator, but three were dead and two more were not expected to survive. Only three of the squad members seemed likely to recover from their wounds. They had apparently reached the elevator first and moved to the back and the sides to make room for the others and were somewhat shielded by the partially closed doors and their less fortunate squad mates.

Wil said, "We need to get the wounded to a hospital and the ISS crew members to the bariatric facility as soon as possible."

Nick replied, "You'll have to go through Gail to get to the wounded. She says the hole generator is their best hope for survival. She says she can remove the shrapnel and repair internal damage faster and with less blood loss than they can at the hospital."

All four men glanced at the controlled chaos at the back of the lab as ISS crew members and IMC volunteers alike moved to Gail's barked orders as they set up an impromptu surgery suite with cafeteria tables and lab workbenches. Off to one side, the German doctor was using Gail's Medi-Monitor to check the blood type of everyone within reach to identify potential blood donors.

Commander Novitski added, "Although I agree that the bariatric treatment for my two crew members is important, I have it under good advice," looking in the direction of Gail and the German doctor, "that they are in no immediate danger ... or perhaps I should say, no greater danger than the rest of us at the moment ... as long as we keep them on oxygen."

Wil frowned, "Commander, are you sure you and your crew want to hang around here? You've seen inarguable proof that this is a dangerous venue at the moment. We're being attacked on all sides by an unknown number of intruders in at least four different groups, and this isn't your fight."

Commander Novitsky smiled, "Please call me Pavel. You say hanging around this place is dangerous ... as opposed to, say, hanging around in a heavily damaged space station running out of oxygen? I discussed this with the crew – they want to stay and help if they can."

Wil frown softened. "Well, if Gail is going to use the prototype in here for surgery, then we'll have to try and make do with the hole generator in the cavern for defense. Commander – I mean Pavel - it certainly would be helpful if you and your people could stay here for a little longer and assist Gail in any way possible. That way, we can take the third squad with us to the cavern."

Commander Novitski responded, "Absolutely. We will do whatever we can."

"Thank you," Wil replied, then turned to the others and said, "Let's go. I want to try to stop Miller next."

The two Labrador retrievers looked at the departing men and then at each other. By some silent agreement, Patti fell in beside the men while Lady moved closer to Gail and her patients.

* * * * *

Randy and his crew were still making cautious progress down the mining tunnel when overhead lights came on. It took several seconds before their eyes adjusted to the sudden brilliance. Although they couldn't see immediately, they could hear.

"Good Morning, Mister Miller. This is Teller County Deputy Sheriff Ahrens. You are trespassing on private property. Ordinarily, I would give you a warning and allow you and your associates to peacefully leave. However, that might be difficult in this instance since the surface currently seems to be controlled by Chinese Special Forces."

Randy switched off his suddenly superfluous flashlight, and looked around for the person speaking, but there was no one to be seen other than his own crew. Looking up, he could see some kind of lighting strips running down the center of the tunnel overhead that now illuminated the immediate stretch of tunnel. Looking ahead and behind this section of tunnel, he could see only darkness.

Having failed to discern the speaker, Randy moved on to discern the message. "Now hold your horses, Deputy ... Ahrens. I am here legally to repossess assets that were stolen from my client and I have filed the required surety bond with the Colorado ... wait a minute, what was that you said about 'special forces'?"

"More specifically, I'm talking about Chinese special forces, Mister Miller. They, like you, are here to *illegally* seize property belonging to MacEwen Systems LLC. Think about it Mister Miller. What proof of ownership did Jimmy Barton offer?"

"He gave me a copy of the title! But how do you know about Jimmy? I didn't tell you my client's name. Come to think of it, I didn't tell you my name either. What's going on here?"

Wil ignored Randy's questions and continued. "He gave you a copy of the title to what? It was the title to the trailer, wasn't it, Mister Miller. It couldn't have been the title to the contents of the trailer, because those contents are clearly stated as the property of MacEwen Systems LLC in the merger agreement with Instrument Technologies Corporation dated May fifth, two thousand eleven, approved, signed and incorporated by attachment to the minutes of the Board of Directors meeting on that date. In the spirit of full disclosure of the legal situation, Mister Miller, I feel obligated to point out that ITC currently stands in violation of said merger agreement, also in violation of a verbal contract to provide long term employment contracts to Mister MacEwen and other senior managers at ITC, and guilty of wrongful termination having bypassed their own written procedures for notice and arbitration.

"But," Wil continued, "returning to the point of our conversation, after being engaged by Mister Barton, you in fact successfully recovered ITC's property - the empty trailer - in Mexicali, Mexico. At that point, the legal part of your assignment was completed.

"By the way, if Mister Barton were to decide to press charges against Mister MacEwen for the theft of the trailer, it would be considered no more than a misdemeanor since Mister Barton himself has already established the value of the trailer as being less than the amount required to tow it back to Texas.

"And that brings us back to 'you are trespassing on private property.'"

Randy was stunned by Wil's detailed declaration of the equipment's ownership, ITC's internal affairs, and knowledge of the trailer's fate - as were Nick and Mike who were listening in.

More than a minute of silence passed while Randy considered all he had heard.

Wil kept thinking, *come on Randy. Work it out. What's the best thing you can do in this situation? I already told you that you can't get back out the way you came in because the Chinese hold the high ground. You are trapped between belligerents, both being more powerful than you, and we are the least likely to kill you out-of-hand ... He's taking too long to make up his mind. I guess a disembodied voice isn't intimidating enough. I'd better use the clincher.*

"Mister Miller, I'm confident that you are not the sort of man who would knowingly break the law. That's why I stopped you for this little chat before you went much further. As an act of faith, I will show you what was waiting for you and your people just ahead.

"First squad, advance and be recognized." *Not quite the correct command for this situation but I'm not sure what would have been more appropriate.*

Randy heard some faint shuffling sounds from the dark tunnel ahead. Then he saw armed men slowly moving out of the gloom into the light. Ultimately, eight men armed with assault rifles of various kinds emerged. They were almost certainly deputized citizens, judging from the way they were dressed and the variety of weapons, but they also had a hard, competent look about them that was very familiar to Randy. *Not oil field roughnecks – miners – but just like roughnecks, familiar with death and not ones to run away from a fight.* Then Randy remembered the automatic weapons fire that he heard earlier. He didn't know if that came from this group or not, but it didn't matter. *We really are outgunned!*

"So, Deputy Ahrens, if there are actually Chinese special forces operating on United States soil trying to obtain the 'contents of the trailer' as you call it, then it must be pretty important stuff."

"True."

"I mean stuff that is important to the United States."

"Correct."

"Well, Deputy Ahrens, there's no greater patriots than me and my crew! Isn't that right, boys?"

The boys didn't look all that enthusiastic about facing Chinese Special Forces.

"So," Randy continued, "how can we be of help to the Teller County Sheriff's Department?"

"Outstanding! Just the sort of response I would expect from any red-blooded, law abiding citizen like you Mister Miller. Here's what I would like you to do. I could really use these Deputies you see before you to help drive some Chinese out of another part of the mine. So it would really help if you and your boys could take their place. Just hunker down right where you are, facing back the way you came. That way you will be in a position to report any incursion from that direction. I really don't expect the Chinese to come in that way, they have destroyed the house but seem to be ignoring the lift house. If anything, they will probably just destroy the lift house also, which would definitely keep them from coming your way. But, if they do come in, don't try to stop them. They are much better armed than you are. Just holler out 'the Chinese are coming' and we will hear you. Then fall back in the direction that you were originally advancing in order to reach our interior lines. Got it?"

Randy replied, "Got em! ... I mean, got it!"

* * * * *

Alfred shut down the outbound audio when Wil made a throat cutting gesture.

Nick glanced over at the third squad members who were spread out sitting with their backs against the cavern wall resting. He didn't want to erode their confidence in their leader by questioning Wil in front of them, so when Nick was satisfied that the volunteers weren't listening, he looked at Wil and murmured sotto voice, "Miller's crew will be slaughtered if the Chinese do come in through the lift house."

Wil also lowered his voice and answered, "Alfred will tell us the minute anyone enters the lift house, and we'll tell Miller and his boys to fall back here to the cavern right away. They can't stand up to the Chinese."

"Then why did you give them instructions to 'hunker down' and 'report incursions'?"

"I'm betting that nothing further will happen in that sector, and I don't want them here in the cavern where they can see us using the hole generator if I can avoid it. This way, I've effectively put them in Time Out."

"Alfred," Wil called out, "tell the first squad to fall back to the cavern for new orders and douse the light in the tunnel. Oh, and be sure to tell me if Miller and his boys start to wander."

Wil turned to look at the security holographic projection to see where the south tunnel intruders were now, and realized he was staring into empty space. They had all come to rely on the holographic display, but it was back in the lab, not in the cavern.

Before he could ask Alfred for an update, Nick pulled Wil aside, looked him in the eye and quietly asked, "Who are you, really?"

* * * * *

Colonel Shi half walked and half slid down the slope. By the time he reached the floor of the valley, he had gained a new respect for the Houston MSS member, now dead, who had lugged the launcher and rounds up to the house earlier. He trudged through the snow towards the west, passed the parked vehicles, and then awkwardly climbed up the slope to where the Los Angeles team waited. He was furious with them for their shoddy mortar work, but as he looked back to the east he could see the burning wreck of the house. One look was enough to realize that it was completely destroyed and no one inside could have survived. He decided that the results are the important part. Besides, there was no real point in returning unspent rounds back to an armory located a third of the continent away. He certainly couldn't see anything else around here worth blowing up.

His sleepless night, the adrenaline surge caused by the assault, and the adrenaline crash afterward, were all starting to take their toll. He stood there mesmerized by the flames and smoke, his eyes unfocused. He suddenly realized that he was close to falling asleep on his feet and mentally slapped himself. As he regained awareness, he noticed a glow on the horizon just a little bit to the right of the burning house. The sun was rising.

Shi turned to the Los Angeles team leader and asked if he had anything to report regarding the San Francisco team. Receiving a negative reply, Shi thanked the man and ordered him to have his team pack up and head back to

Los Angeles immediately, pointing out that the flames and smoke from the house would undoubtedly bring a response soon. Having traveled to Victor by way of south central Colorado, Shi recommended that the Los Angeles team head south on Colorado Highway 67 through Phantom Canyon to U.S. Highway 50 since any emergency response would be coming down from the north out of Victor or Cripple Creek.

He further told the leader to report that the mission almost certainly destroyed the target equipment and killed the inventor, but to make sure, Shi was going to find the San Francisco team and verify that nothing important was in the mine. He requested, and was given, a flashlight from one of the Los Angeles vehicle's emergency road kit. The team leader offered to swap the Colonel's cumbersome RPG launcher for an assault rifle, but he declined.

Shi refrained from telling the Los Angeles team leader that he did not expect to return from this last phase of the raid.

Chapter 44

"I really am William A. Ahrens, and I really am a retired Marine officer, and I really am a Defense Intelligence Agency officer," Wil replied to Nick's question.

Still looking Wil square in the eye, Nick inquired, "Fred?"

Fred replied, "He appears to be telling the truth, but I agree with Alfred. He's been trained and physically altered for the purpose of masking his biometrics."

"Yes, Fred," Wil responded, "and I had to go through all of that because of the abilities of devices just like you. And some of it was pretty painful, I might add."

Nick asked, "How do you know so much about me and ITC and the trailer ... and everything?"

Wil smiled slightly and said, "You've been engaged in classified work your entire career, so you know the old joke."

"Yeah, I know. 'If I told you, I'd have to kill you'," Nick replied in a tone that indicated that he was having none of that.

Wil nodded, "That's right, so I can't tell you *everything*, but I think I won't get in too much trouble if I tell you a few things. And then you, being an intelligent guy and all, can figure the rest out.

"As I said, I am a DIA agent. In recent years, I have been on a long-term undercover assignment investigating fraud on government contracts. Certainly not a glamorous assignment, but an important one, particularly since government spending has declined sharply since the depression began. Many government contractors are desperate these days, and desperate people sometimes do desperate things.

"So," Wil continued, "part of what I do is the same thing that many policemen do. I cultivate informers. Of course I don't call them that to their faces, and they don't think of themselves as such, but that's the vernacular for what they do. Most of them are nascent whistle-blowers, but whistle-blowing is dangerous – by its very nature, it attracts attention to the whistle-blower. There are laws protecting whistle-blowers, and contractors are required to have policies in place to protect them, but I'm here to tell you that none of those protections work. It's odd how our society openly reviles whistle blowers but protects criminals with silence. Everyone should realize that honor among thieves only applies if you're a thief."

"Anyway, a whistle-blower always gets the shaft one way or another, sooner or later. So most of my sources are solid citizen types who see things that they know are wrong, but are afraid to report openly. Like a journalist, I *have* sources because I *protect* my sources. Their identity is the part you're not going to hear from me."

Nick watched Wil's expression carefully as he said, "So you have an informer inside ITC."

Wil laughed and replied, "See? I knew you were an intelligent guy!" But then Wil frowned as he said, "So that explains how I know, and it's obvious how Randy Miller knows. The question that remains is how the Chinese know."

* * * * *

Colonel Shi literally ran into the San Francisco MSS team shortly after he entered the mine tunnel back door. It was a thoroughly awkward encounter. He was on a collision course with the team, but was unaware of that fact until Shi heard a voice ahead of him say, "Turn off the stupid flashlight" in Chinese. Shi instinctively raised the flashlight to point in the direction of the speaker. This immediately overloaded the approaching teams' ultra-sensitive night vision goggles, causing them to either turn their heads away, close their eyes, throw up their hands to cover their goggles or do all three at the same time. This, in turn, caused them to stumble into each other and bounce off of the tunnel walls. The resulting human pinball game ended with two of the team members sprawled on the tunnel floor, one leaning against a tunnel wall and the remaining two holding each other up in the middle of the tunnel.

Shi regarded them with scorn. No one on his Houston MSS team would be so careless as to openly speak in Chinese. Then he remembered that no one on his Houston MSS team would speak any language ever again. This last thought only increased his anger at the San Franciscans arrayed before him. He lowered the flashlight beam, partially to eliminate the night vision device overloads and partially to obscure his view of the ridiculous scene.

Shi controlled his emotions as best as he could under the circumstances, and commanded, "Report! Where have you been? What did you see? Where are you going now?"

His interrogatories were met with silence. There seemed to be a group-wide hesitancy to speak. Just before Shi lost his temper entirely, one of the operatives spoke up - Shi could not tell which one without raising the flashlight beam again. He felt oddly disadvantaged, not being able to see someone who could see him.

"We have been through the tunnels as far as we could go without seeing a ... living soul ... or any kind of equipment - not even mining equipment. We were just now on the way back to report to you."

Shi was not particularly surprised by their findings, or lack thereof, but he needed to be sure. "Does this tunnel run all the way to the vicinity of the house on the mesa like we thought?"

"Yes, sir, we think so. We can't get PIDD signals down here, and so didn't have GPS to go by, but we counted our strides and the distance seemed about right."

"Did you encounter any branch tunnels along the way?"

"Yes, sir, we did, but we did not try to explore them. We didn't have time on the schedule you set."

More uncertainties, thought Shi. *Well, that's why I'm staying – to eliminate any uncertainties. And I don't think these ill-disciplined slackers will be of much help.* "All right, you can return to San Francisco. The Los Angeles team is already preparing to return to their consulate. But I want you to leave me with a stealth suit and night vision goggles. I'm going to do a sweep of the side tunnels to make absolutely sure that you haven't missed anything."

"Yes sir," The operative sounded very relieved.

Shi explained the need for them to make haste and described the southern Colorado route to them.

* * * * *

The first squad, having been relieved by Randy Smith and his crew, was returning to the cavern from the north tunnel as Wil asked, "Alfred, where is the south intruder group now?"

"They are no longer present in any tunnel that I monitor. After retreating from the 'Ghost of the MacNamara Mine,' they continued south and disappeared at the same point that they first appeared on the sensors. The tunnel runs very close to the edge of the mesa in that stretch. My assessment is that there is a breach in that sector which they used to initially enter and subsequently exit."

"So you think that they are back on the surface somewhere to our west."

"That is correct, but I currently cannot access surface sensors for confirmation."

Mike interrupted, "Alfred, I know that you can't access any of the sensors that were in or on the house, but there are other outside sensors, some mounted on the lift house and others mounted in trees around the property."

Alfred replied, "Yes, but I formerly accessed those sensors through a wireless router in the house. My communications with the house have been lost."

Mike continued, "But there is also a wireless router in the lift house for the U-GPS system. You have a separate buried fiber optic connection to that router. You should be able to reprogram the router and connect to the remaining outside sensors."

After a very brief interval, Alfred reported, "You are correct. I now have access to all surviving outside sensors ... I guess there are still some reasons to keep humans around."

That statement sent a chill up the men's spines.

Alfred continued, "I detect no intruders on the mesa other than three inert forms estimated as deceased, with probabilities ranging from ninety-three to ninety-seven percent. Based on prior sensor data, there is also an eighty-nine percent probability of a deceased intruder buried in the ruins of the house."

Alfred continued, "The sun is up now, allowing me to detect the presence of an undetermined number of intruders close to maximum sensor range on the ridge at the far side of the valley to the west. The probability is in excess of sixty-one percent that I am detecting humans, not wildlife. The probability that I am detecting humans increases to seventy-six percent when this sighting is combined with the reverse ballistics calculations for the earlier mortar fire."

"So," Wil stated, "you're saying that the only intruders remaining are on the ridge to the west."

"To be precise," Alfred replied, "I can detect no ambulatory intruders above ground other than the ones on the ridge to the west, but I have no coverage of the valley floor, which could conceal a large number of intruders, although that would be inconsistent with the level of the hostile activity that we have so far experienced. The mine tunnels are clear except for the Miller group in the north tunnel."

Wil rolled his eyes, "Oh, yes, I mustn't forget Blood Hound." He thought for a moment and then went on, "Alfred, please recall the fourth squad from the south tunnel to the cavern."

Nick asked Wil, "Do you think the Chinese are pulling out?"

"Well, they've definitely pulled back, but I don't know if that means they're pulling out. They may be concentrating their remaining forces for a new attack." Wil looked worried. "I have a bad feeling about the south tunnel group. I thought that the Ghost of the MacNamara Mine act might slow them down a little, but I didn't think it would drive them completely out of the mine! I want to get the whole platoon here in the cavern with the hole generator so that we can react quickly and send them where we need them as soon as we know what the Chinese are up to."

Mike asked, "How are we going to find out what the Chinese are up to? They're almost out of our sensor range. We can't really see or hear what they're doing."

Nick smiled and quickly replied, "Oh, I think I know the solution to that problem," as he patted the side of the hole generator.

* * * * *

Colonel Shi was close to total exhaustion as he proceeded through the mine tunnels. He moved very slowly, due in equal amounts to caution and fatigue.

After what seemed like hours, Shi came to a complete halt when he heard a voice ahead. It was just far enough away that he couldn't quite make out what was being said, but shortly thereafter he heard rustling noises accompanied by a few clicks of metal on metal, followed by the sound of shuffling feet. There was a group moving in the tunnel ahead of him! He didn't know who they were or which way they were going; he only knew that they weren't friendly. Standing there holding his breath and listening as hard as he could, Shi finally decided that they were moving away from him. Slowly and carefully, he followed, step by step, determined not to run away again like he did from the porch.

* * * * *

By the time the fourth squad returned to the cavern, Nick had the sensor head mounted back on the near side of the hole and Mike was flying the far side over the west ridge of the valley. The three men watched the video display and listened to the brief conversations between the Chinese MSS team members as Mike maneuvered the tiny hole from group to group.

"They're packing up and leaving!" Mike exclaimed.

"Sure sounds like it," Wil agreed. "Based on what they're saying, they've been ordered out because now that the sun is up the smoke from the house is going to cause a reaction by local emergency response agencies. Maybe they're concerned about the diplomatic repercussions of being caught attacking American citizens on American soil."

Nick responded, "Not concerned enough to refrain from doing so!"

Mike agreed and added, "Little do they know that the only 'local emergency response agency' that's likely to react is the Victor Volunteer Fire Department, most of whose members are currently sitting in this cavern."

* * * * *

There was a light at the end of the tunnel. The light had slowly grown as Colonel Shi followed the group. He slowed even more and fell back further and further in order to remain in the gloom in case someone looked back in his direction. Soon he could hear multiple voices ahead and see well enough to confirm that he had been following a group of armed men who were now entering some sort of a large, well lit cavern. It seemed like there were quite a few men in the cavern based on the sounds of the ensuing greetings. Shi slipped his night vision googles up onto his head and hugged the tunnel wall, silently cursing the San Francisco MSS team, as he slowly moved closer to the tunnel mouth. Then he stopped, and very carefully and quietly loaded his remaining RPG in the launcher.

Nick asked, "Should we just let them go or try to stop them? We can use the hole generator to position the squads anywhere you want out there."

Wil thought it over and replied, "It's tempting, but I'm not convinced that it would really gain us anything. They apparently think that they accomplished their mission by destroying the house. It might benefit us if they carry that message back to their superiors. Besides, somebody around here *is* going to spot the smoke and call it in. If the Volunteer Fire Department can't respond because most of them are already here, they'll call the sheriff. I don't want the sheriff walking into the middle of a bunch of heavily armed Chinese."

Pikes Peak Patti had been lying quietly near the three men as they talked, but suddenly raised her head, looked toward the south tunnel opening and growled.

A moment later, CSM Baker saw Patti slinking towards the tunnel opening with bared teeth and raised hackles and got up to see what was bothering her.

* * * * *

Colonel Shi finished loading the RPG, stepped away from the tunnel wall, and started to raise the launcher. In that instant, he saw a very large dark brown dog crouched in the cavern entrance glaring at him. Standing right behind the dog was a man staring at him with a very surprised expression on his face.

A loud voice came from somewhere in the cavern - the same voice that he had heard on the porch of the house what seemed like a lifetime ago. "Intruder" ... Then everything seemed to happen at once ... "detected" ... Shi continued to raise the launcher to the firing position, ... "in the south" ... The snarling dog sprung forward with startling speed and leapt into the air ... "tunnel!" ... The man turned and dashed away hollering *"Hit the dirt!"*

Colonel Shi managed to raise the launcher to horizontal just as the massive dog crashed into his chest. The momentum of the large animal threw Shi violently backwards as he reflexively fired the weapon. By then, the launcher was almost vertical, pointing at the top of the mine tunnel.

Shi fell back into the dissipating propellant exhaust flame with Patti on top of him as the round tore part way into the rock overhead and exploded, sending rock shards, steel balls and incendiary pellets raining down from above.

The person who had fired the first shot had now fired the last shot of the Battle of the MacNamara Mine.

Even though the RPG had been deflected, the mouth of the tunnel still belched out a quantity of steel balls and incendiary pellets into the cavern.

Thanks to CSM Baker's warning, most of the men had instantly hugged the ground, which greatly reduced the number of injuries. But the CSM did more than just yell a warning - he sprinted across the cavern and hurled himself at what he considered to be the most important person in the crowd, and tackled him, covering him with his own body.

As soon as the steel balls stopped ricocheting, Wil got up and pulled CSM Baker off of Nick. By then, Evan was dead. He took two steel balls in the back in the process of dashing across the cavern. One of them tore through his heart, killing him instantly as he collapsed on Nick. Evan never felt the incendiary pellet that still smoldered in the back of his left leg.

Kneeling, Wil held the body of Command Sergeant Major, United States Army Retired, Evan Baker in his arms. Looking down on Evan's surprisingly composed features, Wil softly said, "Hoo-ah, Top."

Chapter 45

Gail finished operating on the last of the second squad members wounded in the elevator and wearily stood up from her place at the lab workbench. Dr. Scheer, the German doctor-astronaut from the space station, had watched her operate and was completely enthralled with the amazing remote surgical device she employed. With it, she saved all but one of the wounded squad members – without even touching them! She had instructed her helpers to clean and bandage any open wounds before she started, *then* removed foreign objects and repaired internal damage! When asked about this miracle tool, Gail replied that it was just another application of the same device used to rescue the ISS crew.

Their conversation was abruptly interrupted when the sound of Colonel Shi's exploding RPG round reached the lab. Gail, tired as she was, grabbed her Medi-Monitor and ran out of the lab in response. A fine brownish cloud of rock dust billowed down the hall from the direction of the open door to the cavern, so she immediately headed that way with several of the ISS crew and Lady following in her wake.

The cavern was a horrifying sight. The rock dust was heavy in the air and the cavern lights lent the cloud a sickly reddish-brown glow. There were blobs of some sort of burning material splattered on the cavern walls contributing a malodorous smoke to the mix. Men lay all over, some deathly still and others struggling to rise. It struck Gail that the scene was reminiscent of the description of the "Seventh Circle of Hell" in Dante's *Inferno*. She looked around, frantically searching for Nick. Then she saw him ... prone on the floor ... unmoving ... covered in blood.

"*NO!*" she screamed as she ran towards him. *Please, God, no! Don't let him be dead!*

He started to move as she knelt down beside him. *Oh thank you! Thank you!* "Don't move," she commanded, - a seemingly contradictory order since a moment ago she had been so happy to see him do just that - "Let me see where you're wounded!"

Nick appeared dazed, but he protested, "I don't think I'm wounded. I think somebody just ran into me and knocked me down." He slowly sat up and then noticed all the blood on his jacket, shirt and lace jabot and tentatively added, "I think."

Agnes spoke up from her place in Nick's sporran, "He's fine. He was just bowled over. His vitals are good. He'll have a few bruises, but otherwise he's okay."

"Thank God," Gail said as she reached out and hugged him to her tightly.

To Nick's amazement, he hugged her back.

After a moment, Wil spoke up from his position cradling CSM Baker just a few feet away. "Evan saw what was happening, knocked Nick down and shielded him with his body. That's Evan's blood all over Nick. He saved Nick's life."

Gail looked over at Wil and realized that she really hadn't registered the presence of anyone else from the moment she spotted Nick lying in a pool of blood. The depth of her emotional reaction surprised her, but she didn't have time to think about that now. She quickly shifted over to examine Evan, but Wil just shook his head, pointed out the gaping hole in the sergeant's left breast and said, "He's gone, Ma'am. See about the others."

As Gail moved to the next wounded volunteer, Nick slowly rose to his feet and tried to look around. The rock dust and smoke from the incendiaries burned his eyes and the resulting tears blurred his vision. He was a little dizzy and his head hurt. He couldn't seem to think clearly. He wondered if he had suffered a concussion from the fall. Then he saw Mike stand up from behind the hole generator. As Nick stepped closer, he noticed that the console was sporting a number of new dents in its surface.

Mike asked, "What happened?"

Since Nick had no idea what happened, he remained mute.

Alfred replied for him, "A lone intruder in a full-body stealth suit approached the cavern undetected in the south tunnel and attempted to fire an RPG into the cavern. The attempt was only partially successful due to the intervention of Pikes Peak Patti."

"Patti? *Where's Patti?*" Mike asked as he headed for the mouth of the south tunnel. Nick was right behind him with his drawn Smith & Wesson in hand. They both stopped short when they saw Lady lying down with her head on her forelegs, softly crying for her mother in front of a sickening jumble of shattered and charred human and canine remains.

* * * * *

Mike began a flurry of activity to take his mind off of Patti while Nick stood helplessly nearby. There would be plenty of time later for grieving. Mike ordered Alfred to turn on all of the tunnel lights and perform a full sensor sweep to make sure there were no more surprises lurking in the mine. He went on to instruct Alfred to decrease the pixel change threshold settings for motion detection, figuring that a few false alarms here and there were better than another successful incursion. His final step in closing the barn door after the horse got out was to instruct Alfred to leave the tunnel lights off during an intrusion only when it was clear that the intruders were local youth or tourists. Otherwise, he was to deny the cover of darkness to potentially hostile intruders.

When Mike's stream of instructions wound down, Wil, still holding

CSM Baker, interjected a question. "Alfred, what are the intruders on the ridge to the west doing?"

Alfred replied, "I believe they have all departed. Although I could not resolve details, they moved off of the ridge down into the valley. Shortly thereafter, a convoy of vehicles was detected moving south on Phantom Canyon Road. It will require the use of a patrol or a sweep by the hole generator to verify that no one remains in the valley."

Mike sat down at the still functioning hole generator and quickly scanned the valley. "There are two empty Jeeps parked near the road in the valley, but the area is clear otherwise. They're gone ... I guess we've won ... sort of."

Then Agnes's voice rose again from Nick's sporran, this time a lot louder than before - loud enough where everyone in the cavern could hear.

"She kept a stir in tower and trench,

That brawling, boisterous Scottish wench,

Came I early, came I late, I found Agnes at the gate."

Mike asked, "What was that all about?"

Nick, although still woozy, was very familiar with this particular bit of Scottish history. He tugged at his bloodstained jacket, smoothed his bloodstained kilt, and prepared to wax eloquent. "That verse is from a ballad attributed to the Earl of Salisbury after his defeat at the siege of Castle Dunbar in 1338. Agnes, Countess of Dunbar, was the daughter of Thomas Randolph, Earl of Moray, a close ally of Robert the Bruce, and the wife of Patrick, the Earl of Dunbar and March. Castle Dunbar, the fortress of the Earls of March, was the key to Scotland on the southeast border. Her husband left Agnes in charge of the castle's defense while he was with the Scottish army fighting the English. Built on rocks that projected out into the sea, the building was reckoned nearly impregnable. As a result, much of the historic conflict focused on the castle gate."

Nick went on to describe how the Earl of Salisbury tried to crash through the gate with a battering ram, used catapults to hurl rocks at the castle walls and tried to sneak into the castle in the dead of night.

"Black Agnes, so called for her dark complexion, black hair and black eyes, is revered as the Savior of Dunbar Castle. With a force consisting of little more than her handmaidens and a few yeomen, she held Castle Dunbar out of English hands. Outnumbered, outgunned, facing starvation, Lady Agnes never surrendered. She held out to the end, and ultimately won."

Suddenly overcome with a sense of surrealism, Nick stopped and looked around. In the middle of the smoke and dust it seemed that everyone had stopped to listen to him, a man in a Scottish piper's outfit covered in blood and spouting out an obscure history lesson. Even the painfully wounded and the few ISS crew members in the cavern seemed entranced. *Or perhaps morbidly fascinated by the erratic behavior of an obviously brain damaged person.* Then the parallels between the siege of Dunbar Castle and the Battle of the MacNamara Mine leapt unbidden into his mind - the attempt to blast through the front door, the mortar hurling explosive shells at the house, and the sneak RPG attack in the dark mine tunnel.

He looked over at Mike sitting at the hole generator. Then he looked back at the erstwhile miners.

"That's it!" Nick shouted. Pointing at the hole generator, *"That's* not the *Defender, that's* the *Gate!"* Then Nick swept his arm around to indicate the people in the cavern, *"You* are the *Defenders* at the Gate! And just like Black Agnes, you have prevailed even though outnumbered, outgunned and ... well, I guess you weren't really facing starvation." *Now they* know *I've gone bonkers.*

Nick glanced over at Mike, who surprisingly gave him a thumbs-up gesture. Finally, both the invention and its protective organization had names.

"And," Nick looked Mike straight in the eyes, "the official mascot of the Defenders will always be a Chocolate Labrador named Pikes Peak Patti. Pikes Peak Patti II will be available as soon as Lady is old enough to breed."

He could see tears forming in Mike's eyes, so Nick respectfully turned away and tried to look busy.

Then, unexpectedly, from his position on the floor of the cavern still holding CSM Baker, Wil shouted *"Hoo-Ah Defenders!"* And the reply came from the throats of all those present still able to shout, *"HOO-AH DEFENDERS!"*

* * * * *

Thanks to Patti, there were only two fatalities and five wounded out of a total occupancy of almost thirty people in the cavern. The RPG struck the top of the tunnel outside of the cavern, so most of the steel balls spent themselves in an effort to drill into the rock. The rest ricocheted down in a cone pattern all around Colonel Shi and Patti. Most of the balls in the side of the cone facing the cavern entrance hit the rock floor inside the cavern and bounced. Thanks to CSM Baker's warning, almost all of those flew over the reclining men and spent themselves against the rock walls. Of course CSM Baker had not followed his own advice and was not reclining at the time.

The incendiary pellets stuck wherever they hit, which was mostly inside the tunnel, although some made it as far as the cavern walls opposite the tunnel mouth.

They moved the wounded into the lab and Gail and her ISS helpers got back to work. Fortunately, none of the new casualties' wounds were nearly as bad as those from the elevator. Once the patients had been prepped, the assisting ISS crew members were relieved by IMS volunteers, and the astronauts were brought to the cavern Gate for transport to Peterson Air Force Base.

Commander Novitski asked Mike and Nick if they were sure that the ISS crew members were no longer needed, and Mike explained that all of the hostile intruders were either deceased or had departed.

Nick asked Fred, "Exactly where is the hyperbaric chamber facility located on the base?"

Fred replied, "It is in Building 425, directly behind the base pool and bowling alley."

"Okay," Nick said as he sat down at the Gate, "Fred! Call the base commander and announce the imminent arrival of some V.I.P. visitors."

* * * * *

Wil spoke with Randy Miller via the tunnel audio transducers again once the ISS crew had departed.

"Mister Miller, this is Deputy Ahrens again."

Randy replied, "Is everything all right, deputy? We heard an explosion."

"I wouldn't go so far as to say that everything is all right. Causalities were incurred on both sides during the assault. The good news is that the surviving intruders have left the property. Unless you intend to persist in your claim of repossession rights, now would be an excellent time for your crew to exit stage left before the Sherriff arrives and starts counting bodies and asking questions."

"Well Deputy, I've been thinking about what you said earlier. You were right when you said that the title I saw was just for the trailer. I only have Jimmy's word that he owned the equipment inside the trailer. On the other hand, I only have *your* word that the equipment belongs to MacEwen. Now, I hardly know you from Adam - you're just a disembodied voice to me. In comparison, I've known Jimmy Barton since college. Based on *that* ... my boys and I will be heading back to Houston. Uh, what's the best way out of here? Back the way we came?"

Wil just barely managed to suppress his laughter and replied, "Yes, you need to get out the way you came in. The other exits are temporarily blocked. The lift cage will be waiting at Level Two for you. Have a safe trip."

* * * * *

Mike, Nick, Wil and Gail met in the lab as soon as she had done everything she could for the wounded.

Nick asked Gail, "How are they doing? Should we get them to a

265

hospital?"

Gail answered, "They're doing pretty well, all things considered. Performing surgery immediately in such a minimally intrusive way helps immensely to reduce the trauma. Volunteers from the families have arrived to tend the wounded, but there are a couple of more critically wounded that might be better off at my clinic where I have more monitoring equipment."

"Okay," Nick said, "We can use the Gate to move them over there, and then we can leave the Gate open so that you can just walk back and forth between your patients like they were in adjacent rooms."

Gail just shook her head in wonder at the concept of stepping back and forth between rooms that were over a mile and a half apart.

Nick's voice trembled slightly as he asked, "Have the next of kin all been notified?"

Wil answered, "Yes. I went to tell Marcia Baker first, and then she went with me to visit the others."

Nick asked, "She went with you?"

"Yes. Remember, she was Mrs. Command Sergeant Major Baker for many years. This is not the first time she has gone to comfort the families of fallen servicemen. Mrs. Baker has volunteered to take on the task of helping with funeral arrangements and marshalling support for the affected families."

Mike asked, "So who's taking care of *her*? She's one of the 'affected families.'"

Wil answered, "This will keep her busy and in contact with other people. I think that's the best thing for her right now. Besides, I don't think I could have stopped her from doing it, even with a main battle tank."

"I know we've been up all night," Nick said, "but we'll soon be crawling with emergency responders, law enforcement officials, and news media personnel. With smoke visible for miles, dead to be buried, wounded to be treated, and mysteriously rescued ISS Astronauts showing up in the general vicinity, we have truly blown our cover. We need a plan and we need it now. And just to get the conversation started, I have already decided that I am through running. Unless Mike wants to throw me out, I'm staying right here."

The group was momentarily taken aback by Nick's fervor and no one spoke right away.

Finally, Wil said, "What do *you* think we should do?"

Nick sighed. "You all know that I only want the Gate to be used for good, not evil, which probably makes me sounds very naïve. But I know that evil exists in the world and I'm also aware that there are different opinions of what is good and what is evil. I have firsthand experience with that, having worked for people who think only of themselves and have no problem at all with illegal or immoral activities. As far as their concerned, if it benefits them, it is good. If it does not benefit them, it is evil. That's part of basic human nature that can only be modified by socialization. Unfortunately, our current society seems to be bent on suicide, producing large numbers of egotistical sociopaths. Ironically, I became an engineer so I wouldn't have to deal with human nature. I thought I could just work in a laboratory designing neat stuff all by myself."

Nick shook his head slightly and smiled at that.

"I've always been an introvert, so working in isolation sounded really good to me. Of course my career didn't work out the way I thought it would when I was a wet-behind-the-ears recent graduate. I quickly learned that there are significant limits on what you can do all by yourself. As distasteful as it can sometimes be, people have to work together, and over time I think I learned to do it pretty well. It's true that the whole is greater than the sum of the parts. I don't know if that's because of, or in spite of, the parts that are really bad."

Fred chose that moment to interrupt, "That's mathematically impossible, because the sum ..."

"Shut up, Fred," Agnes cut him off.

"Yes, Ma'am," Fred meekly replied.

Nick rolled his eyes and continued, "I also know that we can't put the genie back in the bottle," Nick said as he jerked a thumb toward the Gate. "Once people know that such a device is possible, they will work until they can produce one. Ultimately, we need to be prepared for that event. In the meantime, I aim to strictly control how Gates are used.

"In militaristic terms, Gates are unusual in the sense that they can be used to provide either a potent defense or a powerful offense. I admit that my first inclination is to go on the defensive. But I can tell you from youthful experience that it is very hard to win chess games by always playing defense."

Mike, having frequently been Nick's most aggressively offensive chess opponent, smiled broadly.

"If we are going to maintain control, I think that we have to use all of our strengths, defensive and offensive. There are people out there who want what we've got. We met some of them last night. Pretty soon there are going to be a lot more people who want what we've got. I think the best way to keep them from getting it is for us to use the Gate against them, even if that means we have to use it as a weapon. The time for running is over. The time for hiding is over. The Gate is going to create a lot of chaos. But the potential benefits to the whole human race are so great that we cannot waver. My vote is to make a statement that cannot be ignored, and to make it quickly."

Mike smiled and said, "Sixty-Forty, boss, Sixty-Forty. You don't need a vote. If you do something I don't like, I'll let you know."

Nick smiled back and said, "I have no doubt at all that you will quickly inform me of your displeasure should the impulse arise. I wouldn't want it any other way."

Looking at the others, Nick asked, "What do you think?"

Wil just gave a thumbs-up.

Gail said, "I agree. The benefits trump the difficulties."

Fred 'n Agnes' voices came from the sporran. "We're with you, Boss!"

Nick just shook his head and continued, "So in the midst of tending for the wounded, burying the dead, and fending off the authorities, we have to do two things: We have to get the geothermal generators on line as soon as possible, and we have to ramp up the assembly of new Gates. Just look at the problems we had in the last few hours that would have been avoided if we'd had more Gates. We could have retrieved the second squad from the house and saved lives with just *one* more Gate."

Nick looked down and seemed unable to continue. No one else said anything during the uncomfortable moment. Nick finally collected himself and went on.

"After that, we need even more geothermal generators and even more Gates. If we can do these things, I think we can hold off the world if we have to." Nick paused, and then added, "And we may have to."

Mike glanced at the others and then said, "What do you want us to do first?"

Nick started to discuss how they could train more IMC family members to assemble Gates when Mike interrupted him.

"Not IMC family members, Nick. They're more than that. They're Defender family members now."

Nick - who was still more than a little embarrassed over his outburst in the cavern - nodded and said, "I stand corrected."

They talked about the remaining tasks necessary to get the geothermal generators hooked up. Soon, they all understood what needed to be done and who was going to do it.

Once the discussion died out, Nick looked down at his dried blood-caked clothes. "I don't have a change of clothes. Everything was in the house."

Mike looked surprised, and then said, "Now that you mention it, I don't either! We need to go shopping."

Then Mike and Nick looked at each other with dawning comprehension and said in unison, "The cars!" All of the vehicles were destroyed during the house bombardment. That included Wil's rental car and Gail's Snow Cat out front, as well as Mike's cars in the garage.

Mike looked at Wil and said, "I hope you paid for full coverage on your rental car."

Wil said, "I'll bet it doesn't cover acts of war. Is a Chinese assault on American private citizens an act of war?"

Mike said, "Good point. My homeowner's insurance might not apply either."

Mike looked at Gail and said, "I owe you a Snow Cat."

Nick looked at Mike and said, "I owe you a house."

Mike grinned and said, "I still owe you a pickup truck."

Nick replied, "That's hardly in the same league as a house. Besides," he continued softly, "I owe you Pikes Peak Patti II."

Mike, now also subdued, gruffly replied, "Well, it's not like we don't have the money to handle the loss of a few material things."

After a moment, Agnes offered a suggestion. "I am aware of the types, brands, styles and colors of the clothes Nick and Mike wear on a regular basis, and I know their sizes. I can contact a store in Cripple Creek and have clothes delivered. It's not like it will cost a lot. Both of them would wear the exact same clothes everyday if neither Gail nor I were around to complain about the smell."

That reversed the conversation's trend toward gloominess and brought a few chuckles.

"Sure," Nick said. "Have them put a rush on it. I expect visitors any minute now."

Right on cue, Alfred said, "Two county sheriff's patrol cars have just entered the driveway."

Nick stayed behind to open a Gate to Gail's clinic while Mike and Wil started the long walk through the north tunnel toward the lift house. As they went, Mike asked Wil, "How will Red, White, and Blue react when the news media starts connecting the dots?"

"I know they're not going to be happy. Other than that, I can't speculate," Wil replied. "Actually, I'd better call in as soon as I can. I need to tell them what's going on out here before it hits the news streams. That'll give them a little time to think over their options."

Mike said, "You can do that as soon as we get to the surface. I can handle the sheriff while you call."

The two continued up the tunnel without speaking. When they neared the lift shaft, Wil said, "I'm going to ask for permission to let you and Nick in on what Red, White and Blue are all about. I think we need everyone to understand each other."

Chapter 46

It didn't take long for the news to spread up through the command structure. It started with the colonel of the 21st Space Wing calling the commanding general of the Air Force Space Command. The general then called the Air Force chief of staff, who called the chairman of the Joint Chiefs of Staff and the secretary of the Air Force, who called the Secretary of Defense, Edward Zackerman. The conversations were remarkably similar.

"We apparently have the International Space Station astronauts at the 21st Space Wing Aerospace and Operational Physiology Flight facility on Peterson Air Force Base in Colorado Springs."

"What? Is this some sort of a sick joke? The ISS crew was projected to run out of oxygen early this morning, and neither Roscosmos nor NASA has heard from them for several hours. They're presumed dead. It's all over the news streams."

"They seem to be alive and well, although two of them are undergoing treatment in a hyperbaric chamber for symptoms of decompression sickness. I'm pretty sure that they are the real McCoy. They matched photographs of the current ISS crew posted online. They are either who they say they are, or they have undergone some serious plastic surgery just for a sick joke."

"This can't be! How did they get there?"

"Nobody seems to know. The officer on duty said they just walked in through the door."

"You mean they just walked onto the base?"

"No, they walked through the door into the Aerospace and Operational Physiology Flight facility. The OOD checked with base security who swore that no one even vaguely resembling an astronaut had attempted, let alone achieved, entry to the base. They were all wearing space suits, so they would be hard to miss."

"But how did they get from the space station to Peterson Air Force Base? Has anyone asked them how they returned from space?"

"Yes, sir, but you won't like the answer. Their commander said that they followed a pretty girl through a hatch in the Nauka Multipurpose Laboratory Module that led to a cave. Then there was an underground battle between several different groups and his crew helped tend the wounded. After that they stepped through a hatch in the cave to just outside the door to the facility they're in now."

Silence ... "Sir, are you still there?"

"Yes ... It's got to be an extremely elaborate prank of some sort. Either that, or they really are the ISS crew and their commander has suffered brain damage from oxygen deprivation. Sit on them. Tend to their needs if they're hurt or sick, but sit on them. Lock the facility down. Nobody goes in or out. I've got to bump this upstairs, and I'm going to sound like an idiot."

"I know the feeling, sir."

"I didn't mean to imply that you sound like an idiot, just that I will sound like an idiot. No, I take that back. You do sound like an idiot, but it's not your fault. It's just this idiotic situation."

"Yes, sir; I understand. Good luck with your call."

The last call was from the secretary of defense to the President of the United States, Benjamin Featherstone. It, too, was similar until near the end.

"That sounds like *Alice in Wonderland* mixed up with *Lord of the Rings*. Maybe the guy *is* brain damaged."

"I don't have any specific information on the medical condition of the commander, mister president."

"Ed, is there any chance that this is legitimate?"

"I don't see how, mister president. It's probably some sort of extremely elaborate prank. I wouldn't have bothered you with this if it weren't for the fact that their appearances apparently match the crew photos and we can't figure out how they got on the base."

"Look, Ed ... I know that sometimes in the past there were super-secret, off-the-books type programs that nobody got around to telling the sitting President about. But you and I are more than just president and secretary of defense. We are political soul-mates. We've been through a lot of backroom battles together to get where we are today. I've got to know what's really going on with this astronaut business. I just released a presidential order to fly the flags at half-mast to memorialize those people. I'm going to look pretty stupid if it turns out that we've rescued them with some orbital vehicle that I didn't even know existed."

"Mister President, I can guarantee you that there are no secret orbital vehicles capable of transporting astronauts involved in any Department of Defense program, no matter how highly classified. As you know, both Roscosmos and NASA have some robotic vehicles that can attain orbital altitudes, but they have no life support systems, and the ISS crew was out of oxygen hours ago. Or at least we thought they were."

"What about NASA? Could they have some sort of black program going on?"

"I really don't think so, mister president. I would have heard about it if they did. I have a special relationship with a few very highly placed people at NASA."

"Could Roscosmos have gotten a rescue vehicle launched at the last minute without informing us?"

"Even if they did, mister president, why would they take the astronauts to Peterson Air Force Base in Colorado? Besides, NORAD hasn't reported any orbital launches of any kind worldwide in the last seventy-two hours."

"This is shaping up to be a public relations nightmare, Ed. If we saved them somehow, I'll look bad because I didn't know what my own people were doing. If someone else saved them, I'll look bad for not being able to do so myself. The only way I *don't* get egg on my face is if they aren't really the ISS astronauts.

"All right, Ed. Here's what I want you to do. Keep the lid on that facility they're in. Slap the highest security level on the activities there. Find everyone who has even a hint of what is going on and make it clear to them what will happen if they say anything. Then find some way other than photographs to positively identify the alleged ISS crew members and let me know the results. I hope it goes without saying that I need this done yesterday."

"Yes, mister president. I will get back to you as soon as possible."

"Sooner, Ed, sooner."

"Yes, mister president."

But the speed at which the news spread up through the command structure was nothing compared to how fast it spread through online social media.

Even before the ISS crew entered the Aerospace and Operational Physiology Flight facility, they were photographed and vid'ed coming out of the Gate in front of the building by a group of teenagers heading from base housing to the Aquatic Center for an early swim. The crew was still in their space suits, but they were carrying their helmets, so their facial features were clear. These postings were followed soon after by a running commentary by a civilian technician working in the facility. This series of postings included Commander Novitsky's rendition of their rescue.

By the time the orders from the president made it down to the commander of the 21st Space Wing, local media reporters were already swarming in the Visitor Center at the West Gate, clamoring to be allowed access to the rescued ISS crew. The PIDDs of just about every serviceman, servicewoman and civilian on the base were lighting up with calls from friends and family members wanting to know if they'd seen the astronauts.

* * * * *

Most of the local stringers for the various online news streamers left for Peterson AFB before tips came in from friendly, and promptly compensated, emergency service dispatchers regarding the battle at the mine. The few remaining reporters responded, but didn't arrive until early afternoon due to the remote location. Soon reports of the battle were hitting the net. More postings were added over the hours as the Sheriff's Department and County

Coroner's Office personnel worked the scene. Five local miners had been killed and nine more were wounded.

There were also five unidentified bodies. Two of these were mangled and burned to a degree that would probably make their identification impossible. The other three appeared to be Asian males. Two abandoned rental vehicles were found that might provide clues to the identities of the assailants. There were signs that a large number of assailants were involved, which implied that some unknown number of armed men might still be in the general vicinity, either hiding in the surrounding mountainous region or on the roads thereabouts trying to leave the area. The weapons left with the dead, and the extent and type of damage done to the house indicated that the fugitives might be very heavily armed. The citizens of Victor and Cripple Creek were told to stay in their homes. State-wide alerts were issued. Colorado State Patrol Troopers were summoned, as were agents of the FBI, the ATF, and Homeland Security.

Hits on the news coverage of the ISS crew greatly outpaced the hits on the coverage of the battle at the mine. The latter was largely ignored except in Teller County where it ranked number three behind a $38,000 slot machine jackpot in Cripple Creek and a five car pile-up just west of Woodland Park.

In contrast, the news coverage of the battle at the mine was of paramount interest to the Chinese Ministry of State Security.

* * * * *

"What have you got for me, Ed?"

"I'm afraid it's bad news, mister president. Retina scans and fingerprints of the two American crew members match their records. We don't have retina scans or fingerprints of the others, but the two Americans vouch for them. They really are the ISS astronauts."

The secretary of defense waited silently, knowing that the president was considering his options.

"Who all knows that these people are really the ISS crew? Is it a manageable number?"

" ... I'm not sure I know what you mean by 'a manageable number,' mister president - manageable in what way?"

"I mean manageable in a 'sweeping this all under the table' way ... Manageable in a 'make it all go away' way."

"Sir, I guess you haven't seen the news streams yet. Your orders arrived too late. There are vids of the ISS crew's arrival on the net. Peterson is besieged by reporters. The lid was already off before you even issued the order to keep it on."

The president released a string of expletives that Zackerman tactfully chose to ignore.

"All right, Ed. Let's try and make the best of this unbelievable mess. Put out a press release from your office that we have snatched the ISS crew from the jaws of death just in the nick of time. Don't give any specifics; just say the method of rescue is classified.

"I'll put out an executive order for the flags to be joyously returned to full staff. Tell the secretary of the Air Force to have the ISS crew cleaned up and flown to D.C. immediately. We'll present them to Congress. They'll be the guests of honor at a White House dinner. We'll use them to get good PR without actually letting them talk to anybody except our own interrogators. If anyone comes forward to claim responsibility for the rescue, we'll snatch them up so fast it will make their heads spin and find out how they did it! Is that clear, Ed?"

"Yes, mister president. I'll get right on it."

"You do that. In the meantime, I'll call the secretary of State who will have to handle the headache of keeping the foreign crewmembers here in D.C. for as long as possible without starting a war ... And Ed?"

"Yes, mister president?"

"Put together a team to review every government program and contract we have to look for anything that could have been used to reach that space station and retrieve those astronauts. Put your DIA on it, they're supposed to be hot-shot investigators, right?"

"Yes, mister president ... you know that this will be quite a task, right? There are many thousands of government research programs and contracts to review. It's going to take a lot of time and money to accomplish."

"I don't have either time or money to give you. Rob Peter to pay Paul; I don't care what you do, just make this investigation your top priority."

"Yes, mister president."

Chapter 47

There were two churches in Victor, and members of both were included in the ranks of the deceased. Marcia Baker arranged for the use of the Catholic Church since it was larger than the Baptist Church, and pretty much the whole population of Victor and its next door neighbor Goldfield were expected to attend. There might even be some attendees from Cripple Creek, but it was assumed that not too many people there could take time off from the casinos. The two clerics agreed to co-officiate in a show of ecumenical solidarity in the face of armed violence of a sort that hadn't occurred in their community since the Miner's strike of 1894.

The funeral was the hardest thing Nick had ever done. Family members had requested that he play the bagpipes at the funeral service and lead the funeral procession to the cemetery. Nick just about broke down when he played "Amazing Grace" at the end of the church service. He was all the more emotional for the guilt he felt knowing that these men would still be alive if he had never come to their town.

There were a number of news stringers waiting outside the church as Nick, playing a lament, lead the five sets of Defender pallbearers carrying caskets out to the line of hearses and limousines parked on 2nd Street. Three of the caskets bore American flags in recognition of the veterans therein.

Photography and videography had been banned from the church interior during the funeral service on the orders of the two pastors, but now the reporters jockeyed for position with their PIDDs lifted high to vid the beginning of the funeral procession.

The Cripple Creek funeral home had to do some scrambling to round up enough hearses and limousines. Several came from Woodland Park and even more came all the way from Colorado Springs. It was another expense added to an already expensive event, but the families had all agreed that they wanted a joint funeral. Mike and Nick were paying the tab and wouldn't think of interfering with what Marcia Baker had arranged.

The route to the cemetery was a little over a mile. Nick positioned himself in front of the leading hearse once everyone was ready. As requested, he was wearing his freshly cleaned and pressed MacEwen regalia. The hearses and limousines lined up behind him and matched his sedate walking pace as he stepped out south on 2nd Street towards its intersection with Portland Avenue while playing another of the many laments he would play during the procession.

The Victor Volunteer Fire Department truck was next in line behind the limousines carrying the families of the deceased. Two of the deceased had been volunteer fire fighters, but that wasn't the only reason the truck was in the procession. A handmade casket carrying the remains, such as they were, of Pikes Peak Patti was strapped to the top of the truck. When the firefighters heard how Patti had saved the lives of some of their own, they decided to make her an honorary member of the fire company posthumously. Although Patti would be buried on Mike's land, the fire fighters felt that she should be part of the procession.

Behind the black bunting draped fire truck were cars carrying mourners that weren't family, but unable to walk all the way to the cemetery, followed by the remaining mourners on foot.

As the procession turned west up Portland Avenue, Nick almost stumbled in surprise. He thought that pretty much the whole town had attended the funeral in the packed church, but he was either mistaken or somebody brought in a bunch of ringers. Portland Avenue was lined for blocks by a crowd of men clutching their hats in their hands, teary-eyed women, and solemn looking children. Nick straightened his back and tried to do his best pipes work ever.

It was a bright, cloudless spring day and the air was unusually still. The sky was the perfect cerulean blue only seen at higher altitudes. Even so, there was still a nip in the thin air. Fortunately the street had been plowed and most of the surrounding snow had sublimated, giving a foretaste of the warmer weather to come.

The uphill walk, constant huffing on the blowpipe to keep the bag full of air, and the high altitude all conspired to fatigue him greatly as he crested the hill and turned south on 7th Street. After one block he turned west again, this time on West Spicer Avenue. He was only about halfway to the cemetery, but it was mostly downhill from here and he began to feel better. He had acclimated to the altitude fairly well. There was no way he could have done something like this when he first arrived at Mike's place. ... *How long has it been since I drove into Mike's driveway – an exhausted, unemployed, idealistic fugitive? Now I'm at the head of a procession of the consequences of my actions. The least I can do is to proudly honor these innocent victims now and for as long as I live.*

As Nick approached the cemetery, he saw an inspiring sight. A hook and ladder from the Cripple Creek Fire Department was parked to the left of the cemetery gate, and a hook and ladder from the Woodland Park Fire Department was parked on the right. Their ladders were up at an angle, creating an arch over the gate. A very large American flag was suspended between the two ladders. Nick had to struggle again to control his emotions and concentrate on his playing. When he marched under the suspended flag and through the cemetery gate he saw six people in military uniform standing at attention near five open graves under awnings. As Nick drew closer, he saw that three of the soldiers were wearing Army uniforms - the remaining soldier was a Marine.

When Nick came abreast of the open graves, he turned around and continued to play in place as the procession approached and surrounded the site. He was amazed at how the entourage had grown. The people who had lined the streets must have joined the ranks of the walking mourners.

Once all of the caskets were in place, but not yet lowered, and all of the family members had been seated in folding chairs, the two Pastors took turns reading scripture and praying. After the gravesite service, five of the soldiers lined up and, at the barked commands of the sixth, rendered a rifle salute.

The Marine played "Taps" on a bugle. As the last note drifted away there was silence save for a few muffled sobs. Then one at a time the American flags were removed from the three caskets so adorned. Each one was folded and presented to the appropriate family member. Nick noticed that two of the flags, including the one to Marcia Baker, were presented by one of the Army men but the third was presented by the Marine. Nick realized the third deceased veteran must have been a Marine. He felt a sudden surge of guilt as he realized how little he knew about the men his actions had killed. Nick became determined to get to know all of the Defenders and their family members better, and make sure that none of them suffered any avoidable hardship.

Looking over at Marcia Baker, Nick thought, *Marcia has kept herself busy with the funeral arrangements, but that will all go away as soon as the reception is over. She's all alone now – she and Evan never had any children. What can we find for her to do to keep her from just sitting at home and grieving?* Mike, Gail, and Wil were back at the church helping with the reception preparations. Maybe one of them could offer some suggestions.

Once the ceremony was finished, the crowd started back towards Victor and the funeral reception. Most of the family members returned to their limousines for the return, but Nick noticed that Marcia had decided to walk back, so he hurried to catch up with her.

"Marcia, hold up! Do you want to be alone, or is it all right if I walk back with you?"

"Sure, Nick. I just thought it was such a beautiful spring day that I would walk."

Nick noticed a group of young boys and girls standing next to the road just outside of the cemetery gate. As Nick and Marcia approached, the oldest of the group, who appeared to be no more than a teenager, pushed a young boy towards Nick.

The nervous looking child took his cap off and fooled with it as he looked down at his feet and stammered, "Mister MacEwen, sir ... um ..." and then started to cry as he blurted out, "I was the one that told that man where you were! Those people," he pointed towards the caskets in the cemetery, "are dead because of *me*!" And then he broke down completely.

Marcia immediately knelt down and wrapped the sobbing boy in her arms. Nick knelt beside her, placed his fingers under the crying boy's chin and gently tilted his head up until they were eye-to-eye.

Nick asked, "What's your name, son?"

"Chet," the boy sniffled.

"Who did you tell?"

"I don't know who he was. He was standing in the alley holding up your picture."

"Describe him to me. Did he look Chinese?"

"I don't think so; he was a huge bald guy with a big mustache."

"Okay, listen to me, Chet. The huge bald guy with the big moustache didn't kill anyone. He even helped with our defense. You're not responsible for those people who died." *I'm the one who's responsible for those people who died!*

Chet sniffed and wiped his nose on his shirtsleeve and asked, "Really?"

"Really," Nick answered. After a moment he asked a question even though he was pretty sure he already knew the answer. "Where are your parents?"

"Don't know," Chet said with a shrug. Then, pointing at the oldest boy added, "Gat takes care of us."

Nick stood up and addressed Gat. "Are all of these kids abandoned?"

Gat answered, "Yes, we've all been abandoned by our parents." Then he added with a fierce look, "But we *don't* abandon each other."

Marcia stood up holding Chet's hand, turned towards Gat and asked, "How about we all go to the reception and get something to eat?"

The children all grinned, and Gat, his fierceness suddenly turning to eagerness, asked, "Would Mister MacEwen please play his bagpipe again as we go?"

So, his former fatigue forgotten, Nick filled his bag with air and set off down the road towards Victor at quick time. All of the children pranced happily behind him to a series of jigs and reels. Nick silently laughed at the thought of being a modern day Pied Piper. *But I'm not taking the children away, I'm bringing them back!*

EPILOGUE

Jimmy Barton was in his office at Instrument Technologies Corporation sitting behind his U-shaped, burled walnut desk, waiting for the arrival of the next executive assistant applicant. Sheila Thompson had retired from ITC at the age of seventy, after fifty years of service. Jimmy had gone all out for her retirement party in the cafeteria, even paying for the pizza. Now he was interviewing applicants for her replacement and was none too impressed with the candidates so far. One of them had actually laughed at the telephone sitting on his desk, and all of them had returned blank stares when he mentioned overhead projection transparencies. He hadn't realized how well he had trained Sheila until she was gone.

Sheila's retirement was just the latest change at ITC in the last six months. Ever since the Defender prototype was stolen, Jimmy's uncle Ken had been trying to convince Jimmy's widowed mother Martha that she should sell all of the ITC stock held by the Barton Family Trust. Jimmy surreptitiously bolstered Ken's argument by finagling the financial reports to make the stock appear to be steadily declining and well on the way to being worthless. So when Martha finally agreed to sell, Jimmy was ready. He enlisted Dave Litchfield, who was one of his minority stockholder buddies on the Board of Directors, to help him buy up all of the outstanding shares for a song. This included a token amount of stock held by Ken and a slightly larger number of shares held by Rick Kramer, another old buddy who decided he wanted out. The fact that Jimmy had cheated his own widowed mother, his siblings, his uncle, and an old buddy just sweetened the deal.

It had been a race to see if Jimmy could fire Ken from the post of chairman of the Board of Directors before Ken resigned. Ken won the race. Jimmy became what he always wanted to be, the chairman of the board, president, chief executive officer and majority stockholder of ITC.

Then Dave Litchfield unexpectedly died under suspicious circumstances. Investigators determined that Dave's business relied on relationships with multiple Chinese companies that had unexpectedly severed ties on the same day that Dave's body was discovered slumped over the desk in his office. Dave's company was left with a lot of debt and no revenue. The police eventually ruled it a suicide, based on the business failure aspect and the absence of any other leads. There was one flaw in the ruling - Dave's throat had been cut and they never found a knife. Also a little puzzling was three letters Dave apparently wrote in his own blood on his desk. The letters were S, H, and I. The investigators assumed that he died before adding the last letter to an exclamatory comment on his misfortune.

Dave's business went into receivership and his life insurance contained an exception for suicide, so his widow asked Jimmy to buy back Dave's ITC stock to help with the expense of the final arrangements. Jimmy graciously bought the stock for fifty percent of a song. Now Jimmy had it all. ITC was his and his alone. Life was good.

There was a knock on his office door, and Jimmy got up to open it. This was just another irritating result of Sheila's retirement. She had been the gatekeeper in the outer office; shielding him from the riff-raff and making visitors cool their heels until he was willing to grant them entrance to the throne room. After all, he couldn't leave his office door open. If he did that, anybody, even employees, could just walk in. But now he had to get up and answer the door.

It was the receptionist with the interviewee in tow. The receptionist quickly made the introductions and withdrew, closing the door behind her.

Jimmy noted that the applicant was a very attractive young lady. She was expensively, though not really tastefully, dressed. Her skirt in particular was too short and tight for office decorum and her blouse was too low cut as well.

He waved her toward the couch as he sat down in a leather visitor's chair on the other side of the coffee table. The arrangement made him uncomfortable. He was used to sitting in his leather high-back swivel chair, reigning over visitors from his subtly elevated desk like a magistrate looming over a miscreant. But he had read an on-line article that Sheila had printed out for him that said sitting around a table like equals made people feel more comfortable. *Well, duh! Why on earth did she think he paid all that money to elevate his desk?* Anyway, he needed to replace Sheila soon, so he was temporarily trying to appear as if he wanted other people to feel comfortable.

He glanced across the coffee table and noted that the applicant was looking around his office with an appraising eye and seemed to be pleased. It was a point in her favor that she apparently recognized the signs of wealth and power that he had carefully placed throughout the room. As she took stock of his office, he took stock of her. She really was exceedingly beautiful.

He asked her a few questions about her background and experience. They talked for a while about the job requirements. He purposely mentioned his phone and the overhead projection transparencies to see how she would react. She didn't seem to see anything funny about his phone and said that although she had not worked with overhead projector transparencies before, she was very comfortable with learning new things.

Finally he asked her, "Did you bring references for me, as I asked?"

"Yes," she said, as she handed him a surprisingly thick folder. "You probably know everybody in there."

Jimmy replied, "I know everyone who is anyone, which doesn't mean I know everybody."

He left her contemplating that as he quickly scanned the references. He had already read her resume and knew that she had worked for a number of mid- to large-size companies in the area. A few too many companies in Jimmy's opinion, but the references were all glowing.

"You seem to have worked for quite a few different firms in a fairly short span of time. That's not uncommon in this day and age when so many companies are going out of business. But I am familiar with most of these companies and they are all still operating. Can you tell me why you have changed jobs so often?"

"Well," she answered, "you know how jealous wives can be." Her short skirt rose even higher as she very slowly uncrossed and then re-crossed her legs again in a way that made sure that Jimmy would see that she really *was* comfortable with transparencies.

Just as Jimmy was beginning to think that Sheila's retirement hadn't been such a bad thing after all, and life really couldn't get much better, there was a knock on his office door.

Jimmy angrily called out, "Who's there?"

It was the receptionist again and she seemed very nervous. She said there were several men in the lobby asking to see him.

"I told them that you were in a meeting and couldn't be disturbed, but one of them showed me Environmental Protection Agency Special Agent credentials and told me to interrupt your meeting. I really didn't understand what he was talking about, but he said it had to do with documents from some company named Electronuclear, twenty-seven other companies and a superfund of some sort. Oh, and he said something about responsible parties and piercing the corporate veil, whatever that means."

* * * * *

Sheila sat in her car in the parking lot of the building across the street from ITC and watched as the EPA Agents escorted Jimmy into their waiting vehicle. *I knew holding on to all of those old records would pay off some day. Twenty percent of the amount they recover from ITC a.k.a. the ElectroNuclear conglomerate! That should add up to a nice, tidy pension fund.* Once the agents left with Jimmy, Sheila started her car and drove off to her very comfortable retirement far away from ITC, Jimmy Barton, and her Defense Intelligence Agency controller.

On the way out of town, she dropped an envelope containing a PIDD-Pal memory extension module into a mailbox.

* * * * *

When Colonel Shi failed to emerge from the battle at the mine, Major Ni was briefed into the Defender project and tasked to produce an after-action report on the attack. Ni interviewed each surviving MSS operative individually by secure PIDD and was frankly appalled at the lack of useful information.

It was virtually certain that the Houston team had been wiped out. None returned to Houston or answered their PIDDs. According to the news reports, the assailants left behind three bodies of recognizable Asian males, and two unrecognizable cadavers. Since the other MSS teams did not report any casualties, Ni was assured that the dead accounted for the entire Houston team including Colonel Shi. Because there were no surviving members of the Houston team to interview, it was impossible to know what the team might have seen or achieved.

Remarkably, the Los Angeles team did nothing more than lob mortar rounds at a house and then head back to L.A. when ordered.

The experience of the San Francisco team ended up being a little more interesting. At first, each of the team members insisted they only scouted out the mine tunnels, found nothing, and were ordered back to San Francisco. But, unbeknownst to the team members, Ni was using a voice stress analyzer as a lie detector on the calls. On his second round of calls to the San Franciscans, he made it very clear what would happen if they lied again.

Ni forwarded his report to Beijing and included recordings of the San Francisco team PIDD calls out of concern that his superiors would think he was deranged.

He was very surprised when the Ambassador called Ni to his office several weeks later and instructed him to be prepared to destroy all classified material and evacuate the embassy at a moment's notice.

TO BE CONTIUED IN:

Castle

Book Two of the Defender Series

Author's Note

The Defenders at the Gate novel is set in early Twenty-first Century America during the Second Great Depression. The causes of the depression are not central to the plot and therefore are not included in any great detail within the story itself. Instead, I wrote a fairly lengthy Postscript for those readers who might be wondering how the country got into another depression.

As stated at the beginning of the book, "This is a work of fiction, Names, characters" . . . etc. However, most of the Postscript is based on historical facts. Everything up to the section titled "Awash in Debt" is factual. That section and the sections that follow are - in the author's opinion - reasonable speculations regarding the near future. None of those speculations are intended to offend anyone, but I daresay that it is impossible to write anything these days that won't offend someone - taking offense is now the national pastime. Unfortunately, I'm concerned that the national pastime will soon become trying to stay alive.

On that cheery note, dear reader, press on to "The Genesis of the Second Great Depression" that follows in eBooks, or is available at the link below in order to reduce production costs in the case of print books.

POSTSCRIPT

THE GENESIS OF THE SECOND GREAT DEPRESSION
Subtitle: THE MYOPIC ERA

A popular animated cartoon character created in the mid-Twentieth Century was always cheerfully mumbling to himself as he bustled about getting into trouble due to his myopia – his shortsightedness. The second half of the Century and beyond might well be labeled the Myopic Era in America as the country became progressively more shortsighted (double entendre intended). . .

Visit us online at www.revirescopublishing.com for a FREE download of the complete Postscript!

ABOUT THE AUTHOR:

J. E. "Max" Maxwell was born in the small community of Princeton, Illinois shortly after his father entered the Marine Corps in WWII. His mother lived with her parents on their dairy farm for the duration of the war. Despite his rural beginnings, Max grew up as a city kid in St. Louis and then Dallas. After college, his career carried him to Colorado Springs, Boston, Houston, and Fort Worth where he now lives with his wife, Cindy. They raised five children who have long since flown the nest.

Max became a big fan of Science Fiction in his early teens and regularly rode a bus to a downtown Dallas newsstand where he could buy the latest SF pulp magazines. While Max was still in high school, he wrote a science fiction short story and submitted it to one of the publishers. Soon he received the ubiquitous "your story does not meet our current publishing needs" form letter. The lack of any useful specifics was disappointing, but not a major setback. The show-stopper came when his story appeared in the magazine a few months later under someone else's name.

Smarting from the deep sense of betrayal that only a teenager can feel, Max pursued his original career choice, engineering. He worked as a technician while attending Southern Methodist University in Dallas. After earning Bachelors and Masters Degrees in Electrical Engineering, Max pursued a career in Defence Electronics that ranged from bullpen engineer to the president's suite.

Now, an older-but-wiser Max has returned to his earlier passion for writing Science Fiction.

www.ingramcontent.com/pod-product-compliance
Lightning Source LLC
Chambersburg PA
CBHW081146170626
46809CB00010B/3110